Fairy Dreams

dan Aidan Fairies

Brenna Lyons

PUBLISHER

Dedicated to...

My husband, Rob, who helped me to fly,

My three little people at " *Sidhe Druin,*"

Lisa, who gave me a good kick in the butt when it was needed,

Beth, who sent me an inspirational proofers report on "fai-wies"

And all my SCAdian friends,

Especially Master Efenwealt Whystle and "Perhaps A Dream," without whose inspiration the dream of Fairies would never have come alive in my fevered mind.

NOTE: The towns and estates in this story are fictitious settings. While towns like the ones I describe do indeed exist, and Ballynaclogh (town of stone) and Kinvarra (the head of the sea) are both place names used at various time periods in Galway Co. in Ireland, they are not intended to represent any place currently extent in the country today.

Chapter One

It all started with Xanthe. Life and death, love and hate, innocence and soul-shattering betrayal all came back to one tiny Human female.

For generations, ever since the dark young lord, Bran Blake, brought the golden-haired beauty known as Xanthe home to wed, the family had lived with the curse. No one knew where Bran found such an unknown treasure, but none questioned why he claimed her on sight.

More than a century later, stories of her haunting beauty were still told. Xanthe was a gracious but spirited lady. She rode hell-bent and astride like a man. She was the most beautiful woman anyone in Ballynaclogh had ever lain eyes on until her daughters and granddaughters were born.

The descendents of Xanthe and Bran were not only beautiful. They were formidable women, skilled farmers who were so successful that at times their neighbors cast scornful looks their way. It was a shame that Sean O'Bane had separated Colleen and her child, Darcy, from the land.

Not that Katie was unequal to the task of running the estate without her older sister, Colleen. Far from it, the land flourished under her hand as it had under every Blake woman from Xanthe on. There had never been so much as a hint of disagreement in handling between the sisters in all that time.

Katie was the oldest surviving member in the long line of Blake women. Cadal panned his eyes over her, frail and ill. Her beauty had faded long ago, in the years between his visits. He'd left a vibrant twenty-one year old woman on her wedding day and was summoned back to a woman in her early seventies. It always made Cadal sad to see how quickly Humans faded, especially the good Humans who deserved better from their gods.

Katie coughed, and Cadal moved to her side, offering her what little comfort he could in the form of a medicinal herbal tea.

She took the cup in a shaking hand and waved away his dark look of concern. "I am fine, Cadal. It is not yet my time."

"You should have told me," he whispered.

Katie had confirmed for him that she was dying only the night before. It had taken him months to screw up the courage to ask her. Cadal ached that there was nothing he could do to ease her way.

"I am Human, Cadal. Death comes for all Humans, as it comes for all Fairies."

"But so soon—"

"I know. Were I Fairy, I would still be a child." Her tone was wistful, as it was when she told him about her dreams of flying.

If he had the power, Cadal would grant her the gift of flight for a single night, but not even the Fairy Mistress had power that strong. The Fairy magic could not be given, only taken away.

He cracked a smile. "You are still very much like a Fairy child," he assured her. "You have their purity, and you ask too many questions."

"How long will your Mistress let you stay?" she asked suddenly.

Cadal dropped into one of the soft chairs set before the fire. "Questions, questions. You are always full of questions." He sighed. He didn't know how long he would be able to stay. The Fairy Mistress had said his time was limited, but limited time to a Fairy was surely more than he would need to complete a task in the Human realm. "Morda said I will have time enough."

Katie nodded, her once emerald-green eyes clouded and sad. "I sent for her last night."

His heart pounded in his chest. Katie had put off sending for Mollie for almost a year, reluctant to expose her to Joshua Thornton and his schemes.

"Will she come?" He prayed to The Harmony that she would. He did have limited time, and Mollie was a child. She had years to procrastinate, if she chose to.

She chuckled. "Questions, questions," Katie teased him. "I wonder that you are over two-hundred years old, Cadal."

He blushed. "I must be like your Peter Pan. I seem to lack common sense where the Blake women are concerned."

Or perhaps it was this new world the Humans had crafted for themselves. Televisions showed images in full color now. Automobiles reached speeds of more than ten-times the speed of a horse over distance. Everything was a wonder. Everything was frightening. It was too fast, too easy, too disposable, even life.

Katie sighed and sipped her tea. "I hope she will. I cannot ask you to stay past your time. If that time comes—"

Cadal reached out and placed his hand over hers. "No. I gave my word to keep Thornton from taking your land, and I will do whatever needs done." Cadal was here at the estate, as he'd promised Katie he would be. He'd come to her last year, as some Cadal always had when a Blake woman needed him.

With her husband passed away, Thornton sought to force Katie to sell the estate to him so he could add it to his own holdings. If the land fell untended, it would be sold at auction, and the Blake women would lose their place here, forever. Without question, Cadal knew that could never be allowed to happen.

He had done the only thing he could. Cadal had returned home and made arrangements for an extended stay. He would act as a hands-on trustee, an executor of sorts, until Mollie was comfortable running the estate or, *Harmony forbid*, another of the Blake women came to run it. It was the only way to protect both Katie and the land.

Cadal's mother had been livid that he would choose such a course. Zera always believed that Cadal would fail to come home some day, as his father had failed to come home one day. Cadal had no need of her permission. He had not needed that for many years, but it made him more at ease when their Mistress, Morda, talked his mother into a grudging consent. It would have upset Cadal to have his mother distraught at his leaving, though he did not need her permission to go.

He knew Morda gave Zera her assurances, based on her knowledge of The Harmony's ways and the vibrations that guided them, that he would not be lost to them. In the end, his mother had still voiced an opinion. She believed Cadal was making himself a servant to the women he was drawn to protect when he could content himself to be their friend. In the end, Zera hadn't stood in his way.

"Whatever you can do, Cadal. No more. I can ask no more of you. I have high hopes for Mollie. She is not like her mother. She knows the tales. She lives for the touch of the land."

4

"But she is so young," he complained.

"Cadal, I have told you many times. Twenty-six is many years an adult in Humans. You remember me at twenty-one. Did you think me a child?"

His heart stuttered. No, he hadn't thought her a child. Cadal thought her and her sister both desirable women, but they were both spoken for. "No. You know I did not."

"And neither is Mollie. From what Colleen told me of her, she is all the hellion of her fore-mothers and more."

Cadal smiled. "The land needs such a spirit." But, would he survive losing another Blake woman? Losing Xanthe had all but killed him, and finding that Katie and Colleen belonged to others had not helped his mood.

Katie gave him a searching look. She always knew when dark thoughts weighed him down. "We are more alike now, Cadal. Now that I have lost my John."

He grimaced that The Harmony, or perhaps the 'Christian God,' had never permitted Katie children. "You should have had children," he whispered. Perhaps it was part of the curse that she could not. The family was not being permitted to expand over the years as a normal family would.

"It is the curse. You know it is."

Cadal nodded. Yes, it was the curse.

The villagers believed the Blake Estate was cursed. Every generation produced two daughters, one a spirited lass like Xanthe and the other a quiet, withdrawn lady who was more at ease with her books and chores than with people. Katie Barrett had been such a sister, but she had shocked the entire village when she married John Stuart, the first of the quiet sisters to bind herself to another. That she married at the prodding of Cadal was known only to the Blake family and to Cadal.

No one in the village bothered to call it anything but 'the Blake Estate'. No one bothered to acknowledge the name of the current owners in residence, except when addressing them directly. Over the years, descendents of the Blakes found themselves married to younger sons of other landowners or boys from the village. First sons of landowners saw no merit to the match once it became clear that there would be no male heirs from the marriage. The Blake lands had passed from mother to daughter over the generations. The current family name was irrelevant. It became a given that the estate would simply pass to another daughter who would marry yet another man of a different name into the strange family of women, the Blake women.

Their husbands considered the marriages good matches, despite the fact that they were guaranteed to have no sons. The brides were beautiful and spirited. Known for their peculiar and striking attributes as much as for their wealth, it was an unusual situation all the way around.

"I worry, Cadal."

He trained his youthful eyes on her in concern. "Why? What is wrong? Can I get you something?"

"Why is there only one in this generation? Are we meant to die out?"

Cadal sighed. He wished he had the answers for her. "I know only that your marriage broke the cycle of pain. Perhaps that is why there is only one child."

Katie shook her head. "It broke the cycle of pain for the Blakes, but what of you? How fares your pain?"

Bad, when he allowed himself to think on it. But, he would not burden Katie with that. "It has been more than a century, more than five decades since I found relief from my pain." Morda assured him that his pain would end very soon, that there was another soul for him after all this time.

She raised an eyebrow, unconvinced by his attempt to put her at ease. A knock at the door interrupted whatever comment she was about to make.

Elizabeth entered and smiled, her black curls highlighted in the glow from the fire. "Do you need anything more before I retire, Miss Katie?" she asked in her lyrical voice.

Katie shook her head. "Not for myself, Elizabeth. Thank you. Perhaps for you, Padraic?"

Cadal smiled. "It is William, Katie. Thank you, no, Elizabeth."

Katie blushed. "Dear me, but you do look so like your grandfather, I sometimes forget myself. Forgive me, William."

He nodded with a tight smile.

Elizabeth turned for the door. "Good night to you both, then. Call me if you need me."

Katie offered him a sheepish smile as Elizabeth's steps faded away. "I told you that I always preferred Padraic," she offered by way of apology.

Cadal laughed heartily and retrieved the glass of wine from the table between them. His lies when he came to her were unnecessary. Katie knew he had been drawn to her by a power beyond himself and he would have her best interests at heart. As Cadal, he could do no less. Better, she knew him for what he was, which lessened his burden considerably. He would not have to lie to Katie as he had the first time they met.

The seasons he spent with Katie were among the happiest of Cadal's life. Still, he knew he was unprepared. She would die soon, leaving him without her light and laughter to speed him through this task.

As if reading his sudden melancholy mood, Katie sipped her tea. "It is not my time, Cadal. It is not my time."

* * * *

Mollie Hardy listened to Joseph O'Bane's argument, forcing herself to remain quiet while he rambled on. She tucked one gray-clad leg beneath the other, glad she had opted for the comfortable dress slacks and matching blazer over the white silk t-shirt. A conversation like this one could take awhile. Already, Joseph had been talking for thirty minutes without a break, outlining his latest plan for Bane's Barters, their family's import and old Celtic re-make company.

Mollie sighed as Joseph droned on. She brushed an errant lock of dark auburn hair, escaped from the tight bun behind her head thanks to her endless fiddling, off her face and wrapped it tight around the bun.

His family, she reminded herself yet again. Her family consisted of the poor cousins dragged in to save the butts of the less business-savvy O'Banes. When Sean O'Bane had relocated his wife and child from their estates in Ballynaclogh, Ireland, it was on the pretense that he was to run his uncle's company for him. The truth was, the O'Banes wanted the expertise of the Blake women, the family Sean had the good fortune to marry into.

She scanned her eyes over Joseph. He held controlling interest in the company, but her distant cousin was essentially an idiot when it came to finance, marketing, or any other useful field. He'd majored in Party 101 in college, and it showed in his handling. Undoing the damage Joseph left in his wake monopolized her time most days.

Luckily, Uncle Paul had been a rare jewel for finance, as far as O'Banes went. He'd left the company in excellent standing, which made dealing with Joseph's incompetence possible, if not easy. Of course Paul, like his ancestors, had listened to the Blake women in his employ where Joseph did not.

Today was no different. Mollie could tell that much from the tone Joseph was using and the defensive stance of his six-foot frame. She had yet to open her mouth, and it was war. It was going to be a long day.

Joseph's latest plan was as ill-advised as dozens of others Mollie had heard in the last two years. When Joseph's father died, the useless young man had decided to make a name for himself, all over the company she'd helped build. Mollie massaged her forehead and made notes, prioritizing them on what she should attack — *address, she reminded herself,* first.

Mollie ran a hand over the letter in her pocket for the third time this meeting. If only she could throw caution to the wind and disappear to the family estate. She decided Galway was far enough from Joseph for her liking.

She had never been there herself. Her mother, Darcy, would never permit it when she was young. Darcy had been born there and said her daughter was missing nothing. When Mollie was older, she couldn't afford a trip to Europe.

Still, Nana's descriptions of the lush green hills, the village full of simple people, and the quiet peace of the land calling to a soul, had haunted Mollie all of her life.

As long as she could remember, Mollie had ached to visit the estate she knew only from pictures, stories, and letters from Aunt Katie despite a part-interest in the concern.

Joseph stopped talking and eyed Mollie. It was a challenge, and she knew it. She dropped her pen on the tablet and regarded him silently for a long moment. She was too tired to be diplomatic today, so she decided to be blunt.

"It won't work, Joseph. You'll alienate our biggest clients, and the bank will never lend you the money."

Joseph's eyes became hard and cold. She had seen this look before. He looked as if his eyes were two chunks of coal, but Mollie doubted they could ever be truly warm, even if set ablaze.

"Really?" His shoulders bunched under the stylish dark gray Italian suit and light gray shirt that set off his dark eyes and fiery red hair so nicely.

He's a well-dressed idiot. "Yes, really. I'm sorry, Joseph." She wasn't sorry, but it didn't hurt to say it. "The company's financial position doesn't support this move. Look at the numbers. We can't—"

"It will never support anything better unless we do something drastic."

Mollie shook her head slowly. "We make moderate gains every quarter. Why must you overextend the company in pursuit of more?"

"Because I want to be the best," he thundered.

Mollie fought to keep her temper in check. They had argued this problem many times before. They were a small, family-owned business. If they put up stock, they could compete with the players he wanted to, but Joseph would lose his little castle. If he didn't, it was no use trying to compete with anything but other small, family-owned companies.

"That is not the way," she assured him. Joseph knew why it wasn't. Mollie wasn't in the mood to rehash the whole argument today.

Joseph leaned across his desk. His significantly larger body had given Mollie pause four years ago when she'd graduated and joined the company for her percentage. It had ceased to intimidate her years ago, though Joseph never seemed to clue in to that point. Mollie straightened her five-foot-four height as he started to speak again.

"It's *my* company. I'll say what direction it takes," he growled. Little Napoleon was in rare form today.

Mollie reached her breaking point at last. It was Joseph's company, but she cleaned up his messes as he tried to destroy it, again and again. A sudden image of herself, twenty or thirty years from now, picking up the pieces after Joseph, left her cold and angry.

"Fine. Choose your direction, but do it without me." The words came in a rush, and Mollie was stunned by how good it felt to say them. She felt as if she had been waiting centuries to say them.

Joseph laughed heartily, and Mollie felt a burn in her gut as she fired up for a fight. It had been far too long since she'd felt like this. Had she forgotten what holding her tongue for too long wrought?

"Is that a threat?" he asked in amusement.

"No, Joseph. That is my resignation. If you prefer, I can email it to you, or even type it up in *Word* for you."

"You're quitting?"

Mollie nodded.

"Where will you go?" He still thought she was joking.

Shattering his illusion was going to be sweet. "I have a better offer. I got it just the other day, and I've been thinking it over until now."

"Better than the family business?"

"It's *your* business, Joseph. Remember? It's yours to build or to destroy. I don't want to watch you try to destroy it anymore. I don't want to pick up after you anymore." Mollie reflected that she was going into the real family business. The one he couldn't intrude on, *her* family's business.

Joseph's face turned as vivid a red as his hair. "If that's the way you feel..."

"You know it is. I don't know why I stayed this long."

"Who is it that's offering you more money?"

"It's not more money, Joseph. It's job satisfaction. It's having people listen to what I have to say. It's not seeing you, not having to fight with you every day of my life. A job without you—" Mollie smiled at the thought of such a paradise. It could be in Siberia in winter and an improvement if Joseph wasn't there.

"If you go to work for a competing company, I'll sue on grounds of your exclusivity contract. You better watch what you do, cousin."

"It's not competing. My skills can go almost anywhere."

"You're actually going to do this?"

For the first time, Mollie saw a measure of concern that he was losing his safety net. That made her next move all the sweeter. "Why not? If I stick around here, I won't have a job in a few years. Less if you fire me for telling you when you're wrong."

"Is that what you want?"

"To be fired? It doesn't matter to me. I've already quit. Would you like me to give you two weeks' notice?"

"I don't think that will be necessary."

"Good. Then in two weeks, you'll notice I'm gone," Mollie answered Joseph's scowl. *Less than that*, she hoped secretly. How long would it take Joseph to screw it up?

He didn't need to say there was no coming back. She wouldn't turn back now, even if there were a place for her at the company. They both knew that.

Mollie's smile never faded as she left the building. Her mother would be irritated, but Mollie needed a drastic change. When she reached home, she wrote Aunt Katie and started preparing for her move to the Blake estates. Meeting Katie alone would be worth quitting her job. Nana Colleen's younger sister was, by all accounts, the last sane member of her family, the only one besides Mollie who knew what really counted in life.

By the time Mollie returned with boxes, her mother had left the first of many messages on her answering machine. Mollie looked at the blinking light and laughed hysterically. She was tired of fighting with Joseph and her mother, tired of the rat race, tired of the city, the traffic, and the crime. Twenty-six was far too young to be so tired.

* * * *

"Why?" Darcy Hardy asked for the fifth time in an hour.

Mollie rolled her eyes and took another deep breath.

Darcy continued without waiting for Mollie's answer. "For three generations, we've made our life here. Why take a step backward now?"

"I don't think of it as a step backward, Mother. It's a change, and I think it's a change I need."

"Running away from civilization?"

"Not at all. I just want to do something that will make me happy. Babysitting Joseph doesn't fit into that category. It never did."

"And, if you're not happy?"

"I'll make you a deal, Mother. We'll even make it legal." Mollie smiled. She had been planning this move for the last three days, since she'd walked out on Joseph. It was the only way to keep Darcy out of her hair. Now, Mollie had to hope Darcy's business savvy overpowered her controlling instincts for long enough to make the plan work.

"I'm listening."

Mollie surveyed her mother. Darcy was every ounce the professional woman. Mollie would have to put this in terms she could appreciate. "You sign over your interest in the estate to me, and I'll sign over my interest in the company to you. That way, you'll have the leverage to keep Joseph in line, if you care to take on the job. In the meantime, if I hate farming, I can sell the estate for enough money to start over somewhere. I won't need you to bail me out. It's worth enough to give me a fresh start almost anywhere I want to go."

Her mother snorted in a most unladylike fashion. "That's a deal. The estate will never be worth half of what your interest in the company is worth right now."

Mollie rolled her eyes. It was worth something now, for her share of the quarterly returns as agreed when

Sean brought his family here. But unless someone got a choker on Joseph, next year, it could be worthless.

Of course that wasn't Mollie's motive in this. She wanted sole interest in the estate, so Darcy couldn't interfere with her plans later. Darcy was good at that. Maybe she would forget the alternative in her haste to get the more lucrative interest in the company.

Nana Colleen hadn't wanted to come to America. She had been forced by her husband to leave her beautiful land in exchange for a percentage of a company she'd hated as much as Mollie did. How unfair, to be at the whim of such a man. Mollie would never stand for it again, now that she'd escaped Joseph.

"Is it a deal? Can I call Jenkins and tell him to draw up the paperwork?" Mollie asked.

"Of course it is. Do I look like a fool? I hope you're not making a big mistake. If you do this, you'll have nothing to come back to here."

Mollie shook her head and sighed. She hardly had anything left to come back to since her father died. "Well, there's only one way to find out, I suppose," she commented, turning back to her packing boxes.

She almost added that Nana would have happily gone back the first chance she got. Mollie knew she couldn't push it that far. If Darcy knew Mollie intended to stay at the estate for good, she'd do anything in her power to stop her. It wouldn't surprise her mother, since Darcy believed Nana Colleen *poisoned* her granddaughter with her love for the land, but it would also make Darcy back out of their deal. Mollie was sure of it.

Darcy glanced at her manicured nails in sudden, practiced disinterest. "I still think you're going to regret this. You'll see I'm right when it's too late. You always do."

Mollie hoped Darcy was wrong this time. The young woman wasn't worried about the move, rather about the message she'd received from Aunt Katie. Katie wasn't well, and her executor, Mr. William Cadal, was already running the estate for her. Mollie hoped she hadn't left the service of Joseph O'Bane to find herself in an all-too-familiar situation with William Cadal. She didn't know what powers Aunt Katie had given him over her life. She hoped it was minimal.

* * * *

Cadal wasn't looking forward to Mollie Hardy's arrival. Two days ago, before Mollie started her long trek of planes and trains, Katie had passed away. Cadal had little zeal for the job at hand without his old friend by his side. It became more of a chore than an adventure without her.

Once Mollie Hardy found her feet, Cadal would return home, figure out his final task, and find his true soulmate at last. Surely, his decision to help Katie was his second task.

He knew the young woman would arrive soon. The train would have dropped her in Ballynaclogh half an hour ago, and Liam Brennan, his hired man and the manager of the estates in the Blake's stead when need be, would drive her out to the estate.

Boxes sent ahead had begun arriving a week earlier. They had been stacked unopened in Colleen's old rooms. They must have been sent the same day that

Mollie expressed the letter off to Katie. At least Mollie seemed serious about making a go of it.

Liam entered the stable as Cadal finished brushing down Squirrel, a chestnut mare Katie had bought for her great-niece the very day she found out Mollie planned on coming.

"She is here?" Cadal grimaced at his awkward speech. He was still trying to learn a smoother way to translate into English, but it was slow coming. He had mastered the contractions I'll and I'm, but most of the others were still foreign to him.

Liam nodded, sending a cascade of shaggy dark hair past even darker eyes. "In the house, sir." After all these months, Liam still insisted on calling him sir despite Cadal's dislike for the title.

Cadal raised an eyebrow. "She is tired from the trip, I suppose."

"No, sir. She's actually a mite angry right now, and it seems she's working off the extra energy unpacking."

"Angry? Why is she angry?"

"She asked to see Miss Katie right off." Liam shrugged.

"Angry that Miss Katie is dead?"

Liam nodded.

"She is not upset?"

"I wouldn't know, sir. It's hard to tell with females. Sometimes, they act angry to cover the hurt. Sometimes, they're just plain angry. If I had to guess, I'd say there's anger in there. I don't know what else there is yet."

Cadal nodded and handed the brush off to Liam on his way past. "Perhaps, I should meet this fiery female."

"Perhaps, you should borrow Patrick's motor-cross helmet first, sir."

Cadal frowned at the young man's honest expression and headed for the house. Surely, Mollie wasn't that hard to deal with. Then again, Katie's description of her as all the hellion of her ancestors plus some may have been accurate.

He picked up a tray of bread and cheese from the kitchen and capped it off with two glasses of wine. It couldn't hurt to come bearing gifts. Cadal couldn't afford to alienate Mollie Hardy. Not only had he promised Katie, but also he couldn't stay forever. He had to turn over the estate to this angry young woman and return to the colony. The smoother things ran until then, the sooner he could accomplish his goal.

The sound of boxes being shuffled and ripped open echoed down the stairs. She was at her work furiously. He waited for a lull in the racket.

Cadal knocked on the door quietly. "Miss Mollie?" he called out.

"Please, call me Mollie. It sounds like an oldies song when you say that."

He bit back a chuckle. *Little one, you have no concept what I would consider an oldie.* "May I come in?"

"I'd rather have some time alone if you don't mind," she answered automatically.

"I have brought some food and drinks."

"I'm really not hungry."

"It will go bad if no one eats it."

Mollie sighed deeply. "All right then. If it will get me a few moments of peace, bring it in."

Cadal smiled. Mollie was much more reasonable than he'd expected, given Liam's description of her.

As he opened the door, Cadal got his first look at the young woman sitting cross-legged on the bed. Her hair was dark auburn. He would have thought it was

18

short if it were not for the long tendrils that escaped the style hidden behind her head, brushing over her shoulders. Her deep brown eyes were fixed on the large book in her lap. She wore a form-fitting pair of blue jeans and a green button-down shirt that fell gracefully over her ample chest. Like all of the Blake women, Mollie was exquisite.

He believed Mollie looked much younger than her years, not that he was an expert at guessing Human ages. Cadal remembered what Katie looked like when she was twenty-one. He compared that to Elizabeth, the combination cook and housekeeper Katie employed, at her twenty-fourth birthday earlier that year. If he didn't know she was twenty-six, Cadal would have guessed Mollie at no more than twenty. Maybe less, if he had simply met her on the street. Still, she was marriageable in any culture Cadal knew.

He shook his head to clear the train of thought he found himself following. He found his voice. "Where would you like this?"

Mollie glanced around for a moment. "The night stand seems free of my clutter so far." She returned to her examination of the book.

Cadal set the tray down and picked up a glass of wine. As Mollie accepted it from him, she met his eyes. Her reaction was startling. She was rapt. A blush came up in her cheeks, and she almost dropped the wineglass in her shock. Cadal righted it for her gently.

Her grip tightened, and she snapped her eyes away. As they lighted on the tray, her blush deepened. "Two?" she asked without looking up again.

Cadal felt the embarrassment coursing from her in waves.

"I thought we might talk. Perhaps get to know each other."

Mollie snapped the book shut and leapt to her feet smoothly. "This may not be an appropriate place for that."

He smiled widely. Despite Katie's belief that Mollie was an adult, she was still very much a little girl. "As you wish. Would the library be better?"

She nodded stiffly and left with the book still clutched to her chest like armor.

He followed her down the stairs, holding in a chuckle so that his throat ached in the effort. Mollie might be a spirited woman, but she was also delightfully naïve. Cadal choked off the thought of how much fun educating a woman like that would be.

In the library, Mollie curled into a chair and took a sip of wine. She met Cadal's gaze again. "Now then, what did you want to talk about?" she asked calmly.

Cadal could tell that was a stretch. There was a tension in her that seemed to increase every time his hand passed near and an underlying tremor as she surveyed the length of him critically. Her browsing eyes caused a stirring of sexual interest that almost overwhelmed his confusion with her reactions. What was it about him that unnerved her so completely? What was it about her that caught his interest?

He settled into one of the other chairs and set the tray on a table between them. Cadal took a sip of wine before he answered her. "I heard you were angry. It is my place to make you at ease."

"Is it? Are you Mr. Cadal? I'm sorry. I hadn't expected a man like you to—um..."

"Serve you?" Cadal smiled at her blush. "Do not become accustomed to it. It was a simple courtesy

20

because of your long trip. Please, call me Cadal." He paused and grimaced at the unwanted alternative he must give her. "Or William. I care little for titles."

In truth, Cadal wished he had used the name Padraic a second time, but he had forgotten that Humans named children after living relatives until the mistake had already been made. Like Katie, he had a fondness for the name Padraic. Since he was forced to use a Human name, it could have been one he liked more than William.

"I can appreciate that, but there's no need to worry about me. Honestly, there isn't. My personal upsets are of little consequence." She broke off the comment and stared into the fire for a moment before continuing. "That was unprofessional of me. I owe Liam an apology, and I'll see that he gets it at dinner."

Cadal considered what she said. He knew she wasn't being honest, with him or with herself. Mollie wasn't simply angry. She was lonely and upset. He considered his next move carefully.

"I know Katie wanted you to be happy here. She arranged several surprises for you before..." He sighed and sipped the wine again.

Mollie nodded. "I hoped to meet her, but I guess that's beyond anyone's control."

He could tell that was only a small part of what Mollie really wanted to say, but she stopped herself again.

"Katie would have loved to meet you. She said you were like your grandmother, like her sister. She was looking forward to it, I know."

She regarded him strangely. "I am? I suppose that makes sense. I wanted to meet Aunt Katie because she was like Nana."

Cadal startled. "She was? I was led to believe that they were very different."

They were. Aside from possessing of a stunning beauty, the sisters were complete opposites in body and spirit. Colleen was a fiery woman from her deep red hair to the temper and wit Cadal had sampled when first he met her. Katie was light and laughter, comfort and friendship.

Mollie smiled a wistful little smile. "No, Mr. — sorry — Cadal, they were very much alike."

"Really? In what way?"

She blushed deeply. "Let's just say we all cared for the same things, the things that were important to us, the things we loved."

"Please, tell me."

Mollie didn't answer.

Cadal tried a different strategy. The book in her lap was obviously very important to her. "Does it have to do with the book you are holding?"

He had no idea what gave him that impression, and he'd asked without thinking, much as a child would ask whatever question popped into his head. He thought he'd outgrown that failing more than a century before, but Blake women tended to bring out his forgotten youth in many ways.

Mollie startled then nodded, seemingly seeking for words. "Among other things." She ran her hand over the book fondly. It was very old. "Yes, it most certainly does."

"What is it?"

She laughed. "Fairy tales," she told him, a new-found glitter in her eyes.

Cadal was captivated by how beautiful she was when she offered an honest, happy smile. "Fairy tales? What kind of Fairy tales?" he asked.

"About Fairies, of course."

He smiled uncertainly.

"They're Mima Xanthe's stories. Surely, Aunt Katie told you about them. They're a family tradition."

Cadal felt a stab of regret that he had asked the question.

"There's even a Fairy in here named Cadal," she continued.

Mollie smiled a teasing smile, and Cadal felt a warm rush he had not felt since he'd met Katie. Blake women affected him that way. They always had. It was part of the magic Xanthe and her descendents held over Cadal, the reason he was bound to serve them.

He smiled, surprisingly not a forced smile. "Really? Maybe after dinner, you can read some of the stories to me. I would wager that you are a wonderful storyteller." *Like Xanthe.*

Cadal pushed away the thought. Mollie wasn't Xanthe. He couldn't fall into that trap. He would listen to the stories, because it would put Mollie at ease. It was simply the shock of the first unpromised descendent of Xanthe he had met. Cadal still had a soulmate out there somewhere, maybe in another colony. He couldn't afford to get sidetracked by a girl who reminded him of lost love and longing so effectively, even if she was beautiful and naïve and captivating and...

By the Harmony, stop this! He gulped down a mouthful of the wine, trying to find his center.

Mollie seemed uncertain. "You'd really like to hear them?"

Cadal nodded. "Yes, I really would." He wondered at the realization and found it was true. Perhaps, he merely wanted to know what Xanthe had told her descendents. "Maybe I can tell you a few that my mother told me while we are at it."

"I'd like that. There are quite a few stories, much more than a single night's worth. Are you sure you don't want to read the book?"

"No. Fairy stories should always be told. It loses something in the simple printed word." And his grasp of written English or Gaelic was slightly weaker than his grasp of the spoken word, pitiful as that was when he needed it most.

"Oh, I don't think so. Not if you have a good imagination. If it wasn't for reading them, I wouldn't know half of them. I still get lost in them."

"Really? Did no one tell you the tales? From what Katie said..."

Mollie blushed. "Nana told me some of them before she passed away. She left me the book because she knew..." She looked toward the fire and sighed.

"What did she know?"

She didn't look at him, but she answered. "Nana knew my mother would never read them to me. My mother hated the stories. She could hardly stand that Nana read them to me. If the book had passed to her, she would have destroyed it, I'm sure."

"How sad. I always thought Fairy stories were the best sort."

"Yes, they most certainly are." Mollie smiled and met his eyes again. "I suppose you solved a portion of my upset after all."

"In what way?"

"I was looking forward to sharing the stories with Aunt Katie." She hesitated and looked to the flames, her jaw tightening and loosening as if she fought back a torrent of words.

"Go on," he prodded. Mollie had a habit of not saying what she really wanted to say that Cadal found most intriguing.

"It's childish, but I thought she would be the one person in the family that I could share those stories with, the one person who would understand them, like I do and Nana did."

"And would understand you, as well?"

She met his eyes again and nodded in shock.

"And now she is gone?"

She attempted to smile at his insight, an insight that Cadal didn't understand at all. The problem of Mollie's loneliness and anger was much more complex than he'd first supposed.

"It is not childish. It is very — Human." Cadal sobered at the word. It was very Human, wasn't it? And, she was Human. Why did it surprise him that she acted as a Human would? He shook his head, trying to right his senses.

"I should have come long ago. I've wanted to for years."

"Why did you not?"

"Work, family, responsibilities— I don't know really. I guess I'd finally had enough of it all."

"At least you are here now. I'll do my best to help you juggle until you are comfortable. Unfortunately, there are some vipers here, but I'll help you tame them until you get a handle on them."

Mollie looked slightly shocked. "Thank you. It's more help than I expected."

"That is what I'm here for," he assured her. *That's all I'm here for*, he reminded himself yet again.

Mollie sipped the wine. She was young, but Cadal was certain she was also a formidable woman, as he would expect of any Blake woman, even one that had been separated from her land.

Chapter Two

Mollie spent the rest of the afternoon alone in her room. Most of the boxes were unpacked by dinnertime. There were still two or three small boxes that would arrive, but they were winter clothing and photographs, nothing essential to living. Some of her belongings looked out of place in the ancient house, but it was a comfort to have them around her.

The bright silver and green marble that had accented her black contemporary furniture in Seattle seemed odd when set against the background of stone walls and hand-crafted wood furniture and trims. They were garish somehow, as if she should trade them in for a more homespun look that matched better. Nana's rocking chair had clashed in Seattle, and Mollie found no more need for complete order in her new setting than she had in her old. The pieces of her old life would simply have to find a way to blend with the new and better ones.

Mollie considered Cadal while she worked. She'd learned he preferred to be called by his surname and wondered whether he had encountered the corporate life of being called by that name only. She rejected that. Cadal didn't strike her as corporate. Then again, she'd done the corporate route for years though she hated it. Mollie supposed that meant she wasn't corporate material either. She smiled at the possibility that he'd adopted the use to make her at ease, because of the Fairy tale Cadal more than her background.

She sighed. Cadal must think her some sort of fool for her initial reaction. Mollie flopped onto the bed then realized her mistake. It was so much easier to remember her reaction to him in startling detail on the bed.

Mollie had been unguarded. That was her only excuse.

When Liam brought her out from the train station, she hadn't noticed his sadness, or maybe she'd mistaken it for a reserved nature. Mollie wasn't sure about that now.

She had been caught up in the sights. The little stone houses that lent the village its name were mixed with clapboard homes and stores. It was charming.

She was told the thick stand of trees that surrounded the village went on for miles, winding through neighboring villages and towns with hardly a break anywhere. The trees were bursting with the beginnings of life, though the air was still crisp. The new leaves were budded and bright green, though her breath curled in the frosty air.

The long drive circled in front of the manor house, with its two wings, hand carved oak doors and gardens already cleared for planting. Mollie had found peace in the smell of the soil and the new growth. The whole place had the warm feeling of home, a feeling that had been missing both at her apartment and her mother's house once Dad died.

Mollie knew this place from Nana's stories, but it was more than that. Nana was right. The land called to her. It needed her to be whole, as Mollie needed it to be whole. She'd felt the land sigh in silent relief that she was home. Was this what had been missing her entire life? No, surely it was more than that.

She'd stepped from the car with her backpack, knowing Liam would not allow her to carry her other luggage, that despite her unease with the idea, he already viewed Mollie as the young mistress of the manor.

She'd smiled at the clear blue sky. She belonged here.

Mollie had looked at the house again, knowing its layout intimately. The entry hall, with its stone staircase and polished wood handrails, was behind the carved doors. There were four bedrooms and one bath upstairs. Downstairs to the left, there was a formal dining room. The Blakes used it only when necessary, preferring a cozy meal in the warmth of the adjoining kitchen.

The large rooms to the right were where she would most likely find Katie. Would Aunt Katie be in the library, the parlor, or maybe in the solarium John built for her after a particularly good crop? She'd wondered that very thing aloud.

Liam's whispered answer had filtered into her mind. Mollie had asked him if she'd heard him right. In retrospect, her heart went out to the tortured look on his face. Liam obviously cared a great deal for Katie, but at the time, it seemed her entire world and all her plans had collapsed around her ears.

Mollie was alone. She'd found the courage to give up everything and go to the one person, the one place Nana had assured her would soothe her restless soul.

Then God had played one last joke on her. He let William Cadal literally walk into her barren existence. Cadal wrecked what little was left of her precious calm with his strange, foreign speech and his other-worldly good looks.

His eyes... She'd seen his eyes first. It seemed Mollie had been dreaming of those eyes all of her life.

Her mother had never put much stock in dreams, insisting that they never got you anywhere in life. But Mollie loved her dreams, especially the ones of the mysterious stranger with the haunting blue eyes, so pale it almost seemed that she could literally see through them into his soul. Those eyes were as vibrant as the blue of the morning sky with the reflection of a full moon still visible in their depths. Mollie had spent years looking at men, looking for those eyes, the eyes from her dreams.

All Mollie's dreams were realistic. In the dreams of flying, she felt the wind on her cheek. In the dreams of the land, she felt the soil beneath her feet and heard the whispers of plants and animals in her mind.

Mollie loved the dreams of *him* best. She could never see more than his eyes and the barest outlines of his face, but she'd still felt drawn to *him* from the first dream where *he* appeared.

As she'd looked at Cadal, Mollie had suddenly pictured him in the place of the nameless, faceless stranger who had always resided there. Cadal had flashed simultaneously into a hundred erotic scenes in her mind, and she'd been powerless to stop the progression.

When Cadal had moved to right her glass, the moment was broken. His eyes had shifted away from hers, and Mollie was no longer lost in the depths of them. What was wrong with her? She had barely met this man and she was lost in some adolescent crush. As childish as it sounded, she couldn't talk to him on the bed. It would have been far too easy to fall back under the strange spell of his eyes here.

As it was, it had been almost impossible for Mollie to remind herself that this man was a complete stranger who undoubtedly had no interest in her, even in the safety of the library. She'd found herself considering Cadal's windblown, baby white hair, tanned skin, and his features. The man was boyish and seductive at the same time. Cadal's sleeves had been rolled up to above his elbows and the white shirt clung to his arms and shoulders briefly when he moved, outlining his muscles in a most complimentary way. The shirt had been open at the neck, and Mollie had pulled her eyes away almost painfully to his face.

The more Mollie considered it, the more difficult it became to convince herself that his face could not possibly be the shadowy outline of her dreams. She knew those lines as if they were burned into her soul. Yes, William Cadal was the sort of man who caught her attention, and that was dangerous. Those eyes were dangerous.

Mollie sighed and stared up at the ceiling. Working with Cadal would be more difficult than she'd anticipated but for a totally different reason than she'd first supposed. A fight she could handle, but this attraction bypassed her usual defenses. Tonight, her dreams were sure to be of a new sort. Mollie felt certain that her nameless, faceless stranger would be none of the above. He had a name and a face now, whether she liked it or not.

* * * *

After dinner, Mollie insisted on taking part in the clean-up despite her long day and the existence of the servants. Cadal dismissed Elizabeth and Liam for the night when the work was completed.

Elizabeth's room was a small one behind the kitchen. Cadal understood it was a matter of propriety. An unattached Human woman should have a female servant living in the house with her, especially with a man not of her immediate family living under the same roof.

Liam, though he ate at the kitchen table instead of with the other workers in their quarters, lived in a room in the small house the men shared near the stable. It was a sign of his station that he had his own rooms there, though he was unmarried.

Cadal suggested Mollie collect the book of Fairy tales and meet him in the library. He had stoked the fire before dinner. He tended to it, then poured two glasses of wine from the bottle by the hearth and laid out two cushions by the fire.

As he settled on one of the cushions, he wondered at what he was doing. He wasn't preparing for a tryst, so why had he made the scene so intimate? Cadal did it automatically, with no forethought of what it might look like to Mollie. It was too late, at any rate. He could hear her footsteps in the hall.

She stopped in the doorway and surveyed the scene before her. Even at that distance and in the light from the fire, he could see her color rise. Mollie considered something, but Cadal barely noticed the feeling of her upset and indecision as it assaulted him. He was busy contemplating something else, her hair.

Mollie had let down the tight bun of hair behind her head, and the style had been most deceiving. Her hair reached the small of her back, and the firelight picked up flecks of stunning red in the rich color. She seemed to make a conscious decision. Mollie moved to the other cushion and folded herself neatly into it in a single, fluid motion.

Cadal felt a stab of regret for her discomfort. "Is there enough light for you? I could turn on a lamp, if you need more light to read."

She met his eyes, clearing her throat before she spoke. "No, that's all right. I don't really need to read them anymore, and it's so much more fitting to tell stories by a fire, isn't it?"

"Yes, I think it is at that."

He was glad she refused his offer of more light. Mollie was simply enchanting in the firelight. Cadal found it hard to remind himself that she was still so very young and innocent. *And, she is Human.* That was the part he had to keep his mind on. No matter what fantasies he found himself trapped in, they were impossible. He was what he was. He could not change his life, and Mollie could not become what he needed in a wife.

"So," she broke the moment for him, "where should I start? At the beginning, I suppose."

"No. Start with your favorite story. Which one do you like best?"

Mollie blushed deeply and dropped her gaze to the book in her lap.

"Is that a problem?" he asked.

"No. Of course not." She flipped through the old book and started reading.

Cadal smiled and sipped his wine. He understood her blush now. Her favorite story was about Cadal and the squirrels he loved to ride. Mollie barely glanced at the book or at him. She seemed transported. The story came alive in her words, and Cadal found himself transported as well, back to his youth. The story as he knew it filled his mind.

Cadal's mother marched him before Morda to seek counsel after she caught him riding squirrels through the treetops yet again as a child.

"But, Mother," he argued, "I can fly. What danger can there be?"

Zera paused in their march to the Great Chamber. "Them. The outsiders could see you. Humans! If you wish to ride, I will take you out in Human form and you may ride a horse. Then they would not know what you are."

"Jumping with the squirrels is exciting. Besides, no Human could get close without the sentries seeing them and the Fairy Mistress taking care of it." Cadal dropped his gaze. He could tell by the look on her face that his mother wanted to hear no more of it.

In the end, it proved Cadal needn't have worried about the Fairy Mistress. Morda barely suppressed a smile at the tale, and her eyes glittered in amusement.

Zera's withering look spoke volumes. "I should have known you would be unsympathetic. Really, Morda. When will you take this sort of thing seriously? With all of your close calls, one would think you would see the danger inherent here."

"Oh, Zera. I do. I really do. I suppose when I have forgotten the blush of youth, I will not be amused by it either."

Zera straightened in annoyance. "I see. I have forgotten the blush of youth?" she asked acidly.

"No, Zera. I am sure you still know youth. She glows in your face and skips in your step. You simply forget her humor. Though, even I must admit, your son is handful enough to age anyone."

When Mollie finished, she looked at him expectantly.

"Wonderful," he commented. "Are there any more stories about that Cadal?"

"There are several. Would you like to hear more about him?"

"Do you like them? Would you enjoy telling them?"

Mollie nodded and met his eyes.

Cadal wasn't sure why he asked. Did it really make any difference if Mollie liked a story character? It was another version of himself, someone he could vaguely remember being or being like once, but he couldn't tell her that. So, what did it matter? It did matter, for some reason. Cadal was relieved to learn that she liked the stories. Was this what the Humans called pride?

"Then please do." Maybe, he wanted to know what memories Xanthe left behind of him. Yes, that was the most likely explanation.

Mollie told three more stories with hardly a break between them. She moved through the book, her hands finding the pages without searching. She spoke in a soothing voice, sipping wine at pauses in the tales. When the glass was empty, he refilled it without comment.

Cadal was transported, again and again. Mollie was a magical storyteller. He heard stories about the pond where the young Fairies played, racing raindrops in a summer storm, and riding the wind on a clear moonlit night when ice glittered like jewels on the tree limbs. That one gave him pause. Xanthe was with Cadal that night. He had taken her out to show her the very thing she described in her story.

Mollie placed the book aside and stretched out with her head on a cushion.

"Are you tired?" Cadal asked.

"A little, but..." She looked to the fire. "I know all of those stories about Cadal. Did your mother tell you any Cadal stories? Since we seem to be talking about him anyway."

Cadal bit back his amusement. "Quite a few, actually. Would you like to hear one?"

Mollie faced him and waited for him to tell a tale.

He chose to tell her about a beautiful glade of flowers he'd discovered when he was eighty or ninety years old. As he spoke, he reminded himself constantly to use the third person. He also left out that he'd taken Xanthe to the glade in hopes of pleasing her. Xanthe had loved it, but she hadn't loved Cadal.

At the end of the story, Mollie smiled up at him, and Cadal was struck by the wild urge not to be merely a mentor to his young charge.

"Did Cadal ever fall in love?" she asked. Mollie seemed interested in hearing the answer, though she hid a yawn behind her hand.

Cadal felt a pang of loss at the question. He nodded and stared into the fire. "Yes, he did."

"Was she very beautiful?"

"Yes, she was. Would you like to hear the tale? It is not a very happy one, I'm afraid. I thought I should warn you."

"An unhappy love story? Why is it unhappy?"

Cadal met her eyes again and spoke very softly. "Because she loved someone else."

Mollie shook her head. "Then she couldn't have been the right one for him."

Her answer was childlike in its simplicity. If only the truth were so simple. "Maybe not, but he loved her dearly just the same."

She considered it for a few moments. "I suppose that hurts just as much. I think we'll save that story for another night. I really don't want to hear a sad story tonight. What is *your* favorite story?"

His mind was abruptly a blank slate. Turnabout was fair play, as the Humans said, but he had never really considered the matter before. "I suppose it would be wind dancing."

"Wind dancing? What is that?"

Xanthe didn't write about wind dancing. It shouldn't have surprised him. After all, Xanthe was never in love with another Fairy. She'd never dreamed of the day when it would be socially acceptable to ask or accept the promise. Cadal frowned at that thought before he started talking.

"When two Fairies have been courting, when they are old enough to wed and they are sure of their love for each other, they make a promise to wed. They fly off in search of a wind current that appeals to them and dance together in the wind, a dance of their hearts' own design. After that, everyone in the tree-city knows they are one. They wind dance that day, at their ceremony, and at any time of great joy and celebration for the couple, but a Fairy never wind dances until he has found his soulmate and committed to wed her. It is their promise, and it is their most solemn vow to each other. Even the ceremony is not as important as the promise to have the ceremony. At the ceremony, they are forever bonded to each other. Their souls become one for all time."

Mollie's eyes closed, and she smiled at the image she'd formed in her mind. When Cadal finished his tale, her eyes didn't open again. At first, he thought she was asleep, but then she spoke.

"How beautiful. If only life were really like that."

"Like what?" he asked.

"So simple. So enchanting and beautiful." She yawned deeply, and her voice became slower and more subdued. "If only love really lasted forever. And flying— What I wouldn't give to fly just once."

Cadal was stunned. Xanthe may have wanted to live life as a Human, but her descendent seemed to want nothing more than to live as a Fairy. *If only that was possible...* He had never heard of a case of the transformation being worked in reverse. It took the Fairy magic and the help of The Harmony to convert a Fairy to Human. It couldn't be done in reverse. Mollie didn't have the Fairy magic necessary to the change.

"What do you know about flying?" he asked in amusement, remembering asking Katie that same question at not much younger than Mollie was now.

"Fairies don't use wings, you know. They float on the wind magically. When there is no wind, they..." She furrowed her brow, stammered out an incoherent word then continued. "They *claad* a wind to serve them. It's like floating in a pool of cool water. The wind caresses your face." She sighed in contentment, her expression easing again.

Cadal sucked in his breath, resolved to read Xanthe's book. The sensations seemed far too accurate and personal to have come from anywhere else, and Mollie's use of the Fairy word for *calling elementals* made his head spin. Even Katie's descriptions were never that vivid, and the older woman certainly never spoke a word of the ancient language in Cadal's presence.

He decided to press the temporary advantage he had by asking the sleepy girl another question. "Where did you learn about flying?" he asked close to her ear.

Mollie surprised him by moving closer to his voice in her half-sleep. Her hair brushed his cheek as she moved, sending a wave of warmth through Cadal that he hadn't experienced in over a century, since Xanthe had left his life.

"In my dreams. Nice dreams..."

Cadal's arousal was forgotten. His heart began to pound. Were these dreams simply the result of the years of Fairy tales? Surely not. What could be the purpose of them? He knew, as all Fairies knew, that dreams had a meaning. They served a purpose of sorts. Was it similar for Humans?

Mollie slipped into a deep sleep. She needed the sleep; Cadal decided not to wake her. Rather, he scooped her into his arms. Mollie nestled her cheek to his chest in unconscious response. As Cadal laid her on her bed, he looked at her again and sighed deeply. This duty was going to be much more difficult than he'd imagined. Surely, fate could not be so cruel to each of them. Mollie could never have the Fairy life she dreamed of, and they could never have more than a friendship.

He covered her with a quilt and turned to leave. Cadal had no doubts that Mollie would be more comfortable if he removed more than her shoes, for as long as she slept anyway. But that would be both an unfair assumption to make, that she would welcome such a move on his part, and too hard for him to walk away from.

The door was almost closed behind him when he heard Mollie murmur his name in her sleep. What he wouldn't give to know what Mollie was dreaming. *I'd settle for which Cadal she is dreaming of.*

Chapter Three

Mollie woke suddenly. She ran her hand over her jeans, sighed, then grimaced. She wasn't sure whether she was relieved or disappointed that it had all been a dream.

Cadal had taken his place in her dreams as she knew he would, and she'd greeted him by name, now that she knew the name to use. She shivered, remembering how real the sensations were, but there was no denying that they had been a dream and not a drunken reality. William Cadal was obviously much more restrained or disinterested in person than he had been in her dreams.

Mollie sighed again and swept the quilt back. She glanced at her watch and groaned. She hadn't changed the time from Seattle to New York to overseas. Mollie couldn't remember how many time zone changes were involved, and as a result, had no idea what time it was.

She picked out a lightweight brown sweater, a t-shirt, and jeans and went about her usual morning routine. When she was satisfied with the results of her braided hair and clothing, she went downstairs.

She glanced at the clock in the kitchen and started. It was ten o'clock? "Is that right?" she asked Elizabeth.

"The time? Yes, Miss Mollie."

Mollie made a mental note to ask Elizabeth again not to call her that. She shook her head and reset her watch. "What a lousy first impression," she grumbled. She clicked the set button a second time to start the watch moving again.

"Not at all. You simply have to get used to the time change."

Cadal's voice came from behind her shoulder, and Mollie's body surged in instant awareness to his proximity. What was the matter with her? She was hardly a teenager anymore, but when you have such intimate dreams about someone that are so real, it is hard to turn it off.

"Thank you, but I really shouldn't upset everyone's schedule this way. I'm sure Elizabeth has better things to do than cook special meals for me," Mollie replied without looking at him. Considering the riot in her body already, looking at William Cadal would probably be a very bad move.

Cadal circled to a chair in front of her and sat. "It is not an upset, is it Elizabeth?"

"Not at all, Miss Mollie. Would you like some breakfast? I can make some toast and eggs if you'd like."

No time like the present. "Just toast will be fine, Elizabeth, and please call me Mollie." She glanced at Cadal and smiled, taking a seat across from him. "I don't care much for titles either."

Cadal chuckled. "I'll have toast as well, Elizabeth."

Mollie raised an eyebrow at him. "You just woke?"

"No. I had some work to do, and I decided not to take breakfast earlier with Liam."

She felt the heat rise in her cheeks. "Well, I'm sorry you got stuck with it alone. I'll try to be on the ball from now on. What time do you usually get to work?"

"Six or so, but there is no need for you to be up that early."

"If six is when the work begins, six is when I'll start work."

"There are servants to help you, so you don't have to carry the load alone," Cadal commented, as he accepted a cup of tea from Elizabeth.

Mollie met his eyes, hoping not to lose herself in the depths of blue. "I don't believe in servants. These people are in my employ, and I will delegate responsibilities to them. I believe you should never ask employees to do anything you are not willing to do yourself. If you do, you demean their place in life."

Cadal smiled widely and raised his cup to Mollie. "You will be a formidable land owner."

"Really? Why is that?"

"You are willing to get your hands dirty to get what you want."

"Is that unusual?"

Cadal sipped his tea, raising his shoulder in a half-shrug. "The other land owners may hate it, but your employees will love it."

Mollie sighed. "And making the other land owners happy should rate exactly how high on my list of priorities?"

"I would be friendly. There is no reason to antagonize them, but do not live your life to please them either."

"I see. I've always hated politics, but I suppose there's no escaping it, even here."

He looked wistful for a moment. "I'm sure there is somewhere you can escape it."

Mollie cracked a smile, as Elizabeth set down plates of toast in front of them. "Yeah, the Fairy court, I'm sure." Her smile disappeared as Cadal met her eyes again.

That time, there was nothing warm and inviting about his expression. It seemed Mr. Cadal wasn't what he appeared at all. That shouldn't be a surprise to her. Few men were. If Mollie was reading his expression correctly, Cadal was angry or hurt. But why would he be?

Suddenly, Mollie didn't feel much like eating. Why was she such a lousy judge of character? She picked at her toast and avoided Cadal's eyes.

* * * *

Cadal started his tour of the grounds with Mollie. The young woman was cool and detached. She asked questions and listened attentively to his answers, but her warm, comfortable disposition was gone. Cadal knew his reaction at breakfast was to blame, and he cursed himself inwardly for it.

He knew why he was so angry. It was her joke. It was as if Xanthe had rejected him all over again. As lost in her daydreams of Fairies as Mollie was, she didn't really believe any of it.

He sighed. It didn't matter. Whether she believed it or not, she was Human. *Then again, if a Fairy can become Human, perhaps there is something that could be done.* If she didn't believe it, it could never work. *These flights of fancy are hopeless,* he raged at himself. It couldn't work anyway. The Fairy magic couldn't be given, only taken away.

He showed her to the stables first. Mollie loved her horse and insisted on saddling up to exercise Squirrel while they continued their tour. Cadal could tell she enjoyed riding, though she was not an expert rider. Mollie cracked her first smile since breakfast when Cadal told her the mare's name, but she didn't make a comment. He cringed inwardly at that. She was probably afraid to make a comment because of his reaction that morning.

Mollie loved the landscape. She marveled at how beautiful the land was. She claimed it was beyond her wildest dreams. Whether the fields of grazing animals, lush forest, and rolling hills were really so much more beautiful to her or it was simply the rush of knowing she never had to leave it was unclear to Cadal.

She confided that she had seen farms and forests, despite her mother's complete aversion to anything that resembled nature. The fact that a Blake woman hated nature was shocking to him. How had such a thing happened?

Mollie rattled on and on about every color and texture, every animal and flower, as if they were magical in themselves, and Cadal rediscovered his belief in that very thing. He had to wonder when he'd lost The Harmony's way. Knowing the magic of nature is inborn in every Fairy, yet he had forgotten it. It seemed strange that a Human woman could teach him something so undeniably Fairy.

Cadal saw the deep longing in Mollie's eyes when she looked at the pond in the near grazing pasture, but a glance at her current outfit and a sigh told Cadal that she would be back that way when she was dressed more to the occasion.

Mollie was such a puzzle. At times, she seemed willing to throw caution to the wind and be absolutely free. Then she came crashing back, almost unnaturally, to reality.

Finally, the pair reached the small planting fields. The men were preparing for the spring planting. To Cadal's surprise, Mollie asked to hear the plan. Liam explained what he intended to do, and she shook her head.

"No, it won't work. You need to switch the north and south fields."

Liam regarded her strangely. "No, miss. This crop requires more water. I can water it separately if it's in the north field. If it's in the south field, I'll end up over-watering the north to maintain the south."

Mollie shook her head more forcefully. "You'll deplete the south field if you plant another harsh crop there this year. It has to be this way."

"No offense, miss, but it can't be done. I tried to explain that to Miss Katie."

"And you thought I'd back down easier?" Mollie snapped at him.

Cadal startled at the abrupt change in her. *This was the side of her Liam encountered yesterday. Motor-cross helmet, indeed.*

Liam paled. "No, miss. It's just the watering..." He waved his hand in frustration and looked to Cadal for help.

Mollie rubbed her temples. "How much watering are we talking about?"

"On top of what the other fields need? Probably a thorough soaking every week or so starting with the next few days before we plant to give the crops a good start."

"And how many men do we have on staff?"

"Eight. Why?"

She considered it carefully for a minute or so. "That's fair. We do it my way."

"But Miss, how will we handle the watering?"

"I'll show you."

She marched to the equipment shed. Mollie reappeared, wearing an oversized pair of work gloves and carrying two buckets. She walked up to the stream and filled them.

Liam stared at her in shock. "She's not going to do what I think she is, is she?"

Cadal nodded his head and tried to bury a smile. "I think she is, actually."

Mollie trudged back down the path around the hilltop and dumped the water on the south field. Liam sprinted after her and tried to take the buckets from her hands as she headed back up.

She turned to face him. "If you want to help, get your own buckets. We're planting this way, if I have to water it myself, but I trust I won't be doing this alone."

Liam nodded and hurried back toward the shed to get his own set of buckets.

Cadal watched in amusement as Mollie moved fluidly back and forth with buckets of water. When an hour had passed, she sat down and wiped her brow on the back of a glove before pulling it off with her teeth and flexing her sore hands. Cadal approached her, as she dumped a handful of water over her face and neck.

"Ready to turn it over to someone else yet?" he asked her.

She looked at him with a measure of annoyance. "No, just a break."

Cadal settled to the ground beside her. "Do you mind if I ask you why?"

Mollie stood and stripped off her sweater in favor of the t-shirt beneath it. She dropped the sweater on the ground and pulled her gloves back on. As she hefted her buckets, she met his eyes. "Because none of those men will want to be shown up by a woman. It will be scheduled. Two man teams. When it's my turn, I'll work. Never ask an employee to do something you won't."

He nodded. "Good. Then tomorrow is my turn."

She met his eyes with something resembling suspicion in the depths of her own. "Thank you. You'll work with me."

"What happened to taking turns?" he demanded.

"We will after this first time. These men have to know I'm willing to work like this. Otherwise, I'll be nothing but another useless, pretty face giving them orders."

Cadal nodded though he really didn't understand her drive.

He watched her for the rest of the morning. Mollie took half the breaks Liam did, but she never raised an eyebrow to him for it. Liam was tired. She could see that, but as she predicted, he worked on because she did. Mollie ordered Liam off to lunch, though she claimed she wasn't hungry.

Cadal ordered Liam to take his time about coming back but to bring a tray for the young miss when he did. Liam nodded knowingly and disappeared toward the house.

Mollie was a fiery, stubborn woman, and the Blake estates had been without such a woman since Colleen had left for America. He had to wonder if Ballynaclogh was prepared for the return of this breed of Blake.

While Liam was gone, Cadal took over his place on the field. Mollie eyed him for a moment then seemed to decide that this only served to strengthen her case. For his part, Cadal was trying to ease the amount of work she did any way he could without hurting her pride.

She wolfed down a single sandwich and a glass of milk before pulling her gloves on and taking a set of buckets from Liam. "You're tired, Liam. Go tend to the animals while Cadal helps me for a while. We have to do this again tomorrow. I'll need you fresh."

"I can assign two of the men, miss."

"Assign whomever you like to help me. I will take any help offered."

"Then let me take over, miss."

"No, Liam. I need you ready to plant. I'll rest then."

Liam ground his teeth, nodded, and headed for the stables. Mollie glanced up the hill wearily and set back to work.

Shortly before dinner, the last of the field was soaked. Mollie dropped the buckets and sank to her knees. She pulled off her gloves stiffly and buried her hands in her lap. Cadal could see the shaking she was trying to hide from him. She was exhausted, but she did what she'd set out to do. Her point was made. He returned the buckets to the shed, while Mollie rested. When he returned, he offered her his hand. She shook her head, so Cadal sat down next to her.

"Will you let the men do the work tomorrow?" he asked.

"No, I have a point to make."

"You have made it. You outlasted Liam by double this morning and matched me all afternoon on top of that. It is enough now. It really is."

"It's not. I'm putting them out to do it my way. They have to know I'll sweat and bleed as much as they do and more to make it work. It's not fair to them any other way."

Cadal set his jaw. "All right, but it is going to rain tomorrow. If that soaks the fields?"

49

Mollie met his eyes angrily. "If it's enough rain to soak them, I'll back off. If not, I own a rain poncho."

* * * *

Cadal waited for Mollie to come down to dinner for half an hour before he went in search of her. She had made it back to the house under her own power. How was still a mystery to him, but she did it. Mollie had disappeared into a hot bath and into her room, but she didn't reappear.

He knocked on her door, but she didn't answer. He sucked in his breath and opened the door. Cadal hated to intrude on her privacy, but he was a little worried.

As he might have guessed, Mollie was asleep. She had dressed in a fresh t-shirt and a pair of shorts then fallen asleep across her bed, sandals still clutched in her hand.

Cadal smiled at her. He removed the sandals and dropped them to the floor, then scooped her up onto the pillow. As he pulled the quilt over her, Cadal noticed the marks on her hands. Mollie had worked beyond the point of blisters, until the blisters burst and then bled. He shook his head in wonder and held her hand gently in his own, examining the marred flesh of her palm. It was no wonder Mollie wouldn't take his hand in the field. It would have been agony for her, if she had.

For tonight, he would let her sleep. Tomorrow, Cadal would have to take Mollie in hand. To that end, he had work to do. He would call rain. Cadal would call down the grandmother of all storms, if it would keep Mollie out of the fields tomorrow. He smiled. This was

Mollie. It would *have* to be the grandmother of all storms to keep her out of the fields.

Cadal kissed Mollie's forehead before he left. He had been wrong, after all. She may have Xanthe's spirit, but she was nothing like her ancestor despite it. Xanthe would never have attempted what Mollie did today or what she still planned to do tomorrow, though she knew the condition she was in. Mollie was much more woman than he had given her credit for.

* * * *

Mollie's alarm went off at half past five, and she rolled to her feet with a half-swallowed groan. Every inch of her body hurt.

I insisted on doing that again? She grumbled at her stubborn streak. She wouldn't have done it if she hadn't been so angry with herself for misjudging Cadal. It *was* enough. Mollie knew he was right about that, but she was too stubborn to admit it to him. She didn't need Cadal to baby sit her, and she was going to show him precisely how little she needed him at all.

Except, Mollie did need him to reel her in yesterday, and she hadn't let him. Now, she was stuck between going through with the plan to hand water or admitting to Cadal that she was wrong. She shuddered at the idea of admitting to him that she wasn't smart enough to end this when she should have.

She washed her face, wincing at her battered hands. Watering today certainly wasn't going to help that situation, and she vaguely considered the possibility of padding the gloves somehow before she started work.

A sound intruded on her consciousness. Mollie stepped to the window and swept the drapes aside. *Rain.* It was pouring outside. The fields would be soaked by Mother Nature herself. She laid her head on the glass and thanked whatever unnamed gods sent that lovely rain. It was her salvation. Another day like yesterday would kill her, a fact she would never mention out loud, especially to Cadal.

Mollie blinked back tears and closed the drape over the window. It was time to go to work. She looked at her outfit. It would suffice unless she found outside work that needed done. She padded down to the kitchen on bare feet. The stone floors were cool and relaxing, and Mollie felt the last of the sleep seeping out of her mind.

Cadal was there ahead of her. He looked up from the book in front of him and smiled warmly. "Feel better?"

"A little sore, but I'll survive." Mollie cringed inwardly at the understatement. "Is that Mima's Fairy tale book? I thought you didn't want to read it."

"Yes, it is. I missed hearing them last night, so I thought I might read a few. Maybe tonight, you can read me a few more of them. From the sounds of the rain, we can relax the water brigade."

"What else needs done?"

"Paperwork. I'd like to cover it before the busy time of the month hits us."

"In other words, you want me to take it easy for today, right?" Mollie raised an eyebrow at him over the slight smile that crept out despite her wishes.

"Yes, I do, but I knew better than to say it. After yesterday..." Cadal grinned at her again.

Mollie was struck simultaneously by his knowledge of her stubborn refusal to let him tell her what to do and by how handsome he was, even when she wasn't lost in those wonderful eyes. She nodded and took a seat across from him.

As she settled into the chair, Cadal took her hands gently. Mollie sucked in her breath at the sensation of his warm hands enfolding hers.

"And," he began as his eyes locked onto hers, "I'd like to bandage these."

She didn't need to look at her hands to know what Cadal meant. She couldn't have left the depths of his eyes if she wanted to.

Her blush deepened as much from the feeling of his hand on hers as from her embarrassment. She nodded in response. "You put me to bed again?"

"Just tucked you in. I was worried when you didn't answer me."

Mollie nodded again. Part of her wished he wouldn't leave the next time he did that.

Cadal smiled in amusement and shifted his eyes away. Mollie cursed herself for being so transparent and so affected. Why couldn't she hate him? Surely, Cadal could see right through her. He could play this game forever, and she couldn't stop it.

* * * *

Cadal found familiarizing Mollie with the bookwork of the estate a simple task. It turned out bookwork was her specialty. What he dubbed "unnecessarily complex," she assured him was one of the simplest systems she had ever encountered. He hated to imagine how much worse a system could get.

Shortly before lunch, Cadal left her alone in the library while he checked some numbers with Liam. He returned to find Elizabeth setting out to get him. Cadal didn't wait for an explanation. He felt Mollie's upset and her anger from outside, just like the day he'd come to the estate to help Katie.

He stopped short in the library doorway. Mollie stood behind the desk, a fist cocked and at the ready. Across from her, red-faced and dour as ever, was Joshua Thornton. It shouldn't have surprised him. Thornton caused startling reactions in the Blake women. Perhaps, Cadal would always know when the unhappy neighbor was close by.

Mollie pointed to the doorway without looking at it. "I told you once. I don't care who you are. I want you out of my house right now. If you're still here when the men arrive, I'll have you thrown out bodily."

Thornton scowled deeper. "You don't know what you're doing, I assure you. The men will set you straight when they arrive."

"I doubt it." Her voice was cold and stern.

Cadal stepped into the room and moved to Mollie's side. "I doubt it, too. Now Mr. Thornton, I would suggest you state your business and leave this house quickly."

"Call off that hellcat, and I will," Thornton growled at him.

He startled at the word the irate man chose to describe Mollie, but he wrapped her hand in his own, and she relaxed the fist in response. Mollie lowered her arm, slowly unknotting her muscles under his hand. She didn't look at Cadal. Her eyes remained locked on Thornton.

"What is your business here, Mr. Thornton?" Cadal inquired.

"You know my business. I offer a fair price. You know that. No matter how determined," he spat the word with a certain distaste, "this woman is, she is not equal to running an estate like this, and you know that as well. Talk sense to her."

"I know nothing of the sort. Miss Hardy has proven herself knowledgeable and able, more so than Miss Katie had been for many years."

Thornton's face darkened. "I'll speak to the other owners. Surely, this child doesn't own controlling interest in the estate."

Mollie's muscles tightened under his hand. "I hold sole interest. There is no one else for you to talk to."

"That's ridiculous. What of your sister?"

"I have no sisters."

Thornton appeared shocked beyond words.

"No brothers either," she continued.

"At least that hasn't changed," he commented dryly. "What of your mother? Your aunt? Surely, you're not the only Blake woman left."

"The last, except for my mother."

Thornton smiled in perceived victory.

Mollie smiled wider. "I should mention that she signed her interests away to me before I left. I bought her out."

Thornton looked positively murderous.

"This is my land, Mr. Thornton. Only mine, and after your actions today, I guarantee that I would rather sell my land at a loss to your worst enemy than to you at twice the price you're offering."

"You can't be serious."

Mollie's eyes narrowed dangerously. "I assure you that I am."

"My actions? I could call the constable and report your attack on me."

"Try it. I had grounds, and you know it."

"Wait," Cadal interrupted them. He addressed Thornton first. "She attacked you?"

"She punched me. If she hasn't blacked my eye, I've never been punched before."

Imagine that. Cadal was suddenly sure that these Human hotheads had attacked Thornton on quite a few occasions. But while she was spirited, Mollie had never struck Cadal as the violent sort. He wondered at what Thornton had done to warrant such a response. Mollie had grounds to act. She'd said that only a moment before. He turned to Mollie, but her eyes were still locked on Thornton.

"You goosed me," she stated simply.

"I told you I didn't know who you were," Thornton protested.

"That makes it all right?" she stormed at him.

Cadal whispered close to her ear. "*What* did he do?" He was confused by the strange use of the word goose. A goose was a noisy bird, wasn't it?

Mollie looked at him sharply. She rose on tiptoe and whispered her response close to his ear. "He grabbed my ass."

Cadal felt his face flush. He regarded Thornton coldly. For some reason, the thought angered him. Taking liberties like that with any woman was simply not appropriate, but taking such liberties with Mollie made Cadal's blood boil. "Mr. Thornton, I think you should leave now."

Thornton gaped at him. "You can't be serious. It was a simple misunderstanding. She had no cause to—"

Cadal cut him off. "Mr. Thornton, Miss Hardy has asked you to leave twice. I have asked you twice. If you do not remove yourself, I will be forced to remove you and report your actions to the constable. I think you have Miss Hardy's answer. Have the good grace to accept it, even as you seem to lack the good grace to offer a decent apology."

Thornton offered Mollie a scathing look in parting and turned to go.

Mollie relaxed her cheek against Cadal's shoulder as the front door slammed behind him. "Thank you," she breathed in relief.

Cadal inspected her closely. Mollie was pale and somewhat shaken.

"Are you sure you're all right?" he asked.

She nodded and dropped into the chair behind her. "Yes, I'll be fine. He just made me angry." Mollie inspected the red mark on her knuckles critically and flexed the stiffness out of her bandaged hands.

He crouched to her eye level. "You are sure you are not hurt?"

Mollie laid her hand on his arm and smiled weakly. "Yes. He's a snake. He thought—" Her smile fled, and her face was suddenly very hard. "Well, he thought it would give him the upper hand. He didn't count on my reaction."

"You mean it was not a mistake?"

"Of course not. Elizabeth let him in and pointed him to me. Who else would I be?"

Cadal felt his anger soaring again. "I should have hit him while I had the chance." He cringed inwardly, wondering where the thought had come from and where the anger that drove it came from as well.

Mollie smiled at him in amusement. "No. By law, I was provoked. You weren't. You'd be facing charges if you had. Remember that."

Cadal was stunned at her calm regard for the situation. "At any rate, I think any further visits from the land owners should be directed to me."

"Are you staying forever then?" Mollie raised an eyebrow and waited for a response.

"I cannot promise that." He felt ill at the admission, but he knew it was true. How could he leave? Then again, how could he stay? He found he wanted to stay desperately.

"I thought so." She sighed deeply. "Then I'll have to learn to handle them eventually."

Chapter Four

The next few days passed quickly for Mollie. The planting of the first two fields was well under way, and one of the other landowners paid a visit to meet the new Blake woman at the estate.

Geoffrey Allen was an easy-going gentleman. He didn't press Mollie to sell as Thornton had, but he let her know that the offer was there if she ever wished to.

He also congratulated her on her right jab. Apparently, Mr. Allen wasn't a fan of Mr. Thornton, and the thought of his intemperate rival sporting a shiner was too rich for words.

Mollie felt the need for some time off. She told Elizabeth she was headed out for a walk and set off across the pasture and away from the planting fields. Ten minutes later, she realized where she was headed. She considered going back for a bathing suit but decided that her t-shirt and shorts would suffice. It was a little chilly for a swim, but Mollie found she had acclimated to the colder climate of the estate quickly.

At the pond, she stripped off her shoes, socks, and watch and waded into the cold water. It was not quite as brisk as a few mountain lakes Mollie had managed in her youth, but none of her coworkers at the summer retreats could ever understand how she managed those. The cold water was just what she needed. Mollie dove in and bobbed back to the surface. She realized her t-shirt was now semi-transparent, but it would dry quickly and, after all, it *was* private property.

She had been in the water for fifteen minutes or so when she heard a voice call her name. Mollie bobbed her head up to tread water while she searched the shore with her eyes. There was a strange man watching her from where she entered the pond.

"Who are you? How did you know I was here?" Mollie demanded. A sobering thought occurred to her. No one knew she was here.

The man smiled widely. "Just keeping an eye on you, love," he drawled, too companionably for Mollie's comfort.

She felt her breath catch. Everything about the man looked disreputable and dangerous, from his short, stocky frame to his hard eyes and his ill-fitting clothing.

"This is private property. I suggest you leave."

"Yes, I know it. I heard you're not very hospitable to your neighbors. That's dangerous in these parts."

Mollie felt a stab of fear. She looked around, but there was nowhere to go. Her shoes were close to the intruder. The pond wasn't very big. If she swam to another shore, he'd be close behind her, and she'd be barefoot and half-naked. She met his eyes again. The water was safer. He probably wouldn't follow, and she'd have a fighting chance if he did. Mollie was a strong swimmer, and he would be barefoot like she was.

"Really? How is it dangerous?" she asked.

"Powerful enemies have powerful friends."

"And which are you?"

"Depends on your point of view, now doesn't it? Why don't you be a good girl and come out here where we can talk like friends."

It wasn't a question. It wasn't even a request. He expected her to do it, but there was no way Mollie was going out there with him. He could stand there all day. The water wouldn't bother her, and eventually someone would start looking for her, wouldn't they?

"Come on, love. I just have a proposition for you. That water is mighty cold. I wouldn't want to have to come in after you."

Mollie bit her lip. Why didn't she tell Cadal where she was going? Or Liam? Damn it, why didn't she tell Elizabeth?

* * * *

Cadal was working with Liam at the stable when the first sensations hit him. There was no question in his mind this time. Mollie was in trouble again. She wasn't upset or angry. She was frightened. A chill ran up Cadal's spine.

"Did you see Mollie at the house?" he asked.

"No. Elizabeth said she went for a walk."

Cadal nodded. He strode to Thunder's stall and bridled the stallion then led him outside and mounted him without a saddle. Cadal didn't need the bridle either, but skipping that would be too difficult to explain away.

Liam watched him with a look of concern, but he didn't say what was bothering him.

"I'll be right back. I have to ask Mollie a question," Cadal managed by way of explanation.

He didn't wait for an answer from Liam before setting off at a gallop. Cadal knew where Mollie would go. She had wanted to go to the pond since she'd first laid eyes on it.

The feeling was getting stronger, though whether he was getting closer or she was more frightened, Cadal had no idea. A sudden jolt akin to panic settled in his chest. For whatever reason, Mollie was terrified, and

Cadal had no idea why he could feel it. He topped the rise at a little less than a full run.

There was a man standing at the edge of the pond, calling to Mollie. Both of them looked up sharply at his approach. While Cadal could see the relief in Mollie's face and feel it from her as well, the man's eyes narrowed suspiciously at this new arrival.

Cadal dropped to the ground beside the intruder before Thunder had come to a stop, a move practiced on countless wild animals over two centuries. "This is private property," he informed the man.

The insolent Human grinned crookedly. "So I've heard."

"Then leave."

"I'm leaving. I just came to deliver a message. That done, I'll be on my way."

Cadal glanced at Mollie. "Are you all right?"

She nodded.

"Come out."

Mollie glanced at the strange man and shook her head slowly. She was staying put until he was gone. She was truly frightened of him.

Cadal turned to glare at him. Whatever he had done didn't sit well with Cadal.

The man shrugged his shoulders and started to walk away. "Women. The man who can understand them is worth his weight in the Sidhe's own gold."

Once the man disappeared into the tree line, Mollie cut through the water to the shore in a few strong strokes. She rose from the pond, arms crossed over her chest and shivering. She didn't meet his gaze. Rather, she stared off in the direction the man had taken.

Cadal peeled off his sweater. As he dropped it over Mollie's head, he realized her arms were locked around her chest for more than warmth. He could see the straps of her undergarment clearly through the near-transparent fabric of her shirt. His eyes strayed to her midsection, clearly visible through the non-existent cover. *Harmony alive!* He tried moving his gaze lower, but the sight of water coursing down her slim thighs made him close his eyes, gritting in pain against his instant arousal. Cadal pulled the sweater down over her hips.

"Put your arms in." He kept his voice gentle, belying his scattered state. "Get warm."

Cadal opened his eyes to her face, hoping for a reprieve in the need crushing him, but seeing her in his state of arousal was disconcerting, no matter where on her body he focused.

Mollie met his eyes tearfully and slid her arms into the heavy sweater. She scooped a lock of hair behind her ear and wrapped her arms around her chest again. She fidgeted nervously and averted her eyes. Cadal felt the sick swirl in her stomach growing steadily stronger, but he wasn't sure what he could do to make her feel better. When the tears came, he wrapped his arms around her; she sank into his embrace, burying her face in his chest.

Cadal held her while she cried, and the tears stopped much sooner than he'd thought they would, but the shivering didn't subside with it. Cadal wasn't sure if it was the cold, the embarrassment, or relief, but he wasn't taking any chances.

He lifted Mollie by the waist and set her astride Thunder. He hoisted himself up behind her and wrapped his arm around her to steady her while they rode.

The trip back was torture. Cadal tried to keep Mollie from feeling the force of his erection while holding her close to his body to protect her.

Back at the house, he cradled the young woman to his chest and sent Thunder back to the stable with a smack on the rump. Cadal called Elizabeth on the way in the door and ordered her to bring some hot tea up to Mollie's room.

He directed Mollie into a hot bath. "Dry clothes and hot tea will be waiting for you in your room when you are done. Then I'll ask you to explain, but not before."

She nodded gratefully and disappeared into the bathroom. Cadal sighed as the door closed and went back to the kitchen. As he'd expected, Liam was on his way in the door.

The young man sighed in relief. "You're all right, sir?"

"I am, but Mollie is shaken up."

Liam's eyes went wide in surprise.

"She had a rather upsetting visitor. Once she is calm, I'll get the whole story. Until then, perhaps you could help me identify the man."

"If I can, of course."

"He was a little shorter than you are, stocky, dark hair but balding on top, and badly dressed. He said that he came to deliver a message."

"He went east toward Thornton's lands?"

Cadal nodded.

"That would be Michael Tucker. He's Thornton's hired man."

Cadal set his jaw angrily. He had surmised as much. "Send someone out to the pond to collect Mollie's things, if you would. Then come back here. After I hear her side, I'll decide what is to be done."

Liam nodded and disappeared out the door again.

When Elizabeth informed him that Mollie was settled in with a cup of tea, Cadal went up. Mollie was sitting in bed with the quilt tucked around her. He rolled his eyes. That was most likely Elizabeth's doing.

She smiled grimly as he came through the door. "I guess I should thank you again."

"We can worry about that later. What happened out there?"

Mollie grimaced. "It was a stupid move. I should have told Elizabeth where I was going. I should have realized that private property didn't mean no one would dare cross it. I should have been dressed properly." She shook her head bitterly.

Cadal felt a stab of irritation. She knew it and admitted it, but this discussion was getting him no closer to the information he needed. "We will worry about that later, as well. What happened with Tucker? What did he say?"

"Tucker? So, he has a name now..." She bit her lip lightly. "It was a polite warning not to be so discourteous to my neighbors."

"Polite? You certainly acted as if it was less than polite."

"It wasn't polite, but that's what he'll tell the constable. Just a friendly hello, I'm sure."

"Did he threaten you?"

"Overtly? No. He was smarter than that. I'd wager he's pulled something like this before. It was all very circumspect. How you can make enemies you don't really want to make. That sort of thing."

"What exactly did he say?"

Mollie told him the whole story, beginning to end. Cadal had to admit that her assessment of her situation had been sound. She had been safer in the water than out. Her shaking, he learned, was not at all from the cold but from the fear and shock of her predicament.

Cadal was torn between the urge to deliver a personal message to Mr. Tucker on Mollie's behalf, which he rejected immediately, and the urge to take her back into his arms. He rejected that almost as quickly, though she felt so very right there.

He nodded. "I'll discuss this with Liam. Get some rest."

Crimson colored the high line of her pale cheeks. "No. This is my estate. Any discussion should include me." She started to pull back the quilt.

"All right. Stay there. I'll get Liam and bring him up here."

Mollie raised an eyebrow at the suggestion.

"Don't worry. I'll tell him you are simply recovering from the chill of the water."

She agreed, and Cadal headed down to collect Liam. He knew Mollie was determined to keep up appearances, though he had a poor grasp of precisely what she felt the need to prove.

He took the time to explain the encounter to Liam so they wouldn't have to cover it again upstairs. To his credit, the estate manager looked as angry as Cadal felt. Liam was a good man, as Humans went.

Liam knocked on the door and entered quietly when Mollie called out from inside. "Miss, don't you worry. We'll handle this," he launched into his assurances.

"How?" she asked quietly.

"I'll teach Tucker a lesson he won't forget, personally."

Mollie shook her head. "And the constable will be on his side, and I'll lose my best man or, at the very least, your fines. Right?"

Liam blushed, and he averted his eyes, all but scuffing his boots like a chastised child. "Yes, miss. I suppose that's so."

Morda could have this effect on a full-grown man, but Cadal had never seen it used so effectively by anyone else. Of course, Mollie was her descendent. Cadal suddenly understood why Mollie wanted to do this. Despite what happened, she was thinking more clearly than her headstrong protectors were.

Mollie nodded. "Good. Now that we've settled that, what can we really do? We could call the constable and report Tucker for trespassing. He'll be counting on it anyway. Why disappoint him? It will only be a warning, but at least the constable will know that we're having trouble— Though, I'm sure he already does know it, doesn't he?"

"All true, miss, and we can't touch the big fish."

"You're right about that. I repeat, what can we do?"

Liam smiled. "I could set a few traps along Thornton's property line. Tucker steps into one of them, he won't forget soon."

The color drained from Mollie's cheeks at the suggestion. "No. That's not an option. An animal might get hurt," she decided.

Cadal marveled at her compassion. He doubted many Humans would show such concern.

Liam nodded his head sadly. "Miss Katie would say the same thing. You're quite a bit like her, miss."

"Thank you, Liam. I will take that as a compliment."

Cadal smiled at her heartfelt response. It pleased Mollie to be compared favorably to Katie, and it seemed to please Liam to see the likeness.

"As it was intended, miss." He sighed. "What can we do?"

She shook her head. "We might as well report him. Beyond that..." She chewed on her lower lip, deep in thought. "Thornton thinks he can bully me if I'm alone. Let's not give him the opportunity. If I leave the house for anywhere except the fields where the men are out working, I'll either go on horseback and let Elizabeth know where I'll be or I'll take someone along."

"Or both," Cadal interjected.

"We'll see. Oh, and Liam, let's check the fence lines fairly often."

Liam looked confused. "Consider it done, but might I ask why, miss?"

"Because it's just the sort of two-bit trick I'd expect from them next."

Liam laughed heartily. "Yes, miss. You may be right." He turned to go.

"Liam?" she called after him.

"Yes, miss?"

"Don't get yourself in trouble."

"No, miss. No trouble," he promised her solemnly. His smile returned. "Of course, if Tucker provokes me at the pub— Well, with the proper witnesses, that's another tale, miss."

Mollie waved him away while she tried to stifle the smile that was threatening to take over her face. Her eyes glittered in amusement. As his footsteps disappeared down the hall, Mollie giggled and dropped back on her pillow. She motioned to the door. "See what

I have to deal with? He'll be arrested or at least in a bar fight inside of two weeks. I can guarantee it."

"Then stop him."

"How? You're a man. You should understand that I can't. Until he satisfies his sense of outrage..." She shrugged. "All I can do is minimize it. Now, Mr. Tucker will face a fair fight instead of a pummeling."

Cadal shook his head sadly. "I don't understand it, but maybe I'm not much like other men."

"No, I don't believe you are. You're more restrained, more civil. I can't explain it, really. If more men were like you—" She sighed.

"Well, I'm about to do a very barbaric thing," he answered.

Mollie raised an eyebrow. "Really? And what would that be?"

"I'm about to order you to stay in that bed. I know you want to keep up appearances, but no one will begrudge you some time off to avoid getting ill after the chill you took."

"I don't take orders well, but I will agree on one condition."

"Which is?"

"Stay with me."

Cadal found it hard not to look shocked. From the expression on Mollie's face, he guessed that he failed horribly.

"I only meant to tell Fairy tales and talk," she amended. "We could accomplish that just as well in the library."

Cadal shook his head slowly. Weren't the tables turned? He was acting the little boy, the frightfully naïve child he thought Mollie was a few days ago. "No.

At least I will not have to carry you to bed when you fall asleep."

She cracked a smile that Cadal could tell was strained. "I suppose you won't, at that," she agreed, but he could see the pain behind her easy demeanor.

How did he manage to hurt her so often?

* * * *

Mollie listened to Cadal's stories for most of the afternoon and evening. She enjoyed his company, but her heart wasn't in the activity as it usually was. She had only been angling for companionship, but his reaction had been like ice water in her heart regardless. She found that her temperament and intelligence alienated many men, but his obvious horror at the idea of intimacy was a first in her experience.

She sighed. Maybe it was better to know where she stood, no matter where that was.

That didn't mean Mollie could turn off her feelings. She was still caught every time she was close to him. It made no sense. No sense that she could decipher, at any rate. Cadal was proper, almost aloof, and still Mollie found herself wishing for the most intimate, erotic moments with him and dreaming of them almost nightly. It was maddening.

If she were the type of woman who believed in leading a man in, it would be easy enough for her to tempt him unmercifully. Mollie could arrange any number of 'chance encounters' with his room being catty corner to hers, no one else living in this part of the house, and sharing a bathroom.

But Mollie wasn't that type of woman. If a man wasn't interested enough to show it, what was the point? If she had been interested enough in the knee-jerk reaction she could get, Mollie could have dropped her arms on the way out of the pond, but it wouldn't have been either fair or appropriate, by her own standards.

She glanced at Cadal out of the corner of her eye. Like it or not, she was creating a frustrating fantasy life which could only cause friction in her day to day reality. The worst part was that she had no rational control over the fantasy, even when she was awake. What was it about Cadal that affected her this way? It couldn't just be those eyes.

* * * *

Cadal found that Mollie's assessment of Liam had been fairly accurate. Far short of her allotted two weeks, Liam was sporting several bruises and grinning widely five days later. Mollie scolded him and tended to his wounds personally, but she did smile at Patrick's description of the battle that led to Tucker's very public defeat.

Liam's younger brother was more than happy to report the scene that led Liam to land the punch that rocked Tucker off his feet and started the brawl. Tucker had said any number of inappropriate things about Mollie, including claims of her sexual habits.

Mollie's face darkened, but Cadal knew it was in anger rather than embarrassment. Setting herself up as *one of the guys* had its bad side. Her men were not shielding her from such things as Cadal knew they would have done for Katie. They viewed her as physically vulnerable though able but mentally and emotionally tough as nails.

He grimaced as he realized how very wrong they were. Mollie was fragile. She had merely learned to construct a shell around herself, a very convincing decoy to make everyone think she was what she *wanted* them to think she was. Cadal made a mental note to talk to Liam privately about it. He was sure Mollie would not appreciate the interference if she learned of it.

Cadal found that his motives were becoming confused. On one level, he knew exactly why he was here. He had a task to complete, one of three to find his true soulmate.

When he was young, he had been sure Xanthe was that soulmate. Cadal had been crushed when Xanthe had left the colony and relinquished her Fairy life. She'd left him, left her family, and balked tradition. The only Fairy he had ever met who was not a pretty puff had let him play the fool chasing her before she scorned five hundred years with him for forty with her Human lover.

He had begged the Mistress to release him to a Human life, but she had refused him. In time, Cadal realized it would have only done him harm if Morda had. His pain would have ended sooner, whether he took the Human way and ended his life by his own hand or died a natural death as Xanthe had. The idea of suicide was typically abhorrent to Fairies, but it had sounded strangely appealing in Cadal's darker moments.

Cadal had no chance of winning Xanthe back and sharing her Human life. He'd known she was happy with Bran, even then. One look in her emerald eyes, at her vibrant smile, and Cadal would have lain down at her feet or walked away forever rather than cause her a single moment of unhappiness.

It had taken years of loneliness and self-loathing before he snapped and decided he had to see Xanthe again, but time passes more quickly for Humans. Xanthe was long dead, and Cadal had met her great granddaughter, Colleen, while he was placing flowers on her grave. When Cadal met Colleen, he was struck immediately by her fire and strength. Thus began his fascination with the Blake women.

Colleen was taken, but he'd believed Katie was not, and so he'd had hope for the first time in many years. While Colleen's soul had drawn him as Xanthe's had, her sister was nothing like the other women.

She was, however, a kindred spirit. Katie had needed John Stuart as Cadal needed the soulmate he thought he could never have. Convincing Katie to marry evoked troubling thoughts, but it had also given Cadal a sense of freedom and purpose.

The Fairy Mistress had come to him then. Morda knew he was ready to listen to what she had been trying to tell him for more than half a century. There was still hope.

Xanthe was not his true soulmate. She had never been, but his soulmate did exist. Cadal would soon find his way to her.

He had three tasks to complete. The first had been freeing Katie from the cycle of pain the curse had created. Morda could not tell him his tasks, but she'd assured him that, like the first, he would see his course and act appropriately. If Cadal followed his heart and did not allow himself to be sidetracked, he could not help but choose correctly. Surely, this was his second task, living among the Humans to save the Blake lands and ensure Mollie's inheritance. That was his reason for being here. His heart called him to his task.

On another level, Cadal found himself dreaming of Mollie in a much less than professional manner. The day he'd spent in her bedroom spawned many fantasies for Cadal. If only he really was William Cadal... If only he was Human... Or, if only Mollie was Fairy instead of Human, there might be something between them. For once, even dreams seemed to fail him, because there was little chance that they foreshadowed events to come as he would expect them to.

Cadal didn't know if they could couple, as things stood. Well, there were the tales that young Fairies whispered around, tales of Fairies taking Human lovers without relinquishing their Fairy lives, tales that Xanthe might have tested. That thought sobered Cadal.

Even if the tales were true, what then? If he started a relationship with Mollie, Cadal knew he wouldn't want to leave. It couldn't be loveplay with her. He knew it couldn't. He wouldn't let it be. Yet, he had to leave someday. Otherwise, he would be hurting his mother and others in the colony. Unlike Xanthe, he would miss Fairy life.

He considered that. Cadal really didn't know what Xanthe missed. After all, she had told her descendents those wonderful stories. He'd always assumed she hadn't missed the colony, for no better reason than the fact that she'd turned her back on it. Perhaps he'd done her a disservice in condemning her.

Cadal didn't want a Human life. He didn't like the Human realm, but he wanted Mollie. It was becoming a more difficult choice every day. Was she enough to keep him here past his time? As the days passed, Cadal found the idea of leaving her more and more painful.

He wondered if this was what it was like for Xanthe. Was the Human form what caused this strange unwillingness to leave the Human you found yourself drawn to? Was there something about Humans that drew a Fairy to them, a novelty that was naturally appealing? Or was it something else that Cadal could not even begin to understand?

Chapter Five

Another thing Mollie was right about was Thornton's underhanded ways. Three days after Tucker's defeat, Liam found the first fence section destroyed. Cadal learned then that Mollie had already formulated a plan for this.

While the men prepared to repair the section, Mollie set off on Squirrel with a backpack and a spray paint can. Any questions about what she had in mind were soon answered. Patrick, who was sent along by Liam as a precaution, reported that Mollie numbered the posts and filmed the fence line with a small video camera. The route around the estate took quite a few hours, but she did the whole thing.

Mollie stored the video in her desk in the library. Two days later, the next section was destroyed. She added to the tape and called the constable herself. John McConnell agreed there was no question that the destruction had been malicious, and he did two things that ended the vandalism. He posted a man for a few nights, and he had a very brief, private talk with Joshua Thornton.

Cadal had assumed Thornton would simply give up, but he was wrong. A few weeks later, he got his biggest surprise to date.

A sharp knock on his door woke Cadal from a deep sleep. "Yes?" he called out to the closed door in irritation. What in the world would cause someone to wake him now? The moon was barely falling from its zenith, and his body and mind protested that fact loudly.

"Cadal, it's Mollie. I need your help."

"What's wrong?" Strange how slurring his words naturally gave him a more Human speech pattern.

Still trying to hold to the vestiges of the dream he'd been lost in when she knocked, Cadal was sure he would be happy if the help she needed was a man in her bed. He shook his head to clear the thought away before he did something so crazy.

"Cadal, please," Mollie begged.

He found his sleep torn away by the urgency in her voice. "What is it?"

"Get dressed and meet me downstairs. This is important."

"All right. I'm on my way."

"Thank you." Her voice was very soft through the door.

Mollie moved away and down the stairs. Cadal dressed quickly and pulled on a thick sweater against the chill in the air. As promised, Mollie was waiting for him in the kitchen. She handed him a flashlight, what Katie and Liam had called a torch, and headed out the door without a word. Cadal rushed to catch up.

"Where are we going?" he asked.

"The fields."

"Why?"

"Something's wrong."

"What? Should we wake Liam on the way?"

"Not yet. I need to be sure, first."

"Sure of what?" The conversation wasn't making much sense to Cadal. The fact that Mollie wasn't using the light tucked in her belt didn't make sense. The way she picked out an almost invisible track to follow on the dark night wasn't making sense.

She didn't answer immediately. "Sure that I'm not simply crazy." Her voice was so low that he almost didn't hear her.

Cadal startled and looked at her as closely as he could in the dim light that outlined her from his flashlight beam. "Why do you think you're crazy?" Okay, surprise corrected his speech patterns, too.

She shrugged. "I'm dragging you out here because of a dream. Don't ask me why, please. I really don't know why."

He felt her frustration. What could she dream that would send her to wake him and drag them both out like this? She obviously felt strongly about whatever it was.

"Why take me?" he asked.

Mollie laughed, a strained sound at best. "I don't know. I trust you, and you'd kill me if I went alone."

Cadal smiled. Though he'd never considered murder, the very concept alien to a Fairy, Mollie was the one person certain to drive him to such an extreme. "That one is certainly right."

He looked at Mollie again. She was frightened by what she was doing, though she didn't want to admit it. The knowledge put him on edge. There was something wrong, a feeling of — discord he couldn't seem to grasp.

"What did you dream?" he asked.

Mollie stopped abruptly and turned off the light in Cadal's hand. He shivered at the feeling of her hand as it lingered on his own. She peered into the field closest to them.

"That. Damn it, he's screwing up my fields," she hissed from between clenched teeth.

In the field, Cadal could see two men working by flashlight. Turning his attention to the land instead of her, the feeling of tearing assaulted him...sickness...death. Was this what he'd felt gnawing at him as they walked? No, it was more than this, gut-wrenching as this attack on the land was.

Whoever these men were, they had to be stopped. The mad urge to intervene without reason as he had in his youth assaulted him, and Cadal pushed it away. He'd learned to control these urges long ago. Still, the men had to be stopped...quickly.

He looked at Mollie sharply. "Go back for Liam and Patrick. Tell them to come in quietly. We want to catch them."

Mollie nodded and moved away at a dead run into the dark. She moved silently. Had she moved silently the whole way to the fields? He wished he had taken note of that.

Cadal watched her go. He turned his eyes back to the field, but not his mind. She dreamed this? Mollie knew the land was in danger as she'd known what crops it needed. Over the weeks, she'd known when the extra watering needed done early and when it could wait an extra day or so. Even Liam had been surprised by her expertise. Mollie had not been raised on a farm. There was no accounting for her flawless handling of her land.

Sometimes, rare moments, Mollie seemed more Fairy than Human. When she swam in the frigid pond, when she turned her cheek to a cool breeze, or when she used her unusual insight to keep her land fertile and safe; it was like seeing one of his own in Human form. Other times, she seemed Human. Mollie understood Human nuances that stunned Cadal. Of course, she had been born and raised in the Human realm. If Cadal had been in this world as many years as she had, would he be like Mollie?

Mollie isn't Fairy. Xanthe had been made Human. That meant her descendents were Human. As much as Mollie resembled a Fairy, it could be nothing more than her fascination with Xanthe's Fairy tales and some startling insights into both people and the world around her.

Cadal started. He moved toward the riot in the field. How long had he been lost in thought? Liam and Patrick were already here, and there was little left to do by the time he arrived. Patrick bound the hands of the man he had downed. Liam was still struggling with his.

Mollie knelt next to several small barrels. "Liam, I need to know what this is," she shouted over her shoulder.

"Just a moment." Liam landed a solid punch, and the man beneath him sagged to the earth bonelessly. "Patrick, clean up if you please," he called out. He pushed to his feet and shook the hair back from his face. Then he sprinted to Mollie.

She grabbed his hand as he reached for the barrel. "Don't touch them. Let McConnell."

Liam nodded and studied the spot she was lighting. "Good God. This will kill everything. It's good that we caught them quickly. By morning—" He swallowed the rest of the thought.

"What happens if it gets wet?"

Liam looked around at the field then back to Mollie. "You don't want to know."

"Wake the other men, now. I want shovels and wheelbarrows up here. We don't have time to waste. Send someone to buy them if we don't have enough.

Wake the shop owners. Pay a bonus. I don't care what it takes."

"The rain isn't due until afternoon. Shouldn't we wait for light?"

"They're wrong," she insisted in a panic. "Can't you smell it?"

Cadal stared at her, forcing his jaw shut. Mollie was right, but how could she know that?

"How will we know where they've seeded?" Liam continued.

"Let me handle it. If I'm wrong..." She shot Liam a look of hopeless misery. "Go. We're wasting time. Wake the men. Patrick," she shouted.

The younger brother ran toward her, leaving Cadal to watch over the bound men. "Yes, miss?"

"Shovels, gloves, and wheelbarrows. As many as you can find."

"Yes, miss. Right away." He sprinted toward the equipment shed as Liam disappeared down the path.

Mollie sank to her knees and moved down the hill, tracing her hands over the ground. *One, two, three rows of crops.* He counted them silently as she moved. Mollie stopped abruptly and worked her way across until she reached the far end of the field. When she was done, she bowed her head slowly.

"It's a lot to lose, but it could be much worse," she breathed.

He knew what she was doing, though it was a crude way to accomplish her goal, the way a Fairy child might before she was fully trained. Mollie had found her damaged ground. Cadal was fascinated. Mollie shouldn't be able to do any of this, but she was doing it. It was undeniable. The land whispered the same results to him that she'd accomplished.

Patrick returned with the first load of equipment.

Mollie snapped her head up. Her eyes burned with a fierce determination that Cadal had not seen in their depths before. She motioned to the field above her position. "Tell the men to take everything above this fourth row up to the barrels. I'll be back to help soon."

"Where will you be, miss?"

She glared at him, her jaw tightening in anger, then nodded in understanding. "Checking the other fields. It won't take long."

"I'll go with her, Patrick," Cadal volunteered.

The young man tipped a finger to his forehead, a sign that Cadal had come to recognize as Patrick's acceptance of a command, and went back for another load of tools.

Mollie set off. She walked the fields, moving fluidly, her outstretched fingertips skating over the tops of the small plants. Cadal heard the fields whispering to her, the plants loving her presence in their midst, talking to her like a dear friend. Mollie didn't answer them with more than her touch, but they purred for her, all the same.

When she had circled all of the fields, Mollie faced Cadal and smiled. "They're fine."

He nodded uncertainly. "Yes, I know." *But how do you?*

"Now we have to save the rest." She turned to walk back to the tainted field.

Cadal took her by the arms and bent to meet her eyes. "Mollie? How did you do that?"

Mollie looked around and swallowed hard, her eyes widening. "I don't know."

"But you know the land is safe?"

She nodded, trembling lightly.

"How?"

Mollie opened her mouth to speak, then shut it again, shifting from foot to foot. "I don't know." She glanced around frantically, reaching for the closest plant, meeting Cadal's eyes as his grip prevented her from touching it. "What if I'm wrong, Cadal?" He felt her fear and desperation as if they were his own.

"You're not."

She shook her head and tried to pull back the tears that were welling in her eyes.

"No, you're not wrong. You were right when you woke me, and you're still right. Trust me. You're right." By The Harmony, she *was*, but he wished he knew how.

Mollie wrapped her arms around his chest and held on for a long moment while she got control of her emotions. She backed away, and Cadal was struck by a sense of loss when she left his arms. Worse, his groin ached at her retreat.

She met his eyes. "Thank you, Cadal." Mollie took a deep breath and looked away. "Let's save the rest of it."

Cadal nodded and followed her back, his mind busy and his body complaining.

Mollie was very like a Fairy. Though she wasn't one, it was becoming increasingly clear that whatever his mind told him aside, his body had a very definite reaction he would not hesitate to act on if he could only be sure he wasn't seeing something that couldn't possibly be there.

When they arrived at the field, Mollie picked up a shovel dropped next to Patrick as he rested from his labor and pulled on a spare pair of gloves. She went to work, leaving Cadal to tell the men that the other fields were not a problem.

A quarter of the affected ground had been moved by the time the sun rose. After much discussion, the foul earth was being dumped inside the barn until it could be removed. That way, it would be dry and on the cement floor, where it could cause no more damage.

Mollie watched over her men as she watched over her land. She took few breaks, but she had the men bring a water bucket from the tap, ordered them off the line to eat and rest and complimented their progress as they went. It was all Cadal could do to pull her off the line for a few slices of toast.

"We don't have time," she argued. "I'll eat later."

Cadal removed the shovel from her hands and passed it to Connor as he filed back into the field. "Make the time."

"The rain won't wait. We won't make it." Mollie tried to grab a shovel from Liam on his way off the line.

Cadal brushed her hand away from the shovel and signaled Liam to keep walking. He handed Mollie a slice of toast. "Yes, we will." He brushed away the hair that fell across her face fondly.

Now that the light was better, Cadal could see that what he had assumed was a smudge of dirt was a nasty bruise across her cheekbone. He ran his fingers over it lightly. "What is this?" he asked in a rougher voice than he had intended.

Liam glanced at her on his way back in. "Damn saboteur struck her," he confirmed. "Don't worry. Patrick damn near killed him for it."

Mollie nodded and looked away at the work while she chewed at the toast in her mouth. Cadal took her by the arm as lightly as he could manage to restrain himself to and led her to the stream.

Once they were away from the others, he turned on her. "Why?" he demanded.

"I had to stop them."

She said it simply, quietly, as if he should have known the answer already, and Cadal would have guessed that, if she were a young Fairy instead of Human.

Memories of forcing back his own urge to fight the saboteurs were fresh in his mind. How many times had such urges endangered his life? He couldn't allow Mollie to endanger hers again.

Cadal cupped her chin, and she locked on his eyes. "You come first. You are not getting yourself killed for this piece of land. Understand?"

"I have to—"

He cut her off. "Strike that phrase from your vocabulary. No more chances. Please, I cannot take it anymore."

His eyes strayed to her cheek. Disturbing visions of kissing the damaged flesh melded with even more disturbing visions of testing how easily the one who hit her would bruise...personally.

"I'll try."

Cadal smiled widely and released her chin. "Will you look at what I'm dealing with? You will be risking yourself again inside of a month. I guarantee it."

Mollie smiled at him and popped the last piece of the toast into her mouth. She moved down to the field, grabbed a shovel from one of the men getting a drink, and went back to work. She offered Cadal a mischievous grin as he settled in to work beside her.

She barely noticed John McConnell, as he came and went. Liam and Patrick talked to him, but McConnell promised to return when he realized that

Mollie's time crunch was more important to her than his presence. The offending chemicals were impounded, and the two men were taken into custody.

McConnell didn't ask to speak to Cadal. Cadal wondered about that, but whether McConnell had no interest in him or hadn't been told that Cadal was there was immaterial to him. He counted it as a blessing that he didn't have to deal with the Human authorities either way.

By ten thirty, the rain was threatening and the last load of dirt taken away. Mollie sat in the middle of the freshly-excavated pit and thanked the men for their hard work. She ordered them to do the chores that were absolutely necessary and have lunch. "After that, consider yourselves off-duty for the day. That was good work. Relax. Sleep. Whatever you want. No more work today."

The men filed away with thanks to their employer, and Cadal sank down beside her.

"Nice move. It makes up for that early morning and all their hard work," he complimented her.

Mollie smiled at him. "Why should I punish them for something beyond their control? That's not good for morale."

He offered his hand. "Come on. We should go back to the house."

She lay back on the ground. "I can't move anymore. Maybe I should let the rain recharge my batteries a little."

Cadal appraised her position. "I think your t-shirt would become a bit revealing again." He raised an eyebrow at her. His breath hitched as she took a deep breath and her chest heaved.

Mollie favored him with an impish grin. "You say that like it's a bad thing." She stretched her shoulders and arched her back, offering her breasts for his inspection again.

It was all Cadal could do to tear his eyes away long enough to glance in the direction the others had taken to make sure they were unobserved. He was sure it was her exhaustion talking, but his pulse quickened at the offer. Mollie joked often, but she was rarely this straight-forward about the subject.

"It depends on your point of view. From *your* point of view, it could be a bad thing, especially if all the men got a good look." He lowered himself to his elbow, knowing that another move like the ones she had been making would drive her body into his.

She nodded. "What about your point of view?"

He felt his heart skip a beat. This directness was even more appealing than her gentle suggestion of the possibility. "I don't know." Cadal considered how easy it would be to lower his face to that tempting cleavage. "I know I wouldn't want all the other men to see it," he managed.

Mollie smiled widely and slid from under his body. She got to her feet as Cadal came to his senses and backed off, cursing his reaction to her. Was he insane that he wanted her to touch him intimately, that he encouraged it?

"Well, it's a step in the right direction, I suppose," Mollie commented as she turned away.

She started back toward the house with Cadal following her. He could have caught up easily, but he was enjoying the gentle sway of Mollie's hips.

Cadal berated himself. What he wanted was impossible and distracting. He hadn't thought of his missing soulmate in days. He was allowing himself to be sidetracked. Morda had told him to follow his heart. His heart would know the road, but his heart was leading him off the road. Harmony, if he could ever have what his heart wanted, he wouldn't be concerned about repercussions. Visions of Mollie's body pressed to his own sent shivers through him in imagined ecstasy.

* * * *

Mollie stretched out on the bed after her bath. She knew getting out of bed would be difficult in a few minutes, but she needed to lie down.

John McConnell had returned to talk to her after lunch. His news wasn't good. The men weren't talking. It was his opinion and hers that they were being well paid not to turn in whoever paid them. Mollie was sure McConnell shared her belief that Thornton was doing the paying, though it was left unsaid.

She'd encountered a disturbing moment when McConnell asked her who the first people out to the fields were. She'd only named herself, Liam, and Patrick. For some reason, she wasn't comfortable telling McConnell that Cadal was there. Her actions confused her, because she couldn't find a logical reason for it, but she'd done it anyway. Mollie sighed wearily at the memory of it.

A knock came at the door, and she groaned at the thought of moving. "Come in," she called.

Cadal poked his head in and smiled at her. "Sore?"

"I'd nod my head, but I'm not sure I could move it that far."

He chuckled. "Do you have anything backless?"

Mollie furrowed her brow. "Cadal, I'm sure I'm too tired for dancing right now. Ask me another time, okay?"

Cadal laughed again and shook his head. "Nothing like that," he assured her. "I'll rub your back."

"So rub it, already."

"With a liniment to relax your muscles."

Mollie nodded and a smile touched her lips. "I could just take off my sweater for you."

Cadal pinked up slightly, but he didn't refuse.

"Don't worry. I have a halter top underneath. I wouldn't want to get slapped with a sexual harassment suit, after all."

He turned toward the door, his expression stony. "I'll get the bottle while you take care of that."

Mollie sighed as the door closed. Cadal was so hard to read. She was sure he was interested. She could see how he watched her when he thought she couldn't see it, but any time she approached the subject directly, his reaction was the polar opposite.

The last day or two had been the first times he had wavered outwardly. In the field, Mollie had been sure Cadal would break down and admit that he'd like to see her in a wet t-shirt.

She saw the avid way he watched her while she moved through the water when he joined her for swims; his eyes rarely strayed from her, only when she looked his way. Cadal *preferred* to be the one to accompany her for swims. She knew he told Liam not to assign one of the other men to guard her when she went. When Mollie left the water, Cadal's expression was always one of stark hunger.

Mollie had to admit that his reactions were more than interesting. She found a strange sort of pleasure in knowing Cadal was watching, that he wasn't adverse to the idea after all.

He opened the door, stopped and smiled widely. "You haven't gotten ready."

She glanced down at her sweater as if in surprise. "Oh yeah. I knew I forgot something." It wasn't a complete fabrication, since she had been so lost in thought that she'd honestly forgotten to remove it.

Cadal moved to the bed next to her and set the liniment on the night stand. Mollie reached for the first of the small buttons, but his hands were already there. He smiled wickedly at her surprise, and Mollie relaxed back into the pillow and resolved to let Cadal do whatever it was he intended to do.

* * * *

Cadal wasn't sure what game Mollie was playing, but he decided to tease her back a little. She seemed surprised by his initiative, but she didn't try to stop him. Some place in the back of his mind screamed at him to stop. Very little could be concealed beneath the scrap of her sweater, and Cadal was determined to see what a halter top was, despite the exquisite torture of seeing more of her body.

When all of the buttons were open, he swept the sweater apart and drank in the sight of her. The halter top was barely more than two wide strips of fabric that connected behind her neck and met to form a short stomacher at the lower curve of her breasts before attaching to another band that circled her lower back.

Cadal had to wonder if it was intended as underclothes, as something not meant to be seen in public. He dismissed that idea. Mollie would not be so underhanded.

She surveyed him in heightening excitement. He felt her heart pounding beneath his fingertips, and his own seemed to strain to match the rhythm.

It wasn't as if this was the first time Cadal had seen Mollie this undressed. Her bathing suit covered less, but it was the first time he had undressed her to this point, the first time he had undressed her at all...outside of a dream. Cadal found himself lost in the moment; he wondered what else Mollie would allow him to do, what else he would do, if she allowed it.

He leaned over her, his lips all but brushing hers, savoring the idea of kissing her. He wanted to kiss her. Mollie seemed to expect that he would. Perhaps, any Human man would have.

What had she said once? He was more restrained, more civil. Restrained or not, Cadal found his hold on his actions strained almost to his breaking point. He turned his mind back to his original plan painfully.

He skated his cheek past hers and whispered next to her ear, "Turn over so I can rub your back." Cadal moved away and smiled, his now-pounding heart making him dizzy.

His eyes met hers, and Mollie nodded in understanding or perhaps in challenge. Cadal was playing a dangerous game, and he was going to lose if he wasn't very careful. He wanted to lose, on some elemental level.

She turned stiffly onto her stomach, shedding her sweater as she went. Cadal opened the bottle and warmed a little of the liniment between his hands. There was mint for cooling and blood flow, lavender for relaxation, and several herbs to aid in her healing.

"Smells good," Mollie mused. "Nice combination."

"Old family recipe," he told her. *Very old.* "Now, just relax."

Mollie winced as his hands began to knead her sore muscles. Cadal knew she was in pain. He felt it as acutely as he'd felt her fear and her anger, but as she relaxed under his hands, he felt her arousal growing, overpowering the pain.

If he had ignored it, he could have left then. If Cadal's own arousal had not overridden his common sense, he would have left then. He had accomplished what he came to do. He pushed away the thought and went to work on her shoulders.

"That's better," he told her. "Being tense makes it harder to work out the stiffness."

By the time he told her to turn over again, Mollie was almost boneless in her relaxation. She looked up at Cadal, her eyes soft and dreamy. He met her eyes momentarily and felt a warm rush, though whether it was from her or himself, he wasn't sure. Cadal had Mollie just where he wanted her. If only he knew he could have her, he wouldn't hesitate to take her.

He set to work on Mollie's shoulder. She closed her eyes and rolled her head back at the sensations coursing through her. She was exquisite. Even his dreams weren't this good. Mollie moaned as his hands massaged beneath the straps over her shoulders. Cadal rubbed the muscles of her arms, chest and stomach, brushing by but never actually touching her breasts.

He lost all sense of courtesy. It was a game of sorts. Cadal fed off of her arousal and pushed Mollie to the highest level he could without doing anything irreversibly sexual in nature. He knew all the while he shouldn't be doing what he was. Cadal knew he was, in essence, profiting sexually from something he had no intentions of completing. Still, he found stopping a foreign concept.

When he regained enough self-control to remove his hands from Mollie's body, Cadal met her eyes. His entire body throbbed with a craving for her touch, and he felt her arousal beating at him.

He knew that Mollie would deny him no intimate pleasure. She was his for the taking, if he dared take her. If she kissed him then, Cadal had no doubts that he would test the old tales, but she waited to see what he would do.

Mollie gazed at him longingly, and his smile returned. Cadal found the urge to kiss her almost insurmountable. He reminded himself he couldn't lead Mollie on that way. He couldn't lie to her that way. He kissed the bruise on her cheek gently and did what he should have done much earlier. He walked away.

"Sweet dreams," he called back over his shoulder as he shut the door behind him.

Cadal leaned his cheek against her door, shaking in his need to take her. From inside, he could hear Mollie's frustrated sigh.

"It's going to be a long night."

Her voice was rough, nearly cracking in emotion. He found the sound of it heartbreaking.

He returned to his room and stretched out on his bed. Cadal stared at the ceiling, trying to figure out exactly when he crossed the line in Mollie's room. He had intended to rub her sore back. Nothing more. He had no doubts that his dreams would torture him appropriately for quite some time in retribution for his actions.

"It's going to be a very long night," he agreed.

Chapter Six

Cadal resolved not to test himself like that again. The dreams the first night had him so scattered that he'd found himself standing outside of Mollie's door, contemplating picking up the evening where he had severed it hours before.

In the end, Cadal had set out for a late-night ride on Thunder. He'd groomed the horse properly and given him a treat before returning, much more tired but no more decisive, to the house. He'd looked at her door in longing and sighed before returning to his own room. Cadal had been tortured by the imagined scent of Mollie, the memory of her body under his hands, from the moment his head hit the pillow again.

He needn't have worried about testing himself again. Mollie was very businesslike. To Cadal's surprise, she was friendly, comfortable, but somehow aloof. There were no more jokes about romance, no more raised eyebrows or silent invitations, and no more stolen glances. If it weren't for the fact that he still felt her attraction as strongly as ever, Cadal might have believed her act of complete disinterest. At any rate, it made his job easier in one respect and more difficult in another.

Cadal found his reaction to Mollie was even more distressing when she wasn't making an outward invitation. When he moved close to her to point out something over her shoulder, she would move just enough to avoid his touch. When he offered to walk her to the fields, she would send him ahead and go over some trivial matter with Liam or Elizabeth before leaving the house. When Cadal went to her room to talk to her, Mollie would tell him to come along to the library while she did paperwork. Each time it happened, he felt a deep pang of loss.

What was wrong with him? This was what he wanted, wasn't it? Why couldn't he enjoy the respite?

It came to a head a week after the sabotage in the fields.

The field had been packed with new soil and planted with a short-growth crop to add stability; the last loads of the tainted soil were being sent off. Mollie had assigned herself to the field to help as long as the extra workload existed. As the days wore on, she hadn't slowed down. Her stamina increased, and Cadal saw her carry even more than a fair share of the work on a daily basis. The men were suitably impressed.

Unfortunately, Cadal wasn't prepared for the next impression she made. As usual, Mollie wore a sweater or a flannel shirt to the fields or barn in the cool morning air and stripped it off in favor of the t-shirt she invariably wore beneath as the day got warmer. The sun had been up for hours, and the barn was stifling. Mollie dropped her shovel, pulled off her gloves and peeled the sweater she was wearing over her shoulders. She tossed it aside and grabbed her gloves.

Cadal sucked in his breath audibly. Mollie was wearing the same halter she'd had on the night he gave her the backrub. Her muscles had become well defined by her months on the farm, and her breasts strained against the fabric as she worked. A light sheen of sweat glistened on her skin and ran down the cleavage between her breasts, drawing his gaze.

He looked around the barn.

Liam noticed first. He gaped at Mollie for an instant, then met Cadal's eyes fearfully. Cadal nodded, and the younger man set back to work, avoiding Mollie's direction carefully.

Patrick stopped and stared, then swallowed what appeared to be a lump in his throat. Liam elbowed him roughly, and Patrick took Liam's lead.

Connor was Cadal's breaking point. The young man stopped short and smiled appreciatively at her. Connor's eyes ranged the length of her body, drinking in every curve. Mollie was oblivious to all of it. Cadal felt a nameless rage rising in him. He shouldered past Connor and crossed to her.

Mollie looked at him strangely, then stepped back a pace in confusion. A guarded look settled on her face.

Cadal leaned close to her cheek. "I need to talk to you."

"Talk."

He took the shovel from her hands and wrapped an arm around her waist. "At the house. All right?"

Mollie pulled away from him roughly and headed for the door without a backward glance to see if he was following. Cadal sighed and handed the shovel off to Liam as he passed.

They were halfway back through the woods when she turned on him. "What? What was that reaction for?"

He tried to stay calm, to control his voice despite the tension in him. Cadal was angered as much by Connor's possessive look as by his own drive to lay claim to her in response. Visions of himself pulling Mollie to his chest and silencing her angry words with potent kisses, of taking her off to a warm patch of grass to finish the job, danced in his mind. What type of barbarian was he turning into?

"What are you doing?" he asked.

"I'm working. What the hell does it look like I'm doing?"

Cadal glanced up and down the length of her much like Connor had. He was surprised by the physical effect it had on him. "Like that?" he finally managed to demand of her.

Mollie set her jaw angrily. "It's comfortable. Is that a problem for you?"

"It will be a problem for *you* in twelve hours."

"What are you talking about?" She didn't attempt to hide her annoyance.

"You are already raising eyebrows all over the village, over half the county. You are a woman who handles her land better than most men do. You outwork the men. What do you think is going to happen when *this* one gets around?"

"What one?"

His fury bubbled up. How could she ask that? "Did you see Connor? Patrick? No. You didn't. You were too busy working." He snorted, barely controlling the urge to roll his eyes. "Working, she says."

She paled and crossed her arms over her breasts, looking frightened and unsure.

Cadal pushed back his anger, regaining some portion of his lost calm. "You have to do more than work like a man to win and keep their respect. Keep that in mind. It will make your life easier."

Mollie nodded. "Anything else?" she asked weakly.

"Yes, now that you mention it." Cadal stripped off his shirt and tossed it to her. "Put this on, please." He stood with his hands on his hips and awaited her compliance.

Mollie ran her hand over the shirt then threw it back at him. She started to storm away, then stilled and turned back. "You could have said that you minded a week ago, you know."

Cadal felt a pang of regret. He should have never let that night go as far as it did. "I'm sorry," he told her quietly.

Her face drained of the last of its color. She swallowed whatever emotion she was trying to keep from welling up. "So am I." She didn't storm away that time. Mollie walked away, head up and back straight.

He watched her go. If she had simply been angry, he might not have felt so horrible, but Mollie wasn't angry. She was hurt. Cadal kept promising that he wouldn't hurt her, but he managed to do it, over and over.

He sat down, fighting back misery. He didn't know what he was doing anymore. The excuse he gave Mollie was a decent one. It wasn't the truth by a long shot, but it was a good excuse. He was angry, and he was frustrated, but it had nothing to do with what the villagers thought. It was about the other men looking at Mollie the way Connor had looked at her, and Cadal berated himself for it. She wasn't his.

But she could be.

For how long? In what way? Cadal didn't know if the stories were true. Even if they were, what would happen when his time was up?

Liam interrupted his thoughts. "Went that badly?"

Cadal nodded. "Pretty badly."

Liam sat next to him and nodded to the crumpled shirt in Cadal's lap. "You tried to make her put some clothes on?"

"Yes. I did." He still didn't understand why that hurt her. He would have understood anger at treating her like a child, but he couldn't fathom the hurt.

"She's a fiery woman, sir. Can't give a woman like that orders."

"I noticed. What *do* you do with a woman like that?"

"Given half a chance, marry her."

Cadal startled and stared at Liam in complete disbelief. "What?"

Liam smiled widely. "Be honest, Mr. Cadal. Why do you think I looked to you like that? Everyone knows how you feel about her, except you and her, apparently. You've been hovering over the young miss for months. When she flirted, you watched. When she ignored you, you watched even closer. After today, there's no doubt left. You were murderous, because someone else looked."

He had to admit that Liam had pegged it. He sighed. "What do I do about it now?"

Liam chuckled, looking skyward as if seeking aid or sharing a joke with his God. "You've been honest with me. Be honest with her." He pushed to his feet. "One piece of advice. Put on your shirt first." Liam headed back for the barn, looking smug.

Cadal watched him leave. Every time he thought he understood Humans, something completely unexpected happened. He sighed and pulled his shirt back on. It was time to have a long talk with Mollie.

* * * *

Mollie was sure her day couldn't get worse. Cadal apologized for being interested in her? "What else could go wrong?" she groaned.

"Mollie!"

She cringed at the cordial greeting in a familiar voice. *It can't be. Life isn't this unfair.* Mollie started uttering curses before she even turned to look. "What do you want, Joseph?" She headed for the door, determined to escape as quickly as possible.

Her cousin stepped in front of her. "I had to come see for myself." His smile was patronizing.

Mollie stepped around him and into the kitchen. Joseph followed her without an invitation. That wasn't a surprise.

"See what, Joseph?" she growled at him.

Elizabeth gaped at him. "I'm sorry, miss. I didn't know he was sneaking around waiting for you. Should I fetch Mr. Cadal and Liam for you?"

"No, Elizabeth. I can handle this one by myself. You can get me a glass of iced tea if you have a moment."

The younger woman nodded and stepped away.

"Thank you, Elizabeth."

"Iced tea sounds great," Joseph called after her.

Mollie started washing her hands. "You weren't offered my hospitality."

"Excuse me?"

"You heard me. I'll offer my hospitality long enough to get you on your way, but you do not order my employees around. If you want something, ask Elizabeth nicely. If she has the time, she *might* oblige you."

Joseph clenched his jaw, his eyes cold. "All right, then. Elizabeth, would you *please* get me a glass of iced tea?"

Mollie cracked a tight smile at how foreign the 'please' sounded on his lips. He was certainly out of practice with the word.

"Miss?" Elizabeth was confused and uncertain in light of Mollie's pronouncement.

Mollie shrugged. "If you have the time, Elizabeth. I don't mind. As long as Mr. O'Bane shows the proper respect for both of us, that is."

Elizabeth nodded and turned away.

Mollie glanced back at Joseph. "Now, what do you want?"

"I couldn't believe that you left corporate life to be a farmer, but here you are. Dirt under your fingernails, sweating, and doing manual labor. Where'd you get the shiner, Mollie?"

"I had an accident."

"Fighting off vandals was what I heard."

Mollie raised an eyebrow at him. She wondered where Joseph heard that before deciding it really didn't matter to her. "That's none of your business, is it?"

Joseph eyed her appraisingly. "Nice outfit. Rallying the troops?"

"Getting some sun." She accepted her tea from Elizabeth with a smile and a nod.

"You're being wasted here. Admit it." Joseph didn't even spare Elizabeth a look as she handed him the glass he'd requested. Joseph had always been a bit of a snob.

"I'm happy here. The estate is doing well. I get along with my coworkers. I think I'll stay awhile."

Joseph laughed. "You've got trespassers and vandals. You've lost almost five percent of your crops. Your neighbors hate you. Your whole family line is unpopular." He smiled tightly, and Mollie could read that he agreed with that one in his body language. "The Blake women." He rolled his eyes.

"True, but I like a challenge."

"You caused me a lot of trouble, you know."

Mollie laughed harshly. "I'm so upset. How did I do that? By walking away and letting you sink? That would be *such* a shame."

"No, by signing over your interests to your mother. She's been a royal pain in the arse."

"That's why you're here," she mused.

Joseph darkened but didn't answer.

"Good. At least someone is able to keep you in line. Why are you really here?"

"To take you back."

Mollie felt her irritation blooming. She couldn't believe the nerve of him and of her mother, presuming to run her life this way, as if she would let them.

"The business needs you. Your mother wants you home." He shrugged. "What do you want to come back? I won't offer you a blank check but..." He let the offer hang between them.

"There is nothing you can offer that would make me come back. It's too bad that you came all this way for nothing, Joseph. I gave up on that life. I like it here. Mother will just have to miss me, and you'll have to remember everything I tried to tell you when I worked for you."

"Darcy will disown you. She's already threatened it. She's sent you letters."

"Let her disown me. All she'd leave me is interest in a company I don't want and a house I hate. None of that is a great loss. Maybe you should suck up to her. She can leave her interest to you, and you could have your own way again."

"Mollie, be honest. Everything is against you. Why on Earth would you stay? What possible reason can you have?"

"I don't know Joseph. What reason did I have for sticking around in Seattle all those years? At least I'm happy here. That's a major improvement."

"Give me one *good* reason and I'll walk away. Just one, Mollie, and I'll leave."

Mollie sipped her tea and thought about it. Everything Joseph said was true. In addition, Cadal... Well, it was better not to think about him.

She loved it here, except for Thornton and his vipers. She had a great crew. It sounded like such flimsy reasons when you looked at it that way, but what price could you put on happiness? It was worth a hell of a lot to her, but Joseph wouldn't think so. She set her tea down and searched for an answer Joseph would consider 'good enough.'

The door opened behind her, and Mollie turned to glance at it, gritting her teeth at the sight of Cadal. She hoped he didn't want to get into it again. Then she noticed he was smiling. A wide, honest smile lit his face. Before she could question him about it, Cadal wrapped his arms around her and kissed her.

Mollie's surprise was quickly replaced by the passion that skyrocketed through her at his touch. Her hands, on his chest with the initial thought of pushing him away, wound into his shirt. She pulled him closer. Cadal took the opportunity to run his hand up the bare expanse of her back and to deepen the kiss. Mollie forgot Joseph, as Cadal's touch radiated heat from where his body met hers throughout her entire being.

She lost herself. The passion between them was alive and moving of its own accord. Cadal's mouth searched her, and Mollie opened for him, her body tingling as he caressed her inside and out.

Cadal pulled away, his smile still wide and his eyes locked on hers with an intensity that sent shivers of ecstasy down her spine.

"Feeling better?" he asked, his voice husky.

Mollie licked her lips slowly, savoring the heady aftereffects of his kiss. "Yes. I just needed a cold drink." She needed something cold after that. Or maybe something hot and mindless.

"Good."

Cadal moved his eyes to Joseph, and Mollie felt an odd sense of loss. She wanted to cup his face back to hers, to see those eyes and feel that kiss in her soul again.

"How rude of me," Cadal said more to her than to the other man. "I didn't realize we had a guest." He offered his hand to Joseph with the same wide smile. "I'm William Cadal."

His other hand caressed Mollie's hip in a way that made her dizzy with the same desire that had gripped her when Cadal massaged her. She ran her hand over his breathlessly. Joseph turned red in anger, and Mollie cringed inwardly at Cadal's ruse.

Joseph gripped Cadal's hand for a single, tense pump of a handshake. "I'm Joseph O'Bane. It's nice to meet you."

He lied. This was the last thing Joseph wanted to see, and Mollie knew that as well as he did.

Cadal glanced at Mollie. "Friend of yours?" His mouth twitched in something akin to amusement.

Mollie shook her head. "Not really. Joseph is a distant cousin, and — he's leaving. Aren't you, Joseph?"

Joseph's color deepened again. "I guess I am, at that. I have my answer."

She raised an eyebrow. "Do you?"

Her cousin sized up the larger man. "I think so. Congratulations, Mollie. You had me fooled. I actually believed you were the ice cube you pretended to be."

Mollie tightened her grip on Cadal's hand in reaction to the tensing of his muscles. She wasn't sure if he actually meant to hit Joseph, but they couldn't afford some rash move against her volatile cousin. It was too dangerous. His arm relaxed under her hand in understanding.

Cadal nodded curtly. "Should I have Liam take you back to the village or can you find your way?" His voice was cold, clipped, precision. The invitation Cadal had extended was withdrawn, and there was no question of that.

Joseph smiled widely. He had gotten a rise out of Cadal. That was what he was really after. "I'm sure I can find my way out, if that's what Mollie wants." Joseph looked at her, and Mollie could tell he was gauging her response.

"It is. You know it is." Her mind was still reeling from Cadal's reaction to Joseph's jab at her...and that kiss.

"Then I'll be on my way." Joseph turned and left without another word. The door slammed shut behind him.

Mollie turned on Cadal. "What were you doing?" she demanded in a fierce whisper.

"I kissed you. You seemed to enjoy it, or did I read your reaction incorrectly?" His eyes glittered playfully.

"By the time Joseph leaves town, he'll have someone convinced we're lovers. What then? What eyebrows will I raise then, Cadal?"

Cadal glanced over her head at Elizabeth. "Can we discuss this elsewhere?"

Mollie raised an eyebrow. "Where did you have in mind?"

His color rose a notch though his smile never faltered. "That, I will leave up to you."

She stared at him in disbelief, and her mind whirled. There was no way Mollie was going to her bedroom with Cadal until she knew why this sudden change had come over him. "The library, I think."

Cadal chuckled, turning and leading the way down the hall. Mollie followed him. Despite her anger, she still felt the burn of wanting his touch. She cursed herself inwardly.

Mollie wasn't sure if she was angrier at Cadal for presuming to kiss her after what he'd said or at herself for allowing it to go on. Mollie knew what would happen, and she let herself get swept away.

Swept away, hell! She threw herself at him. She knew Cadal wasn't interested, but she let him get himself in this ridiculous situation because she wanted it. It wasn't merely her reputation on the line here. His would suffer too.

She glanced at him as they walked down the hall. Cadal was unaffected by the whole thing. Why couldn't he be rattled like she was? He was too calm and collected. Mollie sighed. She didn't really know what she wanted anymore.

No, that was wrong. Mollie knew exactly what she wanted and she wasn't going to get it. She wanted Cadal.

Mollie closed the library door behind her and faced him. "Now, why did you do that? If you're worried about Joseph, you shouldn't be. I can handle him on my own."

Cadal met her eyes seriously. "Did you enjoy it?"

"What difference does that make?"

He touched her cheek, and Mollie felt her heart begin to pound. He wrapped his other hand around the small of her back and pulled her to his chest. Cadal feathered his lips over hers, and Mollie found that her reaction was immediate and electrifying. Her hands grasped at the back of his head almost of their own accord and it was she who guided the kiss to a more fervent level this time, opening herself to his questing mouth fully.

Cadal groaned and pulled her tight to his body. Mollie brushed against the rigid length of him, and he shuddered. His movements became more urgent. Cadal was affected, and Mollie considered forgetting the rest of the discussion in favor of exploring that discovery.

When he broke off the kiss, his breathing was ragged and his fingers shook against her cheek. He searched her face then nodded. "Good. Then whatever the villagers say doesn't really matter, does it?" He nuzzled her lips and set Mollie away from him, putting distance between their bodies for the discussion they still had to finish.

Mollie shook her head in confusion. "What about the gossip? You said—"

Cadal met her eyes, and Mollie felt the familiar surge that passed between them every time she was lost in his eyes.

"I lied," he admitted. "Not about the gossip. There will always be gossip."

"What did you lie about?"

"I don't care about gossip." Cadal ran a finger down the neckline of her halter and watched her reaction. "I do not mind you looking like this. I enjoy it quite a bit."

"Then why did you react the way you did?"

Mollie found it difficult to maintain anger with Cadal in light of her reaction to his touch, difficult even to concentrate on the subject at hand. *It's hard to think about what rumors are being started when all you want to do is make sure they're true.*

Cadal traced further down her cleavage. Mollie shifted further into his hand while she savored the progression and the darkening of his eyes. Her breathing hitched.

"When I saw the way the other men were watching you..." He took his hand away and averted his eyes in embarrassment.

"You were jealous?"

He nodded. "I was beyond jealous. I was angry. I didn't want anyone else to look at you that way, to see you like this."

"Then... You're not sorry?"

"Only that I haven't been very honest with you."

"About what?"

"About why I couldn't— Why I can't," he corrected himself bitterly. "I want this. I want you, but there are family matters. I may have to leave. I don't want to, but—"

Mollie nodded. Luckily, she'd had the forethought to make the deal with Darcy. She might have been trapped in just such a situation if she hadn't. "I think I know what you mean. There's no way to work this out, is there?"

He looked at her hopelessly. "I want to. Believe me, I want to, but there are so many complications."

A frightening thought occurred to her. "You're not married, are you?"

Cadal looked amused by the prospect. "No. I'm not married, not promised, not even courting — except you, of course." He sighed. "I'm afraid I haven't even been doing that honorably."

Mollie hoisted herself onto the edge of the desk. "Where does that leave us?"

"Lost somewhere between where we wish we were and where we hope we don't end up," he answered cryptically.

She shook her head. "That's not what I meant."

Cadal sat on the desk next to her. "I know it's not. What do you want?"

Mollie considered it. "I can't have what I want, at least until your life becomes less complicated. In our current situation?" She shook her head. "I hate making life decisions with no information. I don't suppose you could give me more to work with?"

He sighed, shaking his head. "The truth is, I don't know. I could be called home in ten days or not for ten years. I have no idea what type of situation I'll be walking into when I do get called back."

"Then why go?" she asked quietly.

"It is impossible to explain. I have to. It is—"

"Complicated," she supplied for him.

He nodded. "Very."

Mollie took a deep breath. "Why don't we give it a shot? I know I want to. If you're called home—" She felt a pang at the thought of Cadal leaving, especially if she knew he didn't want to go. "I guess we'll have to worry about that later."

Cadal nodded, and she could see the relief on his face. "I was hoping that would be your answer, but we'll take it slow. I know it will be hard, but I won't compromise you."

Mollie smiled at such an old-fashioned idea. She leaned across to kiss Cadal. "Well, we could be a little dishonorable."

He smiled widely and obliged her with a passionate kiss.

* * * *

Zera entered Morda's private quarters without an invitation. The Fairy Mistress had felt her anger coming. She sighed. Zera was becoming more insistent as the seasons wore on, but the time was not yet right.

"Yes, Zera?" Morda asked.

"When, Morda? How long will you allow him to stay?"

"Until the time is right. It cannot be long now."

"Why? The young woman is doing well on her own."

"The vibrations are not yet in harmony."

"You know what has happened, don't you?" Zera accused. "You promised me that this would not be allowed to happen, Morda."

Morda met her eyes. "Peeking in windows, Zera?"

The younger woman blushed.

"At any rate, I only promised that you would not lose your son, that I would not allow him to leave us as Xanthe did."

Zera's disbelief was nearly as strong an emotion as her hatred and anger, strong enough for Morda to feel, even in her weakened state. "He's falling in love, Morda. With a Human."

Morda smiled warmly. "No, Zera. He's *fallen* in love with a wonderful woman who makes him very happy."

Zera was livid, and Morda wished once again that she could tell her the whole truth, but Zera would not believe her even if she did. This was too delicate a thing to have done badly. It had been botched horribly enough already.

"You would return him to me shattered like he was when he lost Xanthe?"

"No. It will not happen that way."

"What other choice is there? A Human cannot become Fairy, can she?"

Morda smiled. That was the real issue here, and it always had been. "You are right, Zera. A Human cannot become Fairy."

Zera waited for an answer the Fairy Mistress could not give yet. The balance had to be protected at all costs, though Morda wished she could toss caution to the breeze, as the Humans said.

"Then what will you do? Surely, Cadal cannot live with this Human until she dies only to return heartbroken to me then?"

"Trust, Zera. If the vibrations are correct, Cadal will return to you whole and happy. I have spoken to Cadal about this matter once. Knowing how stubborn your son is, it may take several conversations before he heeds my words, but that is a risk I am willing to take. Now I must ask you... No, I must tell you something very important, Zera. Do not interfere. The Harmony has a hand in what must happen. Cadal has a destiny. If you interfere, you can only cause pain where there should be healing."

Zera regarded her coldly. "I am hardly a child, Morda."

"You are a mother. You will see things that will make you think you must act, but you must not. Cadal must do what he must do."

She nodded and left, deep in thought.

Morda sighed. Trying to guide one future was exhausting enough, but trying to guide three seemed impossible. Zera still believed Morda had doomed Cadal to unhappiness when she'd allowed Xanthe to leave. Though Zera knew Morda believed in what she was doing, she still wept for her son. When Cadal's hopes and dreams were shattered, so were his mother's.

The only joys left in Zera's bleak world after her husband died had been Cadal's ceremony and the children that would follow. She thought those had been lost when Xanthe left them. Zera had hardened her heart that day...along with Corea and Toril. All of them were effectively lost to her.

If only Morda could have told Zera the whole truth that first night, the mother in her might have been soothed. She might have understood and been patient. She would have felt less pain, but it was guarded knowledge. It had to be, or the fabric of the colony would unravel at the seams. These forays of The Harmony strained the colony to its limits.

Zera, while still her friend, had lost all trust in the Fairy Mistress as a leader. Cadal had suffered a century of torture, and Corea... *Ah, Corea.*

Morda's beloved daughter and Corea's husband, Toril, had never forgiven Morda for allowing Xanthe to leave them. Corea understood even less than Zera and Cadal had how Morda could allow her granddaughter to leave the love and safety of the Fairy realm. Zera and

Cadal would forgive her when the whole truth became clear to them. Corea likely never would. Healing her daughter's wounds was not within Morda's powers. She doubted even her successor could arrange such a magical happening.

If only Corea could have seen Xanthe as she stood in the Great Chamber, awaiting the judgment of the Fairy Mistress that would either crush her or make her the happiest woman in the world. If only she could have heard the young woman's hopes and fears come to life. Morda leaned her head back as her last memories of Xanthe in the colony washed over her.

Xanthe stood in the center of the Great Chamber. Her golden hair fell softly over her green wool dress nearly to her knees and her matching green eyes glanced uncertainly around the Fairy Mistress's throne room from beneath her thick lashes.

Xanthe had been in this room many times before. Everyone in the colony had, but she supposed it was always different when you were one of the called, even if you requested to be one of the called.

She swallowed a lump in her throat and reminded herself that the worst that could happen was that Morda could refuse her request. Xanthe would go miserably back to her life in the tree-city and Bran would go on and marry a local girl from his village.

Bran would do that, wouldn't he? He would forget in time. After all, Humans don't have much time to dwell on things. Their lives demand that they move on or die, and Bran wasn't the type to give up and die.

Xanthe, however, would have centuries of longing ahead of her. Bran was her soulmate. She was sure of it. Without him, she would be miserable, and no other man would fill the void he left. Could she ever forget Bran?

When he was gone to his God in his grave, could she then? Surely not.

Xanthe startled as she realized that Morda had spoken to her.

"I asked," the Mistress repeated, "if you really want this." Morda's gaze was intent. Xanthe could almost read the sadness in those ancient eyes.

Xanthe realized that she must be honest with the Mistress. Morda would know if she wasn't, but it was more than that. She owed her grandmother the truth. Her heart had to speak for her. "Yes, Mistress. Yes, I do. More than life itself."

Morda nodded and straightened on her throne. "That is exactly what you must give. If you choose to live among the Humans, you must be as one of them. You will live and die as one of them, and the doors of the Fairy realm will be forever closed to you. You can never return. You choose this willingly?"

Tears filled Xanthe's eyes as she considered what had been said. Her sisters would be lost to her. Her parents would be as well. Her gift of flight would be relinquished. All of her powers would be forfeit. She would live a Human lifespan and die like one of them.

Xanthe had to admit that none of it mattered if it meant a life with Bran. Resolved, she stood taller. "With a heavy heart, Mistress, but I must."

Morda nodded grimly. "Then go, my child. Go to your love, but never forget us. Though, be warned. Your children..." Morda was far away, listening to another conversation, gauging the harmonies that would lead her home.

"Children, Mistress?" Xanthe was confused. She had no children. What could Morda mean?

"Your descendents, Xanthe." Morda trained her ancient eyes on the young Fairy. "My gift to you, my child, is that your descendents will dream of their true heritage. If any so wish it, they may return to us and leave the Human realm."

Morda turned her gaze to the sky, and Xanthe knew her interview was over. She bowed before her grandmother and ached to embrace her one last time before she left, but somehow Xanthe was sure Morda would never stand for such an emotional outburst. She unbolted the door, left the Great Chamber quietly, and wound her way out of the tree-city.

Morda had felt it all in the way of the Fairy Mistress. It broke her heart, but she'd known at once that this was The Harmony's plan. Xanthe could never have been truly happy in the Fairy realm. Though she missed it and worried about Morda's gift to her children, Xanthe had been happy as a Human.

It was always the same. Xanthe had won her happiness at a horrible cost to everyone else, both those she left behind at the colony and her descendents. Cadal's pain had to be freed. Mollie's pain and Zera's pain had to be freed. Only together could they accomplish such a thing.

Morda had known Mollie would be the one. From the cradle, she was different than the others. From the womb, she'd reached for her birthright.

That fateful day, years ago, Morda had felt her pain. She knew Mollie's heart had been forever changed.

Mollie's life could not have been an easy one since then. Harmony knew it couldn't. It should not have happened this way. Morda longed to give Mollie back those stolen years. It was all in Cadal's hands, and only Cadal could heal her.

Chapter Seven

Cadal found he had a more pressing problem than simply working out the *logistics* with Mollie. He'd considered doing what Xanthe had, leaving the colony for Mollie as a Human. Cadal could tolerate Human life, if Mollie was a part of it. Every time she touched him, kissed him, looked in his eyes; he was more sure of it.

Now that option was lost to him.

He'd wondered at his strange connection with Mollie. Cadal still wondered about it, but there could be no doubt when he started receiving sporadic thoughts and emotions that were not hers.

Cadal was the new Fairy Master. There would be no leaving the colony for him. There was only one born with the gift, and The Harmony, Herself, protected him. If he left, the colony would collapse. Another could not be trained to be what he was, and there would be no leader to take over for Morda. There would be no one to facilitate harmony, to mediate disputes. Their society would cease to be.

This also put a new spin on his situation with Mollie. Why did Cadal connect with her so often? As like a Fairy she was, there was no denying she was Human.

Then there was the problem of his position. No Fairy Master took his place without first marrying his true soulmate. Cadal had become convinced Mollie was his soulmate, but how could she be? He had been wrong about that before. He knew that, but he couldn't be wrong about Mollie. Cadal knew he couldn't.

How much time did he have? If his powers were strengthening, Morda's must be waning. She must begin his training soon. Cadal felt a sick sensation at the thought. He was running out of time. There were so many questions he wanted to ask Morda, but to do so, he would have to admit what he was. Morda must already be looking for her successor. She couldn't know it was Cadal or she would surely have ordered him to begin his training by now.

Mollie knew something was troubling him. Cadal supposed he couldn't hide much from her, but he couldn't tell her the truth about what it was either. She didn't press him for an answer. Mollie cheered him when she could and took his mind off of his troubles in other ways when she couldn't. Cadal knew he couldn't leave Mollie. He couldn't live without her, but staying was beyond his control.

She still kept up her duties on the estate, though she did less fieldwork now that the crisis had passed. Cadal ordered Liam to set the watering rotation so he worked with Mollie on her shifts. Liam smiled knowingly but didn't comment.

Cadal watched her kick into high gear again for the harvest. Mollie worked alongside the men every day until the season ended. She accompanied Liam to the wholesalers' market, and there were record profits for the small estate. Mollie stunned Liam by rewarding each of the employees with a small bonus.

After the harvest, there was a dance in the village. Mollie could tell Cadal had no interest in going, so she sent all of the employees and signed herself and Cadal up for the few duties at home. She explained to Liam that the employees had earned a good time out on the town.

They settled into the library for a quiet night of storytelling in front of the fire once the others were gone. Mollie was enjoying their time together, but she really would have loved to go to the dance despite what she told Liam. Cadal could see it in her eyes.

He looked at her over Xanthe's book. "What do you really want to do?"

Mollie smiled wickedly from her place on the cushion. "If I told you, I still wouldn't get it."

His arousal was immediate and intense. Cadal blushed deeply, taking a deep breath to rein in his errant body.

She sobered. "I'm sorry. Forget I said it. Honestly?"

He nodded.

"Dance with me."

Cadal's heart skipped a beat. He wanted to dance with Mollie, wind dance. He had wanted to for weeks. Every time he looked at her, Cadal could picture nothing else.

Well, almost nothing else. That was something else that was getting harder and harder to avoid.

He knew dancing meant something different to Humans, but Cadal decided dancing with Mollie would mean the same to him, whether it was wind dancing or dancing the Human way. He only hoped it meant half as much to her.

"I don't really know how to dance," he told her. In Human terms, that much was true.

Mollie smiled. "I'll teach you," she offered.

Cadal considered the irony that Mollie, who was so much younger he'd once considered her a child, could teach him something so precious. He nodded slowly, and her smile widened.

Mollie picked out a CD from the stack on the desk and placed it in the player she used while she worked. She moved the cushions and surveyed the room before pushing the play button. As the music started, Mollie stepped to Cadal and took his hands. To his surprise, she placed them on her hips. Then she wound her own around his shoulders. This was more like a kiss than a dance.

His body was instantly on alert. "What now?" he whispered.

"Move together. Sway to the music at first. Then we'll try moving around the floor. That's more difficult, because you end up hitting the other person's feet if you're not in sync."

Mollie began to move her body fluidly against him, and Cadal found the sensation mesmerizing and sexually exciting. Before he knew it, they were gliding and spinning around the room together. Cadal knew that this was what wind dancing was supposed to be. Song after song, they moved together until they were both breathless. The color was high in Mollie's cheeks, and her eyes glittered in the excitement of the moment.

He kissed her. Their kisses were always passionate, but this one was completely unrestrained. He felt the answering call in her, wild and urgent. Cadal knew what he wanted, and nothing was going to stop him as long as Mollie was willing. He swept her off her feet fluidly and onto one of the discarded cushions.

As Cadal covered Mollie with his body, he broke off the kiss and searched her face for any sign of doubt. The eyes that met him were nothing but fevered in her own need. He began undoing the buttons on her shirt furiously, his mouth searching and finding the need in her that matched and magnified his own.

When her bra was uncovered, he reached his hand inside the soft fabric to brush his fingertips over her breast. Mollie pulled her head back and arched to him, her eyes dilating to the sensation. Cadal felt the response of her body beating at his senses, demanding him. He lowered his mouth to nuzzle over the sensitive nipple encased in his hand.

He was jolted out of the moment by a scream of pure rage. It split through his soul, and he recognized it immediately.

"No," he breathed. Cadal searched the room for some sign of Zera, but he couldn't see it. It was real. She was here somewhere. He knew that.

He looked at Mollie miserably. She knew he was about to pull back again, and the loss and longing showed in her eyes already. Her body's plea for him was still at a fever pitch.

Cadal berated himself bitterly. What was he doing? Why did he continue to do this to her? He backed away slowly. He knew he should say something, but he couldn't think of anything to say that wouldn't make it worse. He knew he should hold her, but he couldn't trust himself to hold her. Not yet. He was too raw and involved to do anything but finish what he started if he touched her.

He opened the door to leave the room. Mollie broke eye contact and rolled to her side, arms wrapped around her chest. Cadal knew she was crying softly though he couldn't see it.

He stalked to the door and stepped out into the rain falling outside. Humans talked about cold showers, but as far as Cadal could tell, it didn't help.

The rain became a downpour that matched his mood, but he kept moving. He stopped and looked around slowly. Cadal had no idea where he was going. He couldn't go to Morda. He couldn't face Mollie. He never wanted to see his mother again. He cursed himself for the ill he was wishing Zera even as he cursed her for her part in that night's fiasco.

Cadal sat on the grass, staring into the faint ripples visible on the dark pool. If only he knew what he should do.

Morda's voice came from behind him. "You do know. You always have known. If you would simply stop doubting yourself and your path, this could all pass so much easier."

Cadal turned stiffly and knelt before her. He greeted her as a penitent, slipping into his native language with a sigh of relief. "Mistress."

"Get up, Cadal," Morda barked. "I am your teacher, not your lord. As Fairy Master, you are my equal, not my servant. Now start acting the role."

He started and met her eyes fearfully. "You—" Cadal couldn't finish the thought. He was being a fool. She knew. Wherever he was, whatever his pain, Morda would know it. He groaned and dropped back to sitting, burying his face in his hands.

She sank down beside him and laid her hand on his arm. "Of course I knew, but I could not ask you to leave. What you are doing is vital. Surely, you must feel that."

Cadal dropped his hands into his lap and met her eyes. "I thought perhaps I was simply being selfish. My concern should be Fairies, but..." He shrugged hopelessly.

"What does your heart tell you?"

"Things that make no sense."

"For instance?" she prodded him.

"That Mollie Hardy is my true soulmate."

"She is," Morda said in a matter-of-fact sort of voice, as if it was perfectly obvious.

He gaped at her.

"Why the surprise, Cadal? I told you to listen to your heart." He could see the amusement in her ancient eyes.

"She's Human. Or are the old tales true? About Humans and Fairies coupling?"

"No, those tales are not true. A Fairy must relinquish his or her Fairy life and adopt a Human life to couple with a Human."

Cadal was crushed. If he had tried to couple with her, it would have been a disaster. He *had* tried to. Horror at what he had almost done washed over him. He couldn't conceive of what The Harmony's punishment for such a thing would be. She was not known for kindness when Her laws were broken.

Morda interrupted his train of thought. "Is Mollie truly Human?"

"She must be, and a Human can't become Fairy, can she?"

"No, a Human cannot become a Fairy."

Cadal's heart sank. There was no hope.

Morda interrupted him again. "Are you sure she's Human?"

"Her parents were Human. What else could she be?" Cadal was in a rage, mourning the happiness stolen from him yet again.

"What does your heart tell you?" she prodded again.

"That she's Fairy," he whispered. Harmony, but he wished she was Fairy.

"Why?"

"She speaks to the land. It calls her for help when it's in danger. She knows its pain. She knows our secrets with no logical reason why. I hear her and feel her as if she were Fairy. She loves all of nature and is

willing to sweat and bleed to protect and nurture it—"
Cadal shrugged hopelessly. *If only that were all it took to
be Fairy...*

"Then she's Fairy."

"How? She was born of a Human. Humans cannot
become Fairies."

Morda laughed lightly. "Oh, Cadal. Haven't you
figured that out by now?" she teased him. "Fairies
cannot *become* Human, not fully Human. They retain
their essences. They must. A Human soul cannot be
fabricated any more than a Fairy soul can be. As
Fairies, we can masquerade as a Human. For a time,
we can masquerade as a Human soul."

"But Xanthe?"

"Masqueraded as a Human soul and relinquished
her Fairy life, but her essence was unchanged. That
essence passed, copied if you will, as a part of each of
her descendents. Their physical traits were derived from
mother and father like any child, but in a match like
that, the essence...the soul is of the Fairy. Each of them
appeared Human, and they continued to masquerade
as Human as long as they chose to live as Humans.
Mollie did not choose to be Human, so she is not."

"How could this happen? How could they appear to
be Human and couple with Humans and be essentially
not Human?" His head was spinning from the
revelation.

"A masqueraded soul must eventually return. It
travels in torment until the soul who truly wishes her
birthright claims it." Morda sighed deeply, and Cadal
was assaulted by her pain, a sadness that seemed to
tear at her soul and his by extension. "With Mollie, it
was an accident. It is not supposed to happen this
way." She met his eyes hopelessly. "She doesn't know."

"What?" Cadal managed. "What do you mean, she doesn't know?" How could so momentous a change go unnoticed?

"What have you seen, Cadal?"

He remembered the night the land was poisoned. Mollie's confusion, her fear and her doubt had been no act. "You're right. She doesn't know. How could this happen?" he raged. "How could she survive that way?"

Morda met his eyes again and her tears spilled over. Whatever it was, it affected the Fairy Mistress greatly. Cadal had never seen her like this. He started to call back his question, but Morda had already launched into an answer.

"Mollie was hurt, hurt badly. A Human man that she cared for..."

Cadal felt his blood run cold. A sick feeling settled in the pit of his stomach.

"You can't even imagine the rest, Cadal. It is beyond a Fairy's worst nightmares. Afterward, she retreated back to the old tales that Xanthe told. She knew such a thing would never happen in the Fairy colony. She wished— It was not a flippant joke. Mollie really wanted what she asked for, with all of her heart. The Harmony heard and granted her wish. There was a birthright to be claimed, and she claimed it without knowing she had."

Cadal couldn't believe that fate could be so cruel. In a single blow, he was given his fondest wish and set an impossible task. "What must I do?"

"Convince her of her heritage somehow, then bring her home. Then, and only then, she will be yours. Mollie must be safely back in the colony where she belongs. That is your final task. Your second was to agree to protect her and to find her love. You have completed that task."

"How do I even begin to do that?"

"Love her. Commit to her. The rest is yours to figure out. This is your task to complete. I told you laying claim to your soulmate would not be an easy road."

Cadal found a whole new fear. "How can I?"

Morda met his eyes, her look inviting no argument. "Does her past bother you?"

"No." He faltered, shaking his head. "I mean, yes, but— She's been hurt before. How can I ever make up for that?"

"You can't. Don't try. You're the first man she's been able to trust in all these years. Part of that is her past, but part is the transformation. As a Fairy, she is searching for her soulmate. That is you. You know what you must do. You would have earlier tonight, wouldn't you?"

Cadal favored her with a wearied look. "Do something for me."

Morda laughed. "It has already been done. Zera has been banned from seeing you until you return to the colony."

"Thank you." He considered the current problem. "Why didn't you tell me?"

"You had to discover it for yourself."

"Committing to her may not be easy. I hurt her when I left her tonight. I didn't understand, and I didn't know what else to do. She may not want to commit to me."

Morda smiled. "Speak with your heart. If you do, she will refuse you nothing."

Cadal nodded, praying to The Harmony that Zera wasn't mistaken.

"Go now. It is cold out here and you are soaked to the skin."

He kissed her cheek and headed back to the house.

On the way, Cadal pondered Mollie's past. There were so many things he thought were unimportant. With this single bit of knowledge about her, so many things made sense. She didn't trust men, because she had been hurt by a man. Her reaction to Thornton when he took liberties was perfectly understandable. The way Mollie jumped from the bed when she first met Cadal, her desperate need for the Fairy tales, her need to win the respect of the men she worked with, her reaction when she learned she had invited their attentions without meaning to... It all made sense now.

He cringed at the vision of Mollie in the hands of someone who would hurt her so badly she would beg The Harmony for something she thought she could never have. She'd begged for freedom forever from abuse, a place where such things did not exist, a place where she would be safe. If only she had grown up where she would be safe.

Cadal sighed. The past was past. Mollie's future was a whole new problem. That future could be a future with Cadal by her side, if she wished it. He hoped she wished for it as much as he did.

He went up the stairs and laid his head on her door. *Maybe, I should wait until tomorrow.* No, he had to see her. He knocked on her door.

"Yes?" Her voice was so soft that he almost missed her answer.

"Mollie, may I come in?"

She didn't answer.

"Please, Mollie." He'd beg, if she wanted it. Hadn't Morda said to speak from the heart? Knowing he could have her, he would do whatever she wanted just for the chance to lay claim to her.

"Come in."

Cadal opened the door and stepped inside. At first, Mollie didn't look at him. When she raised her eyes, she sucked in a deep breath.

"Oh, Cadal." She came off the bed and touched his face with trembling fingers that burned against his icy skin. "You're freezing. Get in a hot bath while I make you some tea."

He touched her cheek, swallowing a cry of frustration. Mollie had been crying, and her face was red-streaked and puffy. *My fault. I shouldn't have left her.*

"No. No, I need to talk to you first."

Mollie looked at him as if he were crazy. "You'll have pneumonia if we don't get you warm and dry." She peeled off his sopping sweater and dropped it to the floor with a heavy thump.

"I said I'd never hurt you. I promised—"

"Cadal, we'll discuss this later."

He took her by the upper arms and kissed her, at a loss to say anything of use. Cadal felt Mollie holding back, burying the response her body craved to give him. She had never held back before, and Cadal found it painful. Mollie searched his face and shook her head.

"I shouldn't have left you," he whispered. "Please, don't shut me out. I need you."

She shook her head again and avoided his eyes. "Let's get you taken care of. Then we'll discuss this."

Cadal pulled her to him again. His kiss was more insistent, questing for the response she was hiding beneath the surface. That time, he didn't pull away until she was lost in the kiss with him. Mollie wrapped her arms around his waist and pulled herself to him. Wet as Cadal was, it made no difference to her.

He brushed his lips along her cheek to her ear. "I know what I want, what I've always wanted. Please, tell me it's not too late," he breathed.

His name was all she replied with, but her voice was part longing and part invitation. Cadal returned to her mouth, warming with that little encouragement.

Mollie kissed him. The urgent need had returned. *Soulmates.* Why had he never recognized the melding of their passion before?

Cadal felt her fingers on the buttons of his shirt. Each one she opened seemed to heighten their shared enjoyment. She slid it off his shoulders and ran her hands down his chest to the top of his jeans.

She broke off the kiss and looked into his eyes. "Are you sure?"

"I've never wanted anything more than I want to be with you." And if he didn't have it soon, he'd be lost.

Mollie nodded and undid the button and zipper on his jeans. She never lost eye contact. Cadal wasn't sure if she was afraid he would bolt again if she did or if she was searching for a sign that he was about to run. Regardless, he locked his eyes on hers, feeling her arousal spike with the connection.

Cadal groaned as she reached inside the open jeans to stroke him. He kicked off his shoes and pulled his jeans and socks free with a few tugs at the wet, muddy fabric. He kissed her again, and Mollie's hands cupped the back of his head. He scooped her up and laid her gently on the bed.

He looked down at her and smiled. "My turn." He unbuttoned her shirt, keeping her pinned in his gaze until he had stripped it from her body. This time, there was no halter or bra to obstruct his view of her.

Cadal ran his hands over her breasts, then his lips, his tongue, and finally his mouth; teasing her nipples to hard peaks, laving them, and taking them into the warmth of his mouth reverently.

With each progression, her reaction was more profound. Cadal was captivated by every nuance of her response. Mollie ached for more, and he could not deny her any joy he could offer. The fact that her responses fired his own only intensified the experience.

Mollie bit her lip as she watched him pleasure her. She explored his hair and every inch of his skin she could reach, sending waves of delight through him. Soft sounds of longing left her lips, firing his resolve to bring her to a climax that would satisfy them both.

He removed her panties and roamed the naked expanse of her with his hands before settling at her core, teasing her lightly with his fingers and his tongue. Her response was electric. Mollie moved against him and pulled his head to her in her excitement. She cried out in frustration at the fulfillment her body and soul craved.

Cadal settled over her to give her the release she craved and himself at the same time, but Mollie looked at him in confusion.

"What's wrong?" he asked.

"Can't I do anything for you? Is there something..." She blushed.

Cadal kissed her and brushed a lock of hair from her cheek. "Next time. This time, it's your turn."

Mollie nodded, though the concept seemed to baffle her.

He entered her, cautious, mindful of her past now that he knew it. A light grimace crossed her face. Then Mollie relaxed into the sensations coursing through her. Cadal moved slowly at first, reveling in the sensations he experienced from Mollie's emotional responses and from his own body simultaneously.

Her need matched his own, and he soared with it. Cadal felt the want pulsing at him. *Faster, deeper, harder.* Was it his need or hers? As soulmates in the midst of a first coupling, he wasn't sure there was a distinction. Cadal gave himself over to the commands completely, existing only in the joys of the coupling.

The change in him transferred to Mollie. She cried out as his reactions magnified her own, a tidal wave of pure pleasure now that he gave himself over fully. Nothing existed for her but him claiming her, body and soul. And he would claim her, properly and completely, in the way of the Fairies.

Mollie's climax was pulling at her, and the demands of the coupling became more fevered. Cadal surged into her, clamping her hips to him and tensing for the coming event. The shock wave of pure bliss that passed to Cadal when Mollie climaxed sent him over almost in unison with her. His roar of release sent a tremor of surprise and happiness through her. Mollie threw her head back and arched to draw his essence in. His seed found her open and accepting, and Mollie's hoarse cry at the warmth flooding into her made Cadal shiver in pure need.

A baby. His prayer was as much a craving as his possession of her, as automatic as breathing. *Great Harmony, please. When your plan allows it, let my seed find purchase.* His erection pulsed. He had claimed his soulmate. Surely, The Harmony would bless them. It was customary to ask a blessing at a soulmate's claiming. Cadal wanted that particular blessing desperately.

Mollie clung to him for a long time after. Cadal felt the cascade of emotions from her. Joy, love, comfort, trust... The one that caused him a new pang of anger at her past came last, relief. Cadal knew Mollie was holding back tears. She'd never known it could be this wonderful. While he knew he would be jealous if she had known it, Cadal still felt it unfair that she had been denied knowing.

Cadal kissed her gently. He decided that everything he did would be gentle, for now. Cadal would let Mollie take the lead, except where he had to. When it came to convincing her who and what she really was, he had to take the matter firmly in hand somehow.

Chapter Eight

There were easier lessons to impart and more difficult ones. Since Mollie knew her land, Cadal decided animals would be the next logical choice. She liked animals. They came to her hand as they should and rubbed against her for attention. It was a good first step. Mollie wasn't frightened by their familiarity, though she assumed they had simply become accustomed to people and acted this way accordingly. Cadal knew that was incorrect, which was why he made sure none of the others were close by before he conducted these experiments.

Mollie wasn't doing what she was consciously yet. She was more like a Fairy child. Their defense mechanism from nature was their aura, an aura that nature recognized, an aura of pacification. They had to learn to control that aura and even turn it off when it was necessary. Otherwise, animals might flock to them when they didn't want it.

It was well over two weeks before Mollie did anything that distinguished itself as overtly Fairy. In the end, it was Thunder who got her attention.

Cadal knew the stallion had not been feeling well for several days, but Thunder hadn't given him any indication of his problem.

In all fairness, Cadal hadn't revealed himself to the horse and asked directly. Exerting yourself as Fairy on domestic animals could have unexpected results that the childlike aura would not engender, and he didn't want to waste time trying to repair the damage of Thunder's altered personality if it did, especially when he didn't know how long he would be staying. He walked for several days, hoping the rest would give the animal adequate time to recover from whatever was making him unhappy.

That morning, Cadal took Mollie to the stables to pick up the horses. He planned a ride in the woods. If she could connect with a wild animal rather than a farm animal that was *accustomed* to Humans, maybe Mollie would see what he wanted her to. He needed something concrete that she couldn't explain away any other way to convince her. Cadal knew that she wouldn't believe until she had seen something she couldn't rationally explain.

As they rounded the bend at the top of the hill, Mollie stopped short and gaped at the scene ahead. Patrick and Connor were trying to control Thunder. The horse was panicked and angry. The two men were having a difficult time, but Mollie wasn't concerned with them. Her eyes locked on Thunder.

Cadal felt her awe. She released his hand and walked several steps toward the corral.

The fear. Cadal held his breath and hoped it was a reflection of Thunder's fear and not her own.

The anger. Mollie bolted for the corral before Cadal could stop her. The move was instinctual. No thought process preceded it. Mollie wondered at what she was doing as she ran, but Thunder was in pain. She had to help.

He pounded after her, swearing at himself profusely for not realizing what was happening. Memories of the night the land was poisoned taunted him. It was her reactions he felt, though he'd denied it to himself at the time. The land had been pained but patient, as the land always was. This was an animal, and the call for aid was more primal and harder for a Fairy to ignore.

133

There was a reason Fairy children had keepers and leading strings until they learned to control these urges. Cadal had given his mother more than his share of scares by trying to help an animal he felt needed it.

He was fast, but Mollie was faster, and he had waited too long to react. By the time Cadal reached the fence, Mollie was inside and on her way to the terrified horse. Connor tried to vault after her, but Cadal dragged him off of the top rail. Mollie had a chance in there that Connor didn't, but not if Thunder was in a full panic.

"Patrick, drop your line," Cadal ordered.

Patrick stared at him in confusion.

"Now," he roared, "or he'll kill her."

Patrick's hands relaxed away from the rope and let it fall, and Cadal vaulted into the corral. He only made a few strides when he froze in a panic for her situation.

Cadal held his breath, as Thunder reared up. Mollie stopped her sprint and watched him breathlessly, caught in his display. The horse dropped down and eyed her in mistrust.

Mollie moved slowly. Her hand came up toward Thunder, but she didn't advance. Thunder met her eyes and considered her. He dropped his head in a sign that he accepted her orders, whatever they were, as Fairy. He moved toward her until his forehead brushed her fingertips.

As Cadal started to relax, Thunder pulled away from her and cast a warning call at the fence line. His feet moved defensively. Cadal swung his head around. Connor was trying to approach him again. Cadal waved him back in annoyance, and Connor hefted himself back over the fence and watched the scene warily.

Cadal sighed. He wouldn't reach out to Thunder unless it was absolutely necessary. His sudden appearance as Fairy could send the animal into an unexpected reaction, and he couldn't risk Mollie that way unless she was already in danger. Thunder would have recognized Mollie by her aura the first day, so her control now was no shock to him; Cadal's would be.

Mollie put out her hand in invitation, but the horse backed away, no doubt sure it was some sort of trick. Cadal cursed Connor's interference. She lowered her hand and considered the situation. She backed toward the stable. Thunder watched her with a sort of amused interest. She raised her hand to him again, and Thunder came to her. Cadal smiled at her tactics. Mollie had moved further from the fences and from the Humans.

She stroked his fur and murmured to him. She smiled as Thunder nuzzled her cheek. The horse was safe with Mollie. Thunder knew it, but he wasn't entirely calm yet. Mollie stopped her hand over his ribcage and looked at Cadal in concern.

"He needs a vet." She kept her voice low and soothing.

"One's on the way, miss," Connor called out to her.

Thunder shied away, and Mollie was forced to sidestep as he brushed past her. She favored the young man with a look of irritation at his continued interference.

"Sorry, miss." He lowered his voice that time.

She shook her head and backed nearly to the stable doors. Mollie got Thunder to come to her again. As she stroked his neck, Cadal tried taking a few steps toward them, but the horse eyed him warily. Thunder was comfortable with *his Fairy*, and that was the way he wanted to keep it.

Mollie loosened the ropes around the stallion's neck. Cadal held his breath as she pulled them over Thunder's head slowly. She crooned to him as she did it to keep him calm. Cadal tensed in preparation for forcing his will on the horse if he moved against her while she worked. Mollie dropped the ropes to the ground and smiled in satisfaction at the relief she felt from the great horse. Cadal relaxed his muscles in the giddy release of the fear he had been harboring.

A car pulled up the dirt track, and Mollie's head snapped up. Thunder moved abruptly as she lost her concentration. Mollie had no time to react, and she was knocked off of her feet violently. She panicked as she hit the ground. Mollie couldn't find the concentration she needed to control the horse, and she knew what would happen if she couldn't calm him. Though she knew he didn't mean to hurt her, Mollie knew he wouldn't be able to control his actions.

Cadal moved. He had to do what she wasn't capable of and do it quickly. He vaulted between Thunder and Mollie and waved Connor and Patrick away. Mollie reached for Cadal, frightened for him. She tried unsuccessfully to rally the concentration to protect him from Thunder. Cadal pushed her thoughts away, needing his full concentration for the horse.

He reached his hand and mind out to Thunder. *"Calm, horse,"* he ordered.

The horse reacted in shock to this Human friend who was Fairy in disguise, questioning his perceptions. Cadal nodded, and Thunder bowed his head again. Mollie was experimenting, but Cadal was well versed in what he was doing. Thunder would obey him without question.

"Come to me and be still."

The horse did as Cadal commanded and walked to his side.

Mollie's shock and confusion assaulted him. Already, her mind was attempting to unravel what was happening. Already, she was rejecting the truth.

He laid a hand on the horse's shoulder. "It's all right. The vet is here. You stay calm," Cadal murmured to him.

Thunder shook his mane in agreement and nuzzled Cadal's face before looking sadly at Mollie. The horse hadn't meant to hurt her. It was an accident, and Thunder regretted it desperately. Cadal knelt down to her. Mollie sat stiffly, rubbing her shoulder.

She ran a hand over Thunder's face. "Good boy," she crooned. "Doc will take care of you. I know you're sick."

Doc Smythe waited at the gate. He looked at the trio in concern. "Is everyone okay out there?" he called.

Mollie launched to her feet so quickly that Cadal placed his hand on her waist to steady her. Her voice was strong, though he could see the lingering panic in her eyes. "We're fine, Doc. He just startled. Come on out." She laid a hand on Thunder protectively and looked at Cadal in concern.

Cadal rose to his feet, nodding. "Doc won't hurt him. I promise he won't." He stroked the other side of Thunder's neck and gave the horse a firm warning and his reassurances that it would all be all right. Cadal had met Doc Smythe several times in his months here. He was a good man and would not let a calm animal come to harm.

Doc joined the couple. "Connor said the horse went insane," he challenged them.

Mollie shook her head. "He's in pain. Connor hurt him and scared him. It was an accident, honestly. Thunder needed a gentler hand than Connor was offering."

Doc looked at her closely, seemingly weighing each word she spoke. "Was Connor abusive?"

"No. He didn't realize what was happening until it was too late, and then he panicked." Cadal felt her struggle to think clearly and to keep a light rein on Thunder in case he moved again, but the power she put into it was insufficient to the task.

Doc nodded in understanding and surveyed the calm beast that stood before him critically. "Okay, then. What is wrong with our friend here?"

Cadal stepped in. "He hasn't felt well for several days. I don't think he's breathing well." He took Doc's hand and placed it over Thunder's ribs.

Thunder moved slightly, and Mollie crooned to him, frustrated by her inability to talk to him and fearful that she would lose control of him and Doc Smythe would demand him put down. Cadal reaffirmed his command to the horse. Mollie didn't leave Thunder while Doc examined him. In the end, Doc decided that it was a respiratory infection and medicated him appropriately.

Mollie led the stallion away, and he went into his stall without any cause for concern. She treated him to an apple and hugged his neck for a moment.

Thunder nuzzled Mollie's shoulder lightly, and a sharp pain assaulted Cadal. She was hurt despite her assurances otherwise. She was hurt, but she lied to Doc because she was afraid for Thunder. *How very*

Fairy. She turned her head away and buried her face in Thunder's shoulder so no one could see the pained expression she was hiding.

Cadal moved to them. "It's okay, my friend. She knows you're sorry."

Mollie turned from Thunder and buried her face in his chest.

"Let's go take care of that shoulder," he whispered to her.

She nodded and they moved slowly to the gate and the path beyond with Cadal's arm around her waist. Connor and Patrick were huddled with Doc Smythe. The three men stopped to stare at the couple as they passed. Cadal felt his mouth go dry. At this rate, the rest of the village would figure out what they were before he convinced Mollie of it.

* * * *

The reaction of the men outside the corral wasn't lost on Mollie. She started shaking at the thought of what they had seen. By the time the house was in sight, the shaking was so bad she could hardly walk a straight line.

The pain was blooming in her shoulder like the red glow at sunrise that every sailor dreads. Mollie pushed away that image. *Do I have something to dread?* She shivered in the certainty that she did.

Mollie was suddenly afraid of what she had become. People didn't talk to plants and animals. That only happened in...*Fairy tales?*

She laughed harshly. She was cracking up. Her mother had told her once that this place was haunted.

139

Was it affecting her that badly? Surely, Darcy wasn't right. If Mollie was this far gone, even Cadal couldn't save her from the madness she felt settling into her mind.

She remembered Cadal extending his hand to Thunder. *If Cadal did the same thing I did, would that make him a Fairy too?*

Mollie shook her head miserably. She was cracking up. There was no question now. Cadal was perfect.

Too perfect to be Human? Mollie glanced at him. She considered the snow-white hair, the fathomless blue eyes, and the fit body. *Was there ever such a man? Such a* Human *man?* His speech was becoming more natural, but she remembered how odd it was in the early months. *An accent unlike even the native Irish had?* She winced, half in pain and half in the realization that she was rationalizing her madness by making Cadal a part of her delusions.

Cadal swept her to his chest as soon as the door closed behind them and yelled out a command to Elizabeth to bring an ice pack to her room. He helped Mollie out of her shirt and ran his hands over the ugly bruise that already covered her shoulder.

"It's going to hurt, but there's nothing broken." Cadal barely breathed in his relief.

Mollie met his eyes under her lashes. "Thank you."

"For what?" Cadal asked distractedly as he settled her into bed and started undressing her to make her comfortable.

Her heart sank. She was cracking up. She started to cry.

He tried desperately to calm her. "Mollie, stop crying and tell me what's wrong, please."

"If you don't know what I'm thanking you for, I'm going insane. What difference could it possibly make to tell you and confirm that?" She sobbed miserably, trying to regain control.

Mollie heard footsteps on the stairs and managed to stifle her outburst to a few tenacious tears by the time the knock came at the door. Cadal pulled a quilt over her and went to answer it.

Elizabeth looked around his shoulder as Cadal accepted the ice pack from her. Her eyes went wide at the sight of Mollie. "I'll get the doctor," she said automatically and started to leave.

Cadal took her arm. "That won't be necessary, Elizabeth. Bring up a bottle of wine and two glasses, if you would. Mollie has had a stressful morning, but it's minor."

Elizabeth nodded and left without another word.

He shut the door with a sigh and returned to the edge of the bed. "Mollie, I think I know what you're talking about, but I need to be sure. Tell me what you think happened."

She met his eyes. "Did you or did you not ask Thunder to calm down? He listened to you, didn't he?"

Cadal smiled. "That was your problem. You asked him. I ordered him. You'll have to learn how to do that eventually."

Mollie's mind was whirling. "You...what? Cadal, people don't talk to animals. It's not possible."

He stroked his thumb across her cheek. "You're not losing your mind. You're learning."

"I don't understand."

Cadal settled the ice pack on Mollie's shoulder. "Let's have a glass of wine, and I'll tell you a story."

"What kind of story?" Something in his offer made Mollie want to run the other direction. What could be so scary about a story?

"A sad love story."

The knock at the door came without warning this time.

"Come in," Mollie called.

The door opened, but it was Liam holding the bottle and glasses. He glanced at Mollie and set the bottle on the night stand. "Are you sure you're all right, miss?" There was a hint of something resembling either anger or annoyance in his eyes.

She nodded. "It looks horrible, but I'll be fine. Next time, I won't take my eyes off of a skittish horse."

"If you don't mind my asking, miss... Why did you go into the corral in the first place?"

Mollie sighed. "The ropes weren't the answer. Thunder needed a gentle touch before he hurt himself...or someone else."

"He did hurt someone else. He hurt you." His jaw tightened. He exuded frustration from every pore.

"It was an accident, Liam. I thought he was calm, but Doc's car spooked him. If he was dangerous, it wouldn't have ended there."

Liam nodded in agreement. "True. I trust I can tell the men that you won't be doing that again." It wasn't a question.

Mollie smiled widely. "Tell them that if they don't try to control a horse that way again, I won't try to stop them from doing it."

Liam's smile mirrored her own. "Yes, miss. I understand perfectly." He handed the glasses to Cadal and turned to leave.

"Liam?"

He turned to look at her.

"Thunder doesn't trust Connor. Schedule him somewhere else for a while."

"Consider it done, miss. I'll tend to Thunder personally."

"Thank you, Liam."

He nodded and left the room.

Mollie listened to his footsteps disappearing down the hall and turned back to Cadal. "If you know what's going on, tell me. If you don't, I'm going to know I'm hopelessly insane."

Cadal poured the wine, his expression a void. He met her eyes and handed a glass to her. "The truth may not sound any less crazy."

His warning reminded her of her initial unease. What was she so afraid of? "It can't be worse."

"Unfortunately, it can."

Mollie considered it. She didn't really need to know, did she? *I do. I can't live like this.* She met his eyes fearfully and sipped the wine. "Tell me the story."

"A little over a century ago, a Fairy man by the name of Cadal was lost in love."

She shook her head. "A Fairy tale? Cadal, I don't understand."

He put his fingertips to her lips to still the flow of words. "Shhh. Just listen. Cadal felt sure that this Fairy was his soulmate, the only woman he would ever love as long as he lived. Then news came to him that she was gone forever. He was lost and alone. Life had no meaning to him."

"She died?" They hadn't talked about this story since her first night at the estate, but Mollie remembered some tragedy. It was a sad story. Cadal had told her that more than once.

"No, she fell in love with someone else."

She remembered. Mollie had told him that the woman couldn't have been the right one for the Fairy-Cadal if she had done that.

"The man she loved was a Human. He swept her away, and Morda, the Fairy Mistress, her own grandmother, let her relinquish her Fairy life and adopt a Human life so she could marry her love. Morda let her masquerade as a Human, because she was so very miserably in love."

"What was her name?" Mollie didn't know why she asked. It didn't make any difference, but something told her to ask it anyway.

"Her name — was Xanthe." Cadal sipped the wine, and a tight smile touched his lips.

Mollie laughed nervously. "Is everyone named after Fairies around here?"

Cadal sipped again before continuing. "Cadal thought his life was over. His love was gone forever. He moped about for sixty years or so. By then, Xanthe was long dead. Cadal discovered a friend. Nothing mysterious, nothing shocking, just a friend. She gave him a kick in the pants when he needed it most."

"Sounds like a very nice person." Mollie took another sip of the wine and felt the warmth settle into the task of relaxing her shoulder.

"She was. They remained friends for a very long time, another fifty years or so. Cadal felt good about himself again, but he was still very much alone."

"Did he ever find love again?"

"Yes, he did. He tried to deny that he was in love. He didn't think it was possible, but it was true love and he was fantastically happy."

Mollie was sure she had missed a step. This sounded far too happy to be the sad story he'd promised her. "So, he lived happily ever after?"

Cadal shrugged. "I hope so."

"Was this woman— Was she Human?"

"No, she was Fairy."

"I don't understand, Cadal. What is so sad about that story? It sounds like they get together and everything is fine to me. What am I missing?"

Cadal met her eyes, and a sinking feeling lodged in the pit of her stomach. A sense of vertigo assaulted her before he started talking.

"She doesn't know she's Fairy. She thinks she's Human."

Mollie felt her mouth go dry. "Cadal, that's not funny." It couldn't be anything more than a joke, right?

"No, it's not. It's not funny at all."

"How could someone be a Fairy and not know it?" she demanded.

"Far too easily, apparently. You see, Xanthe was allowed to masquerade as a Human, but she was essentially Fairy. All of her descendents were. All they had to do was choose their birthright rather than choose to be Human."

"Why not someone else? Why her?" Mollie felt the tears stinging her eyes. She couldn't believe that she was even entertaining this. Why was she listening to it? Was she so naïve that she would believe such a thing?

"Every descendent was given the same choice. When this woman was very young, someone hurt her. Someone hurt her so badly that she made a wish. Just a simple wish, *the* wish."

Mollie felt the tears running down her face. Cadal knew? He couldn't possibly know. It was her most guarded secret. Only Mollie knew. Well, that was a lie. *He* knew, *James* and anyone *he* told.

"How? How could you know?" she whispered.

"I didn't until we...ah..." Cadal sighed. "Morda felt your pain. I know this is hard, Mollie. I didn't know how to tell you, how to convince you."

Mollie shook her head. "It's not true. It can't be."

Cadal met her eyes miserably. "Do you really think I'd do that to you?"

"You're saying you're a Fairy?"

He nodded. "We both are."

"Prove it."

"Today wasn't proof enough?"

Mollie couldn't answer. Nothing made sense. She closed her eyes. "What am I supposed to do?"

Cadal sighed. "Live happily ever after."

Mollie sobbed at that. It was too much to ask. There was no such thing as happily ever after.

Chapter Nine

Cadal convinced Mollie to take it easy at the house for the next two days. Those two days and the three that followed were torture for everyone. Mollie hardly spoke. She picked at her food.

Even Liam noticed it. He looked to Cadal worriedly several times. "Is she all right?" he finally asked.

Cadal shook his head. "No, but she will be in time."

"Is it Thunder that has her so upset?"

"Yes, but not in the way you think. If Thunder was well and she was, she'd be riding him." *Probably at break-neck speed as far away as she could get.*

"Then what?" Concern overpowered the anger in his voice.

Cadal shook his head. He couldn't tell Liam that the shock of finding out her life was a lie was killing her. He couldn't tell Liam that being a Fairy was what Mollie had always wished and a jail sentence at the same time. Cadal decided to tell him a very small piece of the puzzle. "It's hard to explain. Mollie knew she had to stop what was happening. She was in control of everything, but she forgot what she was dealing with. She forgot what could happen."

"She forgot that Thunder was a frightened animal, and she let her guard down?"

That was a good reason and close enough to what he was saying to agree to, so Cadal nodded.

"She doesn't like to do that, does she?"

"No, she doesn't. She'll feel better once she's healed and once she's back in the daily routine."

He knew it wasn't nearly that simple. Her healing went a lot deeper than the bruise on her shoulder. Cadal felt all of Mollie's pain, not just the physical. Her shoulder was healing nicely, but her mind was in torment. She didn't know what to believe anymore. She didn't know what to do. Mollie felt trapped. Cadal had tried to give her time to work it out for herself, but she was sinking. She was slipping away from him and from the world.

Cadal was accustomed to Mollie's dark moods when letters arrived from her mother. Each letter demanded her return and made more threats of cutting her off. Mollie had always penned an answer immediately. She sent her love, but she also argued her happiness and her right to choose her own life. Mollie never denied that Cadal was part of the reason she was staying, but she refuted Joseph's skewed version of his visit.

Cadal assumed that it would be more of the same when he saw the letter next to her plate at lunch on that fifth day. For a moment, he considered pocketing it until Mollie was out of this depression. Liam and Elizabeth would understand his motives for doing it. Cadal was sure they would actively encourage it, but Mollie appeared in the doorway before he had a chance to take the letter.

He surveyed her as she came to the table. Cadal found her beautiful despite her haunted appearance. He suspected he would find her beautiful if she were terminally ill; soulmates were like that.

Mollie was pale and she had lost weight. Dark circles stained beneath her eyes, and her clothing was rumpled. He knew Mollie spent adequate time in bed, but sleep was elusive and restless.

Cadal didn't know this first hand. His intimate invitation from his soulmate had come to a screeching halt when she discovered their shared secret. Cadal was sleeping alone these nights, all the more painful for having shared those few wonderful weeks in her bed. Mollie hadn't banned him from her room, but she shrank from Cadal when he was near, and that was too painful to bear.

Mollie took her seat with barely a nod, and her eyes settled on the letter. She sighed and fingered the edge of it for several seconds before resigning herself to opening it. Mollie buried her emotions well, but Cadal could see the muscle twitch at the back of her jaw and the darkening of her soft, brown eyes. Whatever was in the letter was more upsetting to her than Cadal had counted on. He wished he hadn't *considered* taking it for as long as he had.

Mollie pushed her plate away. She folded the letter carefully back into its envelope and stared into space, considering something. When she moved, it was quick and purposeful. Mollie went to the stove and turned up the flame beneath the kettle long enough to light the letter ablaze. She watched it burn halfway down before dropping it into the empty frying pan and walking away.

To Cadal's surprise, Elizabeth tried to talk to her. "Bad news from your mother?" she asked.

Mollie paused on her way out of the kitchen and regarded Elizabeth uncertainly before her eyes hardened again. "I don't have a mother."

Cadal started. "What do you mean?"

"I mean that until I'm willing to give up on this—" She waved her hand at the room. "Fantasy," she whispered. "Until I'm willing to go back to my responsibilities and lead the life I was raised and trained to lead, she doesn't want to hear from me. Since I have no intentions of ever doing that, I guess that is that."

"She'll change her mind." Darcy had to. What mother wouldn't?

"No, Cadal. She won't. You don't know her. I'm doing absolutely everything she despises. That won't change for either of us. I could work in the sleaziest little company, and she'd adjust. But here, like this—" She met Cadal's eyes, and he could see a deep sadness there that he couldn't put a name to.

"She mentioned me?" he asked.

Mollie sighed. "Nothing you need to worry about." She walked away.

Cadal watched her go. He wished he knew what else to do. He hated watching her walk away from him. Cadal met Liam's eyes, hoping for some Human insight into Mollie's reactions.

Liam seemed as lost as Cadal felt. "What now?" he asked, confirming Cadal's suspicion that Human men had no advantage in this sort of thing.

Cadal snapped. He pushed his plate away and headed for the stairs without a word. There was a way to end this. He had to convince Mollie that while her past was crumbling, there really was a future.

He went to her door and slipped in without asking her permission. Mollie looked at him tearfully, but she didn't tell him to go. Cadal moved slowly. Like Thunder, she was spooked. He sat on the bed next to her and met her eyes. Mollie touched his hand, and Cadal shivered in the connection he had missed so much.

"It's all true, isn't it?" she asked.

"Yes. It is. I'll give you whatever proof you want, whatever proof you feel you need. Tomorrow, if you're up to a ride."

"What then?"

"That's up to you. I know what I'd like, but I can't choose for you."

"What would you like?"

Cadal felt her heart pounding. He knew that she already wished it, but she was afraid it couldn't be that easy.

He lay next to her and searched her face. "Marry me. Go back with me. There'll be no more vipers, no more people hurting you." Cadal shrugged and waited to see if she was ready to accept the possibility that it could be that simple.

"I can't just leave." Her argument was weak. He knew it was exactly what Mollie wished she could do, but she couldn't take the chance with the lives of her employees and land.

"You don't have to. I'll have to leave soon, but we have time. Do whatever you need to do first."

"How soon?"

Cadal paused. He wished he knew for certain, but he didn't, and he wouldn't lie to her about it. "I don't know. A few months, maybe. Maybe less."

"What if I don't like it there?"

He smiled. "You will." An idea formed. It would take planning, but it could work. "Would you like to visit?"

Mollie looked at him in disbelief. "I can do that?"

Cadal chuckled. "Of course. All Fairies are welcome in the tree-city."

"I can leave again if I go for a visit?" She was wary, perhaps afraid of being trapped.

"You may not want to, but you can. You can leave any time you want. I don't want you to come there unless you're comfortable. I mean, I want you to more than anything, but I want you to be happy more than that."

"Let's go now," she suggested.

Cadal kissed her, relieved at the glitter that came to her eyes at the possibility. "You have things to learn first, things I have to teach you."

Mollie nodded sadly. "So I don't embarrass you, I suppose?"

"No. So you can go in."

She stared at him, hopelessly confused, and he kissed her again. That time, she responded. For the first time since Mollie vaulted into the corral, Cadal felt that she was truly alive. There was no turning back once her soul touched his. The soaring connection captured them both, and neither questioned it.

Their lovemaking was slow and tender, not as fevered as they had become accustomed to, but it still sparked Cadal's imagination. He couldn't contemplate another day without Mollie's touch. He sank into her arms, momentarily sated. She had to agree. Mollie had to marry him and go with him.

"Cadal?"

He pushed up on his elbows and looked down at her.

"Are the stories true? Is life really so wonderful in the tree-city?"

"It will be. After Xanthe left, I thought I would never be happy, no matter where I was, but that all changed when I realized that I love you. There is work but nothing as hard as what you've already done."

"There is no one like Thornton there?" She paused and shook her head. "No one like..."

"No, there's not. There are disagreements, but everything is very civil. There is no violence in the tree-city. There never has been. All disagreements are mediated by a Fairy Master or Fairy Mistress."

"They're like a king and queen?"

"Not really. It's more like a combination of a religious leader and a parent. The Fairy Mistress is revered, loved, respected, obeyed."

"What if someone doesn't obey?"

Cadal considered it. He would be learning that soon. "I don't know. It doesn't happen often. If there are repercussions, I suppose they're not handled openly."

Mollie nodded. "That makes sense. Always praise in public and criticize in private. Who is the Fairy Mistress? Will I get to meet her?"

He smiled widely. "Absolutely. Morda is still our Mistress, until she passes the seat to another."

"When will that happen?"

Cadal felt a chill. His training had to start soon. Maybe, too soon. Mollie wouldn't be ready to join the colony for quite some time. "I don't know, but I know she wants to meet you."

Mollie furrowed her brow, seeming to search for an elusive bit of information. "Morda? She was Xanthe's grandmother, you said."

Cadal nodded.

"Then, she's—"

"Your great, great, great, great, great grandmother." He laughed lightly. "I think I got that right. Don't mention how many greats there are to her. If Xanthe had married inside the colony, Morda would only be a great grandmother. It might make her feel old."

"Really?" Her eyes widened, and she bit her lower lip.

"A Fairy lives, barring some accident or serious illness, for between six hundred and eight hundred years. We're not considered adults until we're more than a century old, and we typically don't marry until we're at least one hundred and fifty."

"How old are you?"

Cadal blushed. "Do you really want to know?"

She nodded, her expression serious.

"I was two hundred and thirty-five years old last winter."

Mollie giggled. "You're not a spinster, are you?"

"No more than you're a child. When Katie told me you were only twenty-six, I expected a child, a pre-adolescent. Katie scolded me appropriately, of course. Were I to measure your age in terms of a Fairy life, you would be somewhere close to a hundred and seventy-five by now. A little less, perhaps. You're not a spinster."

"You're saying I could live for another four or five even six centuries?"

Cadal nodded.

"With you?"

"Is that a bad thing?" he asked.

Mollie shook her head slowly and met his eyes. Cadal felt the shock wave of passion before her lips met his. That time there was nothing slow about it. Their lovemaking was unrestrained, and her release was shattering, kinetic. Cadal had never seen her so alive. Afterward, Mollie lay over him, her head on his shoulder.

Cadal looked at her smile in wonder. "What are you thinking?" He wished that his link to her were more reliable, that he wouldn't have to wonder what made her happy or angry...or hurt her.

"I just can't believe it's true. It's all so wonderful."

He smiled, wrapping a lock of her hair around his fingertip. "What is? The thought of four or five centuries like this?"

"That too. Humans consider themselves lucky to get thirty years like this." Mollie closed her eyes, sighing in contentment. "I have a grandmother again, don't I?"

Cadal recalled that Colleen had been her lifeline. Now she was without family of any sort in the Human realm. Perhaps Morda's very presence would facilitate healing for her. "More than that. You have a whole family of aunts, uncles, and cousins. Xanthe had a big family."

Mollie seemed stunned by the concept. "I have a family? A whole family?"

Cadal nodded.

"Do you think they'll like me?"

He could understand her concern. If Joseph and Darcy were any indication, she wouldn't trust that family would be a happy affair. "They'll love you. How could they not?" *How could Fairies not?*

In truth, Cadal had been relieved to discover that Joseph was a cousin. When he'd overheard the other man's promise to walk away in exchange for one good reason to do so, Cadal had been terrified that Joseph was a former lover who had come to lay claim to the woman Cadal had finally realized he could not live without.

Mollie met his eyes, her nervousness making his nerves jump in response. "What about your family? I'm not exactly the typical Fairy next door."

Cadal smiled, though he considered the very real possibility that Zera might disapprove. That was something Morda would have to mediate. Or would it fall to him as the Fairy Master?

"They'll love you, too." Cadal hoped it was true. His cousins, Valia and Traden, would love her. He could promise that much.

* * * *

Zera was still seething. It had been weeks since Morda had dictated the terms of her future encounters with her son. Zera had stayed away because of the threat, but she was a constant disruption in Morda's mind.

The Mistress was getting tired. Morda couldn't shield Cadal from Zera's energies forever. Her power was receding, and Cadal would have to begin his training as soon as she could arrange it.

Morda had lost her concentration once. She shuddered at what had almost happened as a result, but Cadal was much better at dealing with his fragile soulmate than even Morda had counted on. Morda had sighed in relief and wept in joy when she felt Cadal claim Mollie in first coupling. The vibrations had shifted much closer to the harmony that was required that night.

Not all of Morda's insights into Mollie's preparations had gone as smoothly as their first coupling. The shock of the incident with the horse had aged the Fairy Mistress half a century. No child since Cadal had been so much trouble. The two were suitably matched.

Morda had worried about Mollie's reaction in the days following her injury. She knew the truth would be hard for the young Fairy to accept, but Morda had never realized how difficult it could be, despite her soulmate's artful handling. Cadal had allowed Mollie time and stepped in as he felt her failing. Morda knew that only Cadal could have pulled her back from the brink like that.

Cadal was taking the task of getting Mollie home seriously. She had agreed to learn what she must to see the colony. Mollie longed to meet her family almost as much as she longed to escape the Human realm. Her drive to come to them was both expected and useful. Morda only hoped that nothing else slowed her progress.

Morda sighed. There was still the problem of Zera. Morda couldn't tell the other woman the whole story, even now. It was up to Cadal to explain, when the time was right. No Fairy Master could take his place without first settling the upheavals of his own life. Zera wasn't making that easy, and her son would have to deal with the upheaval when they returned for their visit. It could not be allowed to fester until they returned to stay, and Zera would address it immediately upon Cadal's return, his first return.

Cadal must be trained before then. It was essential.

She smiled. Perhaps, she should visit Cadal's lessons to Mollie. He could receive his training while his soulmate received hers. In fact, his training could only benefit the method by which he taught her. Morda nodded at the idea. This was exactly what needed done. She was sure of it; the vibrations seemed to hum in agreement, and that was always a good omen.

Morda shuddered, her smile melting away. Cadal's training could destroy him. As Fairy, he was ill-prepared for what he would see. His seasons with the Humans hadn't prepared him, as she'd hoped they would. She had hoped he would take the time to learn what terrors the Human realm held while he was there, that his curiosity would lead him to descriptions of what he must know, but Cadal had insulated himself from the knowledge.

She had not been specific in her warning. Even if she told Cadal what to expect in his training, it would not blunt the effect of what he would see. Fairies had been denied such knowledge for millennia. Morda remembered her reactions when it was revealed to her. It would be worse for Cadal, but it was the only way.

Chapter Ten

Mollie growled in frustration. What Cadal told her to do seemed simple, but she couldn't make it work the way he explained. "Maybe you're wrong."

He sighed. "I'm not. I know I'm not. You are Fairy."

"Maybe I'm a cross-breed or something. Maybe I can do some things and not others."

Cadal kissed her, and Mollie sank into his arms, her body taking up the wild craving for him at his first touch.

He broke off the kiss and met her eyes. "There's no such thing. You are either Human or Fairy. You are Fairy. That means you *can* do everything. I'm going about teaching you wrong."

Mollie considered that statement. "How can you be sure I'm a Fairy? Maybe I'm a Human with some really strange abilities. I mean...it's possible, isn't it?"

He kissed her again and swept her down onto the soft forest floor. His hands explored her body, and Mollie drank in the arousal it brought with it. Cadal fit his body to hers. She knew how hard stopping would be.

Mollie didn't want him to stop. She had denied them both this pleasure for five days. She groaned in the memory of how empty those days had been.

He smiled at her response. "Because, we couldn't couple if you weren't Fairy." Cadal pulled her shirt free from her jeans and ran his hands up her stomach, nuzzling her neck.

Mollie smiled at his choice of words. It was one of the Fairy euphemisms that he couldn't seem to shake.

Cadal had moved into her room the previous night. There was no longer any illusion that they were less than lovers, even from Elizabeth and the others. Mollie found the feeling of Cadal in her bed both comforting and exciting. The knowledge that the others knew didn't faze Mollie in the least, though she knew they'd had enough evidence to form the conclusion that it was so before he moved his things.

The fact that Cadal's bed had rarely been used, and never alone, in the two weeks before Mollie's encounter with Thunder would not have escaped Elizabeth. Nor would the musky scent on the sheets in both rooms. Even Cadal had joked, after making love so many times in the last day in the rush of rediscovery, that he should simply order them breakfast in bed and be done with it.

A sudden thought occurred to her. "What would happen if I was Human?"

Cadal stopped his teasing and considered the matter carefully. "I don't really know," he admitted. He smiled mischievously. "Maybe I wouldn't be able to perform."

Mollie laughed heartily. "You? You can't be serious."

"Thank you. It's nice to know that you think of me as virile."

As if proving her point, Cadal moved the rigid length of himself against her, closing his eyes and drinking in the arousal it brought them both. Mollie untucked his shirt from his trousers and ran her hands up his back beneath. He shuddered at her touch.

"That's not all I think of you. Want to prove me right?" she offered.

Cadal groaned and captured her mouth, tugging up at the back of her shirt. He met her eyes, hopelessly

160

lost in the need now. He had explained that soulmates were like this for their entire lives. Mollie hoped he was right.

His lips had barely brushed over hers again when a new voice entered her consciousness. "I hate to interrupt..."

Cadal startled and rolled away to his back, settling onto his elbows and crossing his legs at the ankles. He sprawled beside her, smiling sheepishly at an old woman seated on a tree-stump ten yards away. Mollie wondered who she could possibly be.

"Just a break to relieve the tension," Cadal told her.

Mollie raised herself up to get a better look at this new arrival. The woman was about sixty-five or seventy, by Mollie's Human estimate. How old that was in Fairy life was beyond her experience so far, and there was no doubt in Mollie's mind that this woman was a Fairy. Her silver hair was in a long braid down her back, much like the one in Mollie's hair. She wore a beige dress with lacing up the front that reminded Mollie of old portraits she had seen years ago, similar to Italian Ren but with sleeves more like an Englishwoman would wear. Her green eyes glittered in amusement.

She laughed a laugh that was far too young for her obvious age. "Cadal, do you really think I don't remember young love? I know exactly what you were doing."

He blushed and nodded. Mollie was sure her face was several shades darker than his was, especially when she caught sight of the obvious bulge at the front of his trousers. It was lessening but still visible.

Cadal glanced at Mollie, seemingly in realization that she was lost. He waved his hand to the old woman theatrically. "This is Morda."

The woman bowed her head as she was introduced.

Mollie's mind wouldn't seem to work correctly. This was the Fairy Mistress? How should Mollie address her? What must Morda think of Mollie to find her like this?

Morda laughed again. "In order. Yes, I am the Mistress. Call me Grandmother, if that pleases you. I know it does, so you might as well. I am well aware of how many greats there are involved in that title, Cadal, but thank you for not mentioning it. And, I think nothing but that you are young and in love. That is a beautiful thing, and you have waited far too long to waste time not appreciating it. There is no shame in what you two share."

Tears pooled in Mollie's eyes.

"Don't weep. You are too beautiful to mar it with useless tears."

She nodded, biting back the urge to shed them.

Morda smiled warmly then turned to Cadal. "You're having a problem?"

Cadal shook his head. "It's new to Mollie. It will come in time."

The Mistress smiled. "May I help?"

"I'd be honored."

Morda turned to Mollie. "It's no fault of yours or of Cadal's. We are asking you to concentrate on being something that you have never been before. Cadal, do you remember when you first tried to take Human form?"

Cadal groaned and dropped to his back. Mollie laughed heartily at the pained expression on his face. He met her eyes, and she clipped off the laughter at the tortured look she saw there.

"Don't laugh," he grumbled. "You have no idea—" His eyes widened in shock. "Yes, you do. You're trying to do the same thing in reverse." Cadal sat up abruptly and looked to Morda for confirmation.

"Exactly right. Do you remember how you finally achieved it?"

"You transferred to me, and I understood."

Morda nodded. "I transfer to nearly every child as a means of teaching them the shift. There are few who can master it without a full understanding."

"Can you do that for Mollie?"

She shook her head sadly. "You are her teacher. The Harmony has decreed that it must be that way, but I can train you. You will have to practice, but I can teach you what you need to know."

Cadal smiled widely, and Mollie was sure that something had passed between the two Fairies that she couldn't comprehend.

He kissed her cheek. "I think this will help." He knelt before the Fairy Mistress and bowed his head.

Morda placed her hands on his temples. For what seemed like a very long time, they didn't move. Mollie looked around the woods. There was no wind. There were no sounds. Nothing moved. All of nature stopped to take notice of something important. But what could it be?

Morda removed her hands, and Cadal dropped his weight back onto his heels. He looked drained, exhausted. A single tear traced down his cheek. Mollie knelt beside him and wiped it away. Cadal met her eyes and wrapped his arms around her. She looked at Morda with a mixture of concern and mistrust as he sank into her arms.

Morda smiled wearily. "It is an effective way of teaching, but it does take its toll. Cadal will recover shortly."

Mollie felt a tight band around her chest. She held Cadal and ran her hands over his back as if she were soothing a baby. She couldn't fathom what could have done this to him, and it frightened her.

Cadal spoke to her, but he didn't move from her embrace. "I'll be fine, Mollie. Don't worry, please."

She nodded, incapable of forming words if she tried.

Morda rose stiffly. "I must go now, Cadal. May I come again?"

He raised his eyes to her. "Yes, Morda. Please do. As many times as you need to."

"It won't take long. You're much stronger than I thought." She smiled a strained little smile.

Cadal nodded and sank back into Mollie's arms. "Thank you, Morda."

"I'll see you tomorrow, then? Here again?"

"As you wish," he answered her quietly.

Morda nodded and started away. She looked back and answered Mollie's unasked question. "You must learn much less than Cadal does, Mollie. Don't fear it. Cadal will be gentle with you, much gentler than I was with him, I am sure."

Mollie wasn't sure what to make of the Fairy Mistress. Morda seemed cold and motherly at the same time. Why would Morda be so rough, if she could be gentler? It seemed at odds with what she knew of Fairies. Mollie was afraid for Cadal, despite his reassurances that he was fine. One thing she was sure of was that she didn't care much for whatever was involved in this way of teaching.

* * * *

Cadal knew how Morda meant to teach him. He knew so much information could only be passed in one way. He hadn't counted on how much there was to learn or how painful and draining such a large transfer would be.

Understanding came quickly. In order to be the Fairy Master, he must be almost omnipotent in all matters concerning Fairies. Cadal wouldn't have to learn every trade, but there was little else he would not have to know.

In this one lesson, Morda had imparted many of her gifts along with a full understanding of them and memory of their uses to her student. She'd also transferred the early history of their colony. It consisted of the memories and emotions of the first five Fairy Masters or Mistresses of Aiden, over two thousand years of the events, lives, intercessions, joys and heartbreaks of his people, now forever etched in his mind. Cadal could feel it, use it, learn from it, and he would pass it on to his successor in due time; though he hoped it would be passed in the usual way, over months of smaller transfers.

Morda had been in constant dialog with him while she transferred the information to his mind. For a terrifying moment, Cadal felt as if he were drowning. Morda had slowed the transfer while she calmed him and taught him to float above the flow that had been passing over him. Cadal knew the transfer was not supposed to go this fast, but Morda explained that time had become an issue for them.

It was his own fault. Cadal knew that. If he had sought her out months ago, he could have slipped out at night and done this the proper way. He chose not to do so, to try and hide from what he was.

Morda had monitored him closely. In the end, Cadal knew that she'd pushed him to his absolute limits, but it had to be done this way. Time was too short to be timid.

Cadal knew Morda would never have pushed him so far if Mollie had not been there to care for him. Morda had honored her, though Mollie didn't know it. To Cadal's knowledge, no one except the former leader and the newer were ever present for the transfers.

When Cadal recovered, he knelt up and hugged Mollie.

"Are you all right?" she asked.

"I'll be fine. It was more than I expected."

"You have to do that again?"

He nodded.

"Why?"

Cadal knew he couldn't tell her yet. He didn't understand why, but it had to be that way. Until the initial transfers were done, he couldn't tell Mollie what the transfers meant. Morda had cautioned him of that in the transfer. Cadal was sure there was some reason for it, due to the particular situation. Other Fairies knew when their soulmates were being prepared. In fact, the entire colony typically knew.

"Morda hasn't given me everything I need yet. She gave me enough to get you started, if you're willing."

Mollie paled at the suggestion.

"Morda's right. I can be very gentle with you. I promise you that it won't hurt."

166

She nodded, but Cadal could tell that she was still nervous. "I trust you."

Cadal placed his hands for the transfer. "Relax. It's just like a backrub."

Mollie smiled. "Speaking of..."

He laughed at the memory. Joking wasn't clearing her mind but it might bring the relaxation he needed from her to do this. He wished that he had someone else to test this on first, though he knew his execution should be flawless. The memories Morda had imparted to him of its use would act as practice to his mind, temporarily taking the place of the memories he would form as he used it personally, easing the way for him and for whoever he had to transfer to.

"I will if you will," he teased her in return. "Now, let's try this."

Cadal closed his eyes. He could still feel Mollie's fear. *Damn it!* This wasn't going to work if she couldn't relax into the sensation.

A sudden inspiration struck him. It would make for an interesting chapter to be turned over to his successor, but it would be worth it. Cadal drew Mollie to him with his hands still placed and kissed her. Mollie relaxed into his chest and he felt her concerns melting away.

Now.

Cadal chose what he sent carefully. He sent memories of various Fairies over the years. Joys and sorrows, daily life, flying, and laughing. He sent the essence of what the life of a Fairy was. Then he sent his own memories of the shift in both directions. There was no reason to do this halfway. While Mollie was relaxed enough to transfer to, he was going to do it right.

Cadal released her from transfer and moved his hands down to her shoulders. When he broke off the kiss, Mollie searched his face. She understood. He could see it in her eyes.

"It's wonderful." Her voice was a mixture of awe and joy.

"Yes, it is." He wasn't sure if she meant the transfer or her new insight into colony life, but she was touched by something that had passed between them.

"Can I try now?"

He moved his hands from her shoulders to his lap and nodded. Mollie closed her eyes. She was trying, but she was still nervous. It wouldn't work if she was nervous.

"Wait," he instructed.

She opened her eyes and looked at him hopelessly.

Cadal took her hands and met her eyes. "Try it with me."

Mollie didn't close her eyes that time. She locked them on Cadal. Even before the shift began, he knew it would work. She was calm, she had what she wanted firmly in mind, and shifting with Cadal seemed less threatening to her.

They shifted slowly, much slower than Cadal had become accustomed to over the centuries. He smiled at the wonder and pleasure Mollie experienced as she changed. *Hundreds of memories of children's first shifts magnified the response, echoing within his mind.*

This was how Morda remained so rooted in youth. She could instantly remember any given situation from hundreds of viewpoints. An amazing empathy came with it. Cadal realized he had been wrong. Morda could not do less than she did. With such a response, how could she ever ignore it?

Mollie looked around at the foreign landscape. She stood slowly and ran her hands over the plants around her. She moved from stalk to stalk in awe. Mollie ran her hands over the petals of a late-blooming wildflower. She stood on tiptoe to brush her cheek against the silky surface. She faced him again, tears spilling down her cheeks. He knew the tears were happy ones, but he went to her and held her anyway.

Cadal closed his eyes and thanked Morda silently for this gift. He understood so very much now. The Harmony knew what She was doing. He had been chosen as both Fairy Master and Mollie's soulmate for a reason. Mollie would trust no one less than her soulmate to lead her through. Cadal had to be Fairy Master to do that. Mollie would never have accepted the transfer from Morda willingly, and he knew now what would happen if she wasn't willing. Cadal shuddered at the thought of her enduring such a thing. He shuddered at the thought of ever having to use that knowledge.

* * * *

Mollie was doing her own share of shuddering. She watched Cadal endure transfers from Morda for three more days. Each time, he came away shaking in exhaustion. Mollie held him and comforted him, each time praying to some unnamed gods that it would be the last.

After Cadal recovered from the transfers, he taught Mollie more. Sometimes, he taught her in transfer, which she came to accept willingly from him. Sometimes, he sat and taught her in a more conventional way. They practiced the shift often. Cadal taught and transferred tidbits of Fairy culture and history, more of the Fairy lore, and the layout of the tree-city.

Mollie learned better control over her link with animals and plants. She learned to call the elements. She even learned the Fairy language. There were many Human words that didn't translate and a few Fairy words that Cadal had to explain. Her biggest problem was in differentiating between the everyday and formal forms of words in Fairy speech, but Cadal assured her she would learn in time as he learned smoother English. Otherwise, the learning was nearly effortless.

Mollie thought practicing her new language was wonderfully enjoyable, and she considered asking Cadal to transfer other languages she found he knew when they had more leisure time. Gaelic held the most allure for her.

As she gained confidence in her new skills, Mollie began to practice the shift alone. Sometimes, Cadal joined her and conducted other lessons while she was in Fairy form. Other times, he watched her moving through the greenery beside him in a mixture of pride and amusement.

The only rough moment came when she encountered an insect for the first time while she was in Fairy form. Mollie hadn't been prepared for the sight of an insect whose head reached to a point above her knee. She scrambled away, and her terrified scream brought Cadal.

He laughed in relief and stepped between Mollie and her admirer. Cadal explained that Mollie was exuding her aura again. He smiled at her reaction to the *bug,* who was still showing a marked interest in her, despite Cadal's hold on it.

"It's not funny," Mollie complained miserably in the Fairy language.

He smiled in amusement. "She's an animal like any other animal. You don't have to fear her."

"You weren't raised Human. It's a *cultural neurosis,*" she interjected in English. Mollie shook her head and continued. She hated slipping English words into the Fairy language. It sounded so tourist. "We're trained to be afraid."

Cadal sobered and regarded her sadly. "Why? You're so much bigger than she is in Human form."

"Humans can't talk to them, remember? To Humans, *insects* are a threat. They eat our food, carry diseases, and hurt us. Their stings and bites are uncomfortable at best and deadly at worst."

He looked slightly ill. "I never realized. Will you show me?"

Mollie regarded him in confusion. "How? I don't know how to transfer. In all honesty, if learning is that painful, I don't want to learn."

"You don't have to. Only one of us has to be able to transfer. It can work either direction."

She nodded. "All right. What must I do?"

"Relax. Let me do the rest."

Mollie smiled. He made it sound like the first time they made love. Cadal chuckled and shook his head as he settled his hands for the transfer. Mollie blushed. She should have known he would sense that thought, considering what he was trying to do.

"Shhh," he breathed close to her lips.

This transfer was different for Mollie. She experienced memories, all flashing through her mind. Her mother scolded her for playing with a cricket she'd brought into the house. There were news reports of mosquitoes carrying meningitis and articles she read. She saw cheesy old horror films about giant insects. She remembered a yellow jacket sting which ended with her arm wrapped in layers of ice and towels while a seven year old Mollie cried. Stories of black death being carried by fleas and rats, anaphylactic responses to venom, and swarms of bees and locust paraded through her mind.

For what seemed like a long time, Cadal accessed anything having to do with insects or spiders of any sort. Some of it didn't seem to make sense, until Mollie realized that Cadal's search was so all-encompassing he was pulling up quotes comparing people favorably or unfavorably to insects. There were stories like the "Ant and the Grasshopper" and "Little Miss Muffet."

Cadal took his hands away. He swallowed a lump in his throat and held Mollie while she recovered from the transfer. She was tired and a little dizzy, but even that transfer was nothing like the ones he'd endured. Mollie never realized how much a person could know on any given subject if you searched hard enough for it.

When she regained her equilibrium, Cadal nodded and touched the spot on her arm where Mollie had been stung. "I think I understand," he said quietly. "As a Fairy, none of that matters. Try to talk to her."

Mollie shook her head and looked away. "I can't yet. Maybe someday."

Cadal nodded and wrapped her in his arms again. "As you wish." He reached out his hand, and the insect moved away. It had been waiting at Cadal's command. She felt a stab of regret for his trouble.

Mollie pulled herself roughly back to the present. Cadal was coming out of transfer with Morda. She caught him, as Cadal fairly collapsed into her arms. Mollie stifled a sob. Every day was worse than the day before. This had to end. Cadal couldn't go on like this. She couldn't go on like this.

She looked at Morda once again. The Fairy Mistress appeared worn after a transfer, but she never showed any concern for Cadal. It was as if his well being was of no importance to her. Mollie wondered that she could be so unfeeling.

Of course, Mollie could never say that to Morda. After four days, she was still caught somewhere between awe, fear, and insecurity where the Fairy Mistress was concerned. Mollie never addressed Morda directly. She answered the few questions Morda asked her as respectfully as she could. Other than that, they had strange conversations where Morda picked thoughts from Mollie's mind and answered them. Mollie still wasn't sure if Morda could hear every thought and chose those she addressed or if she only heard the ones she answered.

Mollie hoped once again that it was over.

Morda answered that thought by addressing Cadal. "Tomorrow will be the last transfer."

Her mixture of worry and relief dissolved into rage as Morda continued.

"There will be little left to teach you, but it will be the hardest for you to learn."

Mollie met her eyes. "No," she offered coldly.

Morda smiled. "Mollie? You addressed me?"

"Damn right I did, and I'll say a hell of a lot more before I'm done."

Cadal raised his head painfully. "Don't, Mollie. Please don't."

Morda laughed that childlike laugh. "No, Cadal. Let her, please."

He nodded and sank back into Mollie's chest, and she felt another stab of concern for his condition.

Morda waved her hand for Mollie to continue. "Now, Mollie, tell me what's bothering you."

Mollie scowled at Morda's motherly smile. *Motherly, indeed.* "*This* bothers me. Every day it gets worse. This is killing him. All right, maybe not killing him, because I don't think you'd go that far, but it is causing him a lot of pain."

"I know," Morda replied sadly.

"Then how can you do it to him?" Mollie raged at her, fueled on by the admission. "Doesn't it bother you? It bothers me."

"Of course it does. I feel his pain, and I feel yours. It gives me no pleasure to see either of you hurt. I do this because I must. I am not blind to Cadal's well being as you seem to think I am. I push him as hard as I do in the interest of time and because he has you to see him through."

"Why is this necessary?"

Morda didn't answer.

Mollie felt her anger rising again. "If this is what it takes to prepare me for the tree-city, then transfer whatever I need to me directly. If it means hurting Cadal for another instant, I won't go. It's not worth it."

Morda shook her head. "I wish it was that simple. Cadal has reached the point in his life when he must learn many things. His training should have started months ago, slowly as he transfers to you. He was unwilling to leave you, so he chose so radical a road. If he does not learn what he must soon, he never will. That would mean disaster."

Mollie looked at Cadal. Tears stung her eyes. "I can't keep watching this."

Morda sighed. "You must, this last time especially. No transfer has ever been done this way. I only attempted it, because Cadal draws comfort and strength from you. Without you, he cannot endure the transfer."

"How can I watch him in pain like this?"

"The same way he watched you. The times you worked until you bled, he did all he could, but he didn't stop you. He called a rain the likes of which no Fairy has ever called to keep you from irreversible harm, but he allowed you to do what you felt you must, even when it hurt you to do it. You must allow him to do the same."

"I see why few people cross you. You're very persuasive."

Morda laughed. "And you are very like Xanthe in many small ways. I missed her spirit. I missed interacting with her. I knew you were not as meek as you presented. I simply had to make you angry enough to tell me so."

"You wanted to make me angry?"

"Xanthe only feared me once, when she thought I might refuse her request to leave the colony and marry her Human. She loved him. I would never have denied her that love, but she feared that I would. I don't want your fear, Mollie. I don't want your admiration. I won't ask for your love and your trust. You must choose to give those when you feel the time is right or not at all. I do ask your honesty. I know your heart. Don't hide it from me."

Mollie smiled. "You want me to let you know when I get ticked?"

Morda laughed and nodded.

"I have to admit it. That's a first. No one has ever wanted to know that before."

Morda sobered. "I must go now. You will be here tomorrow for the final transfer?"

"I will. I hate it, but if he has to do it, I won't desert him."

"I knew you wouldn't."

Chapter Eleven

Cadal found recovering from the transfer very difficult, and the hardest was yet to come. Morda had explained why the last one would be the worst. After tomorrow, there would be nothing Cadal didn't know about the current Fairies of the colony. While Cadal was given an overview of all the previous generations, he would know every nuance of those Fairies within Morda's rule.

"Some of the memories will be painful for you, Cadal. I cannot keep these things from you. I could not, even if I tried to."

Cadal flashed on an image of Xanthe, but she shook her head.

"No, Cadal. There are much more painful things in store for you."

He tried to work through his confusion, but there seemed no logic to her comment. "What will be more painful?"

"I have been shielding you. Perhaps it was wrong of me, but I had hoped it would make what you had to accomplish easier until I could shield you no longer."

"Shield me from what?"

"You will know everyone's thoughts and feelings."

He sighed. "It will fall to me to handle Zera." He had suspected it might. After all, it was an upset in his personal life; as such, he had to settle it before he took his place.

"Yes, it will, but that is not all, Cadal." She hesitated. "You will have everyone's memories. All of them. I can't be selective in what you see."

177

Cadal nodded, though he had no idea what she meant. Of course, he would have everyone's memories.

"Cadal, life as a Human is very difficult."

He felt a sick swirl assault his nerves.

"Humans face much more in their short lives than you can begin to imagine."

"You can't mean the things before Mollie made her wish. She was Human then." He stammered it out, fear gripping him.

Morda shook her head. "No, she was masquerading as a Human. I have been linked to Xanthe and each of her descendents from the womb. She was trapped in a Human life, but Mollie possessed a Fairy soul, Cadal. That was how I knew her pain."

She sighed. "No Fairy Master has ever been asked to do this. None of them were forced to see such things about a soulmate. Even when a Fairy returned, it was with full knowledge and anyone could acclimate him or her to colony life.

"Mollie is different. She always has been. From the womb to the grave, I felt them all. Even in the womb, Mollie was different. She would have come to us eventually, but..."

Cadal felt as if he'd swallowed a fistful of icicles. "Morda, I can't do it."

"Cadal—"

"I can't. You should have warned me," he snapped at her. It was too much to ask. He didn't want to know. He didn't want to see Mollie being hurt.

"Do you love her?"

"You know I do," he answered miserably.

"Then love her. Don't allow yourself to wallow in things you cannot change. Mollie has overcome it. You *must do the same. Years, Cadal. To Mollie, the things you fear are a third of her life ago."*

Cadal agreed, though he felt sick at the thought. Overcome? He must see and feel everything Mollie experienced, face her immediately, and not let it affect him? He suddenly felt very tired.

When Cadal recovered, he lounged for several long minutes, staring at the clear, blue sky.

Mollie lay, her head resting on his shoulder, and sighed deeply. "Can we try something new today?" she asked.

Cadal smiled. "What do you have in mind?" He added an invitation to his tone that made her smile.

"I want to fly."

He sucked in his breath. "That's harder than it sounds," he warned.

Mollie laughed lightly. "I've been dreaming of flying my whole life. I think I may already understand the basics. I want to see how close the dreams were to reality."

Cadal turned over her. "I remember talking to you about this. Did these dreams seem real to you?"

"Very real. As real as the night they poisoned the crops, easily."

He considered it carefully. Maybe her dreams were a doorway of sorts. They often were for Fairies, and even without knowledge that she was Fairy, The Harmony might have led her in such a way. "Have you had any other dreams like that?"

Mollie blushed then nodded, dropping her gaze from his.

Cadal cupped her chin back up. "Tell me," he whispered.

Mollie darkened again. "Let's just say that you weren't exactly a stranger when I met you."

"You met me in your dreams?" Cadal remembered her shock when she first saw him. She knew who he was from that moment?

"Not exactly. We weren't talking at the time."

Cadal smiled widely, her meaning more than clear to him. "Really?"

She nodded.

"I take it that you enjoyed these dreams?" His blood heated at the idea of her dreams leading Mollie to his arms.

"You know I did. They were a nice distraction at first, but once I met you—" Mollie sighed. "It was pure torture. Dreaming about you and not being able to have what I was dreaming was cruel."

"If it makes you feel any better, I had my share of torture. Some nights, I'd end up outside your door or riding Thunder or walking, anything but going to you."

"It serves you right." Mollie said it with an air of finality.

"How do you justify that?" Cadal asked in surprise.

"You knew I was willing."

He laughed heartily. "Yes, but I wasn't sure we were able."

"Ah. I see." Mollie's eyes glittered mischievously.

Cadal knew it was another of her silent invitations, but if she wanted to fly, there was much to do. He got to his feet and took Mollie's hand to pull her up. "Okay. You want to fly. Let's fly."

She smiled widely.

"Shift into Fairy form and we'll go from there."

Cadal tried to explain what to do, but he found that Mollie already knew the steps she had to perform. Of course, knowing and doing were two very different things. Cadal knew he might have to instruct or transfer memories to her more than once before she executed flight correctly. No Fairy managed it on the first try.

He kissed her forehead and stepped away to watch her fledgling attempt at flight. Mollie locked onto his eyes and smiled. Then she rose smoothly into the air on the cool autumn wind. Cadal watched in shock so deep that he almost forgot to be prepared in case she lost concentration, prepared to bring a wind gust that would lower Mollie gently. Once she'd learned how to shift, Mollie could have done this without his help.

Cadal wondered how accurate her dreams about him had been. A strong emotion gripped him, a drive to make her his all over again. He smiled and rose to meet her. Cadal matched Mollie's glide and reached out to touch her hand.

Mollie stopped her forward glide and hovered before him. The wind whipped her hair around her face, despite the long braid behind her head. The color was high in her cheeks, and she practically glowed in happiness. Cadal took her hands and drew her close enough to kiss her.

"Mollie," he began formally. Cadal reminded himself to use the Fairy language. "I'd like you to wind dance with me."

She nodded. "As I recall, *dancing* with you is rather stimulating." She inserted the Human English into their language, an automatic move any time she couldn't find an appropriate translation into Fairy.

Cadal shook his head. "No, Mollie. Remember what wind dancing means. I'm asking you to *marry* me. It's like a Human giving you a ring. If you agree, you're agreeing to wed me." Though he knew she understood the Fairy word for 'wed,' he used the English 'marry' to impress his meaning on her.

She looked uncertain for a moment, and Cadal was afraid she'd refuse, that Mollie would ask him to give her time, maybe until she had seen the colony and knew what she would be accepting. Cadal was sure it was important that she not do that, but the choice was hers. He'd made his promise by asking. Accepting the promise was her choice.

Mollie wound her arms around his neck and kissed Cadal passionately. "Dance with me," she invited in English.

"And everything that goes with it?" he asked quietly, in the Fairy language to emphasize his point.

Mollie switched to Fairy for her response. "I suppose you're stuck with me for the next five or six centuries. Is that okay with you?"

Cadal nodded and kissed her deeply. He drew in his power, and the winds swirled around them. Mollie laid her head back and smiled at the passing scenery, changing the movement slightly to match her mood. When she met his eyes again, Cadal could see that the invitation was still there. He suddenly felt sure, borne up by his almost limitless memories, that there had never been a wind dance like this one, and there would most likely never be again.

Cadal kissed her again as passion gripped him like a wildfire. He had waited so long for this moment. Forever, it seemed. It would be perfect.

He slowed the winds, and they sank toward the forest floor. This would be what it should have been the last time they danced. Cadal undressed Mollie as they sank lower. They would find the clothes later. For now, he wanted to claim his bride properly.

They didn't speak. They lost themselves in the moment, undressing and exploring each other's bodies as if it were the first time. Cadal wished it was possible to make love in flight, but such a thing was impossible. Concentration could not be guaranteed. Still, he could float them a foot or so off the ground while he molded Mollie's body to him and took her breasts and mouth until their need became urgent.

Cadal lay back and lowered them until they floated above a thick patch of moss like those they chose for bedding in the colony. He pulled Mollie over him and she straddled his body smoothly.

"Marry me?" He asked in English this time.

She smiled. "Absolutely."

He groaned in need as she settled her hips snug against his, and they sank into the moss as his control shattered. Cadal surged further into her and watched as Mollie's eyes closed in pleasure. They moved together fluidly, as if they were already one being instead of two separate people.

Had Zera not interrupted, it could have been like this after their first dance, carefree. Before Cadal knew the things he knew, the things he must see tomorrow.

Cadal pushed away the thought and sank into the pleasures of the coupling. Whatever he saw in the transfer wouldn't matter. It couldn't matter. This was the Mollie he loved. It was the only Mollie that mattered.

* * * *

Despite Cadal's self-assurances, he was still afraid of the reaction he would have to the transfer. He found himself contemplating a wholly inappropriate move as he watched Mollie sleeping.

Cadal wondered if he could transfer what he was most afraid of while she slept, but he knew that, conscious or unconscious, Mollie would experience the transfer. It would feel like a nightmare to her. If she startled awake, Cadal would hurt her before he could stop the flow that she would be fighting with her conscious mind. Either way, it would mean inflicting the memories on her in startling detail. If Mollie really had overcome, that would be a cruelty he could never live with committing. It would be better to face it in transfer with Morda and spare her the memories.

He sighed and pulled her closer to him. No matter what was to come in transfer, he had to keep a handle on it. Mollie deserved that much from him.

* * * *

Cadal nearly refused the transfer. It wasn't his nervousness that got to him; it was Morda's choice of how to conduct the final transfer that bothered him. She ordered Mollie to sit and face Cadal while Morda sat behind him. Cadal knew that meant three things.

He couldn't drop his chin to his chest as he had done in previous transfers. Morda's hands, placed correctly, would keep his head up and faced forward. Otherwise, she would be stretched uncomfortably over his back. Mollie would see any outward emotions he presented in that position. Cadal wasn't sure whether or not that was something he could control. And finally, when he opened his eyes, Mollie would be at the forefront of his vision.

Cadal couldn't see the point of it. Why did this entire situation seem designed to make his suffering as momentous as possible? Cadal agreed to Morda's plan. He had to do this to complete his training, and waiting another day to do it would only increase his apprehension.

Morda placed her hands and looked over his shoulder at Mollie. "Hold his hands. Don't let go."

Mollie stared at her in shock then met Cadal's eyes in fear. He could tell she was afraid for him. She was considering asking him not to do this, no matter what the cost might be.

Cadal took her hands and met her eyes. "It will be fine, as long as you're with me. Just promise me that."

Mollie straightened her back. She spoke in fluent Fairy. "We've wind danced. We're one now, remember? How could I do less?"

Cadal smiled widely at the shock he felt from Morda. Her powers had diminished. Morda's shock was not at Mollie's use of their language; she'd heard her granddaughter use it many times. The Mistress hadn't felt their promise. Morda didn't know they were one until Mollie spoke the words.

"Cadal," Morda warned him. "Stop that and stay focused for me, please."

"Yes, Morda." He answered like a chastised child. Cadal felt her annoyance at his tone and pushed his amusement away, lest she remind him in a more tangible way that this was not a joke.

Mollie blushed deeply.

Morda sighed. "You, too. Worry about weddings later."

Her color darkened but she nodded her agreement.

Cadal closed his eyes and shut out the world.

The transfer began. *Cadal perched above the flow with Morda.*

"Remember...don't try to see everything. It will all be there for you to see later," she reminded him.

He nodded. Cadal was certain that Morda would make sure he saw the things she felt were most important right away.

"We'll go chronologically through the Fairies."

"As you wish." Mollie would be among the last Fairies he encountered. Few colony members were younger than twenty-six years.

The lives of the oldest members streamed past him at amazing speed. They were rich, full lives. Morda slowed the stream so Cadal could watch the life of Botor, his father.

Cadal grimaced at that last day. He remembered it vaguely. He was ten years old, a toddler in Fairy years, and Botor and Zera had taken him outside the tree-city to begin his flying lessons.

No one was sure how the Human slipped past the sentries, except Morda, most likely. Botor should have hidden with his family and waited for Morda. She was doubtless on her way, but he looked at his bride, huddled with his son, and decided to try to save them himself. Botor was sure the hunter wouldn't see his defenseless family if he made a spectacle of himself.

He kissed them both and silenced Zera's protest with his fingertips and a shake of his head. Then Botor darted before the Human. The hunter ended Botor's life, and Morda had been forced to commit the ultimate duty of a Fairy Mistress in return. Botor had truly believed it was the best way. If only he had waited, he might have survived the day, but it was a chance he couldn't take.

Zera came next. She and Botor had been born very close together, as he and Xanthe had been. Her thoughts angered Cadal, but he understood her feelings. Zera had been hurt when Botor died, missing that integral portion of her soul that her mate held. It seemed a senseless death to her, and it meant that Zera lost her soulmate far too early. She was left to raise Cadal without him, though Cator and Dalen stepped in dutifully to take his father's place. She would have no more children, and Cadal had been constantly at risk of some catastrophe of his own making which would take him, as a foolish move had taken Botor.

She'd lived only to see Cadal married to his soulmate and to be a grandmother. Then Xanthe had left the colony, and Zera had been convinced that these things would be forever denied them both.

She still believed that. Zera didn't know Mollie was Fairy. She believed Cadal's love for Mollie meant either losing him to the Human world or a life without grandchildren and without peace.

Cadal met Morda's eyes. "Why didn't you tell her? Why didn't you give her peace?"

"There is knowledge that is protected. You will understand when you take your place. There is knowledge that could destroy us if it was known by all, but it's more than that. She's lost her trust in me. Zera doesn't believe The Harmony has a plan. She won't believe any more."

"She'll believe me," he vowed.

"It won't be easy."

"She never was." Cadal smiled at the memory of his mother trying to keep leading strings on him long past the time for them.

"Neither were you," Morda reminded him.

More lives streamed past. Cadal saw his own life. He smiled at his childhood antics. The Harmony always protected the future Fairy Mistress or Master well, but Cadal must have pushed even Her to Her limits. Morda was right. He hadn't been an easy child to raise, and the entire colony seemed to have taken a hand in trying to keep him out of whatever trouble he was in at any given moment. Cadal cringed at his dark years, but Morda skimmed past all but his childhood.

One more Fairy flicked by before Xanthe appeared before him. Cadal watched her life in interest, learning the things he had wanted to know all those years ago. He found it didn't hurt him to know that Xanthe had seen him only as a dear friend and that she'd truly loved her Human husband. She'd been happy as a Human, and Cadal was happy for her. He felt her pain when she lost Bran, her joy in her descendents, her fear of losing them to the Fairy realm, and her regrets at the loss of her Fairy life. Xanthe had missed her life in the colony despite her happiness, so she'd told her Fairy stories to fill the void.

Cadal saw the lives of Xanthe's descendents nestled between the younger Fairies. It saddened him that they lasted so short a time. They were not as carefree as Xanthe had been or as Mollie aspired to be. Each generation was angrier and more out of touch with true peace, moreso when they were separated from the land they had come to love. Darcy was particularly tortured. She actively feared what her daughter embraced.

They'd also shared Mollie's dreams. The gentle sisters only shared her dreams of flying and the land, but her direct ancestors had shared all of her dreams. Cadal startled at the revelation.

He met Morda's eyes again. "Any of them? Any of them could have been my soulmate, if I had been more observant?"

"Not really. It was their torment. Until the right one came along, they would be tortured by their loss."

Cadal groaned. "I prolonged Mollie's torture?"

She smiled. "And your own, without knowing it. You meant to save Mollie from harm. You didn't know the only way to do that was to commit to what your heart screamed for, though I did try to tell you."

Cadal nodded. He should have done this long ago. Had he known, so many things would have gone smoother for them.

Cadal startled, as Mollie's life started to pass before him. Morda was right. Mollie was different from the womb. It was a subtle difference. She was not driven, as her ancestors had been. The torture of her loss manifested itself as a deep longing rather than the fear and anger that had become commonplace among the previous generations.

Her mother tried to squelch it, but Mollie would not be denied. She searched out ways to be one with the world. The results were often amusing. She would come home filthy but happy only to be chastised or punished for her interest.

Other times, the results were frightening. Mollie endured many injuries in her quest to be more Fairy. The Harmony must have had a hand in her survival on more than a few occasions. Mollie loved the old tales and sought to live them as closely as a Human could or closer. Cadal had never broken a bone, and he winced in the knowledge that she had more than once.

They sped into Mollie's adolescence; the dreams of him started, as she had barely reached her sexual maturity. Humans reached that most important stage so very young. Haunting dreams of her soulmate had filled Mollie's mind at an indecent age, an age when, even in comparison to Fairy age, Cadal could never have dreamed of the most innocent sexual experimentation with her. He shook his head in wonder, though he had to admit he had been lost to Xanthe at not much older and not able to effect any more change in the situation than Mollie was.

Mollie found little interest in Human boys, despite her sexually precocious nature and free spirit. She found them too uptight, too competitive, and too unwilling to be carefree. They valued winning over the excitement of the game. She was looking, searching for the man in her dreams. Even then, Mollie was searching for her soulmate, but that soulmate had been a world away.

Then she met James. He wasn't the man of her dreams, but he was carefree in a way Mollie had never experienced in Human men before. Nothing seemed to bother him. James had been content to lie back in the grass while the other young men played sports. When he did play, James played as if he had no idea what the score was and as if he couldn't care less what it was. He'd loved the outdoors.

Cadal felt a deep pain. Mollie had loved James' carefree ways and cared for him deeply. On the surface, he seemed like a Fairy. Maybe that was what drew her to him.

Mollie was still very young. Even by Human standards, she would barely have been considered an adult. As a Fairy, Cadal was not sure that she would have been free of her parents' rule, and she was far too young to marry. As always, Mollie was in love with life.

Cadal felt it hard to breathe. Was this a foreshadowing of what was to come? Surely, Mollie's betrayal had been worse than he'd suspected. If she cared so much for this Human, and he hurt her, it must have been a crushing blow to her.

Before his eyes, Mollie stripped off her sandals and jeans and dove into a secluded lake. She swam in the icy water while James called her from the shore. She came out of the water, grabbed up her jeans and sat down to dress. Her t-shirt was a darker color than the one she was wearing at the pond the day Tucker approached her, so it was not translucent, though it clung to her body, accentuating her curves. It covered much more than her bathing suit did, at any rate, and Cadal knew the bathing suit was a perfectly acceptable form of dress for public display in the Human world.

Mollie didn't see the look on James' face, though Cadal did. It was the Fairy Mistress's awareness of the danger of her situation. He recognized the feeling of discord in The Harmony's web.

The look wasn't amorous. It was calculating, possessive, and yet detached. James plastered on a smile, though his eyes were still hard.

Morda's fear mixed with Cadal's, magnified because she feared in the present as well as the past.

He dropped down beside her and kissed her playfully. Mollie smiled at him and went back to work pulling the jeans over her wet legs, but he wasn't done yet. James pushed her onto her back and leaned over her to kiss her again, a rougher, more ardent kiss. At first, Mollie sank into the sensation, but when he ran his hand up the length of her body to her breast, she pushed at it and wrenched away from his kiss.

"No, James. I told you, I'm not ready for that type of a relationship."

She meant it. There were no coy games involved like Cadal often saw in the Human realm, games that made him wonder how Human men knew when a woman was truly interested. Mollie was already so like a Fairy.

Mollie tried to push past him to sit up, but James was much stronger than she was. She was pushed roughly down again. She met his eyes, and Cadal felt her fear settle in.

"Come on, Mollie," James crooned. "Play nice."

She knew. James' eyes told her everything she needed to know but too late.

She shook her head. "No, James. Let me go." She said it calmly, though she was barely holding down a full-blown panic.

"You can't expect a guy to wait forever."

"Then go date someone else. You've always been free to do that. I'm not ready, but there are plenty of girls who are and who wouldn't mind it in the least. If you can't wait, go find one of them." Mollie stopped suddenly. She realized she had crossed over into a touch of hysterics, while she gushed out that answer. She wanted him to find someone else, now more than ever. He could go and never look back, with her blessings.

James smiled a cold smile. "I've invested a lot of time and effort here."

"You don't want to do this. You know you don't."

"Yes, I think I do." He moved forward as if to kiss her again. "Now, are you going to play nice or not."

Cadal shook his head. That was a taunt. Did James want Mollie to give in to him, or was it some game Cadal didn't know? He wished he understood the nuances of Human relationships better, so he would understand what James was doing.

Mollie understood the game, though she was intent on not playing it. She answered the question by punching and kicking at him, trying to force her way to her feet.

It made no difference to James. Cadal could tell that. If anything, James seemed to view it with a mixture of amusement and excitement. The Human had no problem deflecting her blows and pinning her beneath his body. It was almost too easy for him, as if he knew the most effective way to do it without hurting her in the process. Mollie never stood a chance.

Mollie screamed in frustration as her struggle to free herself from beneath the heavy man proved fruitless. She set her jaw angrily and threw her head side to side, as he tried to force his kiss on her again. Other than that, James was having little difficulty.

She snapped at him, her teeth closing on air as he dodged her attempt to bite him, grumbling curses at him when she realized she had no hope of reaching sensitive flesh. He laughed at that, seemingly amused at her attempt to use the only weapon left to her against him.

His hands roamed roughly over Mollie's body as she tried, with limited success, to pull away from him. Cadal felt outraged that her struggle seemed to enhance James' enjoyment of the act. When James tore her underwear off her body, Mollie screamed again, in desperation that time.

It was her last scream. As James pushed inside her, Mollie subsided into tears. Even the burning pain of her maidenhead being ripped away didn't prompt her into *another scream. She cried and nothing more. Anything else Mollie did only spurred him on.*

She was beaten. James had what he wanted. Nothing could stop that. She looked at the lake through her tears. If only she hadn't come out, she might have been safe. Mollie tried to lose herself in the view, tried to escape what was happening to her body.

Cadal was at his breaking point. The rage and sadness was all consuming. He screamed incoherently inside the transfer. Mollie was hurting, and he couldn't stop it. He couldn't erase it. He was powerless to do anything but watch as James, sated, pushed away from her in the ultimate show of how little she meant to him. Mollie curled onto her side and wrapped her arms around her chest while the tears kept coming.

He flashed on the night Zera interrupted their lovemaking. Cadal had pushed away. He had walked away. Mollie didn't think she meant so little to him at that moment, did she?

The transfer went dim. It wasn't over yet. Cadal knew it wasn't, but Morda was showing pity on him by removing the image from before him.

She leaned close to him. "Look at her, Cadal. Open your eyes and look at her."

"I can't." He couldn't look at her face, the same face. When she made her wish, Mollie had started aging as a Fairy. That was why she'd appeared so young to him when he first saw her. Mollie hadn't aged physically more than a Human year in the many years since that day.

"You must. Remember who she is, instead of who she was, for just a moment."

"I hurt her, Morda." He sobbed at the thought of it.

194

"You didn't know. Look at her, Cadal. Just look at her."

Cadal opened his eyes and stared at Mollie. She was frightened. She was crying, but the emotions were not for herself. They were for him. Cadal realized that he was more real to her than what he was seeing in transfer. He could give her peace. He could take away this pain, even as he could never take away the other.

He touched her cheek gently, brushing away her tears. "It's almost done," he soothed her. "Stay with me a little longer."

Mollie nodded slowly and squeezed his hand. Cadal closed his eyes again and sank back into the dark transfer.

Morda nodded without looking at him. "Can you continue?"

He sighed harshly. "I have to do this eventually, and I won't put her through this again. It might as well be now."

"As you wish. You've seen the worst, Cadal. You've survived the worst."

"No, Morda. She has."

The transfer began again.

James threw Mollie's jeans back to her. "Get dressed." He said it coldly, as if reinforcing how meaningless her pain was to him.

She ran a hand over the jeans, then started pulling them on automatically.

Cadal grimaced. He had seen her do something similar. When he'd thrown his shirt at her, Mollie had stroked a hand over it much as she had those jeans. How many blunders had he made?

Mollie shook lightly. She didn't look at James as she pulled on her jeans. She didn't speak to him. Her fire

195

was gone. Her love for life was gone. Mollie was beaten. As she stared into the lake, she wondered what James would do next. For some reason, the thought that he might kill her didn't seem quite so threatening anymore.

Cadal remembered that feeling of desperation from when Xanthe left. He had been a fool.

"Well, come on," James snapped at her.

Mollie startled and looked at him warily.

"You don't want me to leave you here, do you?"

She glanced around, considering her options. As much as she disliked the idea of being trapped in a car with James, she was thirty miles out and there was no other way back but a two-day hike, unless she was lucky enough to happen across one of the infrequent visitors to the area. This late in the season, that was unlikely, and the temperatures would be close to freezing after dark.

She didn't have much of a choice, really. Mollie stood silently and walked over the hill and down the slope on the other side. Halfway down, she slid. James grabbed her by the arm. Mollie elbowed him roughly and scampered the rest of the way down the slippery embankment like a true Fairy.

James launched after her and pushed her back against a tree. "You still have some fire left after all. Should we give it another go?"

Cadal felt the need to hit something, to scream out his rage again, to empty his stomach. Surely, Morda would have warned him if he had to witness another assault on her.

Mollie set her jaw and looked away with tears in her eyes. Nothing else James could do would touch her. Nothing else could add to it. James backed away, and

Cadal almost cried in relief that it wouldn't happen again.

"Guess not. I thought you had more fight than that. Too bad." He turned and walked away.

Mollie pressed her back into the tree and shook. Her stomach rebelled. She gagged as a wave of dizziness nearly floored her. Mollie considered the freezing temperatures as an honest possibility before she forced herself to start walking.

In the car, she pushed herself as close to the door as she could. She watched James warily as he drove, her hand braced on the door release for comfort.

He stared at her, smiling coldly. "Why couldn't you play nice? It was fun, but it would have been so much more fun, you know."

Mollie shook her head.

James' jaw tightened in anger. "It will be your word against mine. You know that, don't you?" He studied the expression on her face closely. "You have no proof that you weren't a willing participant. I made sure of that. No one will believe you weren't. The way you act..."

Mollie met his eyes, and Cadal felt her heart harden.

James shook his head and looked back at the road. "I can tell that's not going to be a problem, is it?"

He didn't say anything else until he let her out of the car outside of her apartment. As she slammed the car door, he smiled warmly. The smile didn't reach his eyes. "See you around campus, Mollie," he called after her.

Cadal's view shifted to Mollie's as the danger evaporated and it was no longer necessary to see the panoramic view. Mollie walked to her apartment and locked the door behind her. She crossed to the bathroom and started filling a tub of hot water. She pulled off her jeans and stared at the bloodstain that marred them sadly before dropping them in the trash can next to the toilet. Her other clothing followed close behind.

Mollie closed her eyes and pulled off one final thing, a necklace of some sort. She didn't look at it when she opened her eyes. She wrapped it in her fist and considered it for a moment. Her hand wavered over the trashcan. She crossed to the sink and dropped it in the drawer without watching it fall. Whatever the necklace was, it was precious to her. It was so precious Mollie wouldn't see it destroyed, but she would never wear it again.

She climbed into the hot water and hugged her knees close to her chest. Mollie didn't cry. She didn't speak. She simply sat there for a long time before she bathed. She put on a pair of heavy sweats and curled into her bed with Xanthe's book.

Mollie tried to ignore the aches inside her, from her heart more than from James' treatment. As hurtful as it was, he was right. James was expert enough to do little physical damage while he took what he wanted from her. His future freedom depended on it, after all.

Her tears fell on the page as she read. Mollie threw the book across the room and wept into her pillow. Calm again, she recovered the book and held it to her chest.

Mollie stared into the rain outside her window, and a quote from one of the stories flitted through her mind. "The Harmony cries when She feels Her children's pain," she quoted quietly. "Well, She has reason enough to cry today."

She stifled a fresh sob. "Fairies. I wish it was all true. I wish I was a Fairy." Her voice was a choked whisper, and she dissolved into tears one last time. If she could have justified it, she would have gone to the estate that very night. But how would she justify it?

Cadal groaned as he felt the shift in her soul, the shift that granted her innocent wish for her birthright. Mollie didn't feel the shift, not like Xanthe had. Perhaps Xanthe felt it because she knew it would happen. Perhaps it was more jarring, because Xanthe was turning her back on The Harmony's way while Mollie was being welcomed into Her arms.

Cadal saw flashes of James after that. James smiled at Mollie knowingly and glanced at her body as he passed her on campus. He blocked her way with his larger body when he thought he could get away with it. He whispered innuendoes to her, while Mollie pretended to ignore him. Eventually, he stopped.

Mollie never spoke to James. She regarded him coolly while stifling the urge to shake, to scream, to beat at him, or to run. Mollie knew James would give up when he realized that he couldn't provoke her. She was right. James wanted a fight. He wanted to steal her spirit again. Mollie wouldn't allow it. She couldn't let him provoke her, or James would try again. She couldn't stand the thought of it.

Other men tried to get her attention. Some were spurred on by whatever lies James told about her. Her answer was always the same, "Not interested."

Over time, Mollie became the ice cube Joseph referred to. In company, her hair was in the tight bun Cadal saw when he first met her. Mollie was cold, businesslike, and competitive; all the qualities she hated in Human boys. She showed the world an outward side that minimized the chance of falling prey to another James.

Inside was another story. Mollie was fragile, idealistic, and tortured. She missed the land. She craved love, but she wouldn't take the chance of choosing badly again. Mollie wanted to be carefree again, but she knew where that had led her last time.

The dual personality was exhausting. In the end, that was what drove her here. She was tired. Mollie felt old before her time.

Cadal watched her interactions with himself in a mixture of amusement and grief. He was amazed at how much more complex Mollie was than he had supposed. Cadal sighed as Mollie's portion of the transfer faded away. He understood so much more about her now. There would be no more hurting her because he didn't know the story of her past.

He watched the short lives of the two Fairy children younger than his bride was. Then came a Fairy that made Cadal smile widely. It was a babe in the womb. The babe was so young that he barely had a heartbeat. He was so innocent, so perfect. This was the ultimate magic of The Harmony, her most precious gift to them.

Morda laughed at Cadal's enchantment with the child. "It is a special thing to connect with one so young."

"What Fairy is so lucky? He's beautiful." Cadal laughed at the pure joy the babe instilled in his heart.

"So is his mother," Morda observed. "That is your son, Cadal. He sleeps in your bride's womb as we speak."

Cadal stared at her in disbelief then locked on the image of his son, thanking The Harmony for answering his prayer.

Morda held the moment for him a little longer. Then she ended her transfer.

Cadal opened his eyes. Mollie was still there, still concerned for him. He wrapped her in his arms and gathered her onto his lap. That time, his tears were shed in the greatest joy. She would not have to care for him today. Cadal would care for her, for Mollie and for their son.

Mollie turned to him and touched his face. "Are you sure you're all right?"

He kissed her cheek lightly. "Much better today."

She eyed him uncertainly. "Now, I guess, but during the transfer— I don't suppose I should bother to ask what caused those emotions?"

Cadal furrowed his brow. "What emotions?" He hadn't realized that he was projecting anything outside the transfer. Cadal cringed inwardly at the emotions she might have seen.

"Everything. You smiled. You cried. At one point, you looked positively murderous." Mollie shuddered in his arms before she continued. "You even screamed."

"I'm sorry. I hadn't realized you would see any of that, but it doesn't matter now. None of it matters anymore, not to anyone."

Morda chuckled. "That's good, Cadal. I'll go now, but I trust I'll see you soon?"

Cadal met Mollie's eyes and stifled the urge to place his hand over their son. "Very soon, Morda. You have my word."

Chapter Twelve

Cadal held her for long after Morda left. Mollie was sure he would be an emotional wreck, but he wasn't. The emotions he'd experienced in the transfer were so startling and heartfelt, she was sure he would emerge in worse shape than any of the other days.

A look had crossed his face that sent a chill through Mollie's heart and frightened her, not for herself, but for Cadal if he ever gave wings to whatever thought was racing through his mind. When he'd screamed; it was a tortured sound, desperate, and his hands tightened on Mollie's painfully. In the first show of concern for Cadal that Mollie had seen, Morda had stopped the transfer to allow him time to recover.

The rest of the transfer had passed quickly. That was a godsend. After his scream, nothing but a quick ending could have convinced Mollie to stay for more. When his distress ended, a sense of shock followed by wonder had crossed over his face.

Then Morda had removed her hands; Cadal's eyes had opened, and he'd smiled through his tears. Mollie would have assumed it was in relief, but the look he gave her made Mollie believe that she had gifted him with some fantastic joy. Surely, Mollie's mere presence was not so important to him.

Cadal met her eyes. "I think we should make today a short lesson."

"If you're tired, we can skip it."

"No, I want to introduce you to some people you will meet at the colony."

"Introduce?"

"I want to transfer names, faces, and relationships. It will be like a cast listing in a play. I'll let you form your own opinions of them. It wouldn't be fair of me to influence that, but I don't want you to feel you're being bombarded by a room full of strangers."

Mollie smiled. "At least I won't have to ask people's names all day."

She was stunned at the number of Fairies there were in the colony. Mollie 'knew' almost a thousand new people by the time the transfer ended.

Cadal was correct. Xanthe had a huge family. Her immediate family had consisted of Morda, her parents, her three sisters and their husbands, and all of their children. Only one of Xanthe's eight nieces and nephews was an adult Fairy. Gady was one hundred and twelve years old and had been an infant when Xanthe left the colony.

Mollie shook her head in wonder. "I don't understand. What could you possibly have to learn that could take so long and be so intensive? If you can teach me so much so effortlessly..." She shrugged.

Cadal met her eyes. Mollie could see that he was afraid. She was instantly sorry she'd asked the question. She touched his lips lightly in an effort to stop whatever response he was about to make, and he kissed her fingertips.

"You can't tell anyone. Promise me, please. None of the other Fairies can know that I've undergone these transfers or that I've given you your transfers."

Mollie was confused by the request. "But Morda said you had reached an age. Wouldn't everyone?"

Cadal shook his head. "Only those who are chosen undergo the transfers," he explained.

"Chosen? Chosen for what?"

He sighed and ran a finger down Mollie's cheek. "I'm a Fairy Master. It's almost time for Morda to step down. It's past time, but I have delayed it horribly. I'll have to take my place soon."

"Why can't you tell them?"

"If they know, they'll want me to take my place. I'm trained. It's time. They won't want to wait any longer for the transfer of power, but they have to wait. I can't come back without you."

"If it's time—" Mollie didn't really know what she wanted to say. She wanted to offer to stay behind, while he did what he was destined to do. She could follow him later, but the thought of Cadal leaving her made her heart sink.

Cadal nodded. "That's the way I feel too. But there's more. Morda must conduct our ceremony before she steps down as Fairy Mistress. That is one of our traditions. I cannot take my place as Fairy Master until we are wed and until I finish all personal business."

"I'm your personal business, aren't I?"

"You and a few other little things." He smiled and drew her into a gentle kiss. "You may be more work than soulmates usually are, but you're worth it."

Mollie curled her nose, resisting the urge to roll her eyes. That was an offhand compliment at best.

Cadal laughed heartily. "It was meant as a compliment. Maybe I can come up with a better one." He kissed her again, passionately, and laid her back onto the cool grass beneath them. He pulled back slightly to see what she would say of that compliment.

She smiled widely. "Nice compliment. I approve. Now, can you hear everything I think? Do I have any secrets from you?"

"I'm slightly limited until the full transfer of power, but in order, yes and no."

"No secrets, huh?" Mollie smirked. "Well, that does make life interesting. Guess you'll always know what your birthday present is."

"There's only one present I want."

"And what would that be?"

Cadal dropped over her and kissed her again. Mollie wound her arms around him and pulled him closer to her. She was sure that this was a good enough birthday present for her, even if it was the only one she got every year.

* * * *

Cadal felt as if he had to remember not to fly despite his Human form. They weren't visiting the colony for almost a week, but Mollie was already contemplating her options for the estate.

She convinced Cadal to take a midnight flight with her to check out Geoffrey Allen's property. Cadal understood her concern; Mollie couldn't turn the estate over to someone who wouldn't care for it properly, and she couldn't find any good reason to do the type of examination on his fields she needed in any straightforward way. Still, Cadal cringed at the thought of taking such a chance now that Mollie was carrying his child.

The expedition was discouraging. Allen's lands were depleted. If he couldn't run his own lands, he couldn't run the estate. So, who would care for it? Mollie couldn't stomach the thought of dealing with Thornton.

She was having a little trouble stomaching a few things lately.

While Mollie was intent on the fate of her land to the exclusion of almost anything else, Cadal pondered how long he could keep her pregnancy a secret from her. He wanted her to have the joy of discovering it for herself, but every day, it was harder not to discuss it, and Mollie was oblivious to the changes she was undergoing.

Cadal didn't have to wait long. Near the end of the week, Mollie took it upon herself to feed the animals, since several of the men were sick in bed, though she wasn't feeling well herself. By the time Cadal learned from Elizabeth where she had gone and tore off to stop her with a string of curses fanning out behind him in three languages, Mollie was sitting on the stable floor, looking decidedly ill.

She shot Cadal a tortured look. "I think I've come down with something," she complained. "Are the men throwing up?"

He sat and folded her into his lap. "No. I think you have something else."

Mollie groaned miserably. "Whatever it is, I wish it would go away. Every time I lean over..." She swallowed the sick swirl that assaulted her.

He kissed her forehead. "This isn't going away for a little while, I'm afraid."

She favored him with a suspicious look. "What are you talking about?"

Cadal smiled wider. "You remember when I told you that I had a few other little things to take care of? My personal business?"

She nodded then paled slightly. She really did feel awful.

He placed his hand below her navel and rubbed lightly at her womb. "This is one of those little things."

Mollie looked at his face for a moment then stared at his hand. Cadal waited for her answer patiently. A long string of emotions passed over her. She traveled from shock to disbelief to fear.

Cadal swallowed an attack of nerves. What if she wasn't happy about this? Mollie had been raised as a Human, and they had very different ideas about this subject than Fairies did sometimes.

The initial shock wore off. Mollie touched the hand Cadal had laid over their son and wound her fingers through his. A sense of wonder washed over her. She sank into his chest and stared at their hands.

Cadal heard the string of questions passing through her mind as clear as day.

Is it a boy or a girl? A boy would be wonderful.

What am I thinking? How far along am I? Surely, it isn't far. I've only been sleeping with Cadal for a little less than six weeks.

When was my last period? Damn it! Why do I never keep track of things like that? I can remember when I started sleeping with him but not when my period was? Heaven help me! I am hopeless.

Dates danced through her mind without any of them making an impression on her, making her dizziness more acute. The harvest stood out in her mind, the final days of changing blood rags at each break she took.

Before we started sleeping together, obviously. It has never been an issue for us. How could I miss this?

She groaned inwardly at the fact that she hadn't realized it before.

I never considered birth control. What was I thinking? What did I expect would happen if I wasn't doing anything to prevent it?

Of course, it's not as if I've had a lot of practice in this area.

But making love with Cadal repeatedly with no thought of the consequences? Was my brain on vacation?

A tremor of fear settled in her stomach.

Does Cadal feel trapped? Was this why he asked to marry me?

Cadal sighed and shook his head. As usual, her Human mind was complex, skipping from subject to subject almost too quickly for him to follow. He'd grasped at the strange word for a woman's blood, but the concept of preventing a child was chilling to him. Humans had children more often than Fairies, no doubt due to their aging and shorter life spans. Perhaps controlling one's reproduction would be of importance to them. Cadal knew Humans sometimes ended a pregnancy. The horror of that had left him shaken and turned him from Human forms of entertainment and information.

Mollie seemed concerned that he might want her to do that for him or that he might be marrying her for no other reason but that she carried his child. Cadal had been lax in his teaching. Her understanding of The Harmony's way was weak. A Fairy could not reproduce with anyone but a soulmate, and Mollie's gift of his child was the greatest thing she could ever give him, the greatest blessing in all of creation.

"No. That's not why I want to marry you," he assured her. "I didn't know when I asked you to marry me, any of the times I asked you actually. This doesn't change anything except that I'm very happy you're having my child. Now, do you want to know the answers to your other questions?"

She met his eyes and nodded. Mollie groaned again and sank back into his arms. "Remind me not to do that."

He stifled a laugh. "It will get better. To answer your question, the baby is a boy."

Mollie smiled and rubbed her hand over her stomach gently. "Good. There've been enough girls in this family."

Cadal kissed her cheek. "Maybe next time. I wouldn't mind a little girl someday." He met her eyes. "Would you like to see him?"

She looked at him in disbelief. "You can do that?"

"He's beautiful," he tempted her. "I look often. Would you like to see?"

"Yes, I think I would."

Cadal touched her temples lightly and transferred the image of their son. He marveled again at how quickly the child was developing. Cadal held the image for her for several minutes, allowing Mollie to watch his heart beating and his arms moving slightly.

"This is how you knew? You saw this in the final transfer, didn't you?"

"Yes. I did."

"This was why you were so happy when you came out of the transfer?"

"Beyond reason."

"Why didn't you tell me?"

"I wanted it to be a surprise for you. I wanted you to know without my blurting it out, but you've been so distracted, I was starting to think you'd never figure it out on your own."

Cadal ended the transfer.

Mollie sighed deeply and met his eyes. "Guess I should get to work selling this estate. This little one isn't missing a minute with his Daddy, if I can help it."

He scooped her up and headed out of the stable. "I'll settle for you cuddling into bed with some toast and milk until your stomach settles for the day."

Back at the house, Elizabeth tried to make a fuss over Mollie.

Cadal shooed her away.

"I should call the doctor," she protested.

"No, Elizabeth." Mollie waved her off. "I'll be fine, really. I'm just not feeling well."

"If you're sure, miss," she answered uncertainly. "At least, you should stay in bed for a few days."

Mollie raised an eyebrow at Cadal despite her pallor. He read the thoughts that staying in bed was exactly what caused this particular condition and that there were a few of those nights she wouldn't mind repeating when she felt better.

He cracked a smile in response. "If Mollie is up to it, we'll be leaving in a day or two to meet my family. We'll only be gone a few days."

Elizabeth looked at him in shock. "If she is ill, she really shouldn't travel."

"I'll be fine, Elizabeth," Mollie argued.

Elizabeth looked from one of them to the other and shook her head sadly. "I know you will, miss. I know you will. Now, if you'll excuse me, I'll get some milk and toast with preserves for you."

Mollie watched the door close behind her and sighed deeply. "We're not fooling anyone, you know."

Cadal sank to the bed beside her. "We don't have to fool anyone."

"Yes, but it will be easier to handle the sale of the estate if people don't think I'm on the run."

"I'll take your word for it." Cadal had no idea what she meant and wasn't sure he wanted to know. "Are you ready to meet the family?"

Mollie smiled weakly. "I guess we better do it fairly soon. Otherwise, they'll be meeting a very matronly Fairy."

"That makes no difference. We're soulmates. We've wind danced. We're one now. There is no stigma that we're expecting a child before our ceremony."

"I guess Fairy life has a lot of unexpected perks."

Cadal laid his head on her stomach and kissed it lightly. "We simply haven't forgotten what's really important."

Chapter Thirteen

It became readily apparent that word spread around the estate concerning Mollie's *delicate condition* at a rate that alarmed her. The men wouldn't allow her to lift a finger to the physical labors of the farm, much to her embarrassment and Cadal's delight. Mollie blamed Cadal for the change, but he informed her that her culprits lay elsewhere, most likely in the forms of Liam and Elizabeth.

"It's ridiculous. I'm hardly an invalid."

Cadal laughed at her reaction. "It's not a competition, Mollie. In this case, you win hands down. You're doing something the men never can, and they know it. Let them pamper you. Let them do what they can do."

In the end, Mollie grumbled some complaint about all men being hopeless and decided to do some paperwork. Cadal watched her leave the room with a measure of amusement.

He continued to coddle the headstrong young woman as much as she would tolerate, despite her protests. "It's my first child," Cadal told her one afternoon as he ushered her to bed after a violent attack of nausea. "I'm allowed to be overprotective of you." He didn't add that being a *first* child had nothing to do with it. He'd pamper her every time she gave him a child.

Cadal settled the problem of how they should set off on their journey to avoid suspicion by suggesting they take the train as far as Kinvarra and fly in from the other side. Any other mode of transportation would cause some concern. Three days later, armed with backpacks for the necessities, that was exactly what they did.

Mollie was still struggling with almost constant bouts of nausea, and Elizabeth was very unhappy with her decision to travel, but the servant kept quiet about it after Mollie made it clear that she would not be dissuaded. Mollie steadfastly refused to delay the trip, and Cadal had to admit her assessment that waiting for the nausea to end would take far too long was correct, so he agreed.

Cadal knew that Mollie got more and more nervous as the trip wore on, so much so that they had to stop several times to deal with acute bouts of nausea.

He held her while they rested. "Are you sure you don't want to go back?" he offered. "We could say that the train was too much and have Liam pick us up."

"No. I'll be better once we're there. It's just nerves." She slipped into the Fairy language in preparation for the colony.

An hour later, Mollie looked at the great tree in awe. She touched it reverently and looked at Cadal with a sheepish grin. "I've read so much about this place, but I never thought I'd get to see it."

He took her hand and led her to the main doorway. Cadal ducked to step inside, but Mollie stepped through the entryway without a problem, as Xanthe always had. She looked around in confusion at the deserted passageways, barely noting the smooth, tree-oiled and painted surfaces she'd waited so long to see. She'd take note of the designs later, when her mind wasn't so occupied.

Cadal squeezed her hand. "It's all right. By now, everyone will have gathered in the great chamber and the hall to await our arrival."

Mollie looked shocked at the thought of such a crowd. "Why? How?"

"The sentries will have spread the word that we're coming, and Morda knew where we were from the moment we left the estate. It's one of her gifts. This is a very special day for the colony, not as special as when we return for good and have our ceremony, but special."

"A simple visit is so special?" That confused her.

"It's not just a visit. You're a new Fairy to the colony. You are a stranger. They don't meet someone new often. They don't know you were raised in the Human realm. That will be even more of a novelty to them, but even coming from another colony would be cause for celebration."

"There are other colonies?"

"Oh, yes. Once there were five hundred. I know that there are at least twenty more now. We have little contact with each other, and each colony has developed its own identity within the Fairy framework. Visitors are a joyous thing, exciting."

Mollie nodded in a mixture of anticipation and wonder. She knew the layout, and Cadal felt her nervousness peak as they came closer to Morda's throne room.

"Relax. You have me, and you have Morda. We'll know when you need a break."

She nodded, though Cadal knew his words had done little to ease her discomfort.

Zera stepped out to face them as they reached the great chamber. Fury burned in her eyes. "When I heard you brought a new Fairy back, I knew. I just knew."

Mollie startled at the obvious murderous rage Zera displayed. She met Zera's eyes and shrank back against

Cadal. Mollie hadn't expected this. Cadal hadn't really expected *this.*

He looked at his bride in concern. The last thing Mollie needed was this type of greeting, especially in her condition. "Knew what, Zera?" he demanded. "What is it that you think you know?"

She stared at him in shock. "Zera? I'm no longer worthy to be called 'Mother'?"

Cadal felt the sickening sense of vertigo assaulting Mollie's nerves. This was her worst nightmare come true. She was being shunned in the one place she thought she'd be safe and accepted and by no less than Cadal's family. He knew Mollie had hoped she was misremembering the information from the transfer until Zera confirmed her identity.

He squeezed Mollie's hand in comfort before turning on Zera again. "I suppose not. Not when you are acting like such a petulant child and poor hostess."

"I won't allow it, Cadal. I don't know what sort of trick you and Morda have been planning, but I will not accept this ruse," Zera thundered.

Morda appeared from inside the Great Chamber. "There is no ruse, Zera. There is a disagreement. Normally, I would call you into the Great Chamber. Since that is occupied at the moment, we will retire to my quarters until this is settled."

Cadal nodded. "As you wish, Mistress," he answered. He knew it was unnecessary. Cadal was not one of the called. He was the Master, and Morda was the called, but that would become apparent very soon.

Zera scowled at him then Morda. "As you wish."

Morda faced Mollie and smiled in encouragement.

Mollie nodded in understanding. She was called, too. "As you wish." She bowed her head as she said it.

215

Morda looked at each of them in turn. "Good. There being no dissent, we will retire now."

Zera turned on her heel and stalked away with the other three Fairies close behind. Morda met Mollie's eyes and smiled warmly as they walked.

Inside Morda's rooms, the Mistress closed the door and faced the three people gathered in her main room. "Now, I will mediate."

Zera eyed her warily. "What of your conflict? In the past, I have found that you have put your family before my interests. Why should I trust that this is not the case now?"

"Because you are mistaken. It's in your interests and the interests of your family that I attempt to open your eyes before it's too late."

"In my interest to allow this travesty to continue? I am given the choice of losing my son or losing the possibility of family and happiness?"

"There is no choice for you, Zera. Cadal is an adult. He has become promised, sealed in wind dance. He is one with his bride. This is his choice."

"The wind dance is for Fairies. You said yourself that a Human cannot become Fairy. I do not accept the validity of this promise."

Mollie began to shake. Cadal knew she was trying to hold back the tears she wanted to shed. He had to settle this quickly.

"She is not Human," he explained. "Mollie was trapped in the Human world, denied her birthright for many years, but she is and always has been Fairy."

Zera favored him with what she wanted to be a withering look, but Cadal was not about to back down on that point.

"It's not possible, and you know it," she accused. "A Human cannot become Fairy. She was born Human. Anything more is a trick to allow you your bride and Morda her descendent."

Morda sighed and met Cadal's eyes. "I told you it wouldn't be easy."

He nodded. "Xanthe was not Human. Neither were her descendents. They were all Fairies, trapped in the Human world by Xanthe's wish. It was a curse, and Mollie's freedom is a precious gift from The Harmony. It has only happened three other times in ten thousand years."

Zera shook her head bitterly. "Lies," she growled.

Mollie fought back a wave of nausea.

Cadal moved suddenly. He pulled Zera firmly but gently to a chair and motioned for her to sit. She regarded him with concern, then complied.

Once she was settled, Cadal placed his hands on her temples. "I'm going to show you something. You can accept it or not. That is your choice," he warned her.

Zera laughed harshly. "What do you think you're doing?"

"I'm the next Fairy Master."

She looked to Morda for confirmation.

The Fairy Mistress smiled smugly. "It's true, Zera. He is the Master."

"Even if you are, you've had no training. Morda's strength is waning. It's too late."

Cadal lowered his hands and turned to stare at Mollie. She was trying to suppress a gale of laughter at the statement. Her eyes glittered above the hand she had clamped over her mouth. Cadal winked at her, and she stifled another peel of the mirth that was bubbling over within her.

Zera didn't react well to the perceived mockery. "Morda, why do you allow this — Human," she said with a certain venom, "to disrupt this mediation?"

Morda shook her head. "Because this Fairy is involved. She has an interest in this matter, and she knows how very wrong you are."

"I cannot be wrong. Everyone knows it takes months to train a Fairy Master."

Mollie smiled widely. Cadal felt a surge of pride in him from her.

"Five days," Mollie whispered. "He did it in five days. Had I known what he intended, I would have sent him to his training months ago. I wouldn't have allowed him to do it the way he did if I had known, but Cadal was adamant."

Zera scowled. "It can't be done. No one could survive such a transfer. I should have known the Human would lie."

Morda sighed. "I would have agreed with you a few weeks ago. I thought I might be able to complete his training in three weeks. Two, if I pushed him to his limits. Even I didn't know that it could be done. Zera, before this day is out, you may thank Mollie. She is the only reason Cadal survived. She gave him strength and comfort, when he had nothing left to sustain him."

Zera shook her head.

Cadal sighed and placed his hands again. "I will settle this. Will you accept my transfer?"

"You can't—"

Cadal concentrated a single burst of transfer. Zera recoiled, and he released her quickly. When she met his eyes again, Cadal winced at the fear he saw. He'd never wanted to have to prove it that way.

"Will you accept my transfer?"

Zera nodded. "I must. You know I must."

He knelt to her level and placed his hands again. "Relax. I don't want to hurt you. I want you to understand. You must understand."

She nodded again.

Cadal began the transfer.

He transferred the three previous cases.

He transferred Xanthe's final meeting with Morda.

Morda's words drifted through, "My gift to you, my child, is that your descendents will dream of their true heritage. If any so wish it, they may return to us and leave the Human realm."

Cadal chose what he showed her about Mollie carefully. Mollie curled in bed, watching the rain with the ancient book held firm to her chest. "Fairies. I wish it was all true. I wish I was a Fairy," she whispered as tears ran down her cheek.

He showed Mollie calming Thunder, walking the fields looking for poison while the land whispered to her, flying and wind dancing. Cadal showed her Mollie catching him and comforting him as he collapsed after the fourth transfer, arguing with Morda to end his suffering, and holding his hands and crying while he screamed during the final transfer.

Cadal ended the transfer. He knew that she understood.

Tears coursed down his mother's face. She looked at him miserably. "Is she truly a Fairy? In every way? What of children?"

He smiled, unable to contain himself. "She carries my son."

Zera smiled through her tears. She hugged Cadal, laughing and sobbing at the same time. "I recant. I apologize." She met Mollie's eyes over his shoulder. "I apologize to you both. Please, forgive this outburst."

Mollie's relief washed over Cadal.

Cadal squeezed Zera's hand and smiled at her before returning to his bride. He kissed Mollie and met her eyes. "One last piece of business, and we can take our place."

Mollie nodded and wound her arms around him.

Zera called out to them. "I know Morda has arranged quarters for you. For tonight, would you both stay with me?"

Cadal felt the happiness from Mollie at Zera's offer. "It would be an honor," she gushed. Then she looked at Cadal and blushed.

He chuckled then kissed her forehead. "As you wish. You know I'd deny you almost nothing, but you may regret that choice. My bed is not very spacious."

It was Zera's turn to laugh. "Don't be silly, Cadal. You shall have my bed for the night. The two of you shall, I mean."

Cadal looked at her, surprise stealing his words for a heartbeat. "Thank you."

"For your bride and your child, I could do no less."

Morda smiled. "Zera, if you'll join me in the Great Chamber, we'll welcome them properly."

Zera looked at the couple wistfully and nodded. She followed Morda out of the room. Mollie started to follow them, but Cadal took her by the waist and pulled her to him.

"Give them a few minutes. They want to do this right."

Mollie regarded him curiously. "You knew this was coming, didn't you?"

Cadal blushed. "I knew I had to deal with my mother, but I thought she'd address me privately. I didn't know she would..."

"You didn't think she'd involve me in the argument directly?"

"If I had, I would have come alone first. You know I would."

Mollie smiled that impish smile. "You would have left me?"

"For as short a time as I could. A day, if I could accomplish it that quickly. If it would have saved you this scene, it would have been worth it."

She kissed him. "No. It wouldn't, but I would have survived it."

Cadal smiled. "We should go. Everyone will be expecting us."

* * * *

The doors to the Great Chamber opened before them. Mollie took a deep breath and entered, her hand clasped in Cadal's. The room was enormous. It took up more than half the area of a cross-section of the great tree. The perimeter of the room was packed with Fairies standing five deep, all hoping for a look at the visiting Fairy and for a chance to meet her.

At the far end was an ornately carved throne. Morda sat on it, smiling at them as they came. A smaller throne sat next to hers, no less ornate but very empty. Mollie wondered if that was to be Cadal's place until he stepped up. Morda wore a gown similar to the one she had on the first day Mollie met her, though this one was white and topped with a light blue vest. It suited her, though it would look better if the blue was replaced with green to match Morda's eyes.

The murmur, that had started when they first appeared, grew louder as they walked toward Morda. Mollie looked for the cause and blushed deeply. None of the Fairy women wore pants, and Mollie's jeans were a glaring contrast. Cadal wore jeans as well, but they blended easily into the trousers the men wore.

He smiled her direction. "It's fine. You weren't raised here, remember?"

"Once I live here?" She tried to hide her nervousness.

"Wear what pleases you. Wear what's comfortable to you."

Mollie smiled the impish grin that Cadal loved. "Except the halter?"

"Outside of our quarters? Probably not, though you certainly wouldn't get quite the same reaction you did from the Humans."

"What reaction would I get?"

"Curiosity. Maybe a gentle chiding not to walk about in bed clothes." He shrugged. "I'm not sure. It has never come up before."

"Don't worry. I won't be the first to try it then."

Cadal grinned widely and looked back to Morda.

When they were barely an arm's-length away from her, Cadal stopped and bowed fluidly to the Fairy Mistress. Mollie took his lead and curtsied. The move seemed strange to her outside of a dress, but it was well received; though it set off another murmur through the crowd.

Morda raised her hand, commanding silence in the room. "Welcome home, Cadal. This is a special day. We have much to celebrate."

"I believe so, Mistress," Cadal agreed.

"You return from your travels in the Human realm with a Fairy who is a stranger to the colony. As the one who brings this Fairy, it falls to you to introduce her to the colony. Do you accept this task?"

"I do."

"Proceed," she announced.

Cadal looked around the room as he spoke. "Friends, only four times in our long history has so momentous an occasion been celebrated in our colony. A century ago, we lost a young Fairy to the Human realm. Xanthe was sorely missed. Today her descendent, Fairy from birth though exiled in the Human realm, returns to us. Sadly, this visit is a short one, as Mollie has to bring closure to her Human ties. If she is willing, she will then join us permanently. Mollie comes from a prominent line, which she has been denied knowledge of." He extended her hand to Morda. "I return to you your grandchild, Mistress."

Morda nodded and rose to embrace Mollie stiffly. "Welcome Mollie," she said formally. "Your essence has been sorely missed." She met Mollie's eyes and spoke softly. "Tonight, we will be formal. Tomorrow, you will come to my quarters and we will speak."

"Thank you, Grandmother. I'm glad we're finally here."

Morda nodded. "I felt your troubles. You must learn to relax. You will be much less ill that way."

Mollie blushed deeply as Morda returned to her throne. She should have realized that Morda knew. After all, the Fairy Mistress was in transfer with Cadal when he learned about her pregnancy.

Morda addressed the crowd. "That is not our only reason for celebration this day." She motioned to Cadal.

He nodded. Cadal took Mollie's hands in his own and met her eyes. He didn't look at the crowd that time, though his voice was meant to carry to them. "Mollie and I are promised, sealed in wind dance. She has agreed to wed when we return again. She is my soulmate and my bride, one with me always." Cheers went up from the crowd as he planted a gentle kiss on her lips.

Morda motioned them closer, and they knelt before her. "The Harmony blesses the joining of true soulmates. To that, I add my blessings, greater still since I vow that I shall make your ceremony my last act as Fairy Mistress."

Cadal's head snapped up. He hadn't anticipated Morda's announcement. He paled. Mollie guessed he was envisioning difficulties convincing the colony members that he had to leave with Mollie despite his place. He didn't have anything to worry about.

The crowd was in an uproar, no doubt because they were not aware of the training of a new Fairy Master. Cadal had explained that the whole colony typically knew when the training was being conducted.

Morda silenced them with a look. "My time has come," she announced. "My successor has been trained. Once his personal business is complete, I will step down." She took Cadal's hands, and he stood to face her. "Cadal, never bow to me again. My time as your teacher has come to an end. You are my equal, and shortly, you will be my better. Finish the task set to you by The Harmony as She intends and come back to take your place, with my blessings in all things. Protect your bride as The Harmony protects you until you stand before me again."

Cadal tipped his head slightly. "You have my word, Morda."

She sighed and cupped his cheek, a sad smile on her face. "Never has there been such a transfer of power."

"If The Harmony is kind, there will never be the need again."

Cadal put his hands down and lifted Mollie to her feet. "Enough of formalities. This is a celebration. Let us enjoy."

Morda smiled over Cadal's shoulder. "Well done," she told them. "Now, the real work begins."

Mollie looked at her fearfully then decided Morda was joking. "Are there any rules against hugging your grandmother in the colony?"

Morda offered her arms. "I hoped that Xanthe would listen to her heart and hug me goodbye. She didn't. It would make me very happy to have you hug me hello."

Mollie sank into her grandmother's arms and suddenly felt at home. Morda was the family member she had been searching for since Nana died. Morda was the one who would understand her.

She expected a rush of Fairies, but they restrained themselves to a gentle trickle. There were many questions, but few were asked more than once. Cadal explained that the crowd was sharing the information to avoid taxing her unnecessarily.

He watched over her closely, settled her on a comfortable couch, and brought her food even before Mollie realized she was hungry. Cadal curled comfortably into the couch next to her while Mollie met new friends and family, but occasionally he disappeared to provide some comfort for her.

A Fairy couple that Mollie recognized as Valia and Traden, cousins of Cadal's, approached her while Cadal was gone on one of his errands. Like many of the Fairies, they hugged and welcomed Mollie formally before asking her a number of questions about her life in the Human realm. That was everyone's favorite topic.

Traden handed Mollie a cup full of a cool liquid as she spoke to Valia. Mollie thanked him and raised it to her lips, but the smell of strong alcohol assaulted her and she suddenly felt ill. Even if she didn't, she really shouldn't drink that while she was pregnant. She swallowed a hard knot of nausea and set the cup down.

Traden's smile faltered. "It's not to your liking?" he asked.

She had no desire to hurt Traden's feelings. She smiled weakly and nodded her head. Too late, Mollie remembered what a bad idea that was when she was like this. The swirl in her stomach was making her dizzy. "I just need a moment to catch my breath."

Valia looked at her in concern. "We're tiring you," she decided. "Perhaps we should take our leave."

Mollie reached out to pat her arm. "Please, don't go. I enjoy your company." She was telling the truth, but she also knew that as long as she was engaged with Valia and Traden, she wouldn't be approached by anyone new. Mollie didn't feel up to that, at all.

Traden looked at her in confusion. "If you're sure..."

Mollie nodded, and stifled a groan at the fresh spike of nausea it brought with it.

Magically, Cadal appeared at her side. Mollie could tell he already knew what the problem was. He met her eyes and nodded silently. Cadal leaned between his cousins and whispered something. Their reactions were startling. Valia smiled warmly while Traden offered a heartfelt apology and moved away quickly. Cadal settled next to Mollie and kissed her cheek.

She met his eyes nervously. "What did you say to them?" she whispered.

Cadal laughed close to her ear. "I told them that my son was causing you upset tonight." He smiled at her shock. "Tell them the truth next time. It works wonders."

Traden returned with a fresh cup full of a warm liquid that tasted like sweet milk and soothed her stomach wonderfully. Mollie smiled and thanked Traden for his kindness.

He smiled widely at the praise. "This saw Valia through the worst of her early months," he explained. "If I had known—" He motioned to Cadal. "You drink the nectar wine. You really do have a lot to celebrate tonight. Finding your true soulmate, getting promised, becoming Fairy Master, and this blessing on top of it? How do you come by this luck?"

Cadal laughed heartily and sipped the first cup Traden had brought.

Valia leaned close to scowl at Cadal. "Someone should have told us sooner, Cadal," she chided him.

He nodded in reply, sipped his nectar wine, and looked at Mollie pointedly.

"Point well taken," Mollie replied. "I think Cadal was trying to teach me a lesson." She met his eyes. "I've learned it. Satisfied?"

"If you're sure."

"I'm sure."

Valia offered Mollie a wobbling smile. "What lesson was he trying to impart?"

"That Fairies are not like Humans. Here in the colony, there is no stigma that I'm carrying Cadal's child before we're wed."

Valia looked scandalized. "Stigma? What stigma could accompany Cadal's bride giving life to his son?"

"Humans don't always have a soulmate. If they do, they don't always find that soulmate. Men do not always live with or even support their children and the mothers of their children. Even when Humans wed, it usually doesn't last a lifetime." Mollie sighed. There was so much to try to explain.

"Because her mate dies?" Traden asked.

"Sometimes, but more often because they..." She searched for a word in the Fairy language and remembered Zera's words in Morda's chambers. "They recant their promises and turn their backs on their *marriage,* free to do what they wish, even wed another if they choose. It is a difficult situation at best. Even if you love someone and believe you are soulmates, you are discouraged from having a child before *marriage* to try to provide the best chance of a stable home for that child. To do so is deemed unwise and is often frowned upon."

Valia wiped a tear from her eye. "It sounds horrible."

"Humans do many horrible things," Mollie agreed. She knew that better than anyone here. "There are joys, but there are many dangers that simply do not exist in the Fairy realm. It is like a dream here. It is perfection by comparison."

Cadal nodded. "Humans are pressured. They live in a violent, ignorant, frightening place. Many of them have forgotten nature and The Harmony. The separation is so complete that they often resort to violence for petty, unimportant reasons."

Traden nodded somberly. "Thank The Harmony that you found your héritage. I would envy no one that kind of life."

Mollie chuckled. "I would have to agree, Traden. I lived there, and I fully admit that there was little joy for me until I found Cadal. All the joy there was came from my Fairy roots."

She had formed a solid opinion by the end of the conversation. Valia and Traden were going to be good friends when she moved to the tree-city. The trickle of Fairies continued. The news of Mollie's pregnancy spread quickly. Fairies started congratulating them and offering to help them prepare for the baby.

Mollie met most of Xanthe's family, though she learned that children of less than a century were not permitted at this type of function. She would have to wait to meet her younger cousins. It felt strange to think of a child of forty or even eighty years as young.

Cadal explained that many of them would be unrestrained in their curiosity, possibly to embarrassing extremes. "Better that you meet them after their curiosity is slaked somewhat by their parents' explanations."

Corea and Toril were friendly, but Mollie could sense their deep pain at the loss of their daughter, even after all these years. Cadal confirmed that it was compounded by the sight of him with her descendent, a place they had hoped for Xanthe herself.

Harea and her daughter Gady came next. Xanthe's older sister was formidable, but she was also the friendliest member of the family besides Morda. Gady was a bit shy, but Mollie liked her instantly. She was a happy girl and not much younger than Mollie, as Fairies went. The two women were delighted at the prospect of her bringing life to Cadal's son.

Linza, the youngest of Corea and Toril's daughters, was an extremely shy woman, and her husband, Marcan, was much the same. Mollie still felt Linza and Marcan were strangers when they walked away.

Benia and her husband, Witten, visited. She confused Mollie most. "You'll enjoy life with Cadal," she assured Mollie before they moved away. Something in Benia's manner made Mollie uncomfortable, but Cadal wasn't close by, and she forgot to ask him about it when he returned.

Mollie knew Benia was very close in age to Xanthe. She was born only seven years after her sister. That was an unheard of situation in the Fairy realm. The spacing was usually between twelve and twenty years from one child to the next. Corea gave birth to Xanthe seventeen years after Harea, Benia seven years later, and Linza fourteen years after that.

Hours later, Mollie was fatigued. Cadal didn't wait for her to break down. He stepped in immediately and explained that she required sleep. Everyone was gracious and bade Mollie rest for the sake of a healthy baby.

Cadal steered her toward his mother's quarters. Zera had retired for the evening, but she'd laid out a warm quilt for them and a glass of sweet milk by the bedside lamp.

Mollie smiled as Cadal started pulling off his clothing. The sweet milk had settled her stomach effectively, and they had not had an opportunity to make love recently due to her tender stomach. He turned and smiled, then closed the adjoining door between the rooms and stalked slowly toward her.

She raised an eyebrow at the move.

Cadal leaned over her. "You couldn't expect me to pass up an offer like that, could you?"

He kissed her passionately, and Mollie had to admit the sweet aftertaste of the nectar wine in his mouth was like an aphrodisiac to her. Cadal sank to the bed over her, and Mollie pulled at the last of his clothing. He met her eyes in the light from the small lamp. Cadal removed the last of Mollie's clothing, never losing eye contact. He knew what his gaze did to her, and he used it to his advantage, capturing her in the heat of his amorous look.

Cadal kissed her thoroughly, leisurely, and entered her. Mollie felt an incredible shock wave pass through her. He pulled back slightly and locked on her eyes again. Cadal moved slowly, drawing out her pleasure almost painfully.

Locked in his gaze and unable to look away, the sensations swept Mollie away. The rising interplay that always existed between them skyrocketed. Any hopes Mollie had of holding back evaporated as he claimed her slowly. As she climaxed, Mollie cried out despite her attempts not to, and Cadal smiled widely before he shuddered and groaned with the force of his own.

He rolled to the side, pulling Mollie along. She smiled at the satisfied look on his face, and he answered her unasked question.

"I'm thinking that it's good to see you enjoy making love with me so much. I like making you happy."

Mollie kissed him. He moved toward her, and she smiled wider as his hands explored her again. When Cadal met her eyes, Mollie ran her hands down his chest and stomach to pull gently at his hardening member.

"This time, let me make you happy," she crooned.

Chapter Fourteen

Cadal woke to the feeling of Mollie stretching against him. Last night had been more than he had ever dreamed. The attention Mollie had showed him took Cadal far beyond happy into the furthest reaches of ecstasy.

He berated himself for not allowing her free rein to loose the ministrations she craved to give him sooner. He had wasted so much time. Cadal had been so busy trying to pleasure Mollie that he never realized her drive to please him went as far as or further than his drive to please her did.

As inexperienced as he knew Mollie was sexually, she'd still brought him to heights he had not known were possible. Cadal wondered, not for the first time, if her dreams lay as the source of the experience she possessed. They'd connected her to her land and taught her to fly. They'd even steered her course to him. It was not unbelievable that her dreams would direct her to other pleasures.

Cadal had taken a few lovers over the years. By ninety, many young Fairies start to experiment a bit with their soulmates or even with friends, before their soulmates become clear to them. Coupling is not always a part of it.

It hadn't been with Xanthe. Cadal had tried his best to convince her with loveplay much like he used on Mollie. He was sure Xanthe enjoyed what he did, though she never reacted as spectacularly as Mollie did to it. Until Xanthe left, Cadal never took another. In retrospect, it was probably better for Cadal that Xanthe hadn't coupled with him. He wasn't sure he would have survived such a blow.

The two women Cadal took after he lost her were no more than an effort to quell his deep sense of loss. His technique, honed in his pursuit of Xanthe, was such that each of them agreed to couple with him. Each of them had expressed that they would have been more than happy to continue the experience past the two or three encounters he allowed himself with them, but Cadal found the experiences merely relieved the tension in his body for a short time while not touching his heart or soul. The last thing Cadal wanted or needed was another emotionally dead experience in his life. He'd pulled back from the relationships as gently as he could.

Flori was first. Cadal knew why he chose such a pretty puff. It was simple, really. Flori looked like Xanthe. Not exactly like her, but her hair was the same lovely color and her blue eyes could be mistaken for green in the right light. It was a poor reason to choose a lover. Cadal knew it, but he was so lost that any handhold seemed better than oblivion to him. It only lasted twice. After that, Cadal couldn't live with trying to pretend that Xanthe wasn't really gone.

Benia came next. His reason for choosing her was as thin. She was Xanthe's sister, born so close after Xanthe and with a spirit that Cadal hoped would develop into something he could love. Benia looked nothing like Xanthe except a bit in the face. Her hair was honey brown and her eyes were so dark as to appear almost violet. Benia was a wonderful lover, but she didn't touch that place in Cadal that he so desperately needed. Cadal tried three times before he decided that he could never feel for Benia what he should to be so physically intimate.

Each time Cadal took a lover, Zera had hoped for more. Each time he rejected one, her heart had broken for him as well as for herself. Cadal couldn't bear to give Zera false hopes again. He'd vowed he would not take another lover unless he intended to wed.

Cadal pulled himself back to reality as Mollie tried to sit up. She sank back to his shoulder.

"Sick again?" He didn't need to ask. He knew the answer.

Mollie looked at him miserably, reminding herself not to nod this time. "Endlessly."

He smiled. "No, not endlessly. Only until your body adjusts to supporting both of you. In the meantime, I'll get you something to calm your stomach." Cadal kissed her forehead and rose to recover his jeans from the floor and pull them on.

Zera was already awake when Cadal came out. She raised an eyebrow his way and smiled over a cup of warm tea.

Cadal smiled in return and leaned on the counter next to the fire nook. "Yes, Mother," he answered her unspoken comment. "I agree that it's a beautiful thing, and we are very happy. I'm glad you're not upset that we disturbed your rest."

She laughed heartily. "It has been far too long since these quarters have known that type of happiness." She looked past Cadal to the closed door of the adult bedchamber. "Mollie is still asleep?"

"No. She's sick again. I came out to get my clothing. I want to go get her some sweet bread to calm her stomach."

"Then go to the pantry. Gifts of calming foods have been delivered all morning. The potato rolls and sweet milk are best for this. When she recovers enough to join us at the table, there are meats and heavy jellies. That will soothe her best and feed your son very well."

Cadal nodded. "She is in good hands here. It's a shame that we have to return at all. Perhaps I should take some of these things back with me. I have found no Human substitutes that work as well."

He was drawing Zera out. She was disturbed, and he was still trying to get a handle on what was bothering her. She looked away sadly. He'd struck a nerve with something he said. He was on the right track, but he wasn't sure to what.

"Guard her well, Cadal. Mollie is safe here, but out there—" Zera sighed. "I cringe that you must chance so much."

Cadal filled a deep cup with sweet milk. "I know you're afraid. How could I not? I will be much more at ease when we are here and wed, but she has many Humans who watch over her — and myself, of course. I would sooner die than see her harmed. Unbelievably, so would some of those Humans."

He felt two jolts from her, Humans and him dying to save her from some harm. Cadal was beginning to unravel what was wrong.

"I worry. I can't help that where my family is concerned."

He sat across from her. "Botor didn't intend what happened. He only wanted to protect us. If he had realized Morda was so close or that he had an ally in the dog—"

"I know. Just care for her, Cadal. Never forget how important she is, and all will be well."

Cadal nodded. He had formed a mental image of what was wrong. *Dreams.* Zera's dreams the previous night had been tortured. It wasn't Cadal that Zera feared losing now. It was Mollie and her grandson, and she feared losing them to some Human threat. He wished he could reassure her, but his knowledge of the power of dreams left a niggling of unease with him. It was better not to offer lies. Cadal squeezed her hand and disappeared back into the bedchamber to Mollie with the foods to calm her stomach.

Mollie recovered quickly with Cadal's attention and the sweet foods he offered. Once she felt better, he asked her a serious question.

"How long do you want to stay?"

Mollie smiled, a dreamy look in her dark eyes. "Want to? Forever. Realistically? The sooner we leave, the sooner we can come back and you can take your place. But not today. For today, I just want to explore and relax."

"Good. You like it here."

She looked at him in shock. "You're kidding, right?"

"You don't like it?" he teased her.

Mollie rolled her eyes. "Only as much as I *like* you, I suppose."

Cadal laughed heartily at her wit. "Well, I suppose you're not very impressed, then."

She elbowed him lightly in the ribs. "You're talking about the father of my baby like that?" she demanded.

Cadal kissed her. "I like the sound of that. I don't think there is a higher honor than being the father of your child, except perhaps that you love me enough to be his mother."

* * * *

Cadal took Mollie to Morda's quarters shortly after a breakfast of foods that made her feel better than she had in days. Morda met them each with a hug and led them to comfortable seats around a table laden with dried fruits, sweet milk, and meats.

Mollie sampled a slice of roast rabbit. "We better leave soon, or I'll get incredibly fat. Everyone seems to want to feed me."

He laughed. "No, you won't get fat. You will grow a fat, healthy, happy baby."

Morda laughed at the severe look Mollie shot him, which they all knew was for show. "Fortunately, Cadal is correct. Everything you've been eating is very good for you despite how sweet it tastes." She sipped a cup of sweet milk and her eyes glittered over its rim. "And... From what Zera overheard last night, you don't have to worry about too little exercise."

Cadal smiled at the mortified look on Mollie's face. She was having second thoughts about having agreed to stay with his mother for another night.

"Don't worry," he soothed Mollie. "It made Mother very happy to hear it. I think she would have been very unhappy not to. It put her mind at ease that we find so much pleasure in each other."

Mollie cracked a smile. "It's not like we can pretend we've never enjoyed each other's company. Evidence proves otherwise." She patted her womb.

Morda smiled at the joke. "How long will you be here?"

Mollie glanced at Cadal uncertainly. "We'll have to leave soon, but we'll be back as soon as we can. I have to sell the estate to someone who will care for it. If I simply stayed here — disappeared, and I have considered that move, it would revert to my mother's care or worse, to Thornton. She'd accept his offer."

Morda nodded. "I understand. Do what you must. Have Cadal bring your things out when you are ready." She examined Mollie closely. "Look carefully at your options. I think you have a faint idea of the correct answer in mind already."

Cadal looked at Morda in surprise. "If you know, why not tell her?"

"Because The Harmony intends that some lessons be learned not taught."

Mollie twisted her hands nervously. "This is some sort of test?" she asked.

"Not in the way you think. In some things, you must find your own way." She met Cadal's eyes. "You both do."

Cadal understood. This was a test, but not for Mollie. It was part of his final task. Cadal only hoped he would choose his road as well as he had so far. He nodded to his mentor. "Well, if you don't mind, Morda, we will see you at dinner in my mother's quarters. Your granddaughter wishes to see the colony before we leave, and I would like to keep it as leisurely as possible."

"Of course."

As Mollie rose, Morda hugged her then ran her fingertips over her granddaughter's forehead to brush the hair from her eyes. Mollie gripped Morda's shoulder, and Cadal felt the sudden dizziness that assaulted her. As he wrapped his arms around her to steady her, Mollie took a ragged breath. The sensation passed as quickly as it came.

He looked at Morda in confusion, but the Fairy Mistress offered no explanation save a satisfied nod and a smile to her successor. Morda had done something, but Cadal had no idea what it could have been. Whatever it was, he was sure it had to do with his final task. A fleeting stab of fear washed over him as they took their leave.

* * * *

Mollie enjoyed seeing the colony at work and play much more than the party they threw. To her dismay, she discovered that she was forbidden to help in all but the most sedate ways.

"You are doing a very difficult job," Cadal told her.

"Women continue their usual work throughout a healthy pregnancy. They do it every day."

"I didn't say you couldn't do anything. You won't do heavy manual labor right now. No one here will allow it. There are many things you can do. We'll find a few that you enjoy once we're here permanently."

Cadal took her hands and looked deep into her eyes. He'd learned early in their relationship that Mollie had a hard time arguing with him when he did that. It touched some spot deep within her that he couldn't name, but it did come in useful.

"You tend to overdo things at times. I don't want you to bleed to bring crops in. That's not needed here. You've already proven yourself to the Fairies of the colony. Do something you enjoy, or do half a dozen things you enjoy, but stop when you tire. No one will ask more than that of you. Agreed?"

Mollie nodded. "I keep forgetting how simple things are." She hesitated. "How have I proven myself here?"

Cadal smiled. "In many ways. You've survived exile in the Human realm. You have agreed to wed your soulmate. You are bringing two new lives to the colony, your own and our son." He shrugged. "You are who you are."

In the end, Mollie agreed to let Cadal pamper her to a certain extent. He'd hoped the complete change of mindset between the two worlds would convince her to allow it. Mollie would rediscover how to be truly carefree again over time, but Cadal was sure that would be a long way off.

The day passed all too quickly. Mollie wanted to see everything. It was all Cadal could do to convince her to eat and rest. The baby helped his cause by giving her pause whenever she ignored common sense. They had a quiet dinner with Morda, Zera, Valia, and Traden. Cadal was happy to see that Zera seemed to have forgotten both her anger at Morda and the upset over her dreams.

Mollie was nodding off against Cadal's shoulder before dinner was over. He smiled and wrapped his arms around her. She settled into his chest. She was stubborn, but Cadal loved the wonder and passion he felt from her as she discovered her new home.

The conversation quieted as everyone watched the young lovers.

Zera spoke. "Take her to bed, Cadal." He felt a rush of pride washing over her.

Cadal smiled widely and hoisted Mollie up into his arms as he had done many times before. He laid her in the bed, stripped off her shoes and jeans, then his own clothing. Cadal settled next to her and laid his hand over her womb, over his child. The change was beginning to show, a slight softness in her figure and a whisper of warmth radiating from her. Cadal nuzzled her lips, then pulled the quilt over her. He smiled as Mollie shifted closer to him in her sleep.

He sighed, remembering Morda's warning about his final task. Cadal gathered that it would not be pleasant by her attitude. He only hoped the troubling dreams Zera had suffered the previous night were not connected.

Cadal brushed Mollie's hair off her cheek. "I'll guard you well," he told her. "I'll protect you both. I promise."

* * * *

Leaving was much harder on Mollie than Cadal had anticipated. She was upset at going back, though she attested to the need for it. *Perhaps too strenuously?* Mollie hugged Valia and Morda and wiped away a tear as they turned to go.

They had parted from Zera at her quarters. His mother found watching them depart too painful. Cadal knew she'd had more troubling dreams the second night. He admitted to Morda that he would like to deny Mollie the right to return to her land, but he had given her his word that she could leave again, and it was so very important to her.

At Mollie's suggestion, they left behind their clothes in favor of the sweet milk, heavy jelly, and potato rolls Cadal wanted to take back for her. "After all," she rationalized, "we'll be back soon."

Cadal had to admit she had a point. Morda insisted that Mollie carry no pack this time. She was still a fledgling flyer, and the added weight was an unnecessary burden on her, especially while she was getting established in her pregnancy.

The trip back to the estate was uneventful. Liam picked them up at the station in Ballynaclogh. Mollie wanted to hike back to the house, but Cadal steadfastly refused that request. Even with flight, the trip was more than she should be doing for a few more months, until she was well established. She would have exhausted herself on the long walk. Mollie rolled her eyes and agreed.

Back at the house, she made Cadal a deal, the same one she made him after her experience with Tucker at the pond. Cadal didn't balk at it, and they didn't waste time telling Fairy tales. If he wanted her to stay in bed, it was going to be as enjoyable as Mollie could manage.

Elizabeth went back to hovering over Mollie. Cadal watched in amusement as Mollie tried to humor the young woman while retaining some semblance of autonomy over her own life. At times, she closed herself up in their bedroom or the library and claimed she wanted a nap. Cadal knew she was lying, but he also knew Mollie wasn't overworking herself that way.

Cadal refused to let Mollie check out *Sidhe Druin*, the other neighboring estate, the name of which, oddly enough, meant Fairy Ridge. It was too much of a risk. He went alone. Cadal knew Mollie was looking for someone who wouldn't destroy the quality of the Blake estate. It pained him to tell her that *Sidhe Druin* was in no better shape than Geoffrey Allen's property.

He was surprised to find Thornton's land was passably well kept, but Cadal knew better than to point that out to Mollie. She didn't despise the man for his farming, and Mollie would sooner stay here forever than let the estate fall to him.

She started considering her options again.

Mollie used the time to sort out the things she wanted to take to the colony. Cadal found her contemplating the piles one afternoon about a week after they returned to the estate.

He sank to the floor beside her. "Having a problem?"

She bit her lower lip lightly, moving a stack of shirts from one pile to another. "I keep paring it down, but it's still way too much."

"Why?"

Mollie furrowed her brow in confusion.

"Why is it too much?"

"We can't possibly carry all of this. It's not manageable."

Cadal laughed. "I can make several trips. I can even bring a man or two back with me to help carry things. Pack everything, and I'll see how many trips we'll need."

She was uncomfortable with the idea, so Cadal sweetened the pot.

"There is another positive side to the plan. I can bring more sweet milk and rolls when I come back."

Mollie smiled weakly. She had run out of potato rolls days ago, and she was almost out of sweet milk as well. "How long would a trip take without me slowing you down?"

"Six hours. Eight at the most for the round trip."

"Okay. We'll do it. Now I just have to figure out whatever answer Grandmother seems to think The Harmony has planted up here." She tapped her head and sighed.

Cadal kissed her forehead lightly. "You will," he assured her. "Get packing. I'll do the first load tomorrow. We'll do it in two trips plus the bags we'll take when we leave together. I'll get as many men as I need to do it that way." He looked at the frost on the window. "If we can manage this before the first winter storms, it will be much easier and much safer."

Chapter Fifteen

Mollie knew the day without Cadal would be lonely and trying, but she had no idea how trying it would be. Elizabeth knocked on the library door at about lunchtime.

"Yes, Elizabeth?" She looked up from the shopping list in front of her.

"Mr. Thornton is here to see you, miss. What should I tell him?" she asked uncertainly.

"Tell him that I'm indisposed, and I'll be glad to see him the day after tomorrow when my schedule is clear." Mollie raised her eyebrow for effect.

Elizabeth smiled widely. "Indisposed, indeed," she whispered in a conspiratorial tone, her eyes glittering. She knew Mollie was stalling the meeting until Cadal could be there for it. "Yes, miss." She turned on her heel.

Mollie's smile faded as she heard Elizabeth's protests echoing down the hall. He was coming in, despite her orders. Mollie uttered a few choice curses and shuffled her shopping list under a pile of receipts before Thornton appeared in the doorway. She tried to appear oblivious to his presence.

Thornton breezed in with a strained smile. "Miss Hardy," he greeted her, "I was just telling your maid that you could not possibly refuse to see me if you knew I was on my way out of town for a few days."

Mollie eyed him warily. "I'm sad to say you were wrong, Mr. Thornton. Your schedule is of little consequence to me. I have my own schedule to consider. Now, I have refused your company today. If you don't mind showing yourself out—"

"This will only take a moment."

"Elizabeth?"

The young woman ducked past Thornton's shoulder.

"Would you kindly call Liam and Patrick for me?"

Elizabeth nodded and hurried away.

Thornton's face darkened and he puffed up his chest angrily. "That is really not necessary."

"I believe it is. You have until they return. I suggest you speak your mind quickly."

"You did well this past season."

"Thank you." Mollie knew it wasn't that simple. She sat back in the chair and waited for the other shoe to drop.

"You worked like a man, and it paid off for you."

She ground her teeth but didn't take the bait.

"You won't be able to do that this year, will you?" Thornton raised an eyebrow and waited to see what she would say to his implied knowledge of her personal situation.

"Really? I wasn't aware of any physical defect in myself, Mr. Thornton." Where were Liam and Patrick?

He laughed harshly at her poker face. "Come now. You will be unable to, and we both know it. You will be hugely pregnant by planting time and caring for a new infant by harvest. Or are the dates incorrect?"

"What if I will? We won't have to hand water this year. Unless someone poisons my fields again, I can look forward to behaving like any other land owner this year."

Thornton laughed again, and Mollie was struck by how intensely she disliked the man.

"You'll have a baby to tend to. Think about her. Wouldn't it be preferable to live a life of ease? I'll raise my offer by twenty percent. You could live comfortably on that for a decade or more."

Mollie stifled the urge to point out that the Blake women had been running the estate for five generations with no problem. Thornton was simply irked that he had failed to get the estate when Katie was aging and there was no heiress on the horizon. He was watching his chances drop by the day, and he knew it.

"Mr. Thornton, I have no plans of selling this estate. Even if I did, I assure you that I would sooner give it away than sell it to you. As for my ease, don't trouble yourself on my account. I am well cared for."

"I'm sure you are. That is why you find yourself in this predicament. I'm sure William Cadal has taken *fine* care of you. What happens when he leaves? He will, you know. I took the liberty of checking. He's not who he says he is. He wormed his way into Miss Katie's will. Then he wormed his way into your bed. He has no family and nothing to offer you or your daughter."

Mollie laughed. "You'd like to believe that, I know. How sad. The truth is, I've met his family. I've seen what he offers. I find myself in no predicament. Cadal is not leaving us, but even if he did, I would have no problem running this estate and raising our child. Women do it every day. You really should join the twenty-first century, Mr. Thornton."

Thornton leaned across the desk to her. "You poor, misguided child. You cannot see what trouble you are in. You've disgraced yourself. No one will respect you. How will you run this estate? You'll have to sell."

Mollie regarded him coldly. "Never. I'm bringing a new life into this world, and only a crass old fool like you would dare demean that."

"Miss?" Liam said from the doorway.

Mollie had no idea how long Liam had been there, but his timing was perfect. She had no further use for Mr. Thornton, as if she ever had. Patrick was at his brother's shoulder. His face was a mask of concern while Liam's was pure rage.

"Liam, please show Mr. Thornton out to the gates. You two are my witnesses. Mr. Thornton and his employees are banned. Unless they have an appointment with me, I don't want any of them on my land."

Liam smiled at Thornton with cold, dangerous eyes. "If you'll come with me, sir," he said, leaving no room for argument.

Thornton scowled at Mollie. "Remember what I said. You won't have any choice soon. You'll find yourself all alone, and not even your hired hands will be able to help you."

Mollie stared him down though her stomach was in knots. They had to go soon. If Thornton had half a chance, there would either be violence or he would cause trouble for Cadal. It had to end.

"Get out," she said calmly.

Thornton smiled widely and shrugged. "You'll see. No one will offer you what I will." He turned and left without a backward glance.

Mollie felt a sick swirl in her stomach. She lurched past Elizabeth to her bathroom and splashed cold water on her face and neck. Almost as an afterthought, she went to her bedroom and pulled the last of the sweet milk from the backpack next to the bed. What she wouldn't give for some potato rolls to go with it.

The sweet milk had taken the edge off of her nausea when a knock came at the door. "Come in," she called out quietly.

Liam stepped inside. There was concern mixed with his anger now. "Are you all right, miss?"

She nodded. "Yes. My stomach is just upset. Thornton could sour milk fresh from the cow. Thank you, Liam." She met his eyes. "Thank you for getting rid of him."

"Should I call for some toast and tea or maybe some milk?"

"No. I'm not ready for toast, yet." She raised her glass of sweet milk. "This will settle me for now."

Liam motioned to the glass. "What is that? I've seen Mr. Cadal bring it to you when your stomach has been upset."

"It was a gift from Cadal's mother. I think the base is almond milk. I don't know the rest of the recipe, but it works wonders. Would you like to try a taste?"

He nodded and took a sip of the liquid in the glass before handing it back to Mollie. He smiled widely at the flavor. "My grandmother told me about a drink like this once."

She startled. "Someone else makes it? What do they call it? I'm almost out, and it certainly helps." If there was a Human equivalent even remotely close to sweet milk, Cadal wouldn't have to worry about another trip back for more if they were stuck here for a little while.

Liam shook his head. "It had two names. One was ambrosia. The other was Fairy Milk. According to her, you can't get this," he met her eyes before continuing, "unless you know Fairies."

Mollie felt her face pale again. She stared at Liam fearfully for a second before she recovered enough to speak. "Really? How did she come up with that story?"

He took a seat on the chair near the bed and shrugged. "Does it matter?"

"How long have you known?" she asked quietly. The fresh knot in her stomach was worse than the first, and Mollie put the glass down, sure that not even sweet milk would help this pain.

"I had my suspicions about Mr. Cadal before you arrived. Little things, things that didn't add up as they should. You took me by surprise, in the fields the night the poison was planted. When Patrick told me about Thunder, there really wasn't any doubt left about either of you, was there?"

Mollie shook her head and fought back a wave of nausea accompanied by an urge to cry. It was too late.

"It's not safe for you here, is it?"

She wiped away a tear that she couldn't seem to stop. "No, it's not."

"But you don't want to sell to Thornton." It wasn't a question. It was a statement of fact.

Mollie shook her head angrily.

"What about Allen...or Stevens over at *Sidhe Druin*?"

"No. Their lands are a mess. Either of them would ruin this place. I can't allow that."

"What will you do?"

Mollie shrugged. She looked at Liam uncertainly. He had a stake in this. His livelihood was on the line. Liam waited patiently to see what she would say next.

A sudden inspiration struck her. "Liam, what is your fondest wish? If you could have anything?"

He shook his head in confusion. "I don't understand, miss."

"Humor me, Liam. Please tell me. What is your fondest wish?"

He blushed lightly. "Elizabeth," he confided. "To marry Elizabeth."

"Is she willing? Does she love you?"

Liam met her eyes and nodded.

"Then what's stopping you?"

He grimaced. "Money. We won't raise our children in the servants' quarters. We want better for them than that, but I don't have enough money for our own house yet."

"What if you owned a house?"

"I'd ask her tonight."

Mollie nodded. Morda was right after all. "Ask her, then."

Liam looked at her uncertainly. "I don't see how."

Her smile widened in amusement. "If you know where I'll go, you know money is not an issue for me. I need someone who will care for the land. You'll do that. You and Patrick, as a precaution."

He looked at her, his eyes wide in shock, attempting words that wouldn't come.

"I'll take a little money to buy a few things I'd like before I leave, but not much. I'll leave you plenty to run the estate the way we always have, short myself and Cadal."

"Why?" he asked her.

"You'll do it right. You'll care. You'll sweat and bleed for it if that's what is necessary. I know you will, especially now that your family depends on it so directly. Will you promise that?"

Liam nodded. "You're serious?"

"I'll call the solicitor this afternoon. He's done the preliminary work. Aunt Katie demanded it, in case— We'll call it a wedding present."

Liam nodded again. "You have my word," he managed. "Set whatever terms you want. I'll abide by whatever you say."

"Maybe a crop suggestion or two. The land will be yours. You will be the land owner here." She hesitated. "Thank you, Liam. You're making my fondest wish come true, too."

* * * *

Cadal's nerves were alive with a restless itching. Traden was trying to calm him, and he felt badly that it was necessary. The emotions Cadal was receiving from Mollie were disturbing him greatly. His powers were strengthening, but he was still limited, especially when he was widely separated from the sender or when Mollie was in Human form. At the moment, he was frustrated by both handicaps.

Mollie had moved from annoyance to a brutal anger, and he was too far away to help. Cadal felt her sick stomach, much sicker than Mollie had been in well over a week. It was no doubt from the stress. This wasn't good for her.

Finally, he felt the emotion that affected him most, *her fear.* Cadal panicked momentarily, but the emotion was short-lived. *A calm came over her followed by a mild euphoria*, and Cadal relaxed. Her stomach was still troubling her, but Mollie was out of whatever danger she had been in.

Traden matched his glide and peered at him in concern. "What is it, Cadal? What's troubling you? Your reactions are distressing."

Cadal shook his head sadly. "I have to get her out of there, Traden."

Traden looked at him so sharply that he momentarily lost his concentration and dropped slightly before righting himself. "Mollie is in danger?"

"The danger has passed. It was fleeting. I am sure I have one of the Human men who work for her to thank for that. I only leave her at all because I know they will guard her well in my absence."

"Someone would really trouble her now? Are Humans that unfeeling?"

"Not all of them, but some. Some of them take pleasure in exploiting any advantage, even her condition."

Traden paled remarkably. "How can you stand it? I would be a wreck if it were Valia."

Cadal laughed harshly. "Don't think I'm not. I keep reminding myself that she's well guarded, she's usually cautious, and she's more able than most Human men count on."

"Usually? How can she live in such a place and not be constantly on guard?"

"She lets down her guard at times. She forgets how dangerous it is and depends on her self-sufficiency too much. I think it's her Fairy side that takes over and gets her in trouble. At the colony, she can be carefree. She wants so badly to be carefree."

Traden nodded, then he eyed his cousin suspiciously. "What do you mean when you say she's more able than they count on?"

Cadal blushed, smiling sheepishly. "To survive in the Human world for so many years, Mollie has had to learn some skills we don't encourage in the colony. A Human, one who likes to exploit others and is probably the very one responsible for her current upset—" Cadal sighed and his smile disappeared in favor of a hard look that was *foreign and frightening* to Traden. "He tried to take liberties Mollie didn't offer as a means of frightening her into bending to his will."

Traden was shocked into silence for a long moment. "What happened?"

"Before I got there, she defended herself physically." Cadal smiled. "She blacked his eye as a reminder to never attempt touching her again."

Traden laughed nervously. "Violence? Really? She is spirited. What did the Human do?"

"Fortunately, I arrived. He knew he could do nothing. Had the setting been different..." Cadal shuddered. He knew all too well what *could* have happened.

No. He reminded himself that it couldn't. The Harmony, Herself, would have stopped it this time. "He sent back a servant later to corner Mollie while she was alone. The servant threatened her. That, unfortunately, succeeded. Mollie was very cautious after that, but she was in tears by the time I arrived to help her."

Traden looked at him hopelessly. "How do Humans do it?"

He shook his head. "I think that's why their lives are so short, personally. Mollie felt very old for her age for a very long time. I can't say for sure how they all do it. In Mollie's case, she became something she was not. She disguised her true self to survive. As a Fairy, she couldn't exist there. So, she created a shell between herself and the Human realm to hide what she was, even from herself."

"I could see that it would have its uses."

"Yes, but she hid it so well that I was fooled for far too long. Even when the cracks started appearing and I saw glimmers of the true Mollie beneath, I doubted what I saw. Her disguise was that good."

The rest of the trip passed in relative silence. They stuck to the woods to stay in Fairy form as long as they could. When they emerged in Human form, it was a short walk to the house. Cadal's stomach grumbled at the smell of the stew on the stove, but Mollie had to come first.

Liam rose to greet the two men. "Glad you're home, sir. Dinner will be in a little more than an hour."

Cadal nodded. "Thank you. Liam, this is my cousin Traden. He met me in Kinvarra. He'll be spending the night in my old room before returning to my family."

"Welcome, Traden. You might as well come along and get cleaned up for dinner. If you require anything, Elizabeth and I are at your service. The miss is surely waiting for you both." Liam led the way down the hall to the stairs.

"Has Mollie eaten?" Cadal asked.

"Only her Fairy Milk since Thornton left," he replied quietly.

He startled and looked at Liam sharply.

The young man glanced back at him and smiled. "She's fine, really. Patrick and I removed him for her."

Cadal shook his head in confusion. "You said..." Mollie wouldn't tell anyone, not even Liam.

Liam chuckled. "I've known for a long time, sir. Your secret is safe with me, but I hope you brought her more of that milk. Thornton upset her, and that's never a good thing for a woman in her condition."

"Yes, I know."

"I thought you might. Already know her upset, I mean. You seem to have an insight when it comes to the miss."

"Is she all right? She seemed fine when I felt her last."

"Asleep, last time I checked on her. At any rate, she'll be glad to see you both."

They reached the top of the stairs and Cadal met Liam's eyes. "Thank you, Liam, for everything. Please give Traden anything he needs. I need to talk to Mollie."

"Certainly. I'll see you at dinner."

Cadal walked away as Liam showed Traden to the bedroom and bathroom. He slipped into their room.

Mollie was sleeping peacefully. Cadal watched her for several minutes before stepping over her jeans and slipping into the bed next to her. Mollie turned toward him and wrapped her arm around him. Cadal was sure she would fall deeper into sleep, but she opened her eyes and stretched against him.

"Welcome back," she half-yawned.

Cadal rested his hand over their son and checked on him briefly before meeting Mollie's eyes. "You're all right, too?"

She nodded, though she wrinkled her nose. "He made me angry, and I felt ill afterward, but the sweet milk and sleep helped immensely."

"What was it you feared? I felt it. It was fleeting, but you did fear something."

Mollie blushed. "Liam knows," she told him. "He knows about the Fairies, about us being Fairies."

Cadal nodded. "I know. He told me on the way up. Does that scare you?" he asked.

She touched his cheek. "Not anymore. Liam isn't a danger to us. In fact, he's relieved that we'll be safe soon."

"We will?"

Mollie smiled her impish smile and nodded.

"How soon?"

"A week or so, I think. It should be done by then."

Cadal gaped at her.

"Morda was right. I had the answer all along. I just didn't realize it until I was ranting at Thornton."

"So soon?"

She nodded again, her eyes glittering.

"How?" A sudden fear gripped his mind. "You didn't accept Thornton's offer."

Mollie laughed heartily. "Never. Not in a million years. Not for three million dollars." She set her jaw angrily. "Especially after what he said today."

Cadal felt her upset. He kissed her. "Don't worry about that. Tell me the rest."

Mollie shook her head. Cadal was sure tears were not far behind.

"I can't believe he had the nerve—" she choked out.

Cadal kissed her again. Her mind cleared and her passion grew. He sank his face to the buttons on her shirt. Mollie moaned as he started undressing her, pleasuring her with his mouth as her clothing disappeared.

When Cadal was satisfied that Thornton was out of her mind and could be banished again readily, he met her eyes. "Now, who will own the land?"

Mollie traced her lips down his throat. "Liam and Patrick," she told him. She kissed his pulse point, sending a spike of pleasure through him.

"They made an offer?" The shock broke him out of the sensation coursing through him.

Mollie met his eyes in invitation and shook her head. "I'm giving it to them. I'm surprised I didn't realize it before. What do I need the money for?" She ran her hands down his back as she talked. "I'll take some, a little to get a few things before I leave, but the land was always the important thing."

She started unbuttoning his shirt and her mouth returned to the pulse point on his neck while she worked. Cadal's arousal returned with a jolt. Mollie moaned in response.

"Now, can we get back to more important matters?" she whispered.

Cadal nodded his agreement and lowered his head to kiss her again. After their ceremony, he would have to convince her to spend a day or two doing nothing but eating, sleeping, and exploring each other endlessly. They needed a break like that. A time of pure pleasure could only be beneficial in acclimating Mollie to the true freedoms of the carefree life she was embracing.

Mollie undressed him. Cadal sank back into the pillows as Mollie set about returning the favor of pleasuring him. The many dreams of having her in his arms were a joke compared to the reality of her. If Cadal's dreams had been this intense and pleasurable, he would have succumbed to the urge almost immediately. There would be no more wasted time.

Chapter Sixteen

Cadal watched Traden's reaction to Mollie with a touch of amusement. He was waiting in the kitchen when Mollie accompanied Cadal to dinner. Traden rose abruptly and hugged her before asking several times if she was sure she was all right.

Mollie smiled and assured him that she was, and always had been, just fine. When she took her seat, she smiled widely and thanked him. Traden had poured a generous glass of sweet milk and placed two potato rolls next to her plate.

Traden puffed up in pride that he had brightened what he assumed had been a horrible day for her. He was right about that, a fact that Cadal found disturbing because he wasn't there to protect Mollie as he should have been.

Mollie obviously felt better at dinner. She finished her whole plate of stew, most of the potato rolls and all of her sweet milk.

"The baby is hungry tonight," Traden commented with a wide smile. "Your son's going to be a hearty one, Cadal."

Mollie laughed in response. "I don't know about the baby, but I was ravenous. Elizabeth, that stew was wonderful. Is there any left?"

Cadal laughed. "You want more?"

"Not now, but maybe reheated tomorrow," she assured him.

Elizabeth blushed deeply. "I'm glad you like it so much. I was worried when you didn't eat lunch. There's plenty left for tomorrow."

Mollie smiled her impish smile. "I'm going to miss you terribly, Elizabeth. It's not that I can't cook for myself, but you are a fantastic chef and a good friend."

Cadal looked at her in surprise. *What is she up to now?*

Elizabeth looked stricken. "You're leaving?"

Mollie nodded.

"When? Why?"

"A week. Maybe two."

Traden smiled widely. Cadal felt the relief from him at the knowledge that they were leaving so soon.

"We're going to live near Cadal's family. It will be nice to have them close by, especially with the baby coming. Cadal has to return to his own duties. We knew he couldn't stay here forever."

"Who will run the estate?" Elizabeth asked fearfully.

Mollie shook her head and rose to leave. "Let Liam tell you the whole story. I find a full stomach makes me very sleepy." She squeezed Elizabeth's hand and exited toward the library.

Cadal motioned Traden to join him. They followed her down the hall. Cadal knew Mollie was up to something, but he didn't have a clear picture of what it was. She wasn't tired. That part was definitely a lie.

She was stretched out with her head on one of the cushions when the two men entered the room and closed the door behind them. Mollie grinned mischievously, and Cadal found his curiosity mounting.

"What was that all about?" he demanded.

Mollie motioned him to keep his voice down and giggled softly. "I couldn't help it. Liam is terrified. I had to give him a little push."

Cadal shook his head in wonder. "Terrified of what? Push to do what?"

She tried so hard to contain a fresh burst of laughter that she couldn't answer for several minutes. Cadal raised an eyebrow at Traden.

Mollie motioned him closer and met his eyes, whispering her answer. "He can't back down now. They'll be engaged — *promised*," she added in Fairy for Traden's sake, "by morning."

Cadal fought for a breath in his shock. "You arranged this?"

"Not really. It's their fondest wish. They've wanted this forever, but the economics of the situation stopped them. What gives us our freedom also gives them theirs. You see? Besides, Liam told me he was going to ask her tonight. He wasn't getting out of it that easily."

Cadal sank down beside her and leaned over her as he talked. "Why didn't you tell me this?"

She looked up at him innocently. "As I recall, you redirected my attention while I was telling you the story."

Cadal nodded and lay back on one of the other cushions. "You weren't complaining at the time."

"I'm not complaining now. I'm simply explaining why we never got that far into it."

"What do we do?" he asked.

"Give them time alone. Maybe, Traden will grace me with some new Cadal Fairy tales. I'm sure there are quite a few you haven't told me."

Traden laughed heartily and dropped into one of the wingback chairs. "That would be a safe bet. Cadal has a long and illustrious career giving his mother and Morda nightmares with his antics."

Cadal looked at him in shock. "I've long since outgrown that," he protested in Fairy.

Traden followed suit, looking more at ease in his native language. "Yes, but I have at least a century of tales about you, and you know it." He grinned at Mollie. "Cadal was the only child I knew who managed to get called before Morda before he weaned. Zera once commented that Morda only transferred and taught him so much to save his skin."

"Well, she knows about squirrel riding, deep diving, racing raindrops, all of the truly dangerous stories. All you can possibly tell her are childhood pranks."

Traden shook his head and laughed. "I'll wager you haven't told her about the stag. Or have you forgotten that story?"

Cadal groaned and shut his eyes from the memories. "I've *tried* to forget that one. I never got in so much trouble before. Or since. Even Morda scolded me, and she almost never scolded me."

Mollie curled onto his chest and looked down at him. Cadal opened his eyes, and she regarded him with amusement.

"You better tell me. I'll need to know these things before our son tries them." She didn't switch to Human English. Mollie never did when the opportunity to use the Fairy language presented itself.

Cadal blushed. "As if you never did anything dangerous. I've never broken bones."

"I couldn't fly as a child. If I could have, I wouldn't have either."

Cadal sighed and faced Traden. "You might as well tell her. She won't give up until she hears it."

Traden nodded, and Mollie curled down onto Cadal's shoulder to listen.

"One day when Cadal was about thirty-five," Traden began.

"I would have been about twelve or thirteen by Human standards," Cadal interjected. "Keep that in mind, please."

"Oh, no," Mollie groaned. "This definitely doesn't bode well."

"Yes. Remember yourself at that age and keep it firmly in mind."

Mollie gave him a stern look, then looked at Traden with a keen interest.

Traden chuckled and continued. "Cadal slipped away without a keeper and went exploring outside the tree-city. He met a stag in the woods and made friends with the beast. He shifted to Human form and rode around on the stag's back, getting information on the best source for sweet berries. All of the sudden, some Human hunters saw him."

He paused as Cadal groaned and rubbed his eyes. Cadal grumbled a curse on that hunter under his breath, and Mollie snickered.

"They thought he was a ghost or angel or some such thing. He was a young boy with snow-white hair riding a wild animal. What else would they think?"

"What did they do?" Mollie asked.

Cadal laughed. "Two of them ran, but the last one was intent on hunting me along with the stag."

Mollie paled. "What?"

Cadal shook his head. "I knew this was a bad idea, but you wanted to know."

Mollie nodded silently.

Traden continued. "Cadal could have escaped easily, but he refused to leave his friend behind to be slaughtered. It wasn't that he hadn't learned to control those urges. Well, actually, he hadn't, but... Cadal was simply too stubborn to allow such a thing if he could do anything to prevent it. He rode the stag close to the tree-city and attempted something new." He met Mollie's eyes. "You know you can shift objects? Your clothing and such shifts with you?"

She nodded.

"Well, Cadal explained to the stag that he was going to shrink him to help him escape."

Mollie started. "You can do that? Shrink another living thing?"

"It had never been tried before, but it worked, in a manner of speaking."

Cadal laughed. "I wasn't the first after all. In the third Fairy Master reign, a boy named Tuss did it. His subject was a fox, but the results were the same."

Traden shook his head. "You're not getting off that easily, cousin. Well, it worked. Cadal led him directly into the tree-city. That was when it all went wrong."

Cadal laughed. "I wouldn't say it *all* went wrong."

Traden scowled at him. "I'm sure you wouldn't. The stag couldn't handle the shift. The size change was too much for him." He shook his head. "He started running amok inside the tree-city. Cadal was still an amateur at controlling animals though he was very good at talking to them, and he couldn't calm the stag. To make things worse, the hunter's dogs traced the scent of the stag straight to the tree-city."

Mollie tried her best not to laugh at the mental image of a young Cadal chasing the stag through the corridors of the tree-city.

Cadal nodded. "Not a bad guess."

She laughed heartily.

"It's not funny," he assured her.

She laughed harder, remembering how she said the same thing to him when the insect approached her.

Cadal shook his head.

Traden smiled. "At the time, it was terrifying. Now, it is very amusing."

"Especially torturing me with it, I would guess," Cadal grumbled.

"What happened next?" Mollie asked.

Traden shook his head. "Morda had to make a decision. She sent the dogs off first, to protect the colony from that threat. She sent them to a dead-end miles away and instructed them never to come back. In the meantime, Cadal was still trying to stop the stag."

Cadal groaned deeper this time. "You're not going to—"

"Of course I am. Cadal, your bride deserves to know what she has gotten herself into by promising with you and having your child."

"Not what?" Mollie asked.

"Going to tell you about his wild ride."

Mollie glanced at the mortified look on Cadal's face, and he felt the disbelief in her mind.

Traden continued. "The stag got caught up on a doorway, so Cadal jumped on his back and tried to steer him, but the stag was too strong for him."

Mollie sat up and looked down at Cadal. She was frightened and angry. "You didn't," she demanded.

Cadal smiled widely. "Remember *Thunder*?" he asked.

Mollie blushed deeply and nodded.

"Keep that in mind before you say a single word."

She nodded and curled back onto his shoulder without any further thought of outburst.

Traden looked at Cadal and grinned. "I want to hear that tale next. It sounds very interesting."

Cadal nodded, and it was Mollie's turn to groan.

"When Morda was done dealing with the dogs, she went in search of the stag. She came in the east entrance to the Great Chamber, as the stag burst in from the north with Cadal holding on for his life. Morda did the only thing she could. She put the stag to sleep in mid-stride. He went down, and Cadal flew over his head."

Mollie grimaced. "Were you hurt?"

Traden laughed. "He should have been, but he wasn't. Now we know why. It took four of our strongest Fairies to drag the stag outside. While he was still asleep, Morda shifted him to his normal size, and he woke confused by his strange dream."

Cadal sighed. "And I was confined to Morda's throne room with a keeper at each door until she was done and could properly deal with me. She wasn't taking any chances on my slipping away again while her back was turned. I knew how much trouble I was in. Trust me."

"The keepers were stationed to keep Zera from doing you damage before Morda could calm her down. Didn't you ever wonder why your mother was so restrained when they came back?"

"Not really. I was too worried about what would be done."

Mollie nodded grimly. "I can see why you tried to forget it. It was not your finest hour."

Cadal smiled. "I was young and had more ideals than common sense."

"Gee, that sounds familiar," Mollie mused. "I remember I was like that not so long ago."

"Yes, my dear bride, and you too shall grow out of it in time. Hopefully, I won't have to call you before me too many times before that happens."

Mollie gave him a scathing look. "You're some help."

Cadal smiled and rolled over her to kiss her. "Now, let's tell Traden about *Thunder*. He deserves to know what I've gotten myself into by promising to you and giving you a child to carry. There may still be stags around. I may have to assign Traden as your keeper for a short time until you mature."

* * * *

Mollie was sorry to see Traden go. She knew he was going back with some interesting *Mollie tales* that would be passed around the colony, though he claimed he wouldn't pass around the one about Thunder.

She smiled inwardly at the thought that she was going to end up as infamous as Cadal was, if many more were told. After all, he'd had over a century to make a name for himself, but dealing with Humans tended to land you in trouble a lot. Mollie shuddered as she considered some of the tales she could tell the Fairies. She felt sure that Valia and Traden weren't ready for that at all.

Liam asked Mollie to go over the books with him while they had the free time, but she soon surmised he already knew what he was doing.

She met his gaze. "Cadal told you not to leave my side, didn't he?"

Liam blushed deeply and nodded. "He and Traden both, miss."

Mollie shut the book on the desk and shot him a severe look. "If that's all you have to do, I have a better plan for it. Where are the best clothing stores around? Not the most expensive, but the best?"

Liam thought about it for a moment. "There is one in Ballynaclogh I trust. They have a good selection and good quality. There are also two in Kinvarra Elizabeth likes quite a bit. Why?"

Mollie smiled. "Get Elizabeth and get your jackets on. I don't have much time left. I'd like to pick up a few things."

It seemed like a good idea. Cadal and Traden had taken everything she had chosen with them already. The things she had here were intended to stay here for the most part. If she didn't overdo it, she could pack what she chose into a small backpack like the one Cadal brought back with the food in it the day before, the one she had left there last trip.

One small backpack couldn't be a burden on the trip, despite what Morda thought. She had done it before. She knew Cadal's clothing would only take up a large duffel like Cadal and Traden were carrying out today, and there were a few things she wanted to get before she left.

Liam regarded her warily. "I don't think this is what Mr. Cadal had in mind. Maybe you should wait for him to accompany you tomorrow."

"How can I buy anything for Cadal, to surprise Cadal, if he's with me?"

Liam sighed.

"Besides, if you and Elizabeth are with me, I'll be fine. I'd like to see Tucker try something with you there."

Liam nodded and went to get Elizabeth while Mollie pulled on her hiking boots and coat upstairs.

Mollie found shopping in the village frustrating. When she found a beautiful baby boy outfit, the shopkeeper tried to convince her to opt for the little girl

outfit "because you know it must be a girl, Miss Hardy."
She said Mollie's name with a certain distaste, and
Mollie sighed at her emphasis on the 'Miss.' When
Mollie, picked out a negligee that she loved, the woman
raised an eyebrow and commented on how daring it
was. "Don't you think so, *Miss* Hardy." When she picked
out a shirt for Cadal, the woman wrinkled her nose
slightly in disapproval.

In the end, Mollie purchased only those three
things and they left in the car for the other stores.
Mollie had considered not buying anything there, but if
she didn't find anything she liked better in Kinvarra,
she would be stuck returning there. Mollie had no
intentions of doing that.

Shopping outside the village was much more fun.
Mollie bought three maternity outfits, a dress for
Elizabeth, and several more outfits for the baby before
deciding she had extinguished the room available to her
in the backpack. If she packed it tightly, she could fit it
all, plus a few of her oversized shirts that would fit
longer over a growing baby. Mollie was sure Valia and
Zera would supplement with more colony-style
maternity clothes. She had more than enough to be
comfortable.

They returned to the house that afternoon. Mollie
felt wonderful, despite the strange treatment she
received in the village. She reflected over it while she
helped Elizabeth cook dinner.

"Elizabeth, what do the people in the village say
about me?"

Elizabeth glanced at her under her lashes. "They
vary, miss. People always do."

Mollie smiled. "In other words, Cadal told you not to
tell me," she guessed.

"Yes, miss, he did." She smiled weakly.

"Is it that bad?"

Elizabeth shrugged. "I've heard worse. Very little of it's true, so why concern yourself?"

"The true things involve Cadal and me mostly?"

"Some people can only feel good about themselves by casting down another. It's sad but true."

"Translation? Yes, Mollie, they do indeed." Mollie smiled as she cut potatoes into a pot of water.

"You're leaving soon. Does it matter?"

"I suppose not. I just wondered." Mollie glanced at the small ring on Elizabeth's hand. If she was wearing one, no one would dare say a word to her. She was fairly certain about that, anyway. "It seems like such a silly thing to persecute someone for. I wonder, if Thornton wasn't my adversary, would it even be an issue?"

Elizabeth shook her head slowly. "Probably not. You already had two strikes against you. You're a foreigner, and you're a Blake woman. Mr. Thornton was icing on the cake, though a thick layer, no doubt."

"He's going to be very unhappy when he discovers I've given it away from under him."

"I know it."

"You don't mind that the estate comes with that ball and chain attached?"

Elizabeth laughed. "Not at all. He'll learn quickly enough that Liam won't stand for it. No offense, miss, but talking the men out of defending you probably caused you more problems than it solved, in the long run."

Mollie put the pot on to boil. "Maybe so, but I didn't want them in trouble because of me."

"Wouldn't be because of you, miss. If you're attacked, defending you is because of them that attacked you," she reasoned.

"Maybe so. Either way, after Friday, you'll have to watch your back. Be careful. I don't want you hurt, Elizabeth."

Chapter Seventeen

The next few days passed peacefully. At Mollie's request, Liam, Elizabeth, and Patrick kept the impending gift of the estate a secret. She wanted to be safely away when Thornton found out about it.

Patrick started eating at the main table with the others, and dinners became much more animated with his addition. Mollie mused that they should have made that particular move long ago, but Patrick was adhering to a tradition that Mollie couldn't fathom.

Mollie drew up several crop rotations that appealed to Liam. He didn't question that it would be best for the land. With what Mollie was, Liam admitted it would be foolish to assume less from any plan she came up with.

Elizabeth being roughly the same size as Mollie turned out to be a boon. She inherited all of the clothing Mollie wasn't taking. If it weren't for Elizabeth's cap of dark curls, they might have appeared as sisters on some days. Though their friendship was stronger than ever, Elizabeth and the two men couldn't seem to get into the mode of calling Mollie and Cadal anything other than 'miss' and 'sir.' Finally, Mollie gave up trying to correct it.

Mollie agonized over Xanthe's book of Fairy tales. She'd held onto it like a lifeline for so long that the thought of leaving it was painful to her, but it served no purpose in the colony. Most of the Fairies in the stories were still alive. It would simply be memories to them, and she could retell most of them from memory.

Ultimately, Mollie decided to leave Xanthe's book for Liam and Elizabeth. "Read it to your children," she told them. "Let them experience the beauty and innocence. The world needs that, I think."

Elizabeth smiled warmly and accepted it from Mollie's hand. "There are empty pages in here. Maybe we should add the tale of the Blake women and how Mollie fell in love with Cadal and returned home."

Mollie laughed. "Who would believe it?"

Elizabeth suggested writing a book of Human stories, even the sanitized Grimm's tales, for the Fairies, as a lark. Mollie decided against it almost immediately. It would be a book of horrors to them. There would be little amusement when they were read in the colony and likely a few tears.

By Thursday, Mollie was looking forward to signing it all away. She would be free to go home to the tree-city and marry Cadal in little more than a day.

Liam and Cadal had disappeared to the stable, and Mollie was antsy. "I'm going to brush Thunder," she told Elizabeth.

Mollie and Thunder had formed a sort of understanding after his illness. She wanted to ride him, but Cadal wouldn't allow it. Mollie understood his concern. Now was not the time to get thrown from a horse.

"Should I walk you?" Elizabeth asked.

Mollie smiled. "It's just over the hill, and Liam and Cadal are there. If I screamed loud enough, they could probably hear me from here."

Elizabeth nodded. "Don't forget your coat, miss. It's dropping fast out there."

Mollie grabbed it off of the rack distractedly. "Got it," she called out. She set it down to grab a flashlight, which she stashed in the back of her belt for the trip back, and headed for the door lost in thought. "Be back soon," she called over her shoulder to Elizabeth.

The chill outside wasn't as bad as Mollie expected for so late in the day. She set off up the trail and considered the few last-minute things she had to do. A cold blast of wind cut through her heavy sweater, and Mollie realized she hadn't picked the coat up again after she grabbed the flashlight. She muttered a curse and turned back for the house.

Mollie started as she came face to face with Tucker. She turned abruptly, planning to run, but his arms were already around her. One huge hand covered her mouth and the other arm encircled her ribs, pinning her arms to her side. Mollie tried to scream, but it came out as a strangled squeal that was immediately lost on the wind. She started kicking at him, and he tightened his grip in response, until Mollie found it hard to breathe. She settled into his grasp and labored the cold air in and out as effectively as she could.

Tucker leaned his face close to her ear. "That's better. You and me, we're going to have a little talk, a talk we should have had months ago. But first, let's get somewhere private. Too much chance of being interrupted here." He lifted her off the trail and into the woods. Tucker really was stronger and faster than she'd anticipated.

* * * *

Cadal was discussing the animals with Liam when the first shock wave hit him. He sucked in his breath audibly and ground his fingertips into the post beside him as the sense of vertigo washed over him. *Mollie moved fluidly from a mild annoyance to fear to panic.*

He tried to launch for the door, but a crippling band cut off his breathing. *No, her breathing.* Cadal landed heavily on the floor. He shook his head violently to clear enough of the sensation to get moving. Morda didn't suffer this. There had to be a way to control how much of him this took over. Cadal found his feet again and headed for the door in a sort of haze.

Liam appeared beside him and steadied him as another wave of vertigo assaulted him. "What is it?" he asked.

Cadal looked at him and pushed off again. "Mollie. Something is very wrong."

"She's at the house. It can't be bad," he assured Cadal.

He shook his head. It was bad, but he couldn't make sense of the sensations yet.

As they came over the hill, Cadal's heart stopped momentarily. Elizabeth was walking up the trail with Mollie's coat in her hands.

She met their eyes uncertainly. "Where is the miss?" she asked.

Cadal sat down heavily. It was hard to breathe. "She's not with you?" he asked.

Tears filled her eyes and she shook her head slowly. "She left to groom Thunder. She forgot her coat. She set it down and forgot it."

Cadal closed his eyes. He was getting flashes of what was happening from Mollie, but it wasn't enough. He needed more to find her.

Liam stepped in. "How long ago did she leave?"

"Ten minutes."

"Get the men out in the woods. Get them now," Liam ordered.

Elizabeth turned and ran. Cadal heard her pounding back down the trail.

It was still difficult to breathe. Mollie hoped talking was all Tucker intended. She stifled a sob. It probably wasn't. She scanned the woods for Cadal. He had to be able to feel this. As they moved further and further away, her hopes sank. Cadal may know it, but he couldn't find her. If he could, he would have been here by now.

He opened his eyes and locked on something at his feet. It was a flashlight, the one Mollie typically took. He felt her pain and heard her thoughts, more of them all the time.

She had to do something, but what? Mollie toyed with the idea of shifting Tucker, but she didn't know what his reaction would be. What if he went on a rampage and still had her trapped in his arms? To fly, she would have to shift first and either take him with her or be trapped in his arms in Fairy form. It would be too risky and take too long. Rain or snow would take too long to call, and wind would only be good for flying. Wouldn't it? She wasn't sure that she could call a gale capable of damage. She wasn't strong enough to do that yet, was she? The land couldn't help her. Animals? How do you connect with an animal you can't see? There had to be a way.

She was inventorying her Fairy gifts and finding nothing that would help her escape. He couldn't find her. All Mollie could see were trees. There were no landmarks, and she was looking for him to save her. It couldn't be like this. He couldn't sit back and watch while she got hurt again.

Liam bent down to him. "What can you do?"

Cadal heard the bell ringing at the house. Elizabeth was rallying the men to search for her.

He shook his head and set his jaw angrily. "I can feel her, but I can't find her. I don't know how to find her." *Yet.* That was something that passed at the final transfer, but he needed it now.

"Morda," he whispered. Could Morda find her? A Fairy was connected to the Fairy Mistress at a naming ceremony, but Mollie never had a naming ceremony.

Cadal remembered the morning after their arrival. Morda had touched Mollie's forehead. Dizziness had assaulted Mollie, and Morda had smiled and nodded. Did Morda mark Mollie then? Cadal prayed that she had. At the very least, Morda would be able to exact the ultimate duty upon Tucker if need be. Cadal could do that himself if he could find her.

Tucker dropped her roughly. Mollie wrapped her arms around her aching chest and sank to a fallen tree. Her ribs and arms hurt, and the cold was getting to her. If only she hadn't put down her coat.

Mollie shook her head in wonder that she was worrying about a coat when Tucker wasn't going to let her go. He couldn't do that, could he? Then again, James let her go. She shook her head again. She couldn't take the chance. The first opening that presented, she would have to try to get away from him.

Tucker leaned close to her. "Mr. Thornton made you a good offer. Why are you so rude to him? We talked about that, remember?"

Mollie met his eyes briefly before deciding she didn't want to get locked in that cold stare. "I remember."

"You don't want enemies, do you?"

"Not particularly."

"No, you don't want enemies. You have a little someone to worry about, don't you?"

"Yes, I do." Tucker seemed calm enough this way. Maybe if she stayed cool and collected, he would as well.

Cadal buried his face in his hands. He could hear Tucker's words as they echoed in Mollie's mind. She was hurting, she was frightened, and she was so very cold.

"This isn't really a good place to raise a little girl, is it? I mean, working a farm— That's not a life for a little girl."

"I guess not. Working a farm isn't for little girls," she agreed.

"Ah, but that's right. You think this one is a little boy, don't you?"

Mollie cursed her trip to the village clothing store. Tucker couldn't have that information unless he got it there.

"Think you broke the mold? No more girls for the Blake women?"

Mollie lowered her gaze and wrapped her arms closer around her body. "Hope springs eternal. It would be nice—"

"This is a dangerous area. There are vandals. You got attacked in your own fields. It's not safe. You take your eyes off a child for just a minute and who knows what could happen."

Mollie pressed her hands to her stomach, suddenly sick. It wasn't bad enough to threaten her? He was threatening her baby? She had to get out of this somehow. Mollie nodded mutely, dizzy and shaking.

Tucker threatened their baby. Cadal launched to his feet and ran for the stable with Liam close behind.

He grabbed a bridle and slipped it onto Thunder. He had to find her even if he had to do it the Human way. He sucked in his breath as her pain assaulted him.

"It would be a shame if something happened to you. If you and your baby were gone, the land would revert to your mother, wouldn't it? Anyone would have a fair chance at buying it again. Wouldn't they?" Tucker clamped his hand on her chin and raised her eyes to him again.

Mollie felt a stab of uncertainty. If he meant to kill her, maybe she could head him off. "No, it wouldn't," she lied smoothly. "It would revert to Cadal. I have sole ownership and I left it to Cadal. If I die—" She shook her head.

"He has no ties to you." His fingers clenched into her cheeks. "It could be argued. It could be won. It's your family's lands. A judge wouldn't allow it."

Mollie bit back a sob. He had his agenda, and her bluff hadn't been strong enough. She couldn't steer this situation any more than Cadal could steer the stag. It was too big now.

Tucker grabbed Mollie's wrist painfully and pulled her hand in front of her face, her left hand. "He has no ties to you. He has no rights."

Cadal led Thunder out into the clearing.

Mollie blinked back tears. He wanted her to cry or to scream, like James wanted a fight. Maybe if she didn't give him what he wanted, Tucker would give up, too. She almost laughed at how flimsy and ridiculous that sounded. She was grasping at straws.

Tucker smiled at her discomfort. "I've heard you're like a man. I've heard you work like a man. You fight like a man. You think like a man. You can't do everything like a man, can you?"

His hand tightened again, and Mollie tried to shut out the pain. She had done it once, but this pain was more physical.

"No," he continued. "You don't look like a man. You're pregnant. That means you're definitely not a man."

Tucker clamped down tighter on her wrist, and Mollie gritted her teeth against the pain that spiked up her arm. One more like that and the bone would snap, she told herself.

"Maybe I should find out," he mused close to her ear.

Cadal startled at Tucker's threat. *Mollie's logic shut down.* Cadal knew it was the worst thing he could have threatened her with.

Mollie screamed. It wasn't the pain that got to her, though it helped. It couldn't happen. Not again. If she tried to stop him, Tucker could do a lot of damage to her and to her son. If she didn't... Cadal's face filled her mind. That was not an option.

Cadal could hear Mollie's scream in his mind, but it seemed also very faintly by ear. She wasn't far, but there was too much to search. Cadal cursed her panic. Tucker couldn't do it. He could hurt her, even kill her, but he couldn't force himself on her. She didn't remember it.

A sudden thought occurred to her. Thunder. Mollie reached out to him. She knew where he was. She pictured him. She called for his help desperately. He had to hear and help her, but Mollie wasn't sure that Thunder could find her any easier than Cadal could. She prayed her Fairy aura could lead the horse in somehow.

Thunder bolted. Cadal tried to stop him, tried to control him, but Mollie's hold was too strong. They were friends. Mollie and Thunder had formed a child-bond, and she called in on it. Thunder slipped away mentally, then physically as the reins were ripped from Cadal's hand. If Cadal had been on him, Thunder would have carried him directly to her.

He was back at the beginning. Squirrel couldn't follow Thunder, and she couldn't find Mollie. Even if he broke through Mollie's hold after Thunder did whatever she asked of him, the horse would be incapable of telling Cadal where Mollie was. He could only hope that Thunder made it to her in time.

Cadal sank to his knees and screamed in frustration. He couldn't lose her. How could he stop it? He had to stop it.

Liam sank down beside him and watched Cadal worriedly.

Tucker grabbed her roughly by the front of her sweater and dragged her to her feet. "What do you say? Should I find out?"

Mollie shook her head as a single tear spilled down her cheek. He was like James. "No, this is a mistake. This isn't something you want to do."

If he did, there would be no letting her go. This wasn't James. The situation was completely different this time. She hadn't come here willingly. He couldn't expect anyone to believe she had. Mollie prayed that Thunder or Cadal would find her soon.

Tucker smiled coldly, and Mollie knew he had made his decision.

"Mr. Thornton just wanted the land any way he could get it. I like this idea. It's like a fringe benefit while getting the job done."

He kissed her roughly. Mollie pushed at his chest violently, but Tucker anticipated the move and released her wrist so she stumbled backwards onto the frozen ground. He laughed in amusement as she landed.

Mollie scrambled to her feet and launched toward the trees at her back, but Tucker's hand snagged her arm as she moved away. His smile was vicious. He jerked her around to face him. His fist connected with her cheekbone, and colors exploded before her as she crumpled back to the ground.

Like a predator playing with his prey before the kill, Cadal mused.

Mollie sank into a mental fog where Cadal had a clearer image though it was disjointed. Cadal balled his fists and hit the ground beside him as he felt Tucker's hands on her. Mollie barely registered it in her state. He was thankful for that.

Mollie thought that she was imagining the hoof beats. It was a nice dream, a wishful sort of daydream invading the haze she was trapped in.

Tucker moved away abruptly. His hands broke contact with her, and Mollie tried in vain to focus on him.

A flash of something white crossed her field of vision. Tucker disappeared from view. A scream rattled her nerves, but she couldn't seem to work out who was screaming or why before the world faded away.

While Mollie was incapable of connecting the images and sounds she was experiencing, Cadal cringed, then sighed in relief. Thunder ran Tucker down. The images Cadal received could mean nothing less. For the moment, Mollie was safe. Cadal lost contact with her as consciousness slipped away.

He considered his options. Mollie had no coat. By the time they found her by any conventional means, it would be too late.

Cadal reached for Thunder. The horse couldn't tell him where they were. Nor could he be called back to Cadal and find his way back to Mollie without her active participation, but perhaps he could do something useful. The horse had to wake her. Thunder had to bring her home. For a long time, Mollie wouldn't wake. Cadal was considering the futility and danger of a flight, when she opened her eyes.

Mollie startled at the object brushing against her cheek. Thunder's face hung over her. He was nuzzling her. She touched his face.

"Good boy," she crooned in a voice so groggy Mollie hardly recognized it as her own.

Thunder pushed at her shoulder. Mollie didn't understand. She couldn't concentrate. She couldn't talk to him.

She lost consciousness again. Cadal wished he could receive information from Thunder at this distance, but it was impossible. He could only order the great beast and gauge the response from Mollie.

Thunder nudged her again. And again. Finally, it made some sort of sense. Mollie had to get up. She had to move. It was dark and much colder than when she passed out, or maybe it merely felt like it was. Mollie couldn't be sure. She closed her eyes. Thunder snorted next to her cheek.

Mollie touched his face. "I'm going," she grumbled at him.

Once she was awake, Mollie was still incapacitated. It took Thunder an excruciatingly long time to get her to her feet. Cadal cursed and growled as he worked. Mollie lost consciousness between almost every prodding move he had the horse make.

She moved stiffly, slowly. A wave of dizziness washed over her as she got to her feet. She leaned heavily against Thunder's side and wrapped her hand over his back. *"I can't,"* she whispered. *"I can't get up there."*

Cadal ordered Thunder to accommodate Mollie, based on what he felt from her. It was uncomfortable for the horse, but the devoted animal understood that Mollie was injured and needed him, so he complied with Cadal's commands.

Thunder sank to his belly and Mollie lowered herself onto his back. It was awkward for him. She could tell that, but he did it for her. She wrapped her arms around his neck and laid her legs down his sides to drag on the ground. The horse got to his feet and started walking slowly as if he knew she couldn't do more.

"Thank you," she whispered to him. *Mollie flattened herself out as best she could. She drank in the heat from his body as he walked. Mollie closed her eyes to the sway of his body. "Nice dream..."*

Cadal sighed deeply as Thunder started moving. He gave one last order. *"Do not lose her. Bring her home."* before releasing the beast to follow his command. He met Liam's worried stare. "Thunder has her. He has to go slow."

Liam nodded. "She's hurt?"

"Yes. You should call a doctor."

"How far is she?"

Cadal shrugged.

"How badly is she hurt?"

"I don't know. I have no experience with violent injuries."

"What happened to her? Maybe I can take a guess."

Cadal explained briefly the entire sequence of events.

Liam paled and sat back heavily as he spoke. "He's dead? You're sure?"

"If he's not, he will be soon. Thunder was serious about protecting her. He couldn't let Tucker hurt her again. Thunder has a bond with Mollie, a Fairy child-bond. There is no stronger link an animal can form with one of our kind."

Liam looked at Cadal fearfully. "You told him to do that?"

Cadal shook his head. "No, Mollie asked for his help. The rest was Thunder's choice. That was why he ran. You heard her scream?"

Liam nodded. "Faintly."

"So did he. Call the doctor. She can't be far."

"What about you?"

Cadal shook his head. "I told him to bring her here. I'm not leaving."

Liam sprinted for the house. Cadal knew he would most likely be back before Mollie arrived and cursed himself for not telling Liam to bring a blanket back. To his surprise, the young man topped the hill only a few short moments later, and he thought of the blanket himself.

Cadal raised an eyebrow to him. "So quickly?"

"Elizabeth had already called the constable. John is on his way. She's calling the doctor now. I told her to tell him that Mollie is missing, that we found her torch, and that we could hear her scream and fear she's hurt. I couldn't justify any more than that, but Edwards will come quickly with that information. He's a good man."

Cadal nodded again and turned his eyes toward the trees where Thunder had disappeared. He knew the horse's pace was painfully slow, but it had been half an hour since Cadal sent him on his way and there was still no sign of the horse or his rider.

Cadal wished again that he possessed the ability to track her as Morda could. He supposed the Fairy Mistress hadn't made it in time to help her granddaughter. He could imagine Morda's upset at the fact.

While they waited for Thunder, Liam cautioned Cadal about the things he shouldn't say when the constable got around to talking to him. There were things he had to pretend not to know, things he *couldn't* know if he was a Human named William Cadal. Liam finished it up with a short lesson in the Human psychology of the situation, which was not very different than what Cadal was already feeling.

Cadal was across the corral and halfway over the fence before he consciously registered that he could see Thunder coming out of the woods. He touched the horse's face fondly. "Still, old boy. You did fine."

He checked Mollie. She was unconscious on Thunder's back, as he knew she would be. Her legs hung over his sides and her arms were wrapped around his neck loosely, her face pressed to his shoulder.

He eased her off of the horse's back. Liam appeared at his side and spread out the quilt for Cadal to wrap her in. Once she was nestled in his arms again, Cadal ordered Thunder to his stall and added his thanks.

They made it back to the house quickly. Cadal brushed past the stunned constable to their bedroom while Liam tackled the job of trying to explain what had happened to John McConnell to buy Cadal time to do whatever he might have to for her alone.

As he laid Mollie on the bed, Elizabeth breezed in. She pulled Mollie's left hand from the quilt gently. Elizabeth removed the ring from her own hand and placed it on Mollie's. She met his eyes and nodded. "You'll have much less trouble this way," she told him.

Cadal smiled weakly. "Thank you, Elizabeth. Ring the bell. It's cold and dark. The men will need warm food and drinks. Make sure they get everything they need."

She smiled. "The miss would say the same thing. The doctor will be here soon. I'll make some tea for when she wakes."

He nodded, and Elizabeth disappeared from view.

Cadal moved quickly. He had to know how bad it was. He ran his hand over her wrist and her cheek. Nothing was broken, though the bruising was severe. Her sweater was pulled out of shape over her chest where Tucker had dragged her to her feet. Cadal ran his hands over the rest of her. Mollie had bruises on her chest and arms and a few on her legs, but overall, it was much better than he'd expected.

He placed his hand over their son. Cadal held his breath as information poured in. Despite Tucker's threats, despite his treatment of Mollie, their baby was safe and sound within her womb. Cadal sighed in relief and sank to the bed next to her. He pulled the quilt over them both and wrapped her in his arms. Then he started trying to rub his warmth into her. She was so very cold.

Chapter Eighteen

Cadal heard the conversation, as Liam mounted the stairs.

"What more could you want, John?" Liam demanded. "I told you what she said. You know who to ask."

Cadal grimaced at the scene that was coming, but he knew Liam had bought them the time they'd discussed at the stable.

Liam entered the open door without knocking, followed by John McConnell.

The rather gruff-looking constable stopped in surprise. "What is this?" he demanded.

Cadal met his eyes briefly. "I'm trying to warm her. Skin to skin would be far more effective, but I don't want to risk causing her more injury," he lied. In reality, Cadal knew the cold was the only true worry he had for her, but this worked to his advantage. He shouldn't know. Cadal glared at Liam. "Where is that doctor?" he snapped at his friend.

Liam nodded. They had discussed this scene at length. Apparently, Liam approved of how well Cadal was carrying it off. That was a minor relief.

"He's on his way, sir. He'll be here soon."

Cadal shot Liam an irritated look and returned his attentions to Mollie.

McConnell cleared his throat. "I need to ask you some questions, Mr. Cadal."

Cadal glared at him over Mollie's cheek. "Not now."

"I'm afraid I have to, sir."

Cadal looked at Mollie's face and sighed. What he said next wasn't part of the act. "Then ask me here. I'm not leaving her." He sounded as distracted as he was.

If Liam was surprised, he hid it well.

McConnell nodded uncertainly. "I understand. You care for her."

Cadal scowled at him. That time, the anger was real. "We're engaged," he informed the man coldly. "She's my bride."

The constable looked at him in shock and confusion. "I'm sorry. I didn't know." Cadal didn't answer him, so McConnell continued. "Where were you, Mr. Cadal?"

"At the stable with Liam."

"How did you know Miss Hardy was missing?"

"Elizabeth. She came up to deliver Mollie's coat to her and discovered she never reached the stable."

"She came to the stable?"

Cadal understood his intensity. McConnell thought he had something.

He shook his head. "We were on our way down the trail. Elizabeth was coming up."

"What happened then?"

"I couldn't breathe. I know Liam was talking to Elizabeth, giving orders. I can't even tell you what he said. I realized Mollie's torch was lying there on the trail. I had to find her, and I was wasting time. I went back to the stable."

"What for?"

"Thunder. My horse. I could cover a lot more ground that way."

"You didn't leave the stable. Why?"

"I got Thunder bridled and outside, but Mollie screamed. Thunder bolted, and I lost my grip on him."

"Why didn't you take the other horse?"

Cadal hesitated. The real reason was that he was busy trying to affect the situation, but he and Liam had discussed the proper answer to this question. "Liam convinced me not to." He shook his head bitterly. "I was angry, frustrated. I wasn't thinking straight. Liam convinced me I'd be more trouble in the woods than an asset. Besides, I wanted to be where she was most likely to show up."

McConnell nodded stiffly. "She wouldn't come to the house?"

"Mollie might have, but Elizabeth was there, and we'd hear the bell if she went there. She was closer to the stable when—" Cadal shook his head sadly.

"Liam was with you the whole time?"

"Except for a few minutes. He came to tell Elizabeth to call the doctor, after he made sure I would sit still and wait for him. And to bring back a quilt," he added.

"Why the quilt?"

"Mollie forgot her coat, remember? The temperature was dropping," Cadal explained in annoyance. That should have been obvious, and the irritation in his voice was genuine.

"What happened when she came back?"

"I took her off of Thunder, wrapped her in the quilt, and brought her back here."

"The horse? How did Ms. Hardy end up with the horse?"

Cadal shook his head. "Thunder loves Mollie. He'd follow her around like a puppy if he were free to do it." It was one of the dangers of connecting with a domestic animal, especially in the childlike way Mollie did it. "He bolted when she screamed, but he went toward her. Horses are smart. Maybe he did what we couldn't. To be honest, I don't care how it happened. As long as Mollie is back in one piece, I don't care."

"Was she unconscious when she got back to the stable?"

Cadal met his eyes. He remembered what Liam said on the stairs. "No. Almost, but not quite."

"Did she say anything?"

"She mentioned Tucker and something about Thornton."

"What did she say? I need to know."

"I don't remember," Cadal snapped. "I was more concerned with Mollie at that point. She said something about Thornton wanting her land any way he could get it, about him giving Tucker the job of making sure that happened." Cadal knew he told Liam that was said. He hoped fervently that it was close to what Liam told McConnell.

Out of the corner of his eye, Cadal saw Liam nod grimly in agreement. He pretended not to notice. There was no need to draw suspicion.

Cadal locked on McConnell's eyes. "Anything else?" he asked pointedly.

"No. I'll need to speak to Miss Hardy later, but that will be all for now. Thank you for your help."

"Don't thank me. Just find him." Cadal looked at Mollie miserably. "Find him, before I do."

* * * *

The doctor arrived almost precisely as McConnell left the house. Cadal balked at the idea of leaving Mollie.

Liam took him firmly by the shoulders and walked him out. "Elizabeth will stay with her. She'll be fine. Let the doctor work."

Cadal would not be permitted to stay this time, despite his protests.

In the kitchen, Liam sat a glass of amber liquid in front of Cadal. "Drink this and calm down," he ordered.

Cadal smiled weakly at the thought of Liam giving him an order, but the young man had been giving him good advice so far. He grimaced and swallowed the first mouthful. It had the alcohol of nectar wine, but it tasted awful. "What is this?"

Liam smiled. "It's called whiskey, Cadal. The nectar of the gods."

Cadal quickly took another mouthful down. It certainly wasn't getting any better. "Doesn't taste like nectar to me," he commented dryly. "What are we celebrating?"

Liam sobered. "We're not celebrating at all. We're getting you drunk."

Cadal swallowed the third mouthful painfully in his surprise. "Why?"

"To relax you."

Cadal stared at him in confusion.

Liam sighed and sat across from him. "Look, Mollie needs you, but she doesn't need a nervous wreck. I could see you up there. Your anger and irritation were real. You need to take the edge off. People do that sometimes. You don't understand that, and ordinarily I would never suggest it to you, but this one time—"

Cadal pushed the glass away. "Thank you, but I don't want that."

Liam nodded. "Your choice, of course." He picked up the glass and drained the last of it then smiled. "I think you've done enough damage to do the job already."

Cadal looked at him in surprise. "I only had three mouthfuls."

"Which should take the edge off nicely. I'd be happier to get another slug or two in you, but it will do." Liam shook his head. "We need to talk."

"About what?"

"There are a few problems. You're going to have to be prepared to leave in a hurry."

Cadal shook his head adamantly. "Not without Mollie."

"If you must. You know I'll care for her in your absence. I'll even bring her to you, wherever and whenever you need it."

"Why now? Why would there be problems now? We're so close, and we've done nothing to bring further problems."

"Thornton won't go down without a fight. It may be impossible once you two leave. Without Mollie to testify or even with that testimony—" He shook his head and began again. "Thornton knows you're not who you claim to be. He'll use that to take the attention off of himself if he can."

"How do you know that?" Cadal asked quietly.

"I heard him threaten the miss with it the afternoon you left to meet Traden. She didn't tell you, did she?"

Cadal sighed. Maybe he should have listened to what Mollie had to say after all, even if it upset her. "It's my own fault. I didn't let her. I wanted her to relax." He smiled at Liam crookedly. Cadal was beginning to feel the warm glow sinking into his muscles. "There is a lot of that going around, it seems." His smile disappeared. "What else did he threaten her with?"

Liam shook his head. "I didn't hear most of it. I know he threatened that you would leave her and the baby when people found out you were lying about who you were, that she would be abandoned without your love and support."

Cadal cringed at the thought of such a thing. He remembered Mollie's description of Human relationships. Some Human men would do that.

"Don't worry. She laughed at him for that one. Thornton didn't care much for it."

Cadal nodded. "What else?"

Liam scowled and his face darkened. Cadal could guess he was brutally angry about the rest.

"He told her she had been tricked into taking you into her bed, that she'd disgraced herself by allowing it. He told her no one would respect her and she wouldn't be able to run the estate that way. He told her she would be forced to sell when everyone was against her. He's been campaigning for that."

Cadal felt a sick swirl in his stomach. "Campaigning?"

"He's been spreading awful lies about both of you. Miss Mollie asked Elizabeth about it. She wanted to get out and do some shopping, while you and Traden went back. The three of us went to Ballynaclogh." Liam sighed. "She was shunned. It was subtle, but she knew it. The miss pretended to ignore it, but it upset her. In the end, we went to Kinvarra to shop, so she could enjoy herself."

Cadal nodded. "I think you're right. This is a problem."

"You're simply not accustomed to life here. She knew. She saw it coming. Not this, obviously. She knew it was getting ugly, and she wanted out before it exploded. One day, Cadal. She missed her mark by one day."

"As soon as she's able, we're leaving. We have to."

"You may have to go before that."

Cadal shook his head. "I can't do that. It's my job to protect her. I won't leave her again."

"What would be worse? A few days without her, knowing you are both safe, or sitting in a jail cell while they try to figure out where you come from and why you're lying?"

"They wouldn't have to know I was still here. I can arrange that."

Liam sighed. "It would be a chance, but it's a chance you're going to take, isn't it?"

Cadal nodded silently. If it came to that, it was exactly what he would have to do. Getting away was no problem for him. It was Mollie he had to be concerned about.

The two men settled into the library to wait for the doctor to come down. Cadal stared at the fire and considered his options. If he were Human, Cadal had no doubt Thornton would be hurting worse than Mollie was already, even if it landed him in that jail cell. As Mollie said, he was more civilized than that. He had to be more civilized than that. If Cadal ended up in a cage, he wouldn't get back out. He had too much to hide.

Mollie wouldn't be amused if he got himself in that kind of trouble. It would upset her greatly, and Cadal wouldn't do that to her, despite the drive to take care of Thornton and his threats permanently. He had the means to do it. A short flight in Fairy form and a simple touch and thought... Thornton would be found dead, and it would be untraceable to Cadal.

Cadal shook his head. Maybe being in Human form for so long had a down side, or maybe Humans and Fairies were really only separated by environment. Maybe Fairies were no better than Humans were, and the stresses of the Human realm evoked the same responses in Fairies. Was it simply that Fairies were blessed with a functional society?

Maybe it was simply his drive to protect Mollie, though that thought went far beyond protecting her. Mollie's assessment of *just cause* was fairly accurate. Retribution was not a Fairy concept. It wasn't something Cadal could justify engaging in. It would be a different matter if Thornton came within striking distance of Mollie again.

Cadal laughed harshly.

Liam looked up at him sharply. "Did I miss something?"

"I find I'm talking myself into the same conversation Mollie had with you after Tucker frightened her at the pond. I can't go after Thornton, but if he comes near us again—"

Liam smiled. "That would be a sight. You would have to disappear immediately and forever, but it would be..."

"It would be what?"

"I don't know. I keep thinking it would be somewhere between a relief and amusing, but that's not very Christian of me, is it?" He shook his head sadly. "It would be so much easier if I could justify taking people like Thornton out of existence for the greater good, but I'd like to think I'm better than that."

Cadal smiled. "With Humans like you, you have a shot at becoming a civilized race yet, but you have a lot to learn about fermenting drinks. Maybe I'll sneak back a bottle of nectar wine for you someday."

"Good stuff?"

"Imagine your whiskey but it tastes like the sweetest summer fruits."

Liam smiled. "No wonder you seem so unaffected by that drink."

"Not unaffected, but not drunk either. I'm simply comfortable."

"Good. That's what I wanted."

Cadal glanced at the ceiling in annoyance. "What is taking that doctor so long?"

Chapter Nineteen

Mollie moved under the quilt. *Warm.* It felt good to be warm again. She really didn't want to open her eyes, but she wanted to see Cadal. To her surprise, Elizabeth sat over her instead of Cadal. Mollie met the other woman's eyes fearfully.

Elizabeth smiled. "He's downstairs with Liam, miss."

Mollie closed her eyes and nodded in relief.

"The doctor is here. Can you talk to him for a few minutes?"

She opened her eyes again. "Of course," she managed weakly. Mollie tried to put the images together. Everything after Tucker's punch was a strange sort of blur.

"Would you like some tea? I have some here, though it's cooled somewhat."

"If you don't mind, I'd prefer some warm milk."

She smiled and nodded. Elizabeth knew what kind of milk Mollie meant.

Elizabeth met Mollie's eyes and gripped her hand for a moment, twisting a ring. Mollie smiled a tight smile in understanding of the move. They had been telling tales skating on untruths to protect her and Cadal. It wasn't really a lie, so she supposed there was no harm in it.

Elizabeth rose to leave. Once she was gone, the doctor took a seat on the bedside chair.

She decided to take the bull by the horns. "Is my baby all right?" she asked.

The doctor smiled. "It is difficult to hurt one so young. She seems fine, though you should take it easy while you heal."

Mollie scowled. "Would everyone stop calling my baby *she*," she snapped. "It's annoying."

Doc Edwards nodded. "Never annoy a pregnant woman. My wife taught me that lesson far too many years ago."

She smiled. Doc Edwards was easy to like.

"You're going to be fine. There is quite a bit of bruising. That wrist bothers me the most, though I think it's safe to say it's not broken. It certainly seems he was intent on causing you pain. It's going to hurt for quite a while. I can give you something for it, if you like."

Mollie shook her head and ran her hand over her stomach lightly. "I'd rather not."

"I can promise it will be safe."

"I'd rather not."

The doctor nodded. "I'd like to see you stay in bed for a few days. Keep warm. If you run fever, let me know immediately."

She nodded. "I'm sure everyone will keep me quiet, especially if you tell them to."

"Why don't you tell me what happened today." It wasn't a question.

Mollie sighed. "Mr. Tucker grabbed me on the trail. He covered my mouth so that it muffled my scream and his other arm was around my chest." She rubbed her eyes. "He dragged me off somewhere in the woods. I don't know where. At first, he made veiled threats, nothing he couldn't walk away from. You understand?"

"He threatened you?"

Mollie nodded. "And my baby."

"What changed it? He crossed the line at some point."

"I lied to him. I told him I wrote a will leaving everything to Cadal if... It didn't make a difference to him. I thought it might make him back down, make him think twice, but it didn't. He got angry and started squeezing my wrist. I think he wanted to break me, to make me scream."

"What happened?"

"It worked. I couldn't stand it anymore. I hoped we were close enough for someone to hear it, but—" She looked at Edwards miserably.

"They heard you, faintly, but it wasn't enough to find you. What about your other injuries?"

"He threatened to—" Mollie wiped away the tears on her cheeks with a certain amount of irritation and tried again. "He decided Mr. Thornton wasn't going to get the land from me willingly, at least not while I was still alive. He didn't seem to have a problem with that idea, but he got the idea of what he called 'a fringe benefit while getting the job done'."

The doctor paled. "I think I need to call an ambulance."

"Don't bother. He didn't succeed. He tried, but he didn't have time."

"You tried to fight him off?"

Mollie swallowed a lump in her throat. "Yes. I don't remember much after he hit me. I could see his hands—" She hesitated. "But he backed away when he heard Thunder."

"The horse chased him off?"

Mollie furrowed her brow. "I don't know. I heard a scream before I passed out. When I woke up, I could barely make it onto Thunder by standing on a fallen tree," she lied smoothly. Thunder wasn't a trained horse. It was unlikely that Doc Edwards would believe he had lain down to let her on without that type of training. "It was dark. I was so dizzy, I could barely stand, barely throw my leg over a horse. I could barely see Thunder. If Tucker was close by, I didn't know it."

The doctor nodded quietly. "I'll let them know. You get some rest now. I'll send Mr. Cadal back up in a few minutes. John McConnell will want to see you soon."

"I thought he would." She sank back to the pillows as Edwards left the room.

The door opened again and she looked at it expectantly, but it wasn't Cadal. Elizabeth walked in carrying a tray with warm sweet milk, a deep plate of the stew she loved, and potato rolls.

She considered Mollie's expression sadly. "Mr. Cadal will be up in a few moments. The doctor wants to talk to him first. Try to rest now, and eat this food. Mr. Cadal ordered it for you."

Mollie nodded and tried to pull back the tears that were already making tracks down her cheeks. She picked at her food and drank a little of the milk while Elizabeth watched her worriedly. She handed the tray back. "Once I see Cadal," she offered by way of explanation.

Elizabeth nodded and placed the tray on the night stand where Cadal had placed it her first afternoon here at the estate. "Yes, miss. I understand."

"Still sure you want to take this on?"

Elizabeth smiled. "Of course, though we may want to delay it until you're feeling better."

Mollie shook her head stubbornly. "No. The sooner the better. I want to go home with Cadal before something else goes wrong."

"Just a few days, miss—"

"No. It will be one less thing that can go wrong."

"Nothing else can go wrong now."

Elizabeth smiled at her as she said the words, but Mollie felt a cold chill. It could go wrong. There was too much that could still go wrong.

* * * *

Cadal jumped at the sound of footsteps. He had been jumping at the sound of footsteps ever since he and Liam had retired to the library. The first time, he had come face to face with Elizabeth at the foot of the stairs. Cadal knew Mollie was awake, and he had hoped Elizabeth had come to get him, but she was only getting Mollie a drink of warm sweet milk while she talked to the doctor. Cadal had ordered her to take up food as well and turned down her offer of something for himself.

Liam had dragged him away from the stairs and back to the seat in front of the fire. "Come sit down. You'll see her soon."

Cadal stared into the fire and listened to the bits of conversation he picked up from Mollie. He stifled a sob at her description of Tucker's attack. He knew Humans couldn't do what he could, but he had no doubts McConnell would ask all the same questions and more. It seemed unnecessary to make her tell the story more than once.

He heard Elizabeth heading back up, but the door opened again before she reached the top. Cadal lunged to his feet.

Liam pulled him back down gently. "He'll want to talk to you first. Stay put for now."

"I want to see her," Cadal said with an almost uncontrollable urgency.

"In a few minutes. Look at it this way. He's certainly put limits on what she can do. It's your job to make sure she adheres to those limits. He has to talk to you."

He nodded. Doc Edwards stepped through the doorway into the library, and Cadal stood abruptly to face him. The kindly looking man smiled at him grimly, and Cadal felt a stab of fear. He couldn't read Edwards as he did Mollie. If there was something wrong, and Edwards hadn't told her so as not to worry her, would he tell Cadal privately? It seemed likely.

"Sit down please, Mr. Cadal."

Cadal nodded warily and sat next to Liam. He was suddenly glad for that drink. Maybe a little relaxation was all that was keeping him together at the seams.

The doctor sank into a chair across from him and sighed. "She's suffering from some severe bruising and exposure, but otherwise she is physically sound."

Cadal nodded in relief. "Our baby?" he asked. He knew the answer, but he shouldn't know it, and he knew that too.

"Doing well, as far as I can tell. She's showing no signs of distress yet."

"Yet?" Cadal felt an unnamed panic take hold.

"Miss Hardy has suffered a shock. This experience has been and will continue to be very stressful for her. She needs rest, complete rest for a few days at least. The longer you can keep her quiet and relaxed, the less the chance of something going wrong."

"What could go wrong?"

"She could get ill and run fever. She could have problems if she gets upset."

"Problems with the baby?" Cadal asked for clarification.

"It can happen, but it might not. I prefer not to take that chance, personally."

Cadal nodded, thankful for the warning. "Then we won't take the chance," he decided. "Can I see her now?"

"In a moment." Edwards ran a hand over his chin and seemed to consider how to continue. "Mr. Tucker didn't just injure her. He threatened her and the baby. He frightened her."

Cadal nodded. He knew that better than anyone, except perhaps Mollie.

"If she needs to speak to someone, there are people available."

He looked at Liam in confusion.

"He means a counselor, Mr. Cadal," Liam explained.

Cadal nodded though he had no idea what that meant. He met the doctor's eyes. "If Mollie wants one, of course."

The doctor cleared his throat. "Or if you do," he offered. "There's one more thing. It appears Mr. Tucker was intent — that he tried to force himself on her."

Cadal had heard enough. He could feel Mollie's upset. She needed to see him as badly as he needed to see her. He stood abruptly and headed for the stairs. It seemed a good place to cut the doctor off, at any rate.

Edwards called his name and started after him, but Liam blocked him.

"Let him, Doc. He needs to be sure she's all right for himself."

"But what if—" Edwards objected.

"He won't," Liam interrupted. "I know Mr. Cadal. He'd never do anything that would hurt Miss Hardy. He always thinks of her first."

Cadal didn't wait to hear the rest. He took the stairs two at a time and opened the door slowly. Mollie looked up at him and smiled in relief. Cadal sighed and went to her, and Elizabeth slipped away. He wrapped his arms around her, and Mollie clung to him, trying desperately to hold back the tears that came immediately. For a long time after her sobbing stopped, neither of them spoke.

He glanced at the tray of food and smiled. "You haven't eaten."

Mollie darkened, a slight touch of color in her pallor. "I was nervous. I wanted to see you."

"You've seen me. Eat something before you get sick."

Cadal placed the tray on her lap. Mollie ate a little of the food from it, but she was more tired than hungry. He placed the tray back on the night stand without a word when she was done.

"What can I do for you? To make you more comfortable?" he asked.

"Honestly?"

Cadal nodded.

"Get me a nightshirt. If McConnell is coming by, I'd rather not deal with him in my current state of undress. Then lay down with me."

He smiled widely and complied. Cadal handed her one of her long cotton nightgowns from the dresser and pulled off his shirt, shoes, and socks before curling under the covers. Mollie regarded him strangely, probably wondering if he didn't want to meet McConnell in the buff either.

Cadal blushed lightly before he answered her. "McConnell had a problem with my trying to raise your body temperature by sharing body heat, and I was fully dressed that time."

Mollie smiled. "As if I would have minded."

He was happy to see the smile, but she sobered suddenly.

"That's something else you can do for me." Mollie met Cadal's eyes. "Show me our son," she requested quietly.

Cadal nodded and placed his hands on her temples for the transfer. He kissed her. Cadal transferred for several minutes. He felt the relief flooding over her as he did. When he drew back, Mollie was crying again.

He wiped away her tears and tried to calm her. "He's all right. After I made sure your injuries weren't life threatening, I checked him before anything else."

Mollie nodded. "No more chances," she told him. "Until we get to the colony, I'm not leaving your side. I promise."

Cadal pulled her to his chest. "I could stand that. For now, that means resting. No estate. No business. No visitors, beside the official ones we can't avoid. I'll stay with you every minute."

"One exception to that plan. I'm signing those papers tomorrow. I'll do it in bed, but I'm doing it."

He felt the fire of determination burning behind her eyes. Cadal shook his head. "The doctor says you need to relax—"

Mollie pushed away and met his eyes angrily. "I won't relax until we're back home. I can't. If I don't do this, something else will go wrong. I know it will, Cadal."

He considered it carefully. "It will put you more at ease?"

She nodded.

"Okay, this one exception," he conceded.

Mollie folded back into his chest. "Thank you, Cadal. I just want to go home."

He rested his cheek onto her hair. "I know. I want it too."

* * * *

Doc Edwards accompanied John McConnell up shortly after Mollie settled into Cadal's chest again. Mollie insisted that Cadal not be forced to leave. McConnell started to protest, but the doctor took his elbow gently.

Cadal tensed, unwilling to leave Mollie while she needed him. He prepared to argue the point, but Edwards beat him to it.

"John, I'm doing this against my own better judgment. If you must do this tonight, you will do it in a way that won't upset her."

The constable nodded thoughtfully. "All right, but if Mr. Cadal interferes in the least..." He let the threat drop.

Cadal met McConnell's eyes. "Ask what you need to. I know what's happened now. You'll have no outburst from me unless you upset Mollie unnecessarily."

McConnell seemed surprised by the promise. "We'll begin then." He looked at Mollie. "Miss Hardy, why were you going to the stable?"

"To groom Thunder."

"He's Mr. Cadal's horse. Wouldn't you groom your own?"

"Actually, Liam and Patrick groom them both, but Thunder enjoys a good brushing, and we're friends."

"Mr. Tucker stepped onto the trail ahead of you?"

"No, he stepped in behind me. When I turned back to get my coat, he was there." She shivered.

Cadal wrapped an arm around her.

"Did you scream?" McConnell asked.

"Not immediately. I tried to make a run for the stable." She looked at them sheepishly. "I panicked. By the time I screamed, he had a hand over my mouth and his arm around my chest." She shook her head. "He's fast for a man his size and age, not to mention strong."

McConnell nodded his agreement. "Did you fight him?"

"I kicked at him, but between him squeezing on my ribs and my face, I couldn't breathe. He made it fairly clear that he would allow me air if I stopped struggling."

"Did he say what he wanted from you?"

"At that point, he told me he wanted to talk to me privately, apparently the talk he *wanted* to have with me the day at the pond when he couldn't get his hands on me. Either way, he had me this time."

"He dragged you off into the woods?"

Mollie nodded. "He said he didn't want anyone interrupting our talk this time."

"Could you find the place again?"

"No, everything was a flash of trees speeding past to me. I don't even know how long we kept moving."

"What did he do when he got you to the clearing?"

"He dropped me on the ground."

"You didn't run?"

"He was right in front of me. That meant he'd have me again before I made it two steps. On top of that, I was freezing and I had no idea where I was. Given my options, I thought he might do what he said, talk to me and leave. He hadn't really hurt me, only a few bruises. He could have hurt me several times over by that point."

"What did he have to say?"

"At first, it was the same sort of veiled threats he made at the pond. How dangerous it was to be so rude to Mr. Thornton. Reminding me that I had a fair offer on the estate and how I should accept it. Reminding me that I don't really want him and Thornton as enemies."

She sighed, and Cadal rubbed her shoulder in support.

"But he didn't stick to that?" McConnell asked.

"No. He reminded me I have a baby to worry about. He told me working a farm wasn't a life for a little girl." She grimaced at the statement. "He reminded me how dangerous it's been so far. He threatened that if I took my eyes off of my child for even an instant, something bad could happen to her."

"Anything else?"

Mollie nodded. "That was when he started talking about what a shame it would be if the baby and I..." She met his eyes fearfully. "If we both died, the land would revert to my mother, and she would accept Thornton's offer. He didn't seem to have a problem with that idea, so I decided to try to change his mind."

"How?"

"I told him I had a will leaving everything to Cadal. I thought he'd change his mind if he thought it would work against him."

"It didn't work?"

Mollie shook her head. "Tucker grabbed my wrist and pulled the ring in front of my face. He pointed out that Cadal wasn't married into the Blake family yet. Until he was, no judge would give my family's lands to anyone but family."

"But you were lying to him?"

"Yes, I was. I haven't named Cadal in a will yet, but I needed a bargaining chip. It simply wasn't an effective one, I guess."

"What did Tucker do next?"

"He started squeezing my wrist."

"Why?"

"Tucker wanted to make me scream, to prove that he could. He kept talking about how he heard I work like a man, fight like a man, and think like a man. That's when he threatened — to prove I wasn't a man." Mollie dropped her gaze as she said it.

Cadal felt her pulling in sobs again. He ached with her.

"What happened?"

"I was in pain and I was tired of the cat and mouse game. If he was threatening it to get me to scream, which I hoped was the case, I'd give him that victory. If not, maybe he was wrong and we were close enough for someone to hear me. Either way, I screamed bloody murder and hoped for the best."

"What was his reaction?"

"He didn't back down at all. Tucker seemed confident that my scream couldn't possibly bring anyone. He grabbed the front of my sweater and dragged me up by it, until I was face to face with him. Then he asked if I thought he should give it a try." Mollie shook her head weakly, and her face paled at the memory of him so close to her.

"What did you do?"

"I tried to talk him out of it and I started crying." She swallowed a lump in her throat before she continued, very close to tears again. "I knew if he did, there would be only one thing he could do with me after. He couldn't let me go."

McConnell nodded in agreement.

"He laughed at me. He said Mr. Thornton had charged him with getting my land any way it took to do it, and that he would be getting a fringe benefit while getting the job done."

Cadal set his jaw angrily. He looked away momentarily to shield his face from Mollie, got control of his emotions, and brushed his cheek over her hair in comfort. The constable watched his show of restraint in fascination. Edwards met Cadal's eyes and nodded his approval.

McConnell sighed. "What did he do?"

"He started to... He kissed me. I pushed at his chest. He let go of me completely, so that my own inertia knocked me off of my feet." She shook her head in annoyance. "I should have seen that one coming. He tried to grab me again. I gave up on caring where I was and tried to run."

"You didn't make it, obviously."

Mollie shook her head. "He got a grip on my arm and laid a punch on my cheekbone that fazed me pretty good. I remember hitting the ground again. After that, everything is sort of patchy."

"What can you remember?"

"I remember Tucker—" She wiped away a tear and glanced at Cadal hopelessly.

He smiled a tight smile and kissed her forehead. Cadal wished he could manage more for her, but he couldn't.

Mollie took a deep breath and met McConnell's eyes before she began again. "He was leaning over me, and his hands were on my sweater. On my chest," she qualified. "I thought I was imagining the hoof beats, but Tucker reacted too. He pulled away out of my field of vision. I couldn't see him, but I saw Thunder run past me. I heard a scream before I lost consciousness."

"Who took care of you?"

Mollie looked at him in confusion. "I don't understand. I woke up and Thunder was nuzzling my face and shoulder. I'm not sure how long I was out. It was late dusk when I went out and dark when I managed to get to my feet again. I was cold, dizzy, and stiff, but I managed to make it onto Thunder's back before I passed out again. The next clear memory I have was waking up here in bed."

"You didn't see Tucker when you woke?"

Mollie shook her head slowly. "I couldn't see much of anything. I lost my flashlight...my torch somewhere."

"What was Mr. Tucker wearing?"

"Brown. A rough brown coat, an off-white sweater, and brown pants. I think that's why I didn't see him hiding in the trees. He blended too well."

"You said something to Mr. Cadal when you got back to the stable. Do you remember what?"

Mollie shook her head in confusion again. "I don't remember seeing anyone until I woke up here. If I did say something, I was still so far out of it that I don't remember it."

"You didn't see anyone in the woods?"

"Only Tucker."

"No one was riding the horse?"

"I didn't see anyone, and if there had been, why would he or she leave me there to freeze and not bring me directly back? That doesn't make much sense, does it?"

McConnell nodded uncertainly.

Cadal's curiosity got the better of him. "Why do you ask that? You know I was with Liam. Who else would be riding Thunder?"

"We don't know yet, but there were green fibers on Miss Hardy's clothing and on Thunder's hooves, as if he stepped on the fabric. I've seen what you were wearing, Liam, Elizabeth, the other men as they came in to eat. If Mr. Tucker was wearing brown, which the maid at Mr. Thornton's agrees with, and which we found fibers of as well, who was wearing the green?"

"Obviously someone who didn't want to be seen," Mollie noted.

McConnell cleared his throat and met Mollie's confused gaze. "I have to ask this. You understand that?"

"If you're going to ask me if Tucker is dead, the truth is I have no idea. If he's not, he's at least hurt."

He shook his head. "It's not that. There are a lot of rumors about." He darkened considerably. "Your baby? Is it Mr. Cadal's?"

Cadal felt a deep outrage at the question, but Mollie stepped in calmly before he could voice his protest.

"Yes. It is. Who else would the father be?"

McConnell looked at them uncomfortably.

"You shouldn't believe everything you hear. Yes, we are expecting a baby before we're properly wed, but we're not the first and we won't be the last. It is our child. Cadal's and mine. There was never a question about that."

"I notice you don't call Mr. Cadal by his given name."

Mollie smiled. "William never felt like the right name for him. I started out calling him Cadal because of my corporate background, and because he didn't ask me to call him anything else, like many of the people here at the estate did. Over time, it became a habit of sorts."

"There's no one else who would want to protect you?"

"That wouldn't want to be seen? No. If it was one of my employees, he would have brought me back to the house. My family, what little I have, is thousands of miles away."

A sobering thought occurred to Cadal. They weren't all that far away. Both he and Mollie had family not far away at all. At least one family member would know Mollie was in danger before it even happened and would be able to find her the way Cadal couldn't yet. Morda would not want to be seen. She could safeguard Mollie and his son, then fade away, perhaps without Mollie seeing her so she couldn't blurt something out in a daze.

Cadal snapped back to attention. McConnell was talking to him.

"I'm sorry. What did you ask?" Cadal asked.

"You know something? The look on your face—"

Cadal shook his head. "I was just considering that whoever helped Mollie probably feared Thornton enough to try to hide the fact, but I don't know who that would be."

Except a Fairy Mistress whose winter cloak was a rich shade of green when she wasn't in the Master's blue and white for ceremony. A Fairy Mistress who could send a cold wind to make her grandchild turn back in time to see the face of her attacker to warn Cadal or perhaps to save her some more grievous injury?

Chapter Twenty

Mollie humored Cadal by drinking another glass of sweet milk when everyone cleared out. Then she settled into his arms and fell asleep.

Cadal watched her sleep for a long time. He closed his eyes as exhaustion took its toll on him. His dreams were full of Morda. Her time must be coming to a close. Morda went to help Mollie, but she was no longer capable of affecting Mollie's condition, save by the most conventional of means.

They had to go back, but Mollie wasn't ready for the trip. She was so weak, she might not be ready for a week or more. Cadal couldn't leave without her, and he couldn't push Mollie to go before she was ready. He couldn't risk their son that way.

He woke several times and nestled closer to Mollie. Cadal almost lost her again. Until they were away from the Human realm and safely in the colony, that would be a threat. Even then, Mollie could still be haunted by Tucker's assault. The possibility still frightened her. Cadal had to admit that he hadn't cared for his own reaction to the threat of her rape, even as he rejected the possibility of the outcome Mollie feared.

A few of the times Cadal woke, it was to images of Tucker or James hurting Mollie, forcing her. He couldn't imagine what dreams like that must be like for her.

In the morning, Cadal found staying quietly in bed with Mollie was easier than he planned. She was physically drained and had no urge to do anything but talk to Cadal and sleep. He wasn't much better. Cadal had had little sleep the night before, and he snoozed away the morning much as she did, waking only when he felt her moving to use the bathroom or to eat.

The solicitor arrived before lunchtime. He had all of the information Mollie gave him, so the transfer of the land was a matter of more signatures than Cadal could imagine. There were several discussions with the solicitor about her motives, her legal position, and the clauses that had been added to protect both Mollie and the land's new owners from any interference. When the business was completed, he took his leave, and Mollie fairly collapsed on Cadal again. Even that minor exertion had tired her.

When Elizabeth brought up their lunch, Mollie smiled at her sleepily. "You're not my employee anymore," she reminded her friend.

The other woman laughed. "You're right, but you are both my guests. Now lie down and get some rest until you feel better."

Mollie ate. Not as much as Cadal would have liked to see, but she did eat something.

When Elizabeth came to take the tray away, Cadal asked where Liam was. He immediately wished he hadn't.

"Liam gave the men permission to join the search this morning. After lunch with the solicitor, he went out himself."

By mid-afternoon, Cadal knew the search was over. The bell sounded, startling him out of sleep. If the men were being called in this early, it could only mean they found what they were looking for.

Liam arrived an hour later. He looked at Cadal and nodded silently. Mollie closed her eyes and curled into Cadal's chest. When she started crying again, Liam left. Cadal didn't try to discuss it. He simply resolved to hold her as long as she needed it. Mollie fell asleep in his arms.

Cadal didn't sleep that time. He was still holding her when Doc Edwards arrived to check on her.

The doctor raised an eyebrow at Cadal. "Is she all right?" he asked quietly.

Cadal nodded. "Liam came to tell us."

"Was she very upset?"

"Less than I expected. I think it helped that he didn't verbalize it."

"No one will. I doubt there will be many more questions for Miss Hardy. For you— That may be a different matter."

Cadal regarded Edwards strangely. "Why?"

The doctor sat down and glanced at Mollie sadly. "They won't be questioning you today, because of Miss Hardy. I'm forbidding it until she's recovered more of her strength."

"Why? I've told McConnell all I know."

"Doctor Smythe claims that unless a horse is unbalanced or being ridden, he would never run a man down like that. Since Thunder seems to be calm and happy, John is convinced you or someone else — likely you were on that horse."

"I was with Liam. And why would I leave her there? I couldn't do that."

"John thinks you were trying to hide the fact that you rode Thunder. That you, perhaps, covered her with a wool blanket to buy yourself time. Barring that, he thinks you know who did it, and you're hiding his identity from the authorities."

"Why would I do that?" Cadal asked weakly.

His stomach turned. McConnell hit on exactly what he was doing. Of course, if Cadal told the truth, they wouldn't believe him.

"Who are you, Mr. Cadal? Where do you come from? Do you have any papers you can show them to clear that up?"

Cadal felt the sick swirl building, akin to something he would feel from Mollie. He considered checking her, but he would feel it if she woke. Liam was right. Trouble was coming for them and closing fast.

"This is Thornton's doing, isn't it?" Cadal whispered.

The doctor nodded. "Yes, but it doesn't change the fact that you can't prove you are who you say you are, does it?" There was no censure in Edwards' voice, only empathy.

"But apparently it does change the fact that Thornton was so covetous of Mollie's land that he tried to have her killed to get it. Are Hu—" Cadal took a deep breath and reminded himself not to use that term before continuing. "Are the laws going to allow that?"

Edwards shook his head. "Unfortunately, it is a matter of Miss Hardy's word against Mr. Thornton's. That is not usually enough to convict someone. With Tucker, there was other evidence. You understand?"

"People think more of Thornton's word than Mollie's?" Cadal asked incredulously.

"No. You really don't understand this, do you?"

Cadal shook his head angrily.

"Where *are* you from?"

"Very far. Further than seems possible right now."

"Who are you really, Mr. Cadal? Does Miss Hardy know?"

"My name is Cadal, and I'd never lie to Mollie. She knows who I am. Katie knew as well. I've lied to no one about that." Cadal held Mollie closer to him. It was unbelievable. He was being falsely accused of crimes by a criminal, and the Human system would allow it. Not only allow it, but also pardon the criminal's crimes at the same time that they condemned Cadal.

"Why are you hiding? Are you in trouble with the law somewhere else?"

Cadal shook his head. "No. I suppose my problem is that I'm not hiding anything. I never was. I simply have no proof."

Edwards shook his head in confusion. "You must have a birth certificate."

He shook his head.

"Some state ID? A passport? Your ID number?"

Cadal laughed weakly. "People identified as numbers. Such a sad system."

"You can't possibly have been born and raised without them," Edwards insisted.

Cadal sighed. "I have no proof, but I'm not lying to you."

"Then this is going to be very difficult. They won't release you with no idea of who you are. They'll assume you're some sort of illegal, a spy, or that you're on the run from the law somewhere. For the public good, they will lock you up indefinitely."

"How long do I have?"

"I can hold them off for a few days with warnings of Miss Hardy's health. You're not going to run, are you? She's not prepared for that. If you care for her at all—"

"I love her. I would never abandon her."

The doctor nodded. "For now, that's good for her and the baby, but it's not so good for any of you in the long run." He sighed. "I better get washed up and check her. They'll wonder why I've been up here so long." Edwards rose and headed for the bathroom.

Cadal started to lower Mollie to the bed. He started. Mollie stared up into his face, but Cadal hadn't felt her wake. A deep sadness flowed from her suddenly, and Cadal realized Mollie could do one thing no other Fairy could. She could hide her heart from him completely, if she chose.

"How much did you hear?" he asked her fearfully.

"Enough."

"I'll work this out."

"No, we will work this out together."

Cadal nodded and settled her into the pillows. He kissed her cheek lightly as Edwards came back into the room. As the doctor examined her, Cadal wondered how they could possibly work this out.

* * * *

"No," Cadal fairly exploded. "Mollie, no. We're not doing it, and that is final."

She seethed in irritation. "Why not? Don't say it. You're not hiding up here, not even in Fairy form. They'll find you, and I'll lose you forever. This isn't the old west. There is plastic and wire mesh on the windows and motion sensors to keep you from escaping a modern jail. If they take you to a major city, where would you hide if you did escape? And your goddess forbid if they saw you on a camera in Fairy form—"

"You're not ready. You can't possibly be strong enough to fly yet."

Mollie shrugged. "Then we won't fly."

"It's too far to walk, and you're too weak for that as well. This isn't possible."

"We won't walk either."

Cadal stared at her in confusion.

"I'm slow. When I fly, I slow you down, right?"

He nodded.

"Would you say I'm much faster than a horse trots?"

"Horseback? What if you get tired? Or if you get thrown?" He grimaced. "You can't control a horse for that long, and I can't take the chance of you tiring enough not to be able to continue halfway there."

"We'll ride double. Thunder has done it before. You can handle him. I can even sleep if I get too tired."

"It's too cold." Cadal was grasping at straws, and he knew it, but it was too damned dangerous.

"It's only going to get colder. I can wrap up in a quilt while we ride. I can't do that while I'm flying. I'm not good enough, yet."

"Why don't you follow the doctor's orders and rest for your sake and for our son's?"

"I can't relax with the threat of you in jail over my head. If you leave without me, I won't be able to relax because of Thornton. If you're gone, he has nothing to fear. Once you leave, you can't ever come back. You have to disappear without a trace. You know there is only one way for me to relax and that is to get home."

"Liam could protect you for a few days and bring you deep enough into the woods that I can come and bring you the rest of the way," Cadal suggested almost painfully.

"You want that?"

Cadal saw the fear in her eyes. He couldn't lie to her about this. "I hate it, but I won't do anything that risks our son."

"Neither will I. This is the only way, Cadal. There's snow headed our way. I know you can feel it too. You said it would be more dangerous once the snow came. Which is more dangerous?"

He nodded and wrapped her in his arms. Mollie was right, and there was no denying it. The Harmony certainly wasn't making this easy.

"All right," he conceded. "I don't like taking this chance, but we don't have a choice."

"You have to take chances to reach your goals, Cadal. That's life. You took a horrible chance coming here and staying this long. Now we have to get you out of trouble because of it."

Cadal kissed her forehead. "Coming here got me my goal. Let's get some sleep. We'll have a long day tomorrow."

They discovered another problem when Elizabeth brought dinner.

"A guard?" Cadal asked. A guard wasn't a problem for him to slip past since he could shift and fly from one of the second floor windows, but Mollie couldn't possibly fly yet.

Mollie met her eyes. "Both doors?"

Elizabeth shook her head. "No. Just the front, but he'll see you coming out the kitchen door."

She smiled widely. "Only if it's light out. And definitely not in Fairy form in the dark, if the kitchen lights are out for the night."

Cadal looked at her in disbelief. "From here to the stable in Fairy form with no flight? It would take too long. It can't be done."

"Just until we're safely in the woods. We can move silently once we're there, even in Human form. We can't use any lights, but we won't have to. We can do this. It won't even be hard."

He shook his head. "You are hopeless."

"No, Cadal. I'm hopeful. There is a very big difference."

Eventually, Mollie convinced him to try. Cadal fully admitted that he only did so because of how upset she got when he tried to argue the point. He sighed and promised himself things would be back to normal when they reached the colony.

Chapter Twenty-one

At Mollie's suggestion, they waited until long after midnight to leave. In the kitchen, they hugged Liam and Elizabeth goodbye. Cadal felt as if his nerves were wound tight as a spring.

Mollie placed Elizabeth's ring into her hand and smiled. "Thanks for the loan, but you need to put this back where it belongs."

Elizabeth smiled warmly. "Be careful. I'd tell you to come visit, but—"

Mollie nodded. "I know. This is a one-way ticket. Maybe we'll see each other again someday. Maybe in ten or twenty years, when everyone else has forgotten us?" She managed a weak smile.

Cadal grimaced. Leaving them was almost as hard on Mollie as leaving the colony had been.

Liam kissed her cheek. "Take care of him, Mollie. Make sure Cadal doesn't get himself into any trouble."

"I'll try, Liam, but where we're going, it's going to be the other side of the coin. He'll have to be my keeper for a while. Just take care of the land."

He nodded. "You know I will. Be sure Cadal sends back that nectar wine someday."

Cadal smiled. "Absolutely. We'd better go now." He shook Liam's hand one last time. Liam was the most civilized Human Cadal had ever met. Probably the most civilized one he ever would.

Mollie nodded to Elizabeth. "Crack open the door. We'll slip through in Fairy form."

Cadal adjusted the large duffel bag over his shoulder and picked up the dark quilt, tucking it under his arm. He took Mollie's hand. "Ready?" he asked, though Cadal was so frightened by the chance he was taking with her, he knew he wasn't ready himself.

"As ready as I'll ever be."

They shifted slowly for her decreased abilities. Mollie smiled at the stunned looks on Liam and Elizabeth's faces, barely visible in the near-total darkness. They separated and waved to their friends before slipping out the door.

The trek across the lawn was uneventful, though the frost on the grass intensified the chill in the air. Once they were deep inside the woods, they shifted back again. Cadal could tell that Mollie was already tiring, but they were so close. Once they were on Thunder, she could rest.

The rest of the trip to the stable passed quickly. They slipped inside and Mollie released Thunder from his stall. She hugged his neck.

"Thank you, Thunder," Mollie told him again.

Cadal slipped a bridle on the horse and stepped away to unfold the quilt. As he draped it over Mollie's shoulders and tucked it around her backpack, the work lamp switched on. Cadal's hopes sank as McConnell appeared next to the light.

"I thought you might try this, Mr. Cadal. But you, Miss Hardy? It was my understanding that you aren't up to these antics."

"She's not," Cadal answered, "But she refused to let me go alone."

"Go where?"

Cadal shrugged. "Home."

"How did you get past my man at the house?" McConnell demanded.

Cadal darkened.

Mollie started laughing hysterically. She sank to the floor and hugged herself, choking in her mirth. She looked at Cadal. "Do you trust me?" she asked with a glitter in her eyes.

He nodded mutely. Cadal trusted her, but he wasn't sure exactly what she had planned. The images in her mind were scattered. They didn't seem to make sense.

Mollie smiled at McConnell. He was watching her warily and had taken a step further back into the light.

"You're a constable. You trust what you see and you're down to Earth, right?" she asked.

"That covers it," he answered nervously.

"Your constituents wouldn't trust you if you suddenly started imagining things and telling wild stories, correct?"

Cadal caught on. "Mollie, this is a bad idea."

McConnell stared at Cadal in wonder. "What is a bad idea?"

Cadal watched as Mollie started concentrating on the shift, but she was exhausted already. He put a hand on her shoulder and shook his head.

"You're too tired. Let me."

Mollie nodded and touched his hand as he pulled it away.

Cadal straightened and faced the man standing across the room from him. "You want to know how we got past your man? I'll show you." The shift was sudden, spectacular. Cadal sprinted to the other side of Mollie and shifted again.

McConnell stepped back. "What are you?" he asked fearfully.

Mollie took Cadal's hand, and he helped her to her feet. Her voice was soothing. "Think of where you are, John. What stories were you all weaned on?"

McConnell gaped at her in disbelief, then at Cadal. "He was in charge of the horse that killed Tucker his way?"

Cadal raised his hand toward Thunder, but Mollie swept it into her hand smoothly as it crossed her hip.

"No," Mollie assured him. "Cadal wasn't in charge of Thunder."

She touched the horse, and he reared up. Mollie didn't flinch at the movement. He had done exactly what she'd ordered him to do. McConnell, however, scrambled back to the door.

"I was." Mollie touched Thunder again, and he settled next to her and nuzzled her hair. "It was self-defense, John. I was desperate when I called him. He was running wild when he found me. I was semiconscious, and I lost control of him. The only direction Thunder had left was that I needed his help. Neither of us knows who had the green wool, but I can guess as well as Cadal can that it was one of our own."

Cadal nodded his agreement.

"I can't stay here anymore. I belong with my own kind," Mollie continued.

McConnell shook his head in confusion. "Your own kind? You were born in America, in a hospital. I checked. You can't be a Fairy," he insisted.

"I was born of a Fairy who was born of a Fairy who was born of a Fairy. Have you noticed anything strange about the Blake family for the last five or six generations? Always baby girls. All very beautiful and very strange. The Blake women? I'm the last of my line, and I want to go home. I have to go home with or without your approval, John. Please, don't make us go without it. We'll have to now."

McConnell got stiffly to his feet. "Go. I never saw you. Don't come back this way for any reason, and watch your backs." He turned off the work light and opened the door for them.

Cadal wrapped the quilt around Mollie and set her astride Thunder's bare back. He jumped up behind her lightly. Cadal met McConnell's eyes in the dim light, as he wrapped his arms around her. "Thank you, John."

"May I ask you a question?"

"Certainly."

"Why didn't you simply fly out?"

"Mollie is too weak. She's too weak to even shift again. She's barely strong enough to make the trip this way, but—"

"I forced your hand. You have to move now, though she's not up to it?"

Cadal nodded, sadness eating at his frayed nerves.

"I'm sorry. I didn't know."

"I know." He steered Thunder toward the open door.

"Cadal?" McConnell called again.

Cadal met his eyes.

"Why did you come here?"

"For Mollie. Only for Mollie. Loving her and protecting her, then bringing her home when she was ready. That was my only reason for being here."

"You can't do that here. Take her home."

Cadal nodded, and they rode out into the icy night. They had wasted far more time than they had counted on, and it was hard for him not to rush their pace. He gauged Mollie carefully, as Morda had done for him in transfer. When she was at her limits, he slowed their pace to a walk until she recovered. After two hours, he pulled Thunder to a stop and swung Mollie down to the ground in his arms.

"We can't stop," Mollie protested weakly. "We have to keep moving."

"We will." Cadal pulled out a bottle of sweet milk from his duffel and held it up to her lips. "Drink some of this and then we're trying something new."

Mollie smiled a tired but impish grin. "Okay, but I doubt I'll be very energetic."

He laughed lightly. "In a few days, when you're feeling better, we'll see."

"What did you have in mind?"

"You're getting too fatigued riding astride. I'm going to cradle you for awhile. It will slow us down a little, but you'll be able to sleep that way. It will give you a little more body heat as well."

Mollie nodded and took another sip of the sweet milk. "Okay," she announced, "let's move out before we get caught by sunrise."

Cadal sat her on Thunder's back. He swung up behind her and gathered Mollie into his lap. "We should make it nearly the whole way unless something else goes wrong." Cadal kissed her gently and sighed. They would get there, no matter what it took.

Mollie smiled, then frowned and turned her cheek to the wind. "I think something is going wrong."

Cadal nodded. "The snow is coming in fast. I know. We better move. We can't beat it if we're not moving."

* * * *

It turned out they couldn't beat the snow. It started falling an hour later. Cadal turned Mollie to him in an attempt to shield her with his own body, but they were travelling into the snow and she was too tired to ride astride behind him. As a result, the wet snow soaked through the quilt and melted against her hair and cheek. Cadal was frustrated by their lack of headway. The poor visibility had slowed them to a gentle walk.

He raised his hand to Mollie's face. She was cold, but she was asleep, not unconscious from shock or the temperature. They were still almost an hour out from the colony when the sun rose. Cadal hoped it was far enough. The sparse sunlight had one advantage. It improved visibility enough that he was able to increase speed again.

Cadal startled as he came over the next hilltop. There was a man standing below. For a moment, Cadal froze in fear. He couldn't fight and protect Mollie properly at the same time. He couldn't run with Mollie cradled in his arms either. The man raised his face, and Cadal sighed in recognition.

"Ho, Cadal," Traden's voice rang out. "What kept you?"

Cadal maneuvered Thunder down the slope to his cousin. He dropped stiffly next to Traden with Mollie wrapped in his arms. "I'll need your help."

Traden smiled. "So Morda informed me." He bowed formally. "I am at your service, your humble pack horse."

Cadal suddenly understood that Morda hadn't told Traden why they needed his help. His cousin thought they traveled this way simply because Mollie couldn't fly in the snow.

"You're much more than that, Traden. I charge you with protecting my bride and son. Take her directly to Morda and my mother."

His cousin's face paled. "Why?"

He settled Mollie into Traden's arms and kissed her cheek. "Because, dear cousin, I've already led them far too close. I must undo what I have done, and I cannot risk my family to do such a thing."

"Shouldn't Morda—"

Traden swallowed the rest of the question in light of the look on Cadal's face. Morda was no longer capable of what might have to be done. She was not capable of exacting the ultimate duty, and Cadal was. It was understood, but it would never be said. Traden nodded. Transfer of power or no transfer of power, Cadal was the Fairy Master.

"Your bag, Master?" Traden asked formally.

"I can't burden you more. Speed is more important now. I will deal with it."

Traden nodded. "The cold. I understand."

Cadal shook his head sadly and touched the bruise on Mollie's cheek, now an ugly purple. "She shouldn't be out here at all, but she insisted I not leave her behind." Cadal saw Traden's tears brimming over when he glanced up at him.

"Consider it done," Traden promised. He turned toward the colony with a brisk breeze moving behind him.

Cadal watched him go and sighed. He hoped Mollie wouldn't be too upset at him for doing this. He didn't want to leave her, but there was no choice.

He dropped his coat and bag at the base of a tree and led Thunder back to the top of the hill. He called the winds and swept the snow behind him free from tracks, burying his belongings in a bank of snow. Cadal ordered Thunder back along his own tracks while he followed behind, flying on a gust of wind and using it to sweep the tracks away that they left in each direction. If

333

only he could have gauged Mollie and done this at the same time, it would have made this largely unnecessary.

When they had covered five miles, he sent Thunder home by a different route and continued along the first set of tracks. Thunder would leave two sets of tracks that each dead-ended at least seven miles from the colony. The snow would take care of the scent for him.

Cadal was about to turn back when he spotted a search party. He hid in the treetops and watched them come. Cadal had almost forgotten how much fun it was to do this, and the memories of hundreds of Fairy children playing hide and seek with Humans didn't help him take it seriously. He floated along and listened to them as they reached the end of the trail. He was sure they would give up and turn back, but a deep voice caught his attention.

"I don't give a damn if it takes all day, every day for weeks. I will find that little hellcat, and she's going to pay for this," Thornton vowed.

Cadal bristled. There was no way John McConnell sent Thornton out here. He was sure of that. John was misguided, but like Liam, he was a good man underneath. Thornton found out they were missing and he was after Mollie on his own.

Cadal considered the accident he could arrange for Thornton, but he had already argued that with himself. Whether he rendered the ultimate duty or simply arranged for Thornton to be fatally injured by his own horse, Cadal could not justify it unless Mollie or the colony was in eminent danger. Killing him was not an option Cadal could pursue since they were not. But Thornton wouldn't give up easily either. Over days and weeks of searching, he could get close enough to the colony to cause trouble.

An injury that laid him up for a few weeks would have to suffice. Thornton would assume they were long gone by then. Why would he continue to search these woods that long?

Cadal smiled at the plan he had in mind. He gathered the winds and blew a solid wall of snow at the group. Then he reached out to Thornton's horse. The motion was precision. As the other horses shied, Thornton's mount reared up and turned suddenly, sending the overbearing man to the ground. The horse stepped backward lightly, supporting most of his weight on his other legs. Thornton screamed, but Cadal knew it was a simple break. Thornton would be out of his hair for a month. Two at the most. By then, he would most likely give up.

"Thank you, my friend," Cadal whispered over the breeze to the horse.

None of the Humans could hear it, but the horse threw his head in pleasure at the Fairy's satisfaction with his performance.

Cadal flew back to the clearing where he'd left his belongings. He dug them out of the snow in Human form and shifted again. Cadal swept the snow back over the clearing evenly and took flight toward the colony. It was untouched, as it should be. Traden had taken care of his own tracks as he walked. There was no sign left. They had disappeared without a trace, just as Mollie suggested.

* * * *

Morda felt Traden coming. He was angry. Traden was upset, and as he got closer, she felt his confusion. He slowed as he reached the tree-city. *The shift.* He wasn't sure he could do that for Mollie without hurting her. When Cadal shifted the stag, was the problem that Cadal did it for him or that the stag was not a creature that should have been shifted? Traden was suddenly afraid.

Morda set off immediately. She shifted and went to him then placed her hands on Mollie's temples and met his eyes. "Shift slowly. I will lead her through, but she cannot do this quickly."

Traden nodded. They accomplished the transition smoothly.

She turned back and stepped inside the entryway. "Take her to Cadal's bed. We'll care for her from there."

"Yes, Mistress."

Morda moved so quickly that she barely heard his response. She went to Zera's quarters. Zera was not in much better shape than Traden, and it was about to get much worse.

Zera paced the room and met Morda's eyes worriedly. "Where are they? You sent Traden out to them almost three hours ago."

"Traden is bringing Mollie in. Help me get a place ready for her. We'll need to change and warm her."

"Where is Cadal?" she demanded.

Morda sighed. "You know where he is. We don't have much time. Traden is almost here."

"What if something happens?"

"Remember who Cadal is. The Harmony will look after him as She always has. Mollie is the one we have to worry about — and your grandson."

That prodded Zera into motion. She pulled out warm clothing from Mollie's bags and quilts from the shelf. She set them aside as Traden breezed in.

He headed for Cadal's boyhood bed, and Morda realized her mistake.

"On this bed," Zera called to him.

Traden changed direction and laid her on the larger bed. Zera touched Mollie's icy face and glanced at Morda worriedly.

Morda waved Traden away. "Get Valia. Tell her to come here. We'll need a hot meal and warm sweet milk when Mollie wakes."

Traden nodded and jogged away.

She turned her attention to Zera. "Let's get her changed."

Zera started unwrapping the quilt from around Mollie. She noticed the bruise on her new daughter's cheek, but thought nothing of it but that the trip had been a rough one because of the weather. The snow had been heavy, and Mollie's clothing was wet beneath the quilt as Morda feared it was.

Zera started pulling off her backpack and upper clothing, and Morda handled the lower extremities. Morda arranged it this way for a reason. She felt Zera's shock before she heard the curse explode from the younger woman's lips.

"Harmony alive! What happened?" Zera demanded.

Morda didn't meet her eyes. "Quickly, Zera. I'll explain while we work."

Zera nodded and started throwing the wet clothing in a pile atop the soaked quilt. She dried Mollie's hair and body with a cloth then wrapped another around her hair to guard her from a chill.

Morda sighed. The explanation had to be given. "They had to come. They can never go back. Cadal stands accused of several crimes he has not committed."

"What?" Zera paused in the motion of pulling a dry sweater over Mollie's head. She looked back at what she was doing and continued dressing the battered woman. "How could this happen, Morda?"

"A Human attacked Mollie. He threatened her and her child, and as you can see, he hurt her. He intended much more, but Mollie called a horse to help her." Morda sighed. "The Humans don't understand why the horse acted out of character, so they assume Cadal was riding the beast when he ran down the Human and killed him."

"My son is accused of a murder?"

Morda nodded. "Yes. He is, and Mollie is accused of helping him escape the Human authorities." She smiled. "That is the only thing they are charged with that is the truth, running away."

"Why did they come this way?" Zera asked. "Why when it takes so long and leaves a trail?"

Morda knew that Zera already suspected the answer, though she didn't voice it. "Because Mollie could not make the trip any other way. She is too weak to fly. She was almost too weak to shift the few times it was necessary to escape the Human authorities. By all rights, she should not have made the trip at all." She met Zera's eyes. "If they had stayed even another day or two, Cadal would have been lost to us forever. Mollie would not allow it."

Zera nodded. "But to chance so much—"

"They had no other choice. It would have been even more dangerous for him to leave her behind, unprotected, and let her travel alone in worse weather."

When Mollie was dressed and wrapped in dry quilts, Morda touched her cheek lightly, gauging her condition again.

"Will she be all right?" Zera asked.

"With rest, food, and Cadal's love." She turned toward the door. "Let her sleep. The less time she knows Cadal is gone, the better for her."

They had settled at the table by the time Valia appeared at the outer door. She looked past the older women toward the bed where Mollie lay recovering from the trip. "Traden told me—" She looked to Morda uncertainly, then bowed her head.

Morda sighed. "Enough of that. Join us. Mollie won't wake for some time. We will start cooking soon."

Valia sat down, peeking toward the bed again. "Is it true?" she asked quietly, as if not to disturb the sleeping woman. "Did they—" She looked away.

Morda nodded. "Mollie has violent injuries, but she will recover. She won't find her situation as dire as those of us raised in the colony do. You see— Her injuries are not severe, by Human standards. Only her baby is of any concern to them. That is what they fear most for her, but I can tell you there is no problem as long as she gets proper rest. She has survived much worse than this, though not while carrying a child. This was all before she met Cadal, of course."

Valia's expression showed surprise that Morda wished she could feel. She should feel it.

"I didn't know. She told us a little about life in the Human realm, but I hadn't realized how truly barbaric they are. While she carries a child?"

339

"Some Humans feel as strongly as we do about it. Some of those Humans have risked much to protect Cadal and Mollie. Others, care for nothing but themselves. Or worse, for possessions and have no care for any living thing. Such a Human did this to her."

An hour later, Morda knew that Cadal had completed his task. Valia had almost completed the hearty stew she was heating, and Mollie was waking. Morda took a cup of warmed sweet milk to her granddaughter.

Mollie woke slowly, drinking in the warmth, and Morda was sure she would have liked nothing better than to be warm forever. She opened her eyes and smiled at Morda.

"Home," she mused sleepily. Mollie looked around the room, and a panic settled in. "Cadal?" she breathed.

She looked at Morda fearfully, afraid some accident had befallen him as they reached home. Morda sighed in resignation as she felt that fear.

"He's on his way. He should be here in an hour. Two at the most."

"On his way from where?"

"Covering your tracks. Even Humans can track, if they have something to follow."

"He's all right? You're sure?"

Morda nodded. "Now, drink this. It will help you get warm inside. You need to raise your temperature."

Mollie accepted the sweet milk gratefully. She sipped the warm liquid and smiled, meeting Morda's eyes. "It was you in the woods. It was you who kept me warm until I woke, wasn't it?"

"Not warm. Not in those conditions. All I could do was protect you from the worst of the wind. If I could have reached Cadal without being seen, I would have. As it was, I did what I could."

"You know they'll look for us."

"Cadal and I will take care of that."

"If he's found—"

"I know what he's accused of. He won't come to harm. The Harmony protects him, and he's resourceful. Now you must get some rest and stop worrying about Cadal. Food is being prepared. You will eat some while we wait for Cadal. Don't worry him."

Mollie nodded through a mouthful of sweet milk.

Morda smiled.

The time passed more slowly for Mollie than it passed for Zera those two hours. Morda was sure the concept would be difficult for Mollie to shed, this preoccupation with the passage of time. In fifty or sixty years, perhaps she would see the futility of it.

Mollie ate a small portion of the stew and fruits set before her. She looked to the door often, waiting for that first sign of Cadal's arrival. When she heard his voice in the hallway, she smiled widely.

Traden led Cadal into Zera's quarters joyfully. Cadal was drenched and shivering, but he had a smile on his face that looked almost childlike in its purity.

Morda nodded to him. "It went well, I see."

He nodded.

"Good. Go get warmed up before The Harmony forgets to protect you from your foolhardy ways."

Cadal laughed heartily and planted a quick kiss on Morda's cheek before he turned toward the bedroom.

"And don't lay a hand on her until it's warm," Morda warned him.

* * * *

Cadal closed the door behind him and smiled at Mollie. He dropped his wet clothing on the pile and pulled a dry set from the shelf.

"We could share body heat," Mollie offered.

"I don't think you have any to spare yet. Besides, your grandmother would hurt me if you caught another chill that way."

He pulled on his clothes and crawled under the edge of the quilts that Mollie spread out to cover them both. She nestled closer to him and wrapped her arms around him.

Cadal reveled in both the warmth and the way it was given. "Didn't you hear Morda? You shouldn't balk the Fairy Mistress," he teased.

"I'm not," she answered innocently. "She told you not to lay a hand on me. She didn't say anything about me not laying a hand on you."

He chuckled. "Are you going to be this contrary for the next five hundred years?"

"No. I'm not allowed to balk the Fairy Master, remember?"

Cadal planted a kiss on her forehead. "I'm not your master."

"Good, because I intend on giving you grief every time you scare me like that."

"Then I'll try not to do it often."

Mollie smiled. "Will you look at what I'm dealing with? You'll be out there again before the week is out. I guarantee it."

"Almost definitely, but hopefully not much past that."

A light knock interrupted them.

"Yes?" Cadal called out.

"May we come in, Cadal?"

"Yes, Mother, please do. I'd prefer to stay under these quilts until I warm up a little."

The door opened and Morda and Zera filed in. Morda raised an eyebrow at Cadal but offered no comment about the fact that he had not heeded her warning.

Zera smiled at the scene. "I will miss it when you two move into your own quarters," she sighed.

Cadal looked at Mollie and smiled. He could tell that she was thinking the same thing he was. "No hurry, Mother. These quarters have room enough for the next decade or so, unless you get tired of us first."

Zera laughed warmly. "A decade sounds fair. That way, I'll enjoy your company — and my grandson until he starts giving you the worst of the frights you gave me."

He grimaced. "Will no one ever forgive me those days?"

"They are forgiven. I just want you to remember so you'll appreciate what it was like for me when you did it."

"Then I'll be doubly cursed. If he has half of my tendencies and half of Mollie's—"

His bride favored him with a scathing look. "Which, *mathematically*, means you're saying I got into three times the trouble you did."

"I think that's fair. After all, I had a century to get into trouble. You had less than twenty years, and you more than matched me."

"I was a Fairy weaned on Fairy tales, with none of the usual powers, stuck in the Human world and dealing with Humans. You could shift, fly, control weather, and talk to animals. I think you had a slight advantage at getting yourself out of the trouble you got into. Your poor mother probably doesn't know the worst of the things you've done but managed to clean up yourself." She ticked off her points on her fingers.

Morda laughed at their debate. "Oh, yes. The Harmony chose Cadal's mate well. Mollie will keep you in line."

Cadal smiled widely. "I hope so. Of course, I fully intend to make sure she doesn't get into any trouble here."

Mollie shook her head. "I promise to stay indoors away from stags until I'm fully mature. Honestly Cadal, unless Thornton is going to sneak in the back door, I don't think there's much trouble I can get into."

"No. He's out of our way."

Mollie looked at him in shock, and Cadal caught a trace of what she was thinking.

"No, I didn't do what I'm accused of. I simply arranged a riding accident that left him with a broken leg. By the time he recovers, he will have given up the chase."

Mollie nodded uncertainly. "I suppose it's a kinder fate than they planned for me. Overall, it's probably kinder than I could have come up with for him if I had your power."

Cadal touched her face lightly. "Tucker was not your fault. You asked Thunder for help, nothing more. Animals can sense a person's intent. Even Humans believe that. Thunder knew what Tucker was, and he did what an animal will do to protect a loved one. What any creature would do for a loved one. Had I been in his place, I would have exacted the same punishment, tendered in a kinder way, in your defense."

Mollie nodded and sank into Cadal's chest. He felt her sudden exhaustion, and a deep sadness hovered with her over what happened. Perhaps it was better that Cadal hadn't had to exact the duty after all. Cadal wasn't sure Mollie's sensibilities would have managed it well.

Zera met his eyes over Mollie's head. "What did she mean when she said it was a kinder fate than the Humans had planned for her?"

Cadal glanced at Morda. "Can you tell Mother what she wants to know, please? Away from here." He moved his eyes toward his bride, though he knew Morda understood perfectly.

She bowed slightly in recognition of what he was asking. "Come, Zera. They have lived it once. It is better forgotten by everyone. I will tell you if you wish, and you will understand what I mean."

Cadal closed his eyes as the door closed behind them. Best forgotten? No, it was more important than ever that Cadal should remember the vast spectrum of Humans. They were capable of great good and great atrocities. They were also capable of tremendous insight and changes of heart, but until they became fully civilized, they bore careful watch.

No, he must remember, but Cadal would give almost anything to wipe the horrible memories from Mollie's mind. Cadal was still considering the futility of that thought when he joined Mollie in much-needed sleep.

* * * *

Morda cringed inwardly at the favor Cadal had asked of her. Zera was torn between her concern and curiosity and her fear of what she might learn. The Fairy Mistress decided to take it slowly and only answer what Zera felt she needed to know.

Zera waited patiently for several minutes. Finally, she met Morda's eyes. "What did she mean, Morda?"

"Thornton is one of the Humans I told Valia about, the ones who care for possessions above any living creature. He wanted something Mollie *owned.* He wanted her land, given to her by Xanthe, but Mollie knew what he was. She could not allow the land to fall into his hands. Thornton wanted the land so badly that he was willing to sacrifice her life and the life of your grandson to get it."

Zera paled. "This man Tucker wanted the land as well?"

Morda shook her head. "No, he wanted other Human riches that Thornton would give him when the land fell into his hands. If that meant murder, then Tucker would be Thornton's hands."

"Mollie's injuries were the result of his attempt to murder them? Mollie and my grandson?"

Morda sighed. It would be so much easier if she could lie to Zera, but her place as Mistress did not allow that. She could evade an answer, but she could not lie to her people directly. "No, Zera. Some of her injuries were the result of him abducting her before she could reach Cadal, but once Tucker was charged with his course of killing them, he hatched a much worse plan. As a result, he was stopped before he attempted to kill them."

"Worse than taking their lives? What other atrocities do Humans commit?"

"Many atrocities," Morda answered cryptically, hoping to discourage Zera from asking the questions that would lead her into what she felt Zera wanted yet didn't want to know.

Zera looked at her hands, and Morda heard her inner battle. This was territory Zera would rather not tread. She could stop here. The horse had killed a man who intended to kill two of her family. That, in turn, would have killed Cadal, his soul and his spirit. Did she need to know more?

Thornton still lived. If there was a threat to her family worse than death itself, Zera should know it.

She met Morda's eyes with an air of decision. "What Morda? What was threatened that is worse than death?" she asked timidly despite her drive to know.

"Cadal does not fear the act. He knows what was threatened could never be, but the threat, Mollie's reaction as well as his own, angers him and frightens him. Mollie lived as a Human for eighteen years. Some of her fears are deeply ingrained, even those that no longer apply to her. She knows the limits Humans have, but fear is not a rational thing."

"What threat, Morda?"

Morda sighed. Zera would not be put off. "He would have, if he could, forced his attentions on her. He tried before the horse arrived. The worst of Mollie's injuries were his attempt to end her struggle and convince her to submit to his will. Or what he succeeded in, to render her unable to fight him."

Zera stared at her in disbelief. "Heinous, I agree, but you said he threatened her child? If he knew—"

Morda nodded. "That he did."

"Humans would do such a thing?"

"Humans like Tucker, who would attempt such a thing, care nothing about those they hurt. For them, it is not an act of love. It is an act of power and control. Mollie's pregnancy would have meant even less to him than she herself did. He intended to kill them both, so the idea of taking pleasure from her before he did so seemed—" She shuddered as she continued, "Natural to him."

Morda felt Zera's anger and sadness. These were things Fairies had been spared knowing for millennia.

"My grandson could mean so little to someone? My family could be so unimportant that someone would destroy it for a single pleasure? For possession of a piece of land that they can never truly control?"

"Zera, you know now what Humans are capable of, but bury it deeply. Cadal and Mollie need each other, and they need an end to this nightmare. Do not talk to them about this. For them, the less it is an issue, the quicker it will heal."

Zera nodded uncertainly. "How does one heal from something so horrible?"

Morda shook her head quietly. "It is a mystery to me, but Humans do it throughout their lives."

"Cadal and Mollie are not Human."

"No, but Mollie has learned quite well how the Humans survive and how a Fairy survives the Human terrors. To an extent, Cadal has as well, and they improvise together. They provide each other strength in a way few Humans can or do."

Chapter Twenty-two

"How long, Cadal?" Zera pleaded.

Cadal sighed. It had been five days since they'd returned to the colony. At first he'd wanted Mollie to rest in their quarters. He'd accepted that she'd done so for her peace of mind and the continuation of her convalescence.

Mollie was much improved, though she still tired markedly. Physically, Cadal wasn't worried about her. Her emotional state was another matter.

"Soon. Mollie will find her center soon," he promised his mother, praying it was true.

He wanted Mollie to stick close to family. Traden and Valia, Morda and Zera would keep her safe from harm, but Mollie was almost too agreeable to that request. It wasn't her physical exhaustion that convinced her. It was fear, and that was something that couldn't be allowed to continue.

It became apparent on Mollie's first short excursions out into the tree-city after their return that the other Fairies harbored a deep curiosity about her injuries and the story behind them. Mollie's tearful outburst the first time she perceived herself as cornered and questioned about it made it clear she was not comfortable answering questions about the experience.

"Jada came by again to make sure that Mollie wasn't injured," Zera interrupted his musings.

Cadal nodded. "I will speak to Relen again," he promised. *And to Jada.* Relen's mother was convinced the boy had caused Mollie true harm somehow. It was preying on her mind. It was Cadal's job to put the woman at ease.

The Fairies contented themselves with staring quietly at the bruises they could see on Mollie's face and wrist after her outburst, but young fairies are notoriously curious and not mindful of personal boundaries. Relen was a young fairy, only forty-three years old.

His scrutiny had disturbed Mollie deeply, but when Relen brushed his fingers over the bruise on her cheek, Mollie had panicked. Mollie understood the youth was simply curious. She knew Relen wanted nothing more than to see if a bruise from violent action felt any different than a bruise from some accident. None of that had stifled her initial response.

She had startled and moved abruptly to Cadal's side when the boy's fingers touched the spot. Relen had been frightened by her reaction, and Mollie had apologized immediately. Cadal had reassured Relen and sent him on his way. Then he'd wrapped Mollie's shivering body in his arms and carried her back to their bed.

"Cadal," Zera began.

He nodded before she could voice her concerns. Reactions like that disturbed Zera almost as much as they disturbed Mollie. Cadal sensed that Zera was increasingly worried about the lack of intimate relations between himself and Mollie as the days passed.

Cadal knew it wasn't lack of interest but rather exhaustion that was causing the hiatus, but there was no way to convey it effectively to his mother. He held and comforted Mollie, knowing when she was physically ready she would approach him. The waiting wasn't easy, but this was definitely something he wasn't willing to push. She had been pushed too far in that arena already in her life.

"What can be done, Cadal?"

He turned to the bedroom door. Mollie was awake. She was listening to their conversation. "Mollie is doing fine, Mother. She is simply healing. In time, she will find her feet."

Cadal prayed it was true, but true or not, Mollie needed to know that he believed it. He could feel that from her. If what Mollie needed changed, Cadal would know it before anyone else in the colony.

* * * *

After almost a week and a half in the colony, Cadal woke to Mollie's hand on his cheek. As he met her eyes, Mollie pressed her body to him and kissed him, tentatively at first, then more passionately. His surprise dissolved in light of his immediate arousal. Their lovemaking was slow and thorough, amongst the most pleasurable they had ever experienced. To Cadal's delight, not a single thought of any other man or experience marred the moment for Mollie.

Afterward, she lay nestled to Cadal's chest. He felt Mollie's weariness, but she was happier than she had been in well over a week.

They found Zera preparing breakfast when they decided to rise. She smiled at them as they came to the table, and Cadal knew she had few concerns left for their relationship.

"I heard you were awake," Zera explained.

Mollie blushed lightly.

"After all, you and my grandson need a good meal in your belly."

Mollie laughed. "I think your grandson has found his appetite."

"I've noticed. Your sickness is much better as long as you are calm. Once your fatigue eases, your pregnancy will go much smoother."

Cadal shook his head and buried his face in the palms of his hands. He had forgotten that. How ridiculous.

Mollie touched his hand. "Cadal, are you all right?"

He smiled at her over his hands, fighting back a laugh. "Just feeling foolish." She looked at him in confusion, so he continued. "I was being overly concerned. I had forgotten that carrying a child causes such marked exhaustion at first."

"Yes. What did you think—" Mollie darkened a split second before Cadal did himself. "Oh. I think I see. Don't concern yourself about that. I'm jumpy, but it's not making me sick."

"What would I have to do to get you past jumpy?"

Mollie smiled a mischievous little smile. "Get the Humans out of the forest so you can stop running off to lead them away."

Cadal nodded. He knew Mollie hated it when he and Morda went out to dissuade their pursuers. He had been out three times. Mollie was always nervous and worried when he returned. The second time was the worst for her.

Cadal took along one of her backpacks with several delicacies in it.

"What are you doing?" she demanded in dismay.

"Leaving promised gifts for Liam and Elizabeth." His boyish grin usually melted Mollie's resolve.

It didn't work that time. She regarded him stoically. "Isn't this dangerous?" She dropped her gaze, but he knew she could see him through her lashes.

"No. When I'm done, it will look as if it's been there for days."

Cadal flew out and hung the backpack prominently where he told Morda to send the dogs. The more he thought about it, the more sense it made to end their trail this way. Cadal covered the site with a fresh coating of snow blown up by his winds then lounged in the tree limbs, wrapped in a brown cloak lined with thick fleece. The dogs would be here soon, and Liam was with the searchers. He would find his gift when they got that far, when they were stranded at the end of yet another dead trail.

He watched in amusement as the searchers, which included both Liam and John, came to a halt. Their trail had dead-ended again. Liam rode to the tree and lifted down the backpack. Cadal mirrored the wide smile on his friend's face as the other man brushed the snow from the pack.

Liam reached in and pulled out one of the two large bottles inside. He uncapped it and drank in the smell slowly. Then he took a drink and his smile widened. He handed it off to John for a quick drink then placed it back in the pack before zipping and shouldering it. He turned his horse back toward the estate.

There was only one more excursion that came anywhere close to the colony, two days later. Two blessed days had passed since with no sign of their Human hounds. It didn't really surprise Cadal. Liam and John's hearts were not in catching them, and Thornton was out of the game.

He grinned. "I doubt we'll see them again. They figure we're long gone by now. One way or the other."

Mollie smiled one of her impish grins. "You better be sure. After all, you want to keep me out of trouble."

Cadal knew that she was hiding something in an effort to surprise him. He touched her chin. "Explain to me exactly where you think you're going."

She wound her arms around his shoulders. "Well, you said Fairies wind dance during their ceremony. We can't do that with Humans prowling around." She met his eyes, and Cadal felt his instant reaction to the glimmer in hers. "You do want to make an *honest* woman out of me, don't you?"

He nodded then kissed her. "How soon would you like to have our ceremony?" he asked her breathlessly. Cadal hadn't realized how much he had been obsessing over that subject until Mollie brought it up so directly. Their ceremony was never far from his mind.

She feigned serious consideration then smiled. "How soon can it be arranged?"

"Is a week too soon?" he asked without even a thought of how it would be accomplished so quickly. They'd do it somehow. Cadal knew they would.

She put on a pout he knew was all for show. He felt the joy bubbling over from her.

"No. It sounds like a very long time, but I'll survive the wait."

Cadal drew Mollie onto his lap and kissed her. He knew he couldn't contain his arousal much longer. Already, it was like a fever in his blood, and every touch from his bride made it burn all the hotter.

Zera took one look at her son's face and laughed lightly. "Take her back to bed, Cadal. Celebrate. Breakfast will keep for a little while."

Cadal nodded to her with an impish grin that put Mollie's to shame and carried his bride back to the bed. As he swung the door shut with his foot, Cadal met her lips again. Her fingers were busily divesting him of his clothing before they sank into the bed together. Cadal hesitated for a moment before he started undressing her. He had no doubts this would be a ceremony like no other.

* * * *

Valia appeared at the outer door with white fabric draped over her arm before breakfast was over.

Cadal smiled at her. "I should have known. Was it my mother or Morda who sent for you?"

"Morda. I understand you've promised Mollie a ceremony in only a week. You certainly aren't making this easy, Cadal."

Mollie darkened considerably. "If it's a problem, we can push it back," she offered softly. "I don't want to cause upset."

Valia cracked a wide grin intended to put Mollie at ease. "It's not a problem at all. It's a challenge. I simply enjoy teasing Cadal about his hot blood and lack of patience."

"I was the one who pushed for the ceremony to be so soon. I suppose it's my hot blood and impatience that is at fault here. If it's a problem, please tell me."

Valia raised an eyebrow at Cadal. "Traden was correct. You are well mated. I always wondered what information he based that on." Her raised eyebrow announced that her personal speculations and investigations had yielded no answers.

Mollie's blush deepened.

Cadal laughed heartily. "I've been saying that all along. Finally, someone believes me."

Mollie smirked at him. "I still say your son is going to meet a stag someday."

Cadal nuzzled her neck and his smile widened. "Only if your daughter takes on a panicked horse while she's with child."

Mollie's smile disappeared and she paled. "What?" she asked weakly.

Her response was nearly drowned in the shocked replies of the same word from Valia and Zera.

Cadal stared at her, abruptly uncertain. "Surely, you have figured out you were carrying my son when *Thunder*— You have realized that by now, haven't you?"

Mollie shook her head miserably. "It hadn't occurred to me. Honestly, it hadn't. I suppose I would have to have been, but— I didn't realize." She met his eyes. "I'm sorry, Cadal. You know I didn't know yet."

Cadal felt regretful for his teasing. The stag annoyed and embarrassed him, but knowing she was with child when she tackled Thunder horrified Mollie.

He wrapped her in his arms to comfort her. "I'll make you a bargain. I'll never mention it again on two conditions."

"Which are?"

"The first is that you promise never to do it again."

"And the second?"

"That you never mention the stag again."

Mollie laughed. "As long as you promise to keep our children from carrying out either of those *scenarios*."

"Agreed." Cadal kissed her lightly. "Our children. I haven't thought I'd be blessed enough to say that in such a very long time."

Zera laughed. "Cadal, get your hot blood under control, or we will not have time to get this ceremony off the ground."

Valia nodded her agreement. "Traden is waiting for you at our quarters with the others. You better get going."

Cadal sighed. "All right. I'll leave you to tend to my bride." He met Mollie's smile and winked. "We'll discuss this later."

"After dinner," Valia informed him.

Cadal raised an eyebrow at her.

"We have much to do, and so do you. Come back at dinnertime, Cadal."

He nodded and kissed Mollie on the cheek. "I'll see you at dinner." Cadal wound his way down to Valia and Traden's quarters.

His cousin's quarters were teaming with people.

Traden's younger brother, Nolin, would be his third servant. The youth was only one hundred thirty years old, but he was a fine craftsman.

Their father, Berner, would be his second servant. Though Cadal wasn't Berner's namesake, he had taken as much hand in raising Cadal as Dalen and Cator had when Botor died. It was done out of love for the younger brother who died too soon. Berner had always seen Cadal as more of a son than a nephew.

Finally, there was Cessia. Traden's outspoken mother was there for only one reason.

Cadal sucked in his breath impatiently. His fitting would come first. Of all the preparations, Cadal supposed he should be glad to get this detail out of the way quickly, but he was already irritated, and Cessia hadn't even started yet. Cadal tried to relax himself with the idea that it was simply his lack of practice with letting Mollie out of his sight lately bothering him.

Getting the fitting done quickly was unrealistic. Cessia clucked endlessly that the former Fairy Master had been not as broad shouldered or trim around the waist as Cadal was. He smiled at the thought that she could blame Mollie's exertions on the farm for much of the muscle he had put on.

Cadal stood as still as he could in hopes of speeding the process, but Cessia complained that he was never still. A restless itching increased with every moment he stood while his aunt pinned, poked, and lamented her task.

The ceremony outfit would be done in time, but it would require major alterations to be a proper fit on Cadal. With no idea who would be the next Fairy Master, Cadal's clothing had been modeled on the set owned by the former Master months earlier. With forethought, this fitting could have been accomplished when they'd visited last, but they were trying to pack so much into so short a time that it had been overlooked.

Cadal would not deny Mollie or the colony the full effect of this type of ceremony, though he would have preferred the ease of wearing his own clothing. Marriage was a momentous occasion, but the marriage of a Fairy Master or Mistress was even more so. It meant new life for the colony. Cadal would marry in the traditional Fairy Master's ceremonial dress, as each of his predecessors had.

He smiled inwardly at Cessia's assertion that no Fairy Master had ever matched his garb so well. She couldn't know how right she was. No Master had ever had his combination of snow-white hair and blue eyes that complimented the outfit so perfectly.

His stomach was grumbling for a belated lunch when Cessia left with the garments. Cadal sighed deeply and sank into a chair while Traden got him food and drink.

Traden clapped Cadal on the shoulder and placed a plate before him. "Don't worry. That is the worst of it."

"I hope so," Cadal grumbled. He sank into the meal, ravenous.

Berner chuckled at the weariness in his nephew's voice. "Remember, Cadal, it would be an insult to your bride to be less than immaculate for your ceremony."

Cadal nodded gravely as he swallowed a mouthful of the quail. "I know it. That's the reason I put up with it, but three hours? Harmony, how much trouble can it be to fit an outfit?"

Nolin smiled. "In our cases, when the outfit is not much different than any other we own, not difficult. You, however, are the Fairy Master."

Berner's smile grew. "Which means you must adopt your dress of office, and it must be perfect for both your bride and the colony."

Cadal swallowed another mouthful of the bread and fowl that he had fashioned into a sandwich. From the day of their ceremony until the day he turned over to his successor, for any formal occasion, Cadal would don this same outfit. He supposed it should be perfect for that, if for no other reason.

"So," Traden interrupted his thoughts, "what are we preparing as your gift to your bride?"

Cadal smiled widely. "I know just the thing."

* * * *

Mollie tried on the gown Valia brought. It wasn't a style she would have chosen, but it was very pretty.

Valia eyed it critically. "At the very least, we will have to loosen the waist slightly. I'm sure it is uncomfortably snug since your breasts have begun to prepare for motherhood. I modeled it on Gady when I realized your sizes were very close. It's not a bad fit, but it will need a little work. What other changes would you like to make?"

Mollie started. "Oh, there's no time for that, Valia." They had only a week to prepare. The alterations alone, done by hand, would be a formidable job. At the same time, Mollie wished it was possible. It could be a fantastic dress with a few changes to the style.

Valia shook her head. "Your dress must be perfect, whatever your fondest wish is for it. As the bride of the new Fairy Master, this dress will be your ceremonial garb for his entire reign."

Mollie turned to stare at her in shock. "*My* ceremonial dress?"

"Yes. Unless, Harmony forbid, you should die during his reign, you will sit at Cadal's side."

Mollie remembered the smaller throne. She was expected to sit in that place of honor?

"There are stories that a Fairy Master who is at a loss will always find The Harmony's will in his bride's eyes."

Mollie looked at the metal mirror uncertainly. "I don't know what your norms are. What if the Fairies of the colony disapprove of my choice?"

Zera laughed. "Then the other women won't copy your design for their own gowns. What would you truly wish your gown to be?"

"Can I accent it with any color or must it be pure white?" She shook her head in amusement and placed her hand over her son. "A white wedding dress for me, indeed. Right, little boy?"

Valia looked at her in confusion. "We can use some of the Master's blue. See the cloak?" She motioned to the cloak lying across the table.

Mollie ran her hand over the soft blue cloak with the slightest hint of gray in its cast. "Like Cadal's eyes..." She snapped her head up as she realized that Valia had spoken to her. "I'm sorry, Valia. What did you ask?"

"What is the significance of a white ceremony dress to you?"

Mollie blushed deeply. "In the Human culture I grew up in, until recent years, a white wedding dress signified a virginal bride. Even today, there are plenty of jokes when a woman who is very obviously not virginal chooses to wear pure white for her gown. The jokes are considered to be in poor taste, but—" She shrugged.

Valia nodded uncertainly. "Does this go back to the idea of conceiving a child outside of the wedding bed?"

"Partly. Customs change quickly, but ceremonies change very slowly. There are very old customs that have become traditions in the ceremony I speak of. Others come and go.

"Some of the oldest customs involve *ownership* of the bride. A father gives his daughter to her husband, in some cases with a *dowry,* riches and possessions. At some points in history, brides were in such short demand that the husband would pay the father with riches to secure her hand in *marriage.* The idea of the father giving away the bride became a long-standing

361

tradition. It is considered an insult to not allow your father the right to do so while he lives.

"Unless some disease threatened fertility, brides were most prized if they were virginal. They were supposed to be virginal. If she was not, she was supposed to have only coupled with her husband. Humans of my culture have done away with many of these customs in recent years, but many still exist.

"Few times in history, they held that a man should be so sexually innocent going into *marriage*. It's well accepted that he should be experienced. I never realized how complex this is. It is very difficult to explain."

Valia nodded in confusion. "A man owns his bride in your world?"

"Not anymore. At least not in the culture I was raised in. Some cultures still hold to that idea. The tradition of a father giving away his daughter to her husband still exists, but it is no longer a formal arrangement. Her father doesn't own her any more than her husband does. Unless she's below *majority,* but that is a whole new nightmare to explain. In the colony, a woman would not be allowed to marry before she was free of her parents' rule." She sighed and tried again. "The father giving away the bride is a symbolic thing in the culture I come from." She shook her head at the complexity of the system.

Zera looked at her earnestly. "Would you like to include some of your symbols into the ceremony? One of your uncles could give you to Cadal. I'm sure my son would find it amusing."

Mollie laughed. "I'm sure he would. That is definitely not necessary. There are a few symbols I've always liked, though."

Valia looked at her with sincere interest. "What are they?"

Mollie let herself get lost in memories of weddings she had attended over the years. "The *bouquet* of flowers is nice."

"Flowers?" Zera asked.

"Yes, a handful of bound flowers which the bride throws at the celebration after the ceremony."

"To what purpose?"

Mollie smiled. "A game. All of the young, unpromised women free of their parents' rule try to catch the *bouquet* as it flies from the bride's hand. The belief is that the one who catches it will become promised next."

"What else?" Valia asked.

"There is a cake for everyone to share at the celebration. The bride and groom cut the first slices together and feed them to each other. They exchange matching rings at the ceremony and wear them always as a sign of their vows to each other. Or until they recant those vows in the Human world." She shook her head at the idea. It was so easy to fall into the Fairy mentality. It was a horrid system when you thought about it.

"Anything else? It sounds wonderful. I never expected Humans to have so rich a ceremony system for their ideas of the temporary state of being wed."

"Sometimes, the ceremony is the best part of a Human *marriage*," she joked. "Better to make it memorable. When the ceremony ends, they kiss. During the celebration, they dance." She smiled wistfully.

Zera shook her head. "They dance?" She scoffed at the idea of Humans dancing.

"Yes, they do. I taught Cadal how the Humans dance before I knew I wasn't one anymore, before I knew we could wind dance." Mollie smiled at the memories of being in his arms as they whirled across the floor. "Cadal is a wonderful *dancer.*"

Valia giggled. "Cadal danced the Human way?"

Mollie nodded.

"Why?"

She blushed deeply. "He knew it would make me happy, and I think— Maybe it meant almost as much to him as a wind dance. I know I was thinking that."

Zera regarded her curiously, then smiled. "I'm sure you're right. Is that what you would like your ceremony to be?"

"Well, it is winter, so flowers aren't readily available. The cake would be nice, but any sort of sweet bread or pastry would do just as well as the cake. It's the sharing that's important." She looked at her hands. "The rings aren't really necessary, and we'll wind dance, so I guess there's not anything extra to do."

Valia smiled. "Are you sure you don't want to add Human dancing?"

Mollie closed her eyes to join the memory again. "That would probably be out of place here. I think Cadal and I will save that for— Well, privately."

"As you wish. Now, what about your dress?"

"Do you have anything I can draw on? Can I make a sketch? It would be easier than trying to explain it."

Valia fetched some paper bark, a pen, and dye while Mollie removed the dress and laid it gently on the bed. She left the general outline of the high-waisted dress intact. Then Mollie added paneled puffs of the white with the blue in the folds at the shoulders, lowered the neckline to deep into her cleavage and squared it off slightly, and added a sash of the light blue.

Valia nodded her approval. "You wish no other decoration?"

"If there was time, I'd add a four-string knotwork around the neckline, cuffs, and skirt hem in the blue, but that can wait until later. As the sketch shows is more than enough work for the week we have, I'm sure."

Valia smiled widely. "As you wish."

Chapter Twenty-three

Cadal returned to their quarters moments before dinner to find the women huddled around the table. He crept up to surprise Mollie, but she felt his presence and swept the paper bark that was laid out in front of her into her lap as his cheek brushed her neck and he planted a kiss.

He smiled against the warmth of her shoulder. "Something you don't want me to see?"

"Just a surprise."

"You can't surprise me, unless I want you to."

Mollie laughed lightly. "Ah, Cadal *dear*. You know as well as I do that I can."

Cadal met Valia's shocked gaze and nodded. "When you want to," he conceded, "but you have to work very hard at it. I wonder why that is." He lowered his face to kiss her neck again and felt her shiver in response.

"Why what is?"

"Why you can do that and no other Fairy can," he qualified. "It's not your place in the colony. The other Fairy Masters could read their brides as easily as any other Fairy."

Mollie touched his cheek lightly. "It's not my place. It's my training."

"Training?" Cadal was intrigued.

He sat in the chair closest to her as Zera vacated it, then took her hand. Mollie slid the paper bark smoothly into Valia's lap as he settled, but Cadal was beyond interest in that secret. There was a more important secret to learn.

"What training? How does it work?"

Mollie smiled. "Cadal, will you concede that even Humans possess a certain empathy? Or more in some of them?"

He nodded uncertainly. "Liam struck me like that. And Elizabeth, to a lesser extent. They were very good at it for Humans."

Mollie chuckled. "There are many who are much better. Liam and Elizabeth are *amateurs* by comparison. Some are benign and some are the worst sort of *cancer*."

Cadal furrowed his brow. "But what does this have to do with this training? Were you trained as one of these empathic persons?"

Mollie shook her head. "There is no formal training there. I am good at it in the Human sense, but it is more because I have learned to be observant and to read into what is said and done. That is how I knew what Thornton and Tucker would try next. For the most part.

"My real training was eight years of pretending I was something I wasn't so well that I'd be safe from the *cancer* of the Human world. I learned to shield my mind and heart so effectively that I became untouchable. For eight long years, I was completely untouchable, until I let my guard down and forgot to use that training for a little while."

Cadal was hurt. "You would use that training against me?"

Mollie touched his cheek and shook her head. "To shut you out of my life? Never. I may try to surprise you, but as you said, it is very difficult for me to do. Do you know why, Cadal?"

He felt the anger and hurt melting as her touch awakened another deeper feeling. The heat from his cheek radiated like a wave through his entire body. "No," he admitted, "I don't. Tell me." He brushed his cheek over her palm to intensify the sensation.

Mollie's eyes locked on his and Cadal felt breathless. This was typically what she was like when she locked on his eyes. He could understand why it affected her so markedly. Her eyes were soft and alluring.

"Because, Cadal, you are the key that unlocks my soul. You always have been. Do you remember when we first met?"

"I frightened you, unnerved you. You couldn't be close to me," he recalled.

Mollie laughed again. "You never frightened me. I was afraid because I knew who you were. I dreamed of you, remember?"

Cadal nodded.

"I knew you were the one force I could never control, couldn't wall out of my heart, could never escape, and couldn't push away, even if I wanted to, and I didn't want to. I wanted you from the first time I looked in your eyes." She blushed lightly and looked away.

Cadal cupped her chin and turned her face back up until she met his eyes again. "You don't like to let your guard down." He ran his hand down her throat savoring the electricity in the touch.

Mollie cracked a smile. "Putting down my guard for you was probably the only smart time I ever did it in my life. I didn't have much choice, though. I didn't seem to possess much self-control when it came to you."

Valia laughed heartily, breaking the moment. "Cadal is hardly known for his self-control."

Mollie met her eyes with an impish grin. "He damn well should be." She met Cadal's eyes again and her smile widened. "How long did I torture you before you gave in and coupled with me?"

"Knowingly? Maybe three and a half or four months, but I wanted you the first night. I simply thought I couldn't have you."

"Well, that makes two of us. I was disappointed you didn't do more than tuck me into bed those first two nights when I passed out on you."

Zera laughed a low laugh at the thought of her son restraining himself from taking his bride for so long. "How did you torture him?"

"I was horrible. I let him know I was available and interested, there for the taking any time he was ready to pursue the possibility, in almost any way I could. I teased him, strutted around in tight clothing, even outright invited his attentions a few times."

Zera stared at her son in complete shock. "You survived four months of that without wavering? How?"

Cadal laughed harshly. "Oh, I wavered. I wavered often, and Mollie knew it. I just refused to give in. She pulled horrible tricks on me. When I made it clear I wasn't interested— I was lying, of course. She started ignoring me." He shuddered at the memory. "That sent knives through me."

Mollie cocked her head, raising an eyebrow in amusement. "You were jealous, too. I'll never forget you throwing your shirt at me and expecting me to play along and put it on because you said so."

Cadal darkened slightly then smiled. "That reminds me—"

"Yes Cadal, I brought the outfit with me. I wouldn't deprive you of it, but I have another I think you'll like even better."

Her teasing sent a jolt of anticipation through him. "Really? When do I get to see it?"

"I wanted to save it for our wedding night, but there are only so many secrets I can keep at once. Maybe tonight, if you're up to it."

Cadal smiled widely. "Is this one another that's not suitable to wear out around the colony?" he asked with a glimmer of hope.

Mollie's eyes went wide with shock. "Not on a dare. Even in the Human world, I could never— Not in public."

Cadal felt a pulsing tightness grip him. He'd seen what was acceptable in the Human realm. If this outfit covered less than her swimsuit or the halter and a pair of shorts, what did it cover? He couldn't imagine what the purpose of such a garment could be.

"Where do you wear something that is so restricted, even in the Human realm?"

Mollie smiled wickedly and wrapped her arms over his shoulders seductively. "In bed with your husband. It is a frivolous piece of clothing made for only one reason."

"What reason is that?"

"To banish all self-control in him," she answered innocently and sat back in her chair again.

Cadal's head spun. "Why didn't you use this weapon when you were busy torturing me?"

Mollie furrowed her brow. "Because you wouldn't have stood a chance. It would have been unfair of me on a scale you cannot imagine, more or less unfair than any number of things I contemplated doing to change your mind and didn't out of that same sense of fairness. If I couldn't attract you without being so underhanded, I didn't deserve you."

"For instance?" he prodded.

Mollie blushed and shot a glance at the two other women at the table. Valia and Zera stared in avid interest at the couple.

"Why don't we discuss this tonight, in private?" she suggested.

* * * *

Cadal stared at Mollie in a mixture of confusion and arousal.

Valia took her leave with a wide grin at her befuddled cousin, and the paper bark left with her. Cadal couldn't have cared less. He didn't even glance at Valia as she left. His eyes were locked on Mollie. They had been ever since her admission of how fair she had endeavored to be in her seduction attempts.

Cadal imagined Mollie laid back in her bed the night he massaged her. The heat in him coiled tightly as he remembered his hands caressing her skin under the halter while her eyes closed and her head rocked back in pleasure.

His fight could have ended that night easily. Cadal shivered at the idea of his hardness touching her at that moment. The prodding from Morda would have been completely unnecessary. He would have been unable to control his need to cover her with his body and give them both the release they craved. If he had turned slightly and brushed past her, no force in

Harmony's arms could have stopped him from claiming her.

Cadal watched Mollie and Zera prepare a tray of fruit and sandwiches, a concept that Zera found endearing. For all that Fairies were much more civilized, Humans were so very inventive. They tried so hard to pack life into such a short span of time they invariably struck on glimmers of pure genius along the way.

Was that why Mollie was here? Why Xanthe was pushed by The Harmony to leave? Returning Fairies breathed new life into the colony with their almost magical suggestions.

Cadal sighed, then smiled widely. There was no doubt that Humans were experienced and inventive in the area of seduction and loveplay. Even Mollie, with her limited practical experience, would keep him guessing indefinitely. Especially with surprises like the one he was sure to experience after dinner.

The meal passed slowly for Cadal. Mollie glanced at his intent stare several times. She shook her head in wonder at his interest and hunger for what was to come.

Zera smirked at the interaction between them. She spoke suddenly. "Cadal, after dinner will come much more quickly if you eat something."

He glanced at his plate, smiled at his mother, then nodded to Mollie before digging into his meal abruptly. Zera raised an eyebrow in amusement before returning to her own meal.

Cadal finished before Mollie and waited patiently while she finished her meal. When she set her plate on the counter, Cadal was at her back. Mollie chuckled and guided him back to the chair he had vacated. Cadal looked at her in confusion.

"Sit, Cadal," she soothed him. "I'll call you in shortly." Mollie eased him into the chair with pressure on his shoulder.

"Mollie?" Cadal got no further. His need was already more raw than the night of the massage, and he hadn't even touched her yet.

She smiled and touched his cheek gently, sending a shock wave through him. "It must be done right. It won't take long." Mollie turned and walked into the bedroom.

Cadal locked on the sway of her hips and stifled a groan. It better not take long. He wasn't sure how much more he could stand.

Mollie smiled at him from the doorway. "Smile, Cadal. You should have figured out by now that the waiting makes it sweeter." She closed the door behind her.

He didn't stifle the groan that time. Cadal dropped his head to the table atop his hands. Zera started laughing, and he looked at her in confusion.

"You really were in agony for those four months, weren't you? She can tease you unmercifully."

Cadal nodded his agreement, then smiled. "Yes, she can, but she's also correct. The waiting is torture, but the loveplay is all the sweeter for it."

"Hmm. Perhaps you should make an effort to wait more often," she suggested, suppressing a smile.

He laughed heartily. "Never, if I can help it. We waited far too long to begin with. Mollie slows me down when she thinks I need it. Like now, actually."

Zera looked at her son, then away to the closed bedroom door. "The Harmony must have blessed you two almost immediately."

Cadal nodded. "That was Her plan. She knew we had a limited amount of time to accomplish what we must, and we had delayed it painfully already. I'm sure She will take Her time with the next."

"Why was a child essential? Surely, it wasn't simply a means to convince Mollie to come here with you?"

"No. Mollie would have come with me without our son to push her. In fact, she agreed to it with no knowledge that the possibility she was carrying him existed. We committed to our promise in wind dance before either of us knew."

"Then why?"

Cadal sighed deeply. "I think you suspect why, Mother. The Harmony arranged this blessing for you. Look into your heart. Would you ever have believed? Would you ever have accepted Mollie as what she is, until she was carrying my child?"

Zera met his eyes tearfully and shook her head. "Harmony forgive me. Probably not. I have been horrible, haven't I?"

Cadal took her hand. "No, you were trying to do what was right for me and for yourself. Whether you realize it or not, you believed I would be hopelessly unhappy if I had Mollie and we couldn't be blessed with children. You may have been right. In time, I may have been, but even before I knew she could return with me, that I wasn't imagining she was Fairy, I burned for her. My love for Xanthe was an infatuation. I never realized how true love captures you so completely."

Zera nodded. "That is the way of it. If you've recognized that, your love is true. Of course, I had no doubt of that." She met Cadal's eyes. "I saw you dance the Human way."

Cadal scowled, remembering that night, remembering Zera's interruption of what should have been the perfect first coupling. *No.* It was better that he knew Mollie's past. The unexpected relief Mollie felt would have confused and frightened him, marring the experience even worse.

He sighed. "I know."

"I'm sorry for ruining your evening. I should have said that long ago. In hindsight, I should have recognized the way you heard my heart and known it for what it was."

Cadal smiled a tight smile. "If it makes you feel better, you only made us miserable for a few hours. Our evening wasn't completely ruined after all. We still had our first coupling." He smiled wistfully at the memory of the moment when he claimed her as his own. "It was beautiful."

"I have no doubt of it." She hesitated. "The dance was beautiful, too."

"Yes, it was. Wind dancing with Mollie is much better, but I wouldn't mind dancing the Human way with her again. There is something special about it. The movement is mesmerizing."

"You considered it your promise to her, didn't you? When you didn't know she could wind dance? You wanted it to mean the same thing, didn't you?"

Cadal startled. "How could you know that?"

Zera smiled. "I didn't. Mollie did."

He stared at her, working at that comment in mounting confusion.

She squeezed his hand gently. "It meant the same to her, Cadal. She wanted it to just as you did."

"She told you that?"

Zera nodded. "She did indeed. It was right that it should have marked your first coupling. Had I not interfered, it would have."

Cadal smiled widely. "It was perfect. Trust me. I'm glad you caused the delay. If you hadn't, I wouldn't have taken the time to savor it. Our first coupling deserved that much. It shouldn't have been rushed. If you hadn't stopped me, it would have been. Mollie deserved better than that."

Mollie's voice wafted from behind the closed door, calling out for him, and Cadal smiled widely.

"Don't forget to savor whatever surprise she offers, Cadal," Zera reminded him.

He nodded and headed for the door, still half lost in thoughts of their conversation.

Cadal slipped through and shut it slowly. He raised his eyes to Mollie and sucked in his breath at the sight.

The outfit she wore was nearly transparent. A gown of a black material flowed over her body. Her breasts and abdomen were only indistinct lines to him, thanks to the jacket of the same material that topped it, but he could see her breasts, mounded from the top of the bodice in invitation and clearly visible through the single layer of the jacket. Panties covered her, making that same indistinct landscape while her legs were clearly visible, even without the deep slit of the skirt that ended so far above the knee as to almost reach her hip.

"Harmony," he exclaimed harshly, but still Cadal drank in the sight of her without moving.

Mollie's hair, typically in a braid or a bun, hung free around her face and cascaded over her shoulders and down her back. Her eyes glittered in her excitement, and her legs were curled beneath her in a position that allowed Mollie to arch her back slightly, making a stronger offer of her breasts to him.

Cadal licked his lips and tried in vain to clear his mind enough to take advantage of the scene. This near-nakedness was even more enticing than Mollie's naked body pressed to him in invitation. Everything in her manner and position became a cry to enjoy her fully.

"Cadal."

She spoke his name quietly, and Cadal was in motion to her before his mind registered her tone of invitation. His lips met hers softly, and when hers separated to admit his advance, Cadal moaned in ecstasy at the taste of her mouth in his.

He tried to remind himself to keep control. Cadal couldn't get caught up this time. It was too important that he not. Mollie's hand ran up his leg to brush the length of his erection through his pants, and Cadal shuddered at the feeling.

Control. Cadal met her gaze and moved the hand to his back. "Not yet. There's no rush."

Mollie nodded and leaned forward to meet his lips again. Cadal ran a fingertip down her chin and neck to her breast. His thumb circled lazily over her nipple; he felt it harden and press against the thin material of the bodice. Mollie arched further to his touch. A low moan escaped her lips, rumbling against his mouth. Cadal moved to replace the hand with his mouth and sucked greedily at her tender flesh, while his hand moved through the slit in the jacket to cup the other breast, already hardened in her arousal.

Her hand tightened on Cadal's back. She started pulling his shirt up. He moved away slightly and smiled at her heavy-lidded expression. Cadal dragged his shirt off over his shoulders and tossed it aside. He untied the bow at the neck of Mollie's jacket and slid it off her arms. His hands moved the thin straps off of her shoulders and his mouth traced over the bare skin above her breasts, still encased in the bodice but now clearly visible to him without the jacket in his way.

Cadal ran his tongue in circles around her breasts, each in turn until Mollie was shaking in her need for him. He let his mouth trail down her abdomen through the light material. When he nuzzled at the thin panties, she cried out harshly. Cadal felt her arousal reaching a peak. He smiled at the knowledge and kissed her again, allowing her need to diminish slightly.

Mollie wasn't willing to let it go so easily. Her hand moved to his pants again, and she started unbuttoning them to free him. His hand circled her wrist to still her progress. Mollie ran her fingertips over the sensitive length of him and met his eyes. Cadal groaned deeply as the sensation rocked him, then reminded himself about self-control. He moved her hand again.

He smiled at her and eased her back onto the bed. "Oh, no. You wanted to see my reaction. You have to accept what I do in return."

Mollie smiled at him. "I wanted to see you with no self-control, but you're still in control. Very much so. I can correct that for you."

Cadal covered her with his body. "You will. Later. I want to see you completely lose control, for now."

"I'm trying, but you keep stopping my progress." She eyed the length of him suggestively.

He dropped his face to her chest again. That time, Cadal freed her breasts from the soft material and bared her body to her hips. Mollie cried out again, brushing against the length of him.

The shock wave it caused almost crumbled Cadal's calm. Out of control? If Mollie did that again, he would be out of control with no hope of stopping, even of slowing himself in his possession of her.

Cadal took a deep breath to steady his nerves. For once, he was not going to get caught up in Mollie's pleasure. The natural progression of coupling made such control nearly impossible, but it was necessary that he succeed. Mollie would drop her guard completely. Cadal would see to that, and she would learn what she should have had the pleasure of learning long ago, the bliss that came when you didn't hold back.

He turned to the warm flesh of her thighs and parted them gently. Mollie shuddered at the feeling of his fingers so close to the moist flesh between. Cadal ran his mouth up her inner thigh, and her breathing became ragged. He feathered his lips over the fabric of her panties and drank in her scent. As his tongue slipped below the fabric, Mollie tipped her hips to give him a better angle and wound her hands in his hair.

She was close. So close, but not quite there. Cadal sat back, then removed her panties, running his fingers in trails down her thighs. Mollie skated her hand down his chest to the sensitive skin below his waist, then lower. Cadal moved her hand again and kissed the inside of her wrist, feeling her pulse racing below his sensitive lips.

A sound that was half gasp and half sob escaped her lips. "Please, Cadal," she implored him.

He knew her body was in the midst of a riot of sensations and emotions. Mollie craved him. She craved his touch and hers on him and the release Cadal could provide.

"Soon. Very soon."

Mollie nodded, a slightly jittery motion since she was shaking. Cadal moved his hand to tease the silky material over her slowly, then brushed it gently into the depths of her with his fingertips. Mollie's eyes closed and her head rocked back in pleasure. He bit back his sympathetic reaction as her excitement rushed over his nerves and pooled in his groin.

Cadal lowered his mouth to her core and moved the soft material out of his way. He felt drunk on her essence. Her level of arousal added a heavy dose of musk to the spiced taste of her. Mollie voiced his groan for him, as his tongue swirled and darted in and out of the depths of her.

Mollie's reaction was electrifying. Her body rose to meet each caress and she sobbed helplessly. Cadal had employed loveplay on her before, but he had never been so dedicated to drawing her to the edge of the abyss until now.

The wall Mollie had erected against life was visualized in Cadal's mind. Already, cracks marred its integrity. As her sense of control crumbled, so did the barricade. Cadal understood, when she described the method to him that, though she was unaware of it, a portion of the wall was still standing, even to him. From that moment on, he was determined it couldn't be allowed to remain. Erecting little barricades to surprise him was one thing, but the massive structure which hid her innermost self from him could only cause trouble in the long run.

Cadal unbuttoned his pants slowly and pulled them off as he felt her senses cresting toward a shattering release. Mollie cried out in wild abandon, and Cadal felt the last of her wall evaporate into so much dust. He entered her swiftly, and her next cry mixed with his own. He allowed himself to match her rise. They moved together smoothly. Nothing existed outside of themselves. Cadal sank into the dark abyss with her, as she fell again. When the end came, it was explosive. Every nerve bristled with fire and ice.

He sank over Mollie, then raised up on an elbow and stared down into her face. Tears ran down her cheeks.

Cadal wiped them away. "Better?" he asked lazily.

She nodded and smiled weakly, still stunned by the force of release from imprisonment within the walls that held her for so long. Mollie closed her eyes and arched against him as the aftershocks began again. Cadal moved slowly to draw out the sensation for her. Her eyes widened, and she groaned in intense pleasure.

"Isn't it worth it to let your guard down and throw away self-control for a little while?" Cadal ran a hand over her breast playfully and the reaction from Mollie assaulted him so suddenly that he gasped.

Mollie chuckled. "Want to find out first hand?" Her hand brushed between their stomachs, then lower to circle the base of him gently.

Cadal's muscles tightened, and his body spasmed under her touch.

"Oh, you do, don't you?" she crooned to him as her lips trailed from his ear to the pulse point above his collarbone. Mollie ran her mouth back up to his jawline and arched against him, driving Cadal deeper within her as her legs wrapped around him to pull him closer. Her hand traced along his hip to the small of his back and made maddening circles on his body while she nibbled along his jawline and pulled herself onto him again.

Cadal's eyes closed and he surrendered to her hands and mouth as they moved over him. He shivered at the sensation building within him. Suddenly, he was moving inside her again. Cadal pulled back to capture her mouth beneath his own. His pace was fevered, and she drew him higher with every touch and movement. Mollie used her knowledge of the pleasure coursing through him to direct his rise until Cadal's world exploded again then spun out of focus around him.

That time, there was no teasing. There was a comfortable exploration, followed by blessed sleep. They clung to each other in their sleep, and when they woke for fleeting moments, it was only to move closer to each other.

Chapter Twenty-four

Cadal eased out from beneath Mollie and accomplished his morning routine quietly. For today, he would start the day while everyone else slept. Breakfast was cooking when Zera appeared at the table. He set a cup of tea in front of her and turned back to the cook fire.

Cadal felt the smile touch her lips.

"I assume you approved of Mollie's outfit?" Zera asked.

He chuckled darkly. "I have to admit Humans have a unique insight into what will appeal to a man, Human or not." He sat across from his mother. "They are a strange people. Mollie dressed moderately, even in an understated fashion when compared to many Humans of her culture. The things many women wore in public were downright scandalous, by our standards.

"Last night, she was more revealing, more *wanton* than I ever imagined her being. Still, I'm absolutely sure it's an outfit the Humans would consider tasteful, demure, even proper. She seems to stick to presenting herself as a proper Human. She's learning the difference between proper Human and proper Fairy very quickly. For the two of us alone, I have to admit I rather like proper Human on her."

Zera raised an eyebrow. "Though she was proper and you enjoyed her taste in clothing, you tried to make her wear your shirt?"

Cadal blushed deeply. "It was an isolated incident, and I was wrong to do what I did. In fact, I invited it on myself. I liked the outfit." He cleared his throat. "I had seen it privately. Mollie knew how much I liked it. I never envisioned my reaction when other men saw the same outfit. I was jealous. Furious was closer to the truth. In the colony, men would never have looked at her the way the Human men did, even if she was unpromised and not courting.

"I forgot to play Human for a moment, and I forgot I had no claim on her. I wanted one, though. Harmony, how I wanted one. I dragged Mollie off to talk to her privately and came up with some flimsy reason for my reaction. I upset her. Then I threw my shirt at her and told her to put it on."

"What was Mollie's reaction to that?" Zera's smirk announced that she suspected the truth.

"Immediately? She threw the shirt back at me, screamed an insult in my face, and stormed away, leaving me standing in the woods watching her walk out of my life." Cadal sighed deeply. "I hated every second of it. I hadn't merely upset her. I hurt her, and Mollie hated me for it at that moment."

"What did you do about it?"

"I calmed down and put my shirt back on. Then I went after her, kissed her, apologized, and told her how I really felt."

"She never wore the outfit again?"

Cadal smiled widely. "Only for me. I do like the outfit, after all. You may see that one, though she said she would wear an outer layer if she left our quarters." He laughed lightly. "If I hadn't apologized, Mollie may have worn things like it for days to teach me a lesson. No, maybe not. She didn't like the reaction of the other men, either."

Zera nodded. "That's good. She loves you but she's not afraid to speak her mind when you overstep your bounds."

"That's all right. I know how to handle her temper."

"Really?" Mollie commented from the doorway. "And, how would that be?" She leaned against the doorframe, her fist on her hip.

Cadal glanced at her appreciatively. "You wore my favorite outfit." He was trying to sidestep her question and doing a lousy job of it.

Mollie raised an eyebrow and regarded him with an impish grin. "After last night, it's still your favorite?"

He laced his hands behind his head and leaned back. "The outfit last night has, shall we say, limited potential for wear. This one, on the other hand..." His smile widened.

"I didn't ask that. Which do you like better?"

Cadal crossed the room and wrapped his arms around her, laying a kiss on her lips. His hands roamed up the bare expanse of her back. Cadal considered taking the halter off of her slowly in bed. He met her eyes. "Well, I appreciate last night's outfit. I would love to enjoy it many times, but I must admit that this outfit holds a special place in my heart."

Mollie laughed lightly. "I bet it does. Now that you've changed the subject, how do you handle my temper?"

Zera smiled. "She won't forget, Cadal. You should answer her."

He locked onto his bride's eyes and heard her breath catch. Cadal ran a finger down the neckline of the halter. "She knows."

Mollie leaned further back against the doorframe. "That's not fair." Her voice was low and breathless.

Cadal's fingers traced her neckline to the hollow between her breasts. Removing the garment slowly with his mouth alone sounded like a fine idea. He heated at the prospect.

"No, it's not," he admitted. "Neither is kissing you to get you calmed down. That doesn't mean I won't do it for your own good."

She darkened slightly. "For my own good, huh?"

Holding her like this wasn't nearly as easy as Cadal remembered it being. "Yes. When you're taking risks or when you're hurt or need medical aid. Whenever exploiting my advantage is better than the alternative. Have I ever used it for anything else?"

Mollie shook her head slowly. "No, you haven't."

Cadal moved closer and kissed her, breaking the hold he had on her. Then he smiled and backed away. "Come eat. It's almost ready." He started back to the fire.

Zera evaluated what she could see of Mollie's outfit, the front. From her reaction, he guessed that his mother didn't find it too disturbing.

He turned to smile at Mollie as he reached the fire. "We still have a conversation to finish later," he reminded her.

She looked at him uncertainly. "We do?"

Cadal nodded.

"About what?"

"About the many forms of torture you decided not to use on me."

Mollie laughed. "You really want to know this, don't you?"

"Certainly. With as many times as I came close to throwing caution and common sense away to lay claim to you properly, I find the concept that you were holding back in the interest of fairness somewhere between intriguing and enticing."

Cadal pulled a heavy baking crock out of the fire nook with a hook and set it aside to cool for a few moments. He smiled at the mild shock Zera tried to hide, as Mollie sat next to her and his mother gauged the full effect of Cadal's favorite outfit.

He opened the crock and started cutting jelly pastry onto plates. "It's a striking outfit, isn't it?"

Zera was still nodding quietly when he placed the plates before the two women. "I can see why you like it and why you didn't want the Human men to see it again."

Mollie blushed deeply and looked away in embarrassment.

Zera touched her arm. "It is no fault of yours, Mollie. As men are, I am surprised Cadal kept his control. Human men were most likely helpless. You are very beautiful, after all."

Mollie shook her head. "Never assume Human men are helpless," she informed Zera. "Cadal was right. I just forgot that for a little while."

Cadal set his plate down next to Mollie. "I may have been right about what they wanted, but I was wrong about how I handled it. I had no right to say the things I did, and I seem to recall you let me know that rather forcefully."

She smiled a tight smile. "Not a shining moment for either of us. I'm glad you decided to tell me the truth about why you were upset."

He nodded. "For the most part, you were honest with me. I know that. It's still difficult for me to believe how many lies I had to tell to survive there."

Zera gaped at him.

Cadal grimaced. "Yes, Mother. A lot of lies."

Mollie smiled. "You hadn't mastered any other way to handle scrutiny. And, you had to invent a Human life story for yourself. That alone takes a long string of lies. You couldn't exactly admit that you came from a Fairy colony instead of a Human city or that you had no first name."

He laughed. "Cadal is my first name. If I visited another colony, I would be introduced as Cadal dan Aiden."

"dan Aiden?"

"It means son of the colony of fire."

"What would I be called? I'm hardly a son."

"Until you wed, you would be Mollie bas Aiden."

"Daughter of the colony of fire, I assume?"

Cadal nodded.

"What about after our ceremony?"

"You'll be Mollie dannea Aiden." He raised a hand to still her question. "Before you ask, dannea means bringer of sons."

A wide smile lit her face. "What if you only have daughters? Corea had four daughters."

Cadal laughed heartily. "I never said the system was perfect. Besides that, the full title is almost never used...unless you end up at another colony or meet a Fairy from another colony outside the colonies. And, we know you're having at least one son."

"Speaking of names, how does that work here in the colony?"

"You mean as far as naming our son?"

Mollie nodded.

"You choose a name."

"Me? Don't you help?"

Zera laughed heartily. "Cadal? Why would Cadal help choose the name? You are the baby's mother."

Mollie furrowed her brow. "Well, what if he hates the name I choose? I don't suppose I can take the coward's way out and name him Cadal Jr.?"

It was Cadal's turn to laugh. "I won't hate it, even if it's Joseph."

Mollie wrinkled her nose at the suggestion, as he knew she would.

"We don't name children after someone who is alive in the colony at the time. That would get too confusing. Often, the mother forms a new name by using bits of other names she cares for."

"Like what?" Mollie asked.

Zera stepped in. "Cadal was named for my father, Cator, and my husband's father, Dalen."

Mollie smiled, and Cadal knew she had made her choice.

"What is our son's name?" he asked her formally.

"Caden. I want to name him after you and Traden. Is that distinctive enough?"

Zera smiled and laughed in delight. "It's wonderful. Traden will be so happy. It's a very special gift to have a child named for you."

Cadal was speechless for a moment. "You really do want to name him after me."

"I love you. Why wouldn't I want my son to bear the name of the man I love enough to *marry* and bear a son for?"

"For us, it's a blessing to have a child and a gift to have one named after you. To have both in the same child seems too much to ask."

Mollie touched his face lightly. "Not for you, Cadal," she whispered to him. "Do you like it? If you hate it, you know I won't use it. We have months to decide on another name, so tell me the truth."

Cadal kissed her. "I love it. I really do. That is the truth."

"Caden, it is," she announced and wrapped her arms around his shoulders to hug him.

Zera laughed. "Letting a man make the decision on a baby's name? That is original. Let's eat before it's cold."

Cadal ate slowly. He watched Mollie's enjoyment of the pastry with a certain amount of pride. It felt good to provide for her and Caden like this. Cadal was glad to see her eat a second slice.

The more he thought about it, the more Cadal liked the name Mollie chose for their son. She loved him, loved him so much she would name his son after him. Cadal believed Humans named children after their fathers in an attempt to extend their short lives, but perhaps it was more than that. For Mollie, it was an expression of how much she cared for him that she would name her son after him.

After breakfast, Cadal went in search of Traden and the other men. They were waiting at Traden's quarters. Valia was leaving to see Mollie, and Cadal kissed her on the cheek before sending her off to serve his bride.

Traden took one look at the smile on Cadal's face and shook his head. "The outfit last night must have made an impression."

Cadal lounged on a soft chair and laced his hands behind his head. "No."

"What?" Nolin demanded.

Cadal smiled wider at the memory. "Well, it did. She *is* exquisite. But that's not why I'm smiling."

"Then why are you smiling?" Traden asked, grinning with Cadal now.

"Because Mollie chose our son's name today. Just now."

Berner grimaced. "She didn't do the Human thing and name him Cadal, did she?"

"She wanted to, but I explained we don't typically do that in the colony."

Nolin sucked in his breath in shock. "You refused Mollie her right to name your son?"

"No. She asked if it would be well received, and I explained our ways of naming. She wasn't heartbroken. In fact, she chose another name almost immediately."

Berner smiled in understanding. "She made a name? A new name?"

Cadal nodded.

"But she used your name as a part of that name?"

Cadal laughed heartily. "Yes, Berner. That is exactly what she did. She told me she wanted our son to bear the name of the man she loves."

Traden nodded his head in approval. "You are doubly blessed, Cadal. You must be very proud."

Cadal met his eyes. "You should be proud too, Traden. Mollie named our son Caden, after us both."

Traden's eyes went wide. "She would do that for me? She would give me such a gift?"

"She already has, cousin. Congratulations. You have a namesake."

* * * *

Mollie was allowed to do little more than issue orders where her wedding was concerned. Valia brought Harea and Gady for the planning. They were to be her servants for the duration of the wedding preparation and the ceremony. The title bothered Mollie. She preferred to think of them as bridesmaids, despite what they called themselves.

For hours, they talked of nothing but what Mollie wanted. Samples of colony delicacies were offered to her to get an idea of what foods she might like to have served at the celebration. Fabrics were offered as samples of what sheets, towels, napkins and quilts she would like to have.

"This is like filling out a gift *registry*," she joked.

Gady peered at her curiously. "What is a *registry*?"

"When Humans wed, they go to a *store* — a *merchant*..." She gave up trying to find a Fairy word for it and continued. "They choose what they would like for their new home — linens, dishes, cookware, and utensils. Everything in the style they like. They write down what they want and the *merchant* keeps track of what people barter for on the list so they don't get things they don't want or too many of any given thing."

"It sounds like a good system."

"When the people involved are realistic about what they put on the list. I can't imagine needing much. Living with Zera means we're living in a fully outfitted home already. It's going to be a decade or so before we need anything. Well, besides *maternity* clothes and a *crib.* Baby things in general."

Valia smiled warmly. "I'm sure you'll get more baby things than you'll ever need."

Harea looked at her in confusion. "What is a *crib*?"

Mollie smiled. "It's a special bed for a baby or young child who is too small for a bed of his own. It has high sides so the baby cannot fall off and get hurt."

"Don't you want to sleep with your baby?"

"Usually, but a *crib* gives you a place to lay the baby when you want private time with your husband or a safe place to put him when you want to wash clothing or cook. When the baby needs to sleep or play and you need to do something dangerous or disruptive, it comes in handy."

Harea furrowed her brow. "And Humans do this often?"

"Depends on the Human. Some do it far too much. Some only do it once in awhile. In moderation, it's not a bad thing. The baby learns a certain amount of self-comfort and independence."

Gady stepped in again. "Don't Humans have family to help them with their babies?"

"Some do and some *hire* servants to help, but most don't. Chances are that a woman's mother and sisters are working and cannot help. Even if it were possible, I wouldn't be comfortable handing Caden to Zera every time I needed to get something done or wanted to spend time with Cadal. It wouldn't be fair to her. She has her own life and pursuits."

Harea shook her head. "She lives for the chance to hold her grandson. Nothing will be more important to her for quite some time."

Mollie nodded at the sentiment. She realized Valia was staring at her intently. Mollie felt a rush of concern for her friend. "Valia, are you all right?"

"Caden? You've named your son, then?"

Mollie smiled. "Yes, just this morning. I named him for Cadal and Traden." A sobering thought occurred to her. "If that is all right with you. If it bothers you—"

"No." Her face erupted in a wide grin and glittering eyes. "I'm sure Traden will be overjoyed."

"Are you upset by it? Upset at all?"

Valia laughed heartily and shook her head. "It means our families will always be close."

"It does? I like the sound of that, but why?"

"When you gift a man or a woman with a namesake, it is a sign of your trust in that person. Traden will be like another father to Caden. Your son can depend on him as a friend, advisor, and even as a parent if anything should happen to either of you — or both of you. Caden would live with Zera if that happened, but Traden would be responsible for guiding him. Cadal explained none of this?"

Mollie shook her head. "I think I understand. I trust you and Traden that much."

Valia laughed. "Of course, Traden may make a nuisance of himself for a while, making sure you have everything you need to make a happy, healthy namesake for him."

Mollie shook her head in amusement at the idea that Traden would be so attentive simply because she was naming Caden partially after him.

"What else hasn't Cadal told you?" she asked, breaking Mollie's train of thought.

Mollie blushed. "I'm afraid I don't know much about the ceremony yet. It will be different than the announcement, I hope." She grimaced.

Valia looked at her in concern. "What was wrong with the announcement?"

"Nothing, really. But no one was asking my opinion. Morda asked and Cadal answered. I never said a word." Mollie shrugged. "It's difficult to explain."

"You do want to marry Cadal, don't you?"

"Obviously."

"You had already agreed to it? Before he announced it?"

Mollie smiled. "Three times, actually."

Valia shook her head. "You mean you've wind danced three times," she decided.

"No, we've only wind danced once. He asked me to marry him thr..." She furrowed her brow slightly before continuing. "No, four times." Mollie laughed suddenly.

"Why?" Valia asked in obvious confusion.

Mollie blushed. "It's my fault, I suppose. The first time he asked, I was so shocked that I never answered him. Cadal must have been terrified I'd suddenly change my mind or something. He wanted to be absolutely sure."

All of the Fairies looked at her in confusion.

Gady stepped in first. "How are announcements handled in the Human realm?"

"Haphazardly. He tells some. She tells some. His family and her family tell some. There are printed announcements. Some people have a celebration where the bride's father announces it, but their closest friends already know." She shrugged.

Harea smiled. "Well, don't worry. The ceremony is your day."

The three women spent close to an hour explaining the many nuances of the Fairy ceremony. Mollie listened intently. By the end, she was even more disturbed.

"What is wrong?" Harea asked in annoyance. "Cadal had his day. The ceremony is yours."

Mollie considered it. "Does it have to be?"

Valia looked at her strangely. "It can be whatever you want it to be. It's your day."

"But it shouldn't be." Mollie looked at the stunned Fairies. "I mean, it should be, but it should be Cadal's day, too."

"I don't understand," Gady decided.

Mollie sighed and rubbed her temples. "It's so hard to explain this. In a Human ceremony, the official asks if the woman takes the man," she smiled, "for better or worse, *richer* or *poorer*— Forget that one. In sickness and in health, keeping herself only unto him as long as they both shall live. Unless she's cruel or *crazy*, she says 'I do'."

"That sounds close to our idea of a ceremony," Harea huffed.

"Yes, but then the official asks the same thing of the man, and he answers as well. Sometimes, they write their own vows instead of using the standard ones and say what is in their hearts."

"But the man has his say at the announcement," Gady reminded her.

Mollie growled under her breath and gave up trying to explain it. She walked to the pantry and got a big cup of sweet milk to settle her stomach.

Valia touched her shoulder gently. "It means that much to you?"

"I don't know. Maybe it's the reassurance of hearing his vow. It's a very different world here, isn't it?"

"Yes. It is, but it's *your* ceremony. You have hopes and dreams. Every bride does. Do you want a Human ceremony?"

Mollie shook her head. "I want a Fairy ceremony. I'm a Fairy. I should do this right."

"You want Cadal posed the question as you are?"

Mollie met her eyes and nodded sadly. "Yes, I would."

"Then that is what you'll have. I'll speak to Morda."

"That won't be necessary, Valia." Morda was in the doorway.

Valia startled, then bowed reverently. "Mistress."

"Go now. Take the others and work on the arrangements for the wedding night that you have. Leave the ceremony and the celebration to me."

Valia nodded and left quietly with the other two women behind her.

Mollie watched them go. She sank into a chair and buried her face in her hands. "Thank you, Grandmother."

Morda kneaded her shoulder. "Mollie, be calm. You're only making yourself ill."

"I know. I try. Sometimes, what I want or feel seems so insignificant. There is no logical reason I can use to explain it to them. The gap between what is done here and what is normal to me seems so wide. I love it here. Don't get me wrong — but I'm never going to fit in."

Morda placed the cup of sweet milk in Mollie's hand and sighed. "Your feelings, what you want and need, are never insignificant. You must learn to be true to yourself. Don't worry about justifying it. Say what you want. That is enough."

Mollie nodded uncertainly. "I'll work on it."

"As for the other, don't be afraid to make changes. Who says your logic is wrong? Just because we do something here doesn't make it right for you. Or even for us. Don't be afraid to balk tradition. You named your son Caden. That's a good start. Cadal is fantastically happy. You are as well. Is that wrong?"

"I hope not," she grumbled.

"Traditions are fine, but traditions need to flex to live. Sometimes, they need to be broken. Would you and Cadal be where you are today if Xanthe had stuck to tradition?"

Mollie slammed the cup down on the table. "Grandmother, I am not Xanthe. I never was Xanthe," she shouted.

"No, you certainly aren't. Do you know when Cadal first truly loved you? He didn't know it yet, but he truly loved you."

Mollie shook her head slowly.

Morda took a seat across from her. "You watered the fields until your hands bled. You planned to do it again the very next day."

"Cadal hated that."

"Yes. He did, but he also admired you for it. Cadal was only beginning to understand how very unlike Xanthe you were. Xanthe had spirit, but she lacked your drive, your willingness to sacrifice yourself for a greater purpose. Despite his belief that Xanthe was anything more, she was another pretty puff, to use his words. He was beginning to see that."

"He really loved me then?"

Morda smiled. "Almost *irrationally* so at times. He was shocked by his own response. He could have easily hurt both Tucker and Thornton in your defense, even the first time you met Thornton. That frightened him. Cadal would not have to resort to such things here. He had to remind himself constantly not to sink to it there. It was a fight at times to keep from doing something he couldn't hope to justify."

Mollie shook her head in wonder. "It really was as hard for him there as it is for me here, wasn't it? I thought the *bureaucracy* was his only real problem. It seemed so effortless for him."

Morda laughed. "No. There were times when Cadal thought he would never get used to Humans, especially when he thought you were one. You confused him quite a bit. Every ounce of his being told him you were Fairy, despite the fact that you were born in the Human realm. I kept hoping he'd figure it out on his own, but in the end, I had to tell him he was right about you."

Mollie furrowed her brow. "When was that?"

"I think you know when."

She felt her face turn a deep scarlet. "That was when he finally..."

"He would have earlier that night, anyway. Cadal was beyond caring. He needed you so badly, he was willing to test a story the young Fairies tell."

"What story? And why did he stop?"

"The story says that Humans and Fairies are capable of coupling. They aren't. In order for that to happen, the Fairy has to relinquish his or her Fairy life first."

"Like Xanthe?"

Morda nodded.

"What would happen if they tried?"

"Pain. Incredible, intense pain."

"So, if Tucker..." Mollie looked away without finishing, trying to collect herself.

"I believe The Harmony would have been kind to you, since you didn't seek the attention. She may even have heaped a double helping onto him for his punishment. Of course, I can't speak for Her in this matter."

Mollie managed a tight smile. "It would almost have been worth it to let him try, then."

"Almost," Morda agreed. She looked at Mollie in shock. Morda answered her almost before Mollie realized what she was thinking. "Yes, it would have been fortuitous if you had made your wish earlier in life, though I doubt The Harmony would have acted on it until you were both an adult and you truly wanted it."

Mollie nodded sadly. "It doesn't do any good to second guess things like that. I know it, but sometimes I still consider the could-have-beens in life." She shrugged.

"I don't know The Harmony's plan, but I do know you were much more like Xanthe before that day."

"Was I?"

"Yes. You were spirited and carefree. You hadn't developed the drive, determination, and control that make you what you are now."

"I never thought of those as desirable traits, I suppose."

"They serve you well, and Cadal finds them very desirable, unless they are working against him at the time. Without them, you would be very like Xanthe and no more suited to Cadal than she was."

Mollie nodded in understanding. "Why did Cadal stop that night? I was sure he wasn't going to, right up until the second he did."

"Zera interrupted him. Cadal would have claimed you then if she hadn't."

"Interrupted him? How?" she asked suspiciously.

"Cadal was Fairy Master even before his training started. There are gifts he possessed even then, though they were strongest with you. He felt Zera's rage, and he couldn't continue because he knew she was close by."

"She saw?" Mollie buried her face in her hands again. What a nightmare of a thought.

Morda sighed. "She doesn't hate you. You heard all of her objections at your first visit. She only resented you because she thought you were Human. She was afraid of losing Cadal. I'm sure you can appreciate that."

Mollie nodded. "Did he leave to speak to you? Or to her?"

"No. He left to try and reconcile what he was doing. He wanted you, but leaving the colony would be our downfall."

"Because he's Fairy Master?"

"Yes. Cadal couldn't stay in the Human realm with you. He couldn't face the possibility of leaving you and losing you...or even hurting you. He couldn't tell you the truth. Cadal wouldn't admit to me what he was for fear that I would make him leave, though I knew anyway. He hated Zera for reminding him of his situation and stealing that moment of pure joy he had been lost in. He needed to lose himself in it. His soul cried out for it and for you."

Mollie nodded in understanding. "Where did he go? He was obviously outdoors for quite some time."

"When Cadal decided he had nowhere to go, he sat down and stared into the pond, trying to figure out what he should do next. I think he would have sat there all night if I hadn't gone to him."

"How could you get to him so fast?"

"I didn't. Not really. I had just come from intercepting Zera, ordering her away so that Cadal could commit to you in peace. I followed her out, because I knew you and Cadal were at a sensitive juncture in your relationship."

"What do I do about this ceremony?" Mollie asked abruptly.

"Why do you ask me?" Morda's eyes widened in surprise.

Mollie was sure it was feigned. "You came here for a reason. I know you did. Isn't your job to resolve conflict between individuals and within individuals?" She arched an eyebrow at her grandmother and offered her a slightly strained grin.

Morda laughed heartily. "Yes. I suppose it is. Would you like my help?"

"Yes, I really would."

"Very well, then. Will you allow me to conduct a transfer?"

"If that's what needs done. I know it won't be like your transfers to Cadal. He explained it to me."

"Then this will be an easy matter to settle."

"Will you transfer to me or from me?"

"Both. You'll see. May I begin?"

She nodded and moved to the chair next to Morda. Mollie closed her eyes and took a calming breath as Morda's hands were placed.

"Just relax," Morda instructed.

Mollie laughed. "I've heard that before."

"An inspired move on Cadal's part," Morda admitted. "I suppose there is a first time for anything, but don't expect it from me."

Mollie laughed again.

"Clear your mind."

Mollie did as she was told, and the transfer began.

Images of Fairy ceremonies and celebrations over the years passed through her mind. It was more than images. Mollie could smell the smells, hear the music, and even taste the foods.

The transfer changed. Memories of Human weddings flooded through Mollie's mind. Again, the sensations assaulted her.

Morda spoke inside the transfer. "Do you understand what I'm doing?"

"I'm not sure. Are you gauging my responses?"

"Yes. Exactly. When we are done, I will know what you truly want your ceremony and celebration to be."

"Then we write it all down for Valia?"

"No, then I transfer it to those who need to prepare. It will be much quicker and easier that way."

Mollie sank into the information speeding past her and let the time slip away. As when Cadal accessed information on insects, she hadn't realized how much information and how many experiences were stored in her mind on any given subject.

The transfer ended, and Mollie yawned deeply. Gentle as it was, the long transfer was tiring. She could barely open her eyes to look at her grandmother with a bleary sort of understanding.

Morda touched her cheek. "Get some rest, Mollie. Cadal will be home soon."

Mollie nodded and hugged her grandmother before she trudged back to bed. She was deeply asleep before the outer door closed.

Chapter Twenty-five

Cadal wasn't surprised when Valia breezed back into her quarters. He'd felt Mollie's frustration, though he'd actively avoided eavesdropping to find its cause. That wouldn't be appropriate, considering what she was getting accomplished.

Valia crossed to her husband and kissed his cheek. She smiled warmly. "Congratulations, Traden," she crooned to him.

Traden smiled the same wide smile that had been plastered on his face every time he considered his namesake and patted her hip. She disappeared into the bedroom to resume her sewing.

As the door closed, pieces of Cadal's gift reappeared from beneath the cloths that had been hastily thrown over them. The only colony woman who would know what Cadal's gift to his bride would be was Morda. No colony man would be permitted to see Mollie's dress. Having Valia and Traden doing their work in the same quarters was unusual, to say the least.

Cadal furrowed his brow. He felt a string of emotions from Mollie, strong emotions. Weariness and anger were followed by confusion. Cadal fought back his initial response. No matter how raw his emotional state, it would be inappropriate for him to take action against anyone, especially in this matter.

He hazarded a peek at Mollie and discovered that she was talking to Morda. Confident that she was in good hands, Cadal cut off his query before he could learn the particulars of her upset. Cadal sighed. In less than a week, he would be unable to do this. He would be unable to shut anyone out ever again...for his entire term.

It was well over an hour before Morda appeared in the doorway. Cadal glanced around her shoulder in shock, and Traden draped a cloth over their work.

Morda shook her head in amusement. "Don't worry, Cadal. I wouldn't bring her here. Your gift is safe."

Traden moved to uncover the pieces.

Cadal nodded in relief. "Where is Mollie?"

"She's taking a well-needed nap. She probably won't wake for several hours."

"Is something wrong?" Cadal had felt Mollie's upset. If she made herself sick over the preparations, he wouldn't be able to stand it. It wasn't merely the possibility that she might be ill that bothered him. Another delay was not something Cadal could handle.

Morda smiled patiently. "Not at all. She's simply drained from transfer."

Cadal started. "What could be so intensive?" he demanded. He cringed at the edge that crept into his voice. He shouldn't take this out on Morda.

Traden and Berner peered at him. Cadal felt their concern at his outburst. This wasn't Cadal's usual way, and they knew it. Nolin actively avoided meeting his eyes.

Cadal waved a hand to Morda in apology.

The Mistress sat down with a sigh. "The ceremony planning was wearing her down, both physically and emotionally. It seemed the quickest way. Now, she can relax. There is little left for Mollie to do, and she will be rested enough to enjoy her own ceremony."

Cadal nodded. "I felt her anger and frustration. I hadn't realized it had gotten that bad."

"She'll be fine. We talked extensively, and the transfer went well," Morda added pointedly to soothe his fears that Mollie wouldn't accept it as smoothly from anyone but Cadal. "I need to see Valia and the others. A short transfer to each of them will end any further debate."

Cadal ground his teeth. No wonder Mollie was frustrated. There should be no discussion involved. Mollie's wishes should have been carried out without question. "Debate? What debate could there be?" he asked as calmly as he could. Cadal was having trouble hiding his rage.

"Mollie is unconventional. You have a few surprises in store. The other Fairies were concerned that her ideals are often at odds with our traditions. What she wants is more beautiful than I ever imagined in both its ceremony and in what it means to her to have it that way. It is priceless to her. Mollie was simply at a loss to explain it properly to Valia and the others. Change does not come easily to us."

"You formed an image of the whole, and now you'll tell each of them what she wants?"

"Precisely. Now, if you'll excuse me, I have to get the women working on what must be done."

Cadal nodded, and Morda disappeared into the bedroom with Valia. The men's heads snapped up at Valia's squeal of pure delight. Almost in unison, they turned to smirk at Cadal. He felt his face start to burn, shrugged, and went back to his work.

Traden handed him an etching tool. "It sounds as if you have some very interesting surprises in store for you," he commented. Traden raised an eyebrow in amusement.

Cadal managed a tight smile. "With Mollie, life will be a series of surprises, and I intend to enjoy every single one of them as much as I can. If I wanted no surprises, I could have stayed here and surrounded myself with pretty puffs. As I recall, I have been rather popular when I chose to be."

"No, you couldn't. Your soulmate was calling to you. You had to go to her. Besides, while the ladies may have enjoyed your attentions, you never really enjoyed theirs. Until now. Mollie has captured a place in you that no woman ever has or ever will again. You could never be happy, here or anywhere, without her."

Cadal nodded and managed a real smile that time. "You're right about that, but having a spirited woman means that I'll have all of the temper and inspiration that is a part of the package. Somehow, I think that makes the having all the better."

Morda passed back through the room and smiled at Cadal. "This is going to be the finest celebration in millennia. I think you'll appreciate your bride's sense of style."

Cadal's smile widened and he raised an eyebrow at his mentor. "I'm sure I will. I enjoy her taste in clothing, and it's a stretch not to peek at that dress every time I'm here. She will have exactly what she wants. I'll simply sit back and enjoy my surprises."

"Yes, I think you will at that." With that, she left to find her granddaughters.

Berner and Nolin chuckled at the thought of the Fairy Master being surprised by anything.

Cadal gave them a stern look that was not for show. His temporary reprieve from his moodiness was over. "I allow myself to be surprised for the enjoyment. I like surprises, especially the ones my bride arranges."

Traden laughed uproariously. "That's not what I heard."

"She can keep a secret with enough concentration. It comes from her time in the Human realm. She can't do it at all sometimes, and she can't keep secrets that hurt. All of her secrets are playful, so I let it go when I know she's keeping one."

Nolin nodded. "You are going to have a very interesting life. Much more interesting than you ever counted on."

Traden smiled. "Cadal has always had an interesting life. If The Harmony wasn't protecting him and his bride—"

Berner laughed heartily.

Cadal sighed. This was another annoyance that would never end. "Berner, don't say it," he warned. "I finally got Mollie to drop that subject. Don't make me order you. Understood?"

"As you wish, Master," Berner replied reverently, but with the glimmer of the withheld comment still in his eyes.

Cadal sighed again. "The Humans have a saying. With friends like you, who needs enemies? You know, I never really appreciated the sentiment until just this moment."

Traden looked at him in surprise. "Cadal, you don't mean that."

"You know I don't," he snapped. "Neither do the Humans. It is a sign of annoyance with someone they really do care for, but I understand it much better now."

Cadal fingered the etching tool, then ran a hand over his chin. He looked away from his family. "I know who the enemy is. I broke his leg to save my family and my colony. If *Thunder* hadn't gotten to Mollie first, I would have arranged much worse for Mr. Tucker." Cadal sighed and rubbed his temples roughly. "Perhaps worse than what did happen to him. I know that shocks you, Traden, but what he threatened and what he did would shock you much worse than what I would have done to him."

Traden dropped a hand on Cadal's shoulder. "Go see your bride. I think you need the rest as much as she does."

Cadal met his eyes and nodded. "You're probably right about that. I think I will lay down for a little while." He pushed the etching tool toward his cousin and turned to go.

"Cadal?" Traden called after him.

He stopped and looked back wearily.

"Try sleeping this time. It works wonders."

Cadal laughed a brittle little laugh. "Not likely, Traden, but I will try."

On the way back to his quarters, Cadal listened to the conversation of the men he'd left behind. He knew they were worried about him, but until Cadal took his place and Morda stepped down, there would be no peace for him.

Morda was failing. He had felt it for days. If Mollie hadn't approached the subject of their ceremony, Cadal would have had to very soon. Only Mollie calmed the wild buzzing in his head and ache in his soul.

Cadal passed through their empty quarters. Zera was with the women preparing for the ceremony. Only the women of Mollie's family, Zera, and Valia would know what Mollie had planned.

That was fine with Cadal. Whatever she chose would be wonderful, and they would be one at last.

Anything Mollie chose would be precious to him for marking the end of his long journey. Once they were wed, he could take his place. Once Mollie's day was over.

He watched Mollie sleep for several long moments before he stripped off his clothing and slipped into bed beside her. As she did the first night Cadal knew her, Mollie moved closer to him in her sleep and her hair brushed his cheek. They had come so far since then. He wrapped his arm over her and kissed the top of her head gently. Mollie murmured something and turned to his chest. Cadal smiled at the thought that, even the first night, he would have been fantastically happy to have Mollie in his arms like this.

Cadal rested a hand over Caden to check on him, then sighed in contentment that his son was healthy and safe after everything that had happened.

As he fell asleep, Cadal considered the peace that Mollie gave him, a peace that was elusive any time she was not in his company. He would spend as little time away from her as he could until he took his place. If Cadal could figure out a way to arrange that, it would be a feat of magic.

* * * *

Morda knew the problem. She was simply at a loss when it came to a solution. Cadal was correct in his assessment, but she had no more clue than he did how to solve the dilemma.

She made her way to Traden's quarters. If it had come to this, she would admit what she had come to say to him and live with the embarrassment of the admission. It was more important that Cadal find the peace he was denied until he could take his place.

Traden bowed his head to her and continued his work.

"Berner and Nolin have gone to dinner?" she asked.

"Yes, Mistress."

"How is it coming?"

"Just fine. The gift should be completed in two more days at the most. More than enough time."

Morda sat down facing the young man. She chose her words carefully. Morda wished she could read him, but as her powers diminished, only powerful emotions were passing to her without the benefit of the transfer. Rather, they were passing to her, but her mind was no longer capable of dealing with the flow effectively. Only those powerful enough caught her attention.

"Traden, how long would it take without Cadal's assistance?"

His head snapped up. Traden's concern was strong. She could feel that much.

"Is there a problem? Is Cadal or Mollie— Are they ill?"

Traden had seen Cadal's irritation and weariness. Of that she had no doubt. Traden loved his cousin, and such a thing would not have escaped his attention.

Morda flitted her hand in dismissal. "Not at all. This is a difficult situation, Traden."

"What is, Mistress?"

"Traden, my time has come. Passed, actually. I am Mistress in little more than name now."

Traden looked away and tried to hide the deep sorrow he felt at her admission. He was hiding more. Traden was hiding his nervousness.

"You knew this already?"

He nodded. "Yes, I do," Traden whispered. "This is not something we should discuss. It is not appropriate that I should have this confidence."

"It *is* appropriate. We must discuss this, for Cadal's sake."

Traden locked on her eyes. "Why his sake?"

"Cadal has only the final transfer before he can take his place. His entire being screams to take that step. Cadal is in pain, pain as real as he felt when Xanthe left him. You remember those days?"

Traden grimaced at the memory, nodding.

"You hurt with him, because you love him."

"Yes, I remember. What can be done?"

"As always, he draws comfort from his bride. Cadal must be allowed as much time in her arms as we can arrange. Every moment he isn't there is agony for him. There is little left for Mollie to do. We need to free Cadal from his duties as much as possible. Tell him it is my wish that he keep Mollie calm. I will shield him from your true intentions. It's dishonest, I know. It's simply the best I can come up with to help him now."

"Then I was right to send him to her earlier?"

"Yes, you were."

"Cadal seemed strained, irritated. I thought he was simply tired."

"He's weary, but the sensations are also uncomfortable. Cadal's nerves are worn thin. He is trying to control his gifts without the transfer he needs to do so."

"Can the transfer be done sooner? Can we end this?" Traden asked urgently.

"No. It's difficult to explain, but the nature of the transfer requires Cadal to be complete. It cannot be accomplished before the ceremony. His soul must be whole." She smiled sadly. "We've already sidestepped quite a few traditions on the way, those that are a good idea but not required."

Traden smiled. "Like Mollie's presence at the former transfers?"

Morda winced. "Zera told you?"

"Yes. The images of Cadal's pain disturbed her. We understand it would cause concern, so it's considered a family secret." He started and looked at Morda abruptly. "Can the transfer be done on the ceremony day?"

She shook her head.

"Do they need to consummate their ceremony before the transfer?"

Morda chuckled. "No. I think it's safe to say they've consummated their union."

"Is it a tradition then?" Traden asked pointedly.

"Yes, but it's one I will not ever balk."

"What tradition is it?"

"Nothing will be allowed to detract from Mollie's day. It cannot. Her day must be as she truly wishes it to be."

Traden nodded in perfect understanding. "The very next day," he decided.

"Yes. It will have to be. You will help until then?"

"You know I will."

* * * *

Cadal woke to the smell of another rich stew. Mollie liked the stews the women prepared for her. She ate them more heartily than anything save the jelly pastry he made for her, so the women kept making variations of it in hopes that her appetite would remain a good one, for her sake and Caden's.

His stomach rumbled, and Cadal realized he was famished. Zera would come to wake them soon.

He snuggled closer to Mollie and smiled at the feeling of having her in his arms, even when she fell into bed fully dressed and wearing her shoes. Her presence soothed and comforted him. Dinner could wait. Like the night Cadal had massaged her, the idea of removing his hands from Mollie was a foreign concept to him.

Mollie moved inside the circle of his arms. She pressed a kiss to his throat and wound her arms around his chest. "I like waking up like this. Maybe we should schedule a nap together every afternoon."

She settled closer to his chest, and Cadal realized Mollie had removed the halter when she put on the shirt she wore. His sense of loss evaporated as her breasts brushed the skin of his chest through the soft material of her shirt.

Cadal smiled, then remembered the reason for this nap. "It sounds good to me. Are you sure you're all right? I was worried about you."

She nodded. "I was tired before the transfer. It just made me more tired. I feel much better now."

"How much better?" he teased, running his hands under the back of her shirt.

Mollie giggled and moved against him purposefully. "Very much." She nipped at his ear and her whisper rumbled through him.

Voices wafted through the door. Valia was discussing something with Zera, and Mollie strained to hear what it was.

"I'm sorry, Valia. Cadal and Mollie are resting. Can it wait until tomorrow?"

"I suppose. I had hoped to speak to her alone for a moment."

Mollie groaned and started to sit up.

Cadal wrapped his arms tighter and pulled her gently but firmly against his chest. "Don't go. Whatever it is, it can wait. Can't it?" He searched her face for confirmation.

"She said it would only take a few minutes. If we'll have peace for the rest of the night, isn't it worth it?"

He sighed. "I suppose so. Go on, but just a few minutes." Cadal released her and kissed Mollie's neck as she rose to go.

"I promise."

Cadal smiled at the sway of her hips as she left the bedroom. Mollie had a way of gliding as she walked that he had never noticed in another woman.

Mollie touched Valia's shoulder.

Traden's wife looked past her to Cadal, then blushed deeply at the sight of him covered to the waist by the quilt that she had stolen Mollie's warmth from. She bowed to him reverently. Then Valia took Mollie's arm and led her out of sight.

Cadal furrowed his brow and swore fluently under his breath. Something was going on that shouldn't be. He knew that, but he shouldn't pry into it if it had to do with the ceremony. He retrieved his clothes from the floor, growling in irritation as he pulled them on and left the bed.

As Cadal expected, Valia had removed Mollie from their quarters for their discussion. *Damn!* He couldn't wait for their ceremony. There would be no reason for this type of annoyance after that.

And, if whatever Valia was talking to Mollie about was another dismissal of Mollie's rights to choose her ceremony, a judgment would come due. Cadal reined in the thought that his beloved cousin would have to answer to the new Fairy Master for it this time.

* * * *

Mollie stared at Valia in confusion.

Valia seemed sincere in her need to talk, but she'd remained silent for the entire walk to the meditation room. Once inside, she bolted the door for privacy.

"Valia, what's wrong? You bring me here, the one place where we cannot be overheard without leaving the colony. We cannot be interrupted, even by Cadal or Morda. Something isn't right. This goes way beyond any secret about the ceremony, so what is it that you need to say?"

Valia met her eyes nervously. She was frightened by something, and Mollie felt a sudden fear for her.

"You are correct. I have no right to ask what I am going to. I will understand if you are angry with me afterward. I know Traden will be. Morda as well. I only hope you and Cadal will be more understanding with me." She had switched into a very formal mode of the Fairy language while she spoke.

"Sounds like you're *going out on a limb* for me. Go on."

"I want to ask you to add something to your ceremony, at the end, just before the celebration begins. It is your day. You can refuse. That is your right."

416

"What should I add? I've already kept almost all of the traditions, though I am adding some of my own. What more could I need?"

"I am not *going out on a limb,*" she said the strange phrase awkwardly.

Mollie was sure she didn't really understand what it meant.

Valia sighed and continued, "...for you. You are my friend, but what I do now, I do for Cadal. Traden and Morda are so concerned with tradition, they will not ask what I must. I am sorry that I must."

Mollie folded herself onto a large cushion on the floor. "For Cadal?"

Valia nodded. "I cannot claim to know you better than Morda, but I have seen your love for Cadal. I have heard the tales of you ordering Morda to stop his pain during the transfers. You traveled with him in a grievous condition rather than see him locked in a cage."

Mollie shook her head. "Valia, I don't understand. Please, explain this to me."

"I know you would do this for him, if only someone would ask it," she blurted out. Valia covered her mouth with a hand, her eyes wide.

Mollie felt a cold pain settle into her stomach. "Tell me, Valia. If Cadal's in trouble, you know I will help in any way I can."

"It is not trouble. Cadal is in pain. He needs to undergo the final transfer and take his place. Every day he does not do it is harder on him."

"Then he should do it now, tonight," she decided.

Valia shook her head sadly. "He cannot. He cannot take his place until after the ceremony."

Mollie felt her anger rising. She took to her feet and motioned to the door bitterly. "The traditions can be damned. He's taking his place tonight if I have to drag him to Morda myself."

"It is not a tradition. The transfer depends on Cadal being completed, linked to you through the ceremony. If we keep him with you as much as possible between now and the ceremony, he will be fine until then. You have a calming effect on him."

Mollie flashed on the memory of Cadal's reaction to her leaving his side to talk to Valia. There was a touch of desperation in him at that moment. He should have told her. He knew and he didn't tell her.

"I won't leave his side again until then," she decided.

Valia grimaced. "You must for a short time tomorrow."

"Why?"

"The last of the arrangements need to be made."

"Which arrangements?"

"Furnishings, decoration, and household goods."

"Cadal can help. He has to live with those decisions too."

"He cannot," she gasped in shock.

"Valia, I'm about to show my Human roots. If I offend you, I'm sorry. Cadal will help. He'll be an equal partner and have his say in these matters, like Humans. Anyone who has a problem with this decision can refuse to be a part of it. Understood?"

Valia nodded in amazement. "As you wish."

"Good. Cadal will be getting upset at my absence. I need to make a quick stop on the way back. Come with me," she ordered.

Valia unbolted the door and followed Mollie out into the corridor. "Where are we going?"

"To set my grandmother straight," Mollie replied with an edge of ice she was sure she had never let Valia see before.

Valia paled, probably at the thought of anyone taking on a Fairy Mistress. "I was afraid you were going to say that. Why do you need me?"

"You *went out on a limb* for me and for Cadal. I'm going to return the favor."

Valia looked at her in confusion.

"You'll see."

At Morda's quarters, Mollie knocked on the door sharply and barely waited for Morda's call before barging in.

Morda looked up in surprise. "Mollie? Valia? What's wrong here?"

Mollie looked from Valia's sheepish embarrassment to Morda's confusion, and her anger grew considerably. "Grandmother, you wanted to know when I get *ticked*. You've done it. How could you hide Cadal's pain from me?"

Morda looked at Valia in shock. "You didn't," she fairly exploded.

Valia cringed and dropped her gaze.

Mollie stepped between them and stared at Morda coldly. "Don't you dare chastise Valia for this. She is my one true friend. A true friend will tell you something like this, like Valia did. Someone who would keep a secret like this is not worthy of my trust.

"I'll forgive you the deception this time because you didn't know my feelings on the matter. I'll assume that's true and give you the benefit of the doubt. Now, you know them. I've said what I want. I will not justify it. Do

419

not ever keep something like this from me again. Understood?"

Morda nodded in shock. "As you wish."

"I also wish to add Cadal's succession to the end of our ceremony. Despite popular belief, the ceremony is not mine. It is ours, Cadal's and mine. I won't be able to enjoy my day unless I know it marks the end of his pain as well. Is there any problem with that? If so, tell me now and be prepared to plug your ears, because what I have to say won't be kind."

Morda smiled weakly. "You really want this?"

"I do."

"Then it is done. Cadal will be getting upset. You should go."

"I know that now. No more interruptions tonight. I will see you both tomorrow."

Morda nodded, and Mollie saw a glimmer of some deep emotion in her eyes. Was it pride or satisfaction? Mollie was suddenly unsure about whether or not her grandmother had engineered this scene. She pushed the thought away and hurried back to Cadal, hoping that Morda wouldn't decide to answer her.

Chapter Twenty-six

Cadal paced the main room. If he was this *antsy,* to use one of Mollie's insect terms, when Mollie had been gone a little more than half an hour, how could he possibly survive the next few days of wedding plans? They must be separated according to tradition, though not for his own duties.

Traden had stopped by to let Cadal know that Morda had asked their help. She felt Mollie was getting too emotionally drained and frustrated with the preparations. Morda had ordered Berner, Nolin, and Traden to complete Cadal's gift for him while Cadal attended to the more important task of keeping his bride relaxed. Still, the women would exile him for all of Mollie's sessions.

Traden's sudden appearance and his nervousness led Cadal to the realization that there was more to the situation than Traden was saying. Morda had asked Traden's help. Perhaps, she did at that. Spending time with Mollie would calm her, but it would also calm Cadal. As weak as Morda had grown, she could still feel Cadal's pain.

He was sure she could, because despite Cadal's attempts to read Traden, there was a block keeping him from seeing the truth in his cousin's heart. Morda could do that for the other Fairies, as Mollie could do it for herself.

The most disturbing thing for Cadal was Traden's reaction to the news that Mollie had mysteriously disappeared at Valia's request. Traden had assumed she was still asleep after the transfer. Cadal's announcement had sparked embarrassment and irritation that was not lost on Cadal, despite Traden's attempts to control his reaction and Morda's block. Traden had taken his leave abruptly and disappeared.

Cadal had garnered two brief glimpses into Traden's mind. Traden was looking for his wife, and he was angry for something he believed Valia shouldn't be doing. Cadal growled at the idea that Valia was attempting to push Mollie into changing her wishes for her ceremony. What else could cause such a reaction in his cousin?

Mollie appeared in the doorway and regarded Cadal with a look of honest concern. Then she came to kiss him on the cheek and wound her arms around his waist with a satisfied smile.

"Just a minute, huh?" he complained, though her touch was already soothing his battered nerves.

"No more work tonight."

"What did Valia need?" Even if Mollie didn't tell him the truth, her emotions would help Cadal decide how upset with Valia to be.

"Morda neglected to tell me something, and I had to make a quick change to the ceremony."

Cadal knew there was more to it, but Mollie hadn't lied to him, to his relief as much as hers. His interest was still piqued. While Mollie was gone, Cadal had felt her anger and her fear. The latter had almost sent Cadal scrambling to find her until he remembered where they were. It couldn't be a fear that could bring Mollie harm.

She'd loosed her temper on someone. If it was Valia, Cadal might not have to say a thing to her. Mollie was not known for mincing words when she was angry enough. Not looking into what was going on had been more difficult than Cadal ever imagined.

"It's taken care of now?" he asked quietly.

Mollie nodded and brushed her cheek against him. "Let's eat. I'm starving. Then—" She raised an eyebrow at him. "We'll get back to the discussion of how much better I'm feeling after my nap, if you're still interested."

"First, we'll get back to the discussion about your fair seduction tactics."

Mollie blushed but agreed.

Dinner passed quickly, though Mollie had two plates of stew. Zera nodded her approval. Mollie favored Cadal with a beguiling look, and he removed her plate to the sink.

He helped her to her feet. "Ready for that discussion?" he asked.

"I am, but I'm not sure that you are."

Cadal raised an eyebrow in amusement at the thought that there was much more Mollie could have done to attract him. He followed her into the bedroom. Mollie kicked off her shoes and curled her legs under her at the head of the bed. Her eyes glittered playfully, and Cadal felt the urge to postpone this discussion yet again.

She was so very enchanting. What else could Mollie possibly do to make Cadal want her more than he already did? Cadal pulled off his boots and sat at the foot of the bed facing her. He was sure if he sat next to her, they would never get to the end of the discussion and Cadal wanted to get that far this time.

"What could you have done that you abandoned out of fairness?"

His breath caught as Mollie unbuttoned the top few buttons on her shirt.

"There were a lot of things I could have done, Cadal," Mollie purred seductively. She leaned forward onto her hands.

Cadal was struck by the landscape of her breasts he could see through the open shirt neck. He locked on the rosy nipples, taking a shuddering breath.

"I could have leaned across my desk like this...or across my bed." Her voice was pure invitation.

Cadal nodded in understanding. His mouth went dry, and his arousal was instantaneous. Unfair wasn't the word for what this would have done to him. "Was this the worst? Or was there something more unfair?" he managed weakly. Keeping himself from reaching out to capture her breasts with his hands or his mouth was almost impossible at this point, but Cadal had to know.

Mollie sat back on her heels, no doubt satisfied that she had made the proper impression. Cadal groaned for the view that disappeared as she did.

"That was the least of what I considered. The most fair."

Cadal met her eyes in shock. "This? For Humans?" He couldn't seem to ask the question.

Mollie shook her head. "Even for Humans, the behavior I'm talking about wouldn't have been proper. It's used often, but it's considered inappropriate to use it on a man to gain his attention. Once you have a relationship, it's a perfectly acceptable way to entice him into bed with you, to show your interest in coupling."

Cadal nodded, though he barely registered the implications past the one that startled him. Mollie had considered throwing caution to the wind as he had. "What else did you consider?"

"I've never worn a *mini-skirt* for you," she mused. She smiled at Cadal's confusion. "A *mini-skirt* is a skirt but as far above my knee as my *shorts* tend to be."

"That would be unfair?" *Harmony, yes! It would be unfair. What am I saying?*

"Not just wearing one. They're perfectly acceptable wear for Humans, even in public."

"I don't understand." *There is something more unfair than simply wearing it?*

"You would if I bent over in one in front of you or sat with my legs slightly parted and acted as if I didn't notice." Mollie blushed deeply.

"There's more to this, isn't there?"

"Wearing little or no underclothes would help to get your attention."

"It would have done more than that." Keeping the fire that was building within him reined in was getting difficult. "What else?"

"Arranged scenes would be next in line, I think."

Cadal peered at her.

"Things like having my towel drop or slip on my way back from a bath."

"Leaving you naked or near-naked as I passed by?"

She nodded sheepishly.

"Is that the worst?"

"No, it's not."

Cadal was intrigued. "What else could you do that is even more unfair to me than that?"

Mollie's blush deepened. She smiled at him. "I could have arranged touching you accidentally."

"Like what?"

Cadal moved closer to her. Mollie's breathing quickened, and Cadal could smell the musk of her arousal. Talking about the many things she wanted to do to seduce him was a sort of loveplay for them both.

"Like stopping in front of you and leaning to pick something up, which would brush my backside against you as if it was accidental. Or reaching past you and brushing my fingers or wrist over you as I did. I could even have tripped into you wearing few clothes, so you would be forced to catch me."

"What if that didn't work?" Cadal asked. His voice had dropped to a husky growl. Not taking her was maddening.

"I could always touch you on purpose and see how you reacted to it."

"For instance?"

Mollie met his eyes. Her hand touched his leg and ran upward to brush over his growing erection. Cadal groaned in pleasure at her touch.

"I could run my foot up your leg under a table or the desk and stroke you that way or run my hands under your shirt when we were close. Any intimate contact I thought I could get you to stand still for. If you didn't stop it, I would simply progress until you stopped it or until you took me to bed and finished it."

"I wouldn't have stopped it," he breathed. "I wouldn't have been able to stop if you did that."

Mollie nodded and moved the hand to her lap.

"Was that the most unfair thing you considered?"

She shook her head slowly.

Cadal felt the need to claim her overriding his ability to hold himself in check quickly. "What was the most unfair thing you considered? Tell me." *Tell me quickly.*

"The night you gave me the massage..."

Cadal smiled. "I remember the night well. I ended up outside your door several times. I had my fair share of fantasies about going to you in the night and finding out how far the invitation in your eyes really extended. Anything you would have done to me that night would have had the effect you wanted quickly."

"Then you'll understand what I wanted to do." Mollie took a deep breath. "I wanted to go to your bed naked and do whatever it took to change your mind. Anything it took, any of the things I mentioned and anything else."

"All it would have taken was you in the doorway. I would have taken you to my bed without a backward glance."

Cadal ran his fingers over her breast through the fabric of her shirt, and Mollie gasped in delight. Her head rocked back.

"Why didn't you do it?" he inquired.

"I was afraid you'd turn me away, and there would be no hope left."

Cadal unbuttoned a few more of the buttons on her shirt and swept his hands inside to fully cup her breasts. "How close did you come to doing it?"

Mollie smiled secretively. "Why don't you transfer that answer?" she invited him. She pulled her head forward.

Cadal met Mollie's eyes. Transfer? *He searched what Morda transferred to him.* Why had he never thought of that before? What she was saying wasn't there. None of it was. At first, Cadal wondered if the scene was an elaborate tease, but he realized there were holes in the transfer, holes he was meant to fill in later.

Morda claimed she couldn't do that. Was she lying? No. Morda couldn't lie to him. Was this beyond even her doing?

Why would Mollie suggest a transfer? Cadal wasn't sure what Mollie had in mind, but he stopped wondering when she kissed him passionately. As aroused as he was, that was Cadal's breaking point. He no longer cared how it could happen.

Cadal pulled away slightly, as Mollie started removing his shirt. He startled, realizing hers was already gone. She finished removing the shirt, then knelt up to go to work on her jeans. Cadal moved her hands away and took over undressing her. When she lay naked beside him, Cadal leaned to kiss her.

"Now, why should I transfer the answer?" he asked.

"Call it an erotic experiment. I know what I was feeling. I want to see what reaction you have to it."

"Where did you come up with that idea?"

"I'm creative. Are you interested, or should I just tell you?"

Cadal shook his head, then removed the rest of his clothing. He kissed Mollie passionately and settled over her. Cadal met her eyes again. "Are you ready?"

"Oh, yes. I think I am."

Cadal placed his hands, and the transfer began.

To his confusion, Cadal found he was watching himself massaging Mollie, running his hands over her body and watching her response to it. He eased his hands away, and Mollie's eyes opened in that look of longing and invitation that coiled his desire until it was almost painful. This time, he kissed her. His hands returned to her body, and they undressed each other. Their efforts were fevered in their need, Cadal's mouth claiming hers urgently as he stripped her.

Finally, the scene made sense to him. Cadal had dreamed it that night, before he rode Thunder, before he stood outside her door and considered doing exactly what he had in the dream. The dream-Cadal entered her, and Cadal moaned in the imagined pleasure of it.

Mollie's arousal teased his mind. Cadal couldn't separate her arousal in the transfer from her current arousal. She was out of control. His body's response to the transfer was striking, a maelstrom of their typical sexual rise doubled.

The image shifted, and Cadal felt a pang of anger and loss from himself as much as from Mollie. She snapped awake, denied even her illusion. Mollie beat at the pillow beside her in frustration. She wished the images were real.

Mollie argued with herself for a long time about what she wanted to do. Cadal wanted her. She knew that, but his refusal to accept her offer confused her. Dozens of plans she had considered and rejected flashed through her mind, and Cadal shuddered at the vivid images of her actions and his reactions. Mollie formulated the move she wanted to make. It was an all or nothing move. If Cadal turned her away, there was no chance. If he didn't... More images coursed through her mind. Mollie shivered in expectation of his touch.

She sighed. Any chance had to be better than this torture. Mollie peeled off her clothing and sat on her bed for several long moments, criticizing herself for this course of action. She knew better than this. What was she doing?

Mollie stood abruptly and headed for the door to the hall. "Making up my own mind for once," she whispered with an air of decision.

Cadal watched the gentle motion of her walk as Mollie made her way down the hall to his room. He was fascinated. Mollie made it that far. She stopped outside his door, and Cadal was sure she would back out. Mollie had made it as far as he had. She turned the doorknob and stepped inside.

He felt her disappointment. The bed was empty. Cadal was riding Thunder. She hadn't backed out after all. If Cadal had been there, he would have claimed her that night.

Mollie laughed harshly. Did Cadal know her intentions that well, or was this all some cosmic joke? The laugh choked off as Mollie considered the possibility that she would never be allowed to change anything important in her life. Whether she chose it or not, was she destined to be alone?

She curled onto Cadal's bed. Mollie drank in the scent of him on his pillow and sighed again. She could stay there in his bed, but her confidence fled. Mollie went back to her own bed.

But not without leaving her scent in Cadal's. It had tortured him when he'd returned, though Cadal had never realized it was really there and not a figment of his imagination.

Mollie curled beneath her quilt without recovering her clothing from the floor.

Enough was enough. If she couldn't change anything, what was the point of trying?

That was why Mollie started avoiding him? Cadal was stunned.

Mollie sank back into a restless sleep. Another dream took hold of her, and another dream Cadal held her in his place.

Cadal sobered. What he was seeing was both troubling and fantastic.

He released her from the transfer and met her lips gently.

"I didn't expect you to go so far," she admitted. "I should have remembered what came next. I'm sorry."

"Don't be. It was a coincidence that I wasn't there. I was riding Thunder and trying to talk myself out of doing what you had the courage to do. You really didn't back down."

"Yes, I did. If I hadn't left your bed—"

Cadal's smile widened. "If I would have come back and found you in my bed, that dream would have been a joke in comparison to the night we would have had."

Mollie smiled and arched to roll her hips against him. The moist warmth of her brushed over the tip of

Cadal's erection, and he plunged deep inside her in an almost reflexive motion. As Cadal struggled to regain some semblance of control over himself, Mollie moved to drive him deeper.

"Show me," she pleaded.

His self-control shattered. Cadal moved at a frenzied pace. The sensations were like nothing he'd ever encountered, with her or with the others. Mollie matched him, movement for movement. Her legs wrapped around his hips and pulled him deeper within her, and Cadal moaned at the feeling of himself sheathed in her arms, legs, and within her.

Cadal drew back onto his knees with his hands under Mollie's back and lifted her smoothly. She settled onto his lap as Cadal changed position. Her eyes closed, and Mollie sank into her enjoyment of the new sensations this position offered. She leaned back into Cadal's hands and bared her breasts to his attentions. Cadal thrust into her and marked her tender flesh lightly with his mouth and hands. Their mutual enjoyment soared.

He was shocked by how rough he was being. Cadal would never have pursued this type of scenario had Mollie not initiated it, but he found it an irresistible force once he embarked on the road. Cadal was drawn into a release that rocked him to the core of his being. The sheer force of it was magnified by Mollie's ragged cry as she collapsed into his chest, shaking in the aftermath of her own climax.

Cadal drew her closer to his chest and sank to the bed. This was the true calm he needed. The few hours away from her were getting harder each time he had to do it. Cadal sighed. If only he could eliminate the need to leave her until the crisis had passed, but there seemed no way to do that.

"What's wrong?" Mollie asked in a lazy voice.

"I'm going to miss you tomorrow. I wish we could spend the day like this."

She searched his face in confusion. "You're going somewhere?"

"Valia may have a soft spot for me because of Traden, and Gady is intimidated by me, but Harea will have me banished while you have your planning session. It's *tradition*," Cadal informed her in a conspiratorial tone, which shocked him thoroughly.

When did he decide the traditions were less than appropriate? When they started working against him?

Mollie smiled and kissed him, sending fresh shock waves through Cadal's body.

"No, she won't. I've forbidden it."

"You've what?" Mollie couldn't do that, could she? It sounded too easy to be true. Why hadn't he thought of it? Of course, all Cadal could do was forbid Mollie's exclusion from his planning, not demand his inclusion in hers. That was Mollie's choice, and she'd made it.

"I've forbidden it. The ceremony is settled thanks to Morda. All that's left is a short discussion of household goods. You have to live with the decisions. I told them you would help make the choices. I — umm — *drafted* you. Sorry," Mollie finished in a tone that said she wasn't sorry at all.

"But tradition says it must all be as you wish. What I want doesn't matter."

"It matters to me. Cadal, tradition says it takes months to train a Fairy Master. Tradition says only the old and new leader can be present for those transfers. Tradition be *hanged*," Mollie exploded. "Since when have we been mired in tradition?"

Cadal met her eyes cautiously. "You know, don't you?"

"Yes, I do. You should have told me yourself, Cadal." Mollie's eyes were sad despite her anger. "You didn't tell me," she repeated in a much lower voice. He'd hurt her again.

"How did you find out? It was Valia, wasn't it?"

"Valia has a soft spot for you, and she knew I would want to know. She's a good friend, the best."

Cadal could tell it was important to Mollie that he not vent his anger at Valia for what she did. "If you're not angry with Valia, who did you loose your temper on?"

"Grandmother. I took her advice. I let her know when I was *ticked*. I stood up for what I wanted, and I allowed no argument."

He laughed heartily. It took several minutes to recover. "I'll bet that surprised her."

"I'm not sure, but I think she was proud of me for it."

Cadal nodded. Mollie was probably right about that. She and Morda could never have a healthy relationship until Mollie was willing to balk her authority.

"Will you help me pick out our household goods?" Mollie moved against him.

Cadal gasped at the feeling of her warmth moving around him again. His softening body hardened in response.

"I'll make it worth your while," she offered.

He turned to trap Mollie's body beneath him and pushed deep within her. She gripped Cadal's arms in the spasm of pleasure that coursed through her.

"You make everything worth my while just by being here. Now my pretty bride, if you move against me one more time, I promise you I will make it worth your while."

Cadal knew even before the smile curved her lips that Mollie intended to test that threat. He thought of Morda's childlike personality. Would life always be this carefree and energetic between them?

Chapter Twenty-seven

Cadal was more stunned when he learned that Mollie had insisted on adding his succession to their ceremony. He started to question whether or not Mollie was sure she wanted to make the change, but she rose up on her knees in the bed. Mollie towered over Cadal, fists on her hips in a pose that declared she would stand for no argument and displayed her body in a most complimentary fashion.

Instead of arguing, Cadal wrapped his hands around Mollie's waist and drew her into a gentle kiss. He rested his hand over the soft patch of her womb that showed their son growing within her. Cadal eased her back onto the bed and dropped his cheek to the spot.

Mollie wound her hands through his hair and sighed in contentment. "After today, when everything for the ceremony is done, do you think anyone would be upset if we spent a day or two like this? Before you have to be Fairy Master and I have to decide what I want to do with my time?"

Cadal kissed the swelling mound of her stomach tenderly. "I was thinking the same thing, and no one will mind if we do exactly that. I'd like it." Cadal didn't mention that he had wanted to do that before they even came to the colony. "We should eat breakfast before the women arrive. After they leave, let's come back here."

"In a minute. I'm enjoying this too much to leave yet."

Cadal smiled at the expression of comfort and at her unwillingness to leave the embrace. In the end, he allowed himself to savor the moment far too long. They were still eating their breakfast of potato rolls, which

Mollie devised a means of toasting, with heavy jelly and sweet milk when the women arrived.

Valia smiled widely at the scene. "Late night?"

Mollie shook her head. "No, but I think our son is making me lazy. It seems I'm spending a lot of time napping and lounging these past few days." She looked at the plate in front of her and grimaced. "And eating."

Valia laughed. "Caden is making up for lost time. It took quite a while for you to find the appetite to support both of you."

Cadal cleared his plate to the wash counter and returned to sit next to Mollie.

Harea regarded him in surprise. "Cadal, we have much to do here. You should go to Traden and the others."

Mollie snapped a look at Valia, swallowing a mouthful of sweet milk. "You didn't tell her yet?"

Valia blushed lightly and shook her head. "I couldn't. Such a thing should come from you."

Mollie nodded. "Very well. Harea, Cadal is staying. He will help me make the rest of my choices."

Harea turned deep scarlet. "He can't. Tradition says—"

Mollie silenced her with a severe look that she'd inherited from Morda. No wonder it had looked so familiar the few times Cadal saw her use it on her employees at the estate.

"Tradition says this will be as I wish it, any way I wish it. I wish Cadal to be present to help me make the decisions that affect us both in our daily lives. If that bothers you, I'm sure Grandmother can ask Benia or Linza to take your place. I would be sad to see you go, but if that's your choice in this matter..."

Cadal watched as Harea turned an unhealthy shade of pale. Gady covered her face to hide the wide smile that came unbidden at her mother being chastised so effectively. Valia tried to hide a look of deep shock at Mollie's words. Cadal heard Valia's mind clearly.

It isn't done. It simply isn't done. It is an honor to serve a bride, to be one of those chosen to do so.

Valia hadn't told Harea of Mollie's choice, because she already suffered the older woman's scorn. Morda had chosen their servants for them before they even returned to the colony. She'd explained to her family patiently that Valia would be one of Mollie's servants, despite being a member of Cadal's family, for three reasons.

Mollie had few friends in the colony, and even fewer she trusted as of yet. Valia was her closest confidant. In the Human realm, a woman's closest confidant would serve her in this way, despite her allegiances. Mollie would expect that it would be so. Finally, Mollie had adopted the Human custom of accepting Cadal's close family as her own. To Mollie, Valia was her cousin as Zera was her mother, even before the ceremony was complete.

Harea shook her head and bowed to Mollie. "All shall be as you wish. If this is your wish," she sighed, "then Cadal will be welcome as your equal here."

Cadal smiled widely. "Don't worry, Harea. I won't let it go to my head."

She rolled her eyes for effect. "I would never presume that it would, Master."

Mollie handed Cadal her empty plate and grinned mischievously. "If you don't behave, I may change my mind, Cadal."

Cadal felt a stab of panic, though he knew she was teasing.

Mollie's smile faded at the look on his face. "Don't worry. I wouldn't really do that," she assured him.

He nodded soberly and cleared the plate. Cadal sank beside her, wrapped an arm around her, and drew Mollie to his chest. "I'll behave," he promised. "Now, let's see what decisions have to be made before you take a nap."

The time passed quickly. Mollie didn't understand why they had to choose so many things when they had enough of everything at Zera's home to last them the decade they would be there.

Valia explained that their quarters were being set up despite the fact that they would not take immediate possession of them. The fact that they would not be expected to live there for so long simply meant the craftsmen had so much more time to make it a true work of art.

Cadal leaned close to her. "They'll still be our quarters. After our ceremony, we'll retire there for the night. At any time, we can go there for privacy, to spend an evening alone or have a meal alone. We can take up residence whenever we choose to."

"That sounds intriguing," Mollie replied calmly.

Cadal felt the excitement she was masking. They weren't hiding their physical relationship, but he knew a completely unrestrained night held appeal for her.

"Can we store things there, like clothes I won't be able to wear until after Caden is born?"

"We may use the space in any way we choose to use it," he said.

Mollie nodded uncertainly. "It seems a fantastic extravagance, but I suppose we'll need these things eventually."

Valia cut in. "Besides the usual beds, table, and chairs, is there any furniture you would like in particular?"

Mollie considered it carefully. "An *armoire* and a *rocking* chair," she decided.

The other women looked at her in confusion.

Cadal stepped in. "An *armoire* is a large cabinet for storing clothing, and a *rocking* chair is a comfortably wide chair with armrests that is set into bowed wood called *rockers* so that it can be pushed back and forth while you sit in it."

Gady looked stunned at the concept. "Why would you want to?"

Mollie laughed. "It's very soothing. It's also useful for calming a cranky infant. You pat the baby and rock and sing." She looked wistful at the thought of it.

Cadal was struck by how lucky his son would be to have Mollie for a mother.

Valia chuckled. "I'll let Traden know. He'll want that to be his personal gift to his namesake, I'm sure."

"I'd appreciate that. It's just as soothing for the mother as it is for the child."

They talked about decorations and colors. Cadal's input on this subject consisted of one proclamation. No horses or stags. Mollie laughed heartily. She chose rich greens and beige coupled with accents of squirrels for decoration.

Their work was almost done by lunchtime. The final decision had to do with styles of furniture. Rather than attempting to explain it all, Cadal offered to transfer images of several of the styles he liked to her and speed the process.

"After all, if she was familiar with the styles, this could all have been completed by now," he reasoned.

Even Harea had to admit that Cadal was correct about that.

Cadal placed his hands and *transferred four different styles to her. Mollie decided almost immediately on the one she liked, then she decided to tease Cadal a little.*

"I like our other use for this better," she crooned *inside the transfer.*

"Later. Let's get rid of our guests first." Cadal ended the transfer and smiled at Valia. "Mollie likes the knotwork."

Valia made a note of it. "I should have known."

"Valia," Mollie cautioned her. "We are keeping *some* secrets."

"I remember. I apologize. We'll be going now. Eat lunch and relax for a while."

All three Fairies smiled secretively and walked away.

Cadal turned to Mollie and raised an eyebrow. "I don't suppose you're going to explain that comment?"

Mollie laughed and shook her head.

"I can find out."

She smiled crookedly. "No, you can't."

He leaned close to her ear and nuzzled her. "Yes, I can. Valia can't block me."

Mollie gaped at him. "You promised."

Cadal pulled her into his lap and kissed her neck. "I won't, but one good tease deserves another."

Mollie leaned back in his arms to nuzzle up his neck to his chin. "Cadal, if a tease is what you really want..." she invited him.

* * * *

The next three days passed in a relaxed sort of blur. Mollie and Cadal spent hours lying naked in each other's arms. They slept and talked, punctuated by lovemaking whenever the mood struck and eating whenever they were hungry. Both hungers struck them often, and satisfying them was the most joy either of them had experienced in their respective lives. Cadal's daydreams of this scenario were never this good.

On the rare occasions they dressed, Mollie expressed concern that even her loose jeans were uncomfortably tight when she sat or bent over. Mollie packed them away with a sigh and unpacked loose sweats and what she called *maternity* clothes, though she claimed she would not need them for several months to come. Cadal was struck by both the inventiveness of the outfits and the limited potential for wear. Humans were strange people.

Cadal took the opportunity to reassure Mollie that he found her more desirable every day; never despite her softening midsection, sometimes because of it, and always regardless of it. He knew Mollie was moody because of the child she carried. As Cadal understood her treatment of Morda and Harea, he also understood Mollie's occasional melancholy and soothed her as best he could when she succumbed to it.

On the day before the wedding, Valia interrupted their leisurely lunch to insist that they attend to the final fittings of their ceremony clothes. Cadal glanced at the blue fabric of the cloak folded to hide the dress from him and smiled. He was sure Mollie's sense of style would show through, even in a dress such as the one she would be expected to wear.

He fled to Traden's quarters with the thought of completing his fitting quickly, but Cessia still clucked over all the small adjustments she planned to make overnight. Cadal's outfit must be perfect, after all.

"Cessia," he pleaded. Cadal's annoyance had clawed at him before she started adding pins to the material to mark the corrections. It quickly became unbearable.

"Cadal, be patient. It will be a grievous affront to your bride, if you don't let me finish. Besides, Valia will be doing the same thing with Mollie. Even if you left here now, you couldn't go to her."

Cadal nodded. Cessia was right and he knew it, but he still felt the separation chewing at his nerves. Cadal startled when he felt Mollie's pure delight surge through him, and Cessia shot him a venomous look. Apparently, Mollie's fitting was a much happier affair than his was shaping up to be.

Traden looked at the smile that spread across his face with a keen interest. "What caused this sudden change?"

"Valia must have done an excellent job. Mollie is very happy."

Berner sucked in his breath and snapped his head up. "You can't do that," he protested.

"I can only turn off what Mollie sees and hears, not what she feels. I cannot help but know how happy she is," his smile widened, "and Mollie is very happy."

Traden laughed. "Good. A happy mother makes healthy babies."

Cadal nodded. "That's true, and Caden is a very healthy baby."

"Cadal, do you know what a *rocking* chair looks like? I'd like it to be perfect."

Cadal nodded and glanced at Cessia. She was busy on the trousers, so he waved Traden closer. "I might as well do this the easy way," he commented. "Will you accept a short transfer?"

Traden nodded, then bowed his head to accept Cadal's hands.

He transferred a view of the rocking chair in the library at the estate. Then for comparison, he added an image of Mollie with one foot braced on the edge of the chair and her knee up, supporting Xanthe's book on her thigh, while the other hung down to rock the chair gently with the ball of her foot as she read. Mollie's long legs poked out from the shorts she wore, and the light sweater clung to her curves invitingly. Cadal was sure that the memory of her perfection probably passed with it, a part of the memory.

When he released Traden, his cousin met his eyes gratefully. "Perfect," he agreed.

Cadal blushed at the thought that Traden might be agreeing with his assessment of Mollie and not the image of the chair, but Traden had his own soulmate. His wonder would not last long after the transfer faded.

"I don't think I'll ever get used to the fact that you can do that." Traden shook his head. "She really does love that chair, doesn't she?"

"Yes, she does," Cadal agreed.

"When was that image?"

Cadal smiled a tight smile. "Before we coupled but after I started courting her properly. I enjoyed watching Mollie from the moment I first laid eyes on her, though."

Traden nodded. Cadal heard the unspoken thought that if she was dressed like that often, he had a hard time believing the four months Cadal attested to waiting before laying claim to her. Even from the transfer, Traden could feel Cadal's need to take that step.

"What was she reading?" Traden asked, changing the subject smoothly.

"Xanthe wrote a book of tales, Fairy tales about life in the colony. It has been passed down to each of her descendents. It was Mollie's only comfort until I found her."

Traden looked at him in surprise. "They were about us?"

"Some of us. Most of them were about Morda and about me. I asked Mollie to tell me her favorite tale our first night together at the estate. She was embarrassed because it was a tale about me."

"Not the stag. She didn't know that one."

"No. The squirrel riding." Cadal smiled at the memory of that night, but avoided the memory of his instant arousal as she brushed past him. That was a memory for a time when Cadal could act out what he'd wanted to do at that moment.

"She couldn't know that you were the same Cadal," Traden stated uncertainly.

"Not really. Maybe even then she had musings of it, more of a flight of fancy her rational mind would not accept as fact. Mollie was infatuated with the character in the book before she met the man behind the character. She was fascinated with me before she even knew my name. I suppose on some level, Mollie always knew. She was much more in touch with the fact that our coupling, our being one, was imperative than I was."

"Mollie was fascinated by you before she knew your name? How? Why?"

"She knew me. All of Xanthe's descendents knew me. Each of them were tortured by dreams of me from sexual maturity on, Mollie included. As she once explained it to me, I wasn't a stranger when she met me. The first time she looked in my eyes, she knew who I was or at least who I would be to her."

"Was that why she pursued you so intently?"

Cadal nodded, glad for the momentary distraction Traden was offering him. "She knew. Every ounce of her being cried out for me. I felt the same way, but I was too obstinate to believe it." Cadal sighed, the anger gnawing at him again. "Mollie was displaying all the first powers a Fairy child does, and I still managed to talk myself into believing she was Human." He shook his head in annoyance at how he was paying for it now. "I wasted so much time actively arguing my way out of the obvious truth of the situation," he berated himself in a low voice.

"Well, that's all past," Traden soothed him. "You can be with Mollie without any interference now."

Cadal glanced at Cessia working on his vest, then scowled. "If I ever get out of this fitting, you mean."

* * * *

Mollie wasn't simply delighted. She was amazed. Despite her assurances that the knotwork could wait, Valia's crew had completed it along with the rest of the work. The bodice fell low over the tops of her breasts, and the thread of Master's blue that made up the embroidery shimmered with silvery light against the white background. The blue sash and panels added the perfect accent of color, and the white boots that matched the outfit were soft and comfortable.

Mollie surveyed her reflection in the polished metal critically, then laughed in the realization that it really was herself she was appraising. Mollie moved to one of her bags and dug through until she found the small wooden box that held the sum total of all the jewelry she had ever owned.

"What are you doing?" Valia asked in amusement.

"Just getting my medallion. I want to wear it."

The velvet bag laid heavily in her hand, and Mollie smiled at the remembered weight against her chest when she moved. She hadn't worn the medallion Nana left to her since...

Mollie cut off the thought painfully. She knew why she'd stopped wearing it. It was the only thing Mollie wore that day that she didn't have the heart to throw in the trash. That didn't matter now. She was wearing the medallion to get married in, and the bad memories would be banished forever.

She placed the large piece of jewelry over her head and felt the chain settle against her neck, the cool weight warming to her skin. The medallion had felt like a part of her from the first time Nana had dropped it over her tiny shoulders as she read Mollie the Fairy tales in the rocking chair close to the fireplace in her living room. The intricate knotwork etched into its face was like none she had ever seen before or since, and it always made her feel at peace. Mollie checked her reflection again and smiled widely. The medallion was perfect. She knew it would be.

Valia touched it gently. "It's exquisite work. It almost looks like something a craftsman here in the colony would create."

Mollie laughed in realization that it could well be. "It's possible, I suppose. I don't know how old it is. I know my grandmother, Colleen— My real grandmother had it passed to her when her mother passed away. She never told me who the original owner was. I don't think even she knew that. It may have belonged to Xanthe. Even if it wasn't made here, she may have commissioned a Human craftsman to recreate it. It's not as refined as a Fairy craftsman would usually put out. I honestly don't know." A sudden thought occurred to Mollie. "Valia, can I borrow your bracelet for the ceremony?"

Her friend looked at her in confusion. "It's a trinket. If you like it, you may have it," she offered.

"No. That defeats the purpose. It must be borrowed, not given. Never given."

"I don't understand."

"It's an old Human charm for a bride. A bride will have good luck if she wears on her person something old, something new, something borrowed, and something blue. The medallion is old. The dress is new, and the sash is blue. I need something borrowed, just for the day, to complete the charm."

Valia smiled widely again. "An enchanting tradition. Yes, you may borrow my bracelet for your ceremony."

Mollie hugged her. "Thank you, Valia."

"Now, let's try the cloak."

* * * *

Cadal's mood deteriorated as the fitting wore on. When Valia returned with the heavy fabric folded over her arm, Cadal sighed deeply. "Cessia, will this take much longer? Mollie is done."

Cessia shook her head. "She probably stood still for her fitting."

Valia laughed as she came back from storing the dress in the bedroom cabinet. "She didn't either, but there was little left to do."

Cessia offered a wide smile. "It looks good?"

"Like no other ceremony dress ever seen. It's fantastic." Valia's eyes glittered in pride.

Cadal sighed again. "Can we talk about this later?"

Cessia regarded him sternly. "If you will stand still for one more pin, you can go." She glanced at Valia.

"Was he always this impatient? I don't seem to remember it."

Valia erupted in a fresh burst of laughter. "Cadal never stood still long enough to be impatient, Cessia."

The older woman chuckled in return, and Cadal realized that no one in the room would dispute that comment, even Nolin, who hadn't been alive long enough to form an opinion on the matter.

Cessia eyed her work critically. "Go take it off. Carefully so you don't disturb the pins. Then you may go, Cadal."

Traden rose to follow him into the bedroom, and the other men followed his lead.

Cessia eyed them warily. "What's this?" she demanded.

Berner touched her face fondly. "We simply have to discuss Cadal's gift to his bride. You know it must be done privately."

His wife nodded her agreement. "Bring me the clothes when you've finished."

The men disappeared into the bedroom and closed the door. While Cadal carefully removed his ceremony clothes, Traden recovered a carved wooden box from one of the shelves. He opened it and presented the gift to him.

Cadal sucked in his breath. "It's perfect, Traden. Thank you all. I could never have completed it on time alone...or half as masterfully."

Traden beamed. "I'm glad you approve." He replaced the lid reverently and placed the gift back on the shelf he had taken it from.

Cadal started pulling on his jeans and the shirt Mollie had bought him before they left the estate. He met Traden's eyes sadly. "I never thanked you properly for making the last one. I should have, long ago."

Traden nodded. "You were distracted, and then it hurt too much to think about. I wondered why you chose to use the same design, but I decided not to mention it."

Cadal smiled a tight smile. "I made that design for my soulmate, Traden. I was simply wrong about who that soulmate was. Mollie deserves something so beautiful. At least I helped make this one."

* * * *

Mollie placed her medallion back into the jewelry box and stretched out on the bed. Tomorrow, she would be married to Cadal. She sighed in satisfaction.

Only one thing bothered her...the pre-ceremony preparations. Mollie learned that, because of their situation, the fact that they had started their courtship and promise living away from family together, the idea of the family gatherings to say goodbye to the individuals had been declared a useless measure by Morda. However, their servants would still expect to prepare them according to tradition. That meant hours of separation Cadal should not have to endure.

She was still considering the problem when Cadal opened the door to the bedroom. He was in a bad mood, but he managed a smile for Mollie as he crossed the room and curled next to her on the bed. He flipped his boots off impatiently as his arms wound around her.

"It went that badly?" she asked.

Cadal grumbled in annoyance. "It looked fine to me, but to hear Cessia tell it, it was an affront to you and to the colony. Maybe I should have had Valia do my sewing. She seems much easier to deal with."

"I've met Cessia. I'm sure you're correct. Your aunt is driven."

"Yes, and I know where she is driving me," Cadal growled.

Mollie laughed weakly at the joke.

Cadal examined her expression. "What's the matter?"

"I'm just worried."

A look of panic crossed Cadal's face.

"Calm down," she soothed him. "I'm not worried about the ceremony or being *married* to you. I'm worried about you."

Confusion replaced the panic. "Me? Why are you worried about me?" He tucked his arms around her and pulled Mollie to him smoothly. "I have what I need."

"They're not going to let us skip the preparations. You know that as well as I do. It will take hours."

Cadal groaned. "I know. I've been trying to figure a way out of that without a general announcement of the problem, which would not be a good idea. It doesn't seem possible."

"Will you be all right?"

He nodded. "I'm not going to be pleasant, but I'm sure I'll survive until I see you again. Traden will understand and intervene for me if I require it."

"If you're sure, I'll stop worrying."

Cadal smiled. "No, you won't. That is one of the many reasons I love you."

Chapter Twenty-eight

Cadal and Mollie had barely finished breakfast when Valia and Traden appeared at the outer door.

"Are you ready?" Traden asked.

Cadal nodded. "Everything I need is at your quarters." He hesitated and kissed Mollie gently. "I'll see you in a few hours."

Mollie glanced at Traden. "Take care of him for me."

Traden bowed formally. "As you wish. I will deliver him safe, if not relaxed, to you in a few hours."

Mollie nodded. Traden understood her perfectly. He would care for Cadal.

Valia smiled widely as the men left, then turned to Mollie. "Are you ready?"

"Are we coming back here?"

"No. Most of your preparations will take place in Morda's quarters. Bring whatever you'll need with you," Valia instructed her.

Mollie collected the few things she needed into one of her backpacks and followed Valia into the corridor. "What do we have to do?" she asked nervously. Mollie hoped Cadal would do all right while they were separated.

"You do nothing but allow yourself to be pampered for a little while." Valia smiled at her surprise. "We will massage you with oils, bathe you, arrange your hair, and dress you."

Mollie raised an eyebrow at her friend. "No."

"What? Why not?"

"I don't mind the massage. I don't mind someone washing and styling my hair, but I absolutely draw the line at anyone else bathing me." She smiled wickedly. "Unless that someone is Cadal, but since it's not—"

Mollie broke off the thought before she explored it too carefully. Now was not the time for that. "I don't mind help getting the dress over my head and getting the buttons done, but I will dress myself otherwise."

"This is another cultural difference, isn't it?"

"Absolutely."

Valia sighed. "Harea isn't going to like this."

Mollie smiled a mischievous little smile. "Who cares? It's my day, not hers," she whispered in a conspiratorial tone.

Valia looked at her in shock, then laughed heartily. "If you look at it that way, I suppose you're correct."

"You shouldn't let Harea bully you. You're my *matron of honor*. You outrank her."

"I'm what?"

Mollie flitted her hand. "It's a Human custom. The bride has an envoy, a go between, or an *enforcer*." She considered that one carefully. "Someone who will carry out her will, face down people who upset her, and will serve her completely as all of them."

"You wish me for that place of honor?"

"I told Morda that you're my one true friend. No matter how close a family is, only a bride's one true friend is worthy of that position."

Valia nodded in understanding. "Thank you. I'll try to be equal to the task." She opened the door to a spring room and waited for Mollie to pass by before closing them in.

Morda, Harea, and Gady were there waiting for her.

Morda smiled widely. "Well, the day is upon us," she announced.

Mollie nodded and dropped her pack under the table. "Yes, it is. *Well, time's a wastin',*" she drawled in English before switching back to Fairy again. "I guess we should get moving."

Valia laughed. "We'll massage you first."

Mollie nodded and started stripping off her clothes.

Morda took her shirt as she handed it off. "How is Cadal?"

Mollie smiled. "Good, I think. He made a joke about drinking some nectar wine as a *sedative*. I told him not to drink and fly."

Mollie glanced around. Only Morda was smiling.

"Sorry," she mumbled. "Human joke."

Mollie found the massage less expert than Cadal offered, but it was still relaxing to her body if not her mind. The first disagreement came up after the massage.

"What do you mean, no?" Harea demanded.

Mollie sighed.

Valia stepped in as the perfect Matron of Honor, before Mollie could launch into an explanation. "It's a cultural difference. Brides in Mollie's experience do some things for themselves we don't normally do. Mollie will bathe herself and dress herself to the outer clothes. Our major interest will be her hair, washing and styling it."

Harea cast Valia a cool look and opened her mouth to protest.

Morda silenced Harea with a look. "Well said, Valia. As befitting a true *Matron of Honor*. Well, get to it." She hurried the surprised younger woman along. "Remember, not too hot because of the baby."

Valia bowed and moved to the spouts to make a hot bath. She gauged it carefully, perfected over years of drawing a bath this way.

Mollie grimaced, remembering her first attempt at controlling the flow of water. She'd splashed cold water over herself in an attempt to redirect the flow valve into the deep pool and out of the catch basin that collected water for a shower. Then Mollie had made the water far too hot and had to overfill the pool to cool it enough to let a little of the water out and complete her bath. Cadal had laughed at her attempt when he heard. He'd offered to teach her, but Mollie decided she had made enough practical mistakes to figure it out at that point.

She sank into water that was the perfect temperature due to the mixture of water from the lake and the hot spring Valia directed into the pool. The scented oils mixed with the hot water and surrounded her in a fragrant mist that soothed her senses. Mollie sank under the water and ran her fingers through her hair. The others were staring at her curiously when she surfaced again.

Gady barely surpressed a giggle. "This isn't a swimming pond, Mollie."

"How do you wash your hair?" Mollie countered dryly.

"Under the water spout."

It figured. They would have a specific use for the catch basin here. It was typical.

Mollie smiled and dunked her head again. "You don't know what you're missing. *Showers* are for washing off the dirt. Baths are for pure enjoyment. Try it sometime. You might find you like it."

Harea sniffed impatiently. "Another strange Human custom, I suppose," she commented grimly.

Mollie smiled wickedly. For some reason, she found Harea's disdain for Humans grating today. She might not be one now, but Mollie had spent years as a Human. "Don't forget, I've lived as a Human. I've not only played Human. Not only as a Fairy pretending to be Human but also lived as a Human. They deserve a lot of credit. For all their limitations, they pack more life into twenty years than Fairies do in a century. Ask

Cadal sometime. He'll be happy to tell you about it. Humans may do things you consider strange, but they know how to enjoy themselves, despite their destructive side."

Valia smiled. "I've heard Cadal's description of some of your antics as a Human. It's a good thing for you that The Harmony knew who you were soulmate to and extended Cadal's protection to include you."

Mollie shook her head. "Not likely. I got hurt often. I paid the price for my antics. I wasn't *immune* like Cadal was."

"Well," Valia decided, "why don't you sit back on the bench and soak while we work on your hair?"

Mollie obliged her and let the water relax away the last of her tensions as the ladies massaged a fragrant solution into her hair. When Valia announced she was ready for a rinse, Mollie stymied Harea's move toward the basin by laying back smoothly and shaking her hair around her like ribbons on a breeze to wash out the last of the solution. Mollie sat back on the bench and ran her hands over the silky hair left behind. What Humans wouldn't give for this recipe.

Morda smiled. "Comfortable?"

"Intensely."

"Have you decided how to wear your hair?"

Mollie nodded.

"We should get started on that," Morda noted.

Mollie wondered whether Morda knew the style and was commenting on the time it would take or not.

"We've spent quite a bit of time here already," Morda commented, letting Mollie know she wasn't going to answer that one.

Mollie grinned and climbed out of the pool. Valia and Gady were waiting with a thick robe to wrap up in for the trip back to Morda's quarters. To Mollie's surprise, Harea placed her folded clothes into the backpack and shouldered it for her. Mollie walked in the procession, Morda and Valia ahead and Harea and Gady behind.

People cleared the way as they walked the corridor, bowing respectfully. Mollie assumed they were bowing to Morda, but her grandmother explained that it was a show of respect for Mollie as the bride of the new Fairy Master. The thought made Mollie uncomfortable. The concept of servants had been difficult enough for her. This respect, not even for herself but for the machinations of Fate that placed her with Cadal, was disconcerting. She breathed a sigh of relief as they reached Morda's quarters.

Mollie took a seat in a soft chair and sipped sweet milk while Harea worked on her hair. Knowing Cadal would be enchanted by it, Mollie had decided to wear her hair down and requested as much curl as Harea could manage. An hour later, her entire head was a mass of long curls framing her face and cascading over her shoulders and down her back.

Valia leaned close to Mollie's ear. "You should dress now. It's close to the time we must leave."

Mollie nodded and scooped up her backpack while Valia laid her outer clothes on Morda's bed. She dressed at a leisurely pace, knowing Valia would leave her enough time to do so. Gady blushed deeply at her lace underwear, matching strapless bra, and thigh-high pantyhose. Mollie guessed that no Fairy would be caught dead wearing such underclothes. Or maybe they would, if something like it had been introduced before. Fairies were open-minded about many things Mollie didn't count on.

Valia smiled widely as Mollie pulled on her boots. "I can see why Cadal enjoys your sense of style."

Mollie stood, a hand on her hip and a touch of a smile on her lips. "If you ever want to give Traden a surprise, let me know. I have things that will fit you."

Valia eyed her critically for a moment before she started laughing. "I might inquire about that later. For now, let's get this dress on."

Gady and Valia settled the dress over Mollie's head, while Harea pulled her hair away from the fabric gently. Mollie slipped her arms into the sleeves and held them out, while Harea lifted her hair and Gady buttoned the back of the dress. That accomplished, Mollie added a spritz of perfume and a touch of lip balm for the cold outside. She dropped her medallion over her head. Valia fastened her bracelet on Mollie's wrist.

Gady stared in wonder. "You're giving Mollie your bracelet?"

Valia smiled. "Just lending it to her for the ceremony."

Morda laughed from under her own ceremony dress. "Something old, something new, something borrowed, and something blue. I always thought that was a beautiful tradition."

Mollie laughed lightly. "Eavesdropping again, Grandmother?"

"Not at all. I recognize it from Xanthe's wedding. She was enchanted with the idea of Human charms for luck."

"You went to Xanthe's wedding?" Mollie asked in shock.

"Of course, I did. She was my granddaughter. It was touching. Not as touching as your ceremony will be, but I suppose a happy bride is a beautiful bride." Morda draped her cloak over her shoulders and hugged Mollie quickly. "I must go now." She hurried out before Mollie could thank her.

Harea smiled patiently. "Gady, get her hair. Valia, drape the cloak over her shoulders." As she fastened the clasp on the cloak, Harea's eyes locked on the medallion settled on Mollie's breast. "Where did you get this?" she asked, peering at the piece of jewelry.

"Blake family heirloom." Mollie met Harea's eyes. "Is there a problem?"

"No. I suppose not. It just seems...familiar."

Valia nodded. "It looks like colony work, but it's more rough than an adult craftsman would produce. More like an apprentice. Mollie suggested that Xanthe might have found a Human craftsman to create it as a reminder of home."

"It's possible," Harea conceded, but she seemed unconvinced, bothered by something she didn't voice. She tugged the cloak down over Mollie's shoulders until it covered the bodice of her gown, protecting her skin from the bracing wind Mollie would no doubt meet outside. "That will keep you warm until the end of the ceremony. Are you ready?"

Mollie smiled at the sudden realization that she was nervous. She nodded sheepishly. "As ready as I'll ever be."

Valia handed off a small bouquet of blue and white flowers to her.

Mollie met her eyes gratefully. "How? Where did you get this?"

Valia laughed. "The Mistress has many powers I don't understand."

Mollie smiled. Her grandmother would make sure it was perfect.

* * * *

Cadal was surprised at how difficult it was. Those three long hours felt like days. When his servants massaged him, his muscles grew more tense. The hot water he usually found so calming was an irritation to him, and he cringed at the feeling of the men bathing him. Cadal climbed out of the water and put his arms out for the robe without thanks or even comment about their care.

Berner watched him warily. "Cadal, are you ill?"

Cadal put out a hand to still Traden before his cousin could tell the lie on the tip of his tongue. "My succession is today. What you're seeing is my body's reaction to it. It's difficult to control." Cadal met his uncle's eyes. "I'm sorry I have to concern you this way."

Berner looked at Traden intently. "You knew this?"

Traden nodded sheepishly.

Berner shook his head, tapping down his anger. "Is this why Cadal has been absent from the usual formalities?" he demanded.

Cadal grimaced. "Yes, it is. Traden didn't tell anyone, because Morda and I didn't wish it. We didn't want to detract from Mollie's ceremony any more than we had to. Morda will perform our ceremony, then she will step down. She must step down. It's overdue. That's why my body and soul ache. Mollie stills the fire in my blood. Until I take my place, she's the only thing that can. If I'm unpleasant, I apologize."

Berner bowed his head. "We will go. The sooner you take your place, the sooner all will be well."

They made their way through the corridors. Traden led the way, and Berner and Nolin trailed behind. Cadal kept his eyes locked on Traden as they walked. Looking at the crowd as they bowed to him created a strange sort of vertigo in him.

The other men left Cadal in peace to pace the floor in Traden's main room while they watched him worriedly from the bedroom. As time passed, the sensation turned from an annoyance to pain. Time seemed to stand still. Cadal kept pacing, willing his body to be patient until he took his place, until he had his bride back in his arms to pacify the need searing his soul and his mind.

When Traden told him it was time to dress, Cadal tore off his robe and pulled on his ceremonial garb quickly. Traden took down the gift for Mollie and tucked it inside his own cloak before straightening Cadal's cloak, then his collar. Traden nodded and swept his hand toward the outer door.

Cadal wasted no time. The corridors were empty as they made their way to the meadow outside the tree-city, and he was only vaguely aware that his servants had to run to keep up with his frenzied pace. The meadow was swept free of the deep snow until the piles that surrounded the crowd lent a white backdrop that was three times Fairy height.

Morda was waiting, surrounded by a crowd that seemed impossibly huge and caused a spike in the pain that still held Cadal in its grasp. Zera stood behind Morda and to husband's side, the place of honor that Botor should have shared. Dalen stood to Zera's left, a sign of his place since Cadal was his namesake, a place Cator would have shared had he lived to see this day.

Cadal was all too aware of the empty spot to bride's side. Mollie had no parents or advisors to fill that place of honor. It was something Cadal wished he could have solved sooner, but the time was not right for that reunion yet. Cadal sighed at the thought that Mollie would be satisfied with Morda's presence.

A gasp of awe went up from the crowd at the sight of Cadal in the white jerkin and boots that matched his hair so well and the blue vest, trousers, and cloak that reflected perfectly the blue of his eyes. Cadal embraced Morda then turned back to look to the entrance to the tree-city.

The bridal party moved up the slight embankment. Cadal could barely see the blue and white of Mollie's garb past the line of her three attendants. When they reached Cadal, the three parted and bowed to him, dropping behind his bride and revealing her to him.

Cadal's eyes locked on Mollie. Harmony! She was beautiful. How could Mollie get even more beautiful in those three hours away from his side? Her hair hung in curls all around her face, framing her pink cheeks and dark eyes. Though he couldn't see the dress clearly yet, Cadal was sure her cloak was pulled low over the bodice for a reason.

At first, Mollie didn't meet his eyes. Her eyes roamed over his ceremonial garb with an appreciative cast. She looked deep in his eyes and took Cadal's hand. The pain unfurled slowly, and Cadal breathed in relief. He felt Berner's muscles relax almost as vividly as he felt his own.

Morda raised her hands for silence from the crowd and began to speak. "Cadal and Mollie come here today to become one as sealed in wind dance. A promise was made. A promise was accepted. Cadal, so that none may question, ask Mollie once again before these witnesses that they may see and hear your promise."

Cadal barely registered the handful of blue and white flowers Mollie handed off to Valia in preparation for the promise.

He took both of Mollie's hands in his own and sighed at the calm she brought him. "Mollie, I would like you to wind dance with me. Will you consent?"

She smiled widely. "Yes, Cadal. How could I not? I love you so."

Cadal knew the last part was her own touch, but he was glad for it though it was not necessary to the ceremony.

Mollie released his hands and lifted gracefully into the sky. Cadal watched her in the same wonder at her instant expertise that had enthralled him the last time they promised. He rose to Mollie and floated before her. Cadal placed his hands on her hips and drew Mollie to him as she wrapped her arms around his neck. He focused the winds and bade them swirl around them. They danced in the wind for several long minutes until Cadal felt Mollie begin to shiver in the arctic chill. He stilled the winds and they sank together to the ground before Morda. A cheer went up from the crowd in appreciation of the beauty of their promise. Cadal felt a pang of loss as Mollie lowered her arms to her sides and took a single step back from his embrace. Morda's words broke him from the emotion.

"The Harmony blesses all unions of true soulmates, and She has already blessed you both. The term dannea is truly appropriate of Mollie. She brings the colony a new soul. She blesses Cadal with a son of his own. This is a true sign of healing. What was once shattered is now made whole for the colony as well as for Cadal and Mollie." Morda faced Mollie. "Mollie, do you accept Cadal as your husband, your soulmate, one with you always?"

Mollie met Cadal's eyes. "Longer than always. Longer than forever. Until Time ends."

To Cadal's shock, Morda turned to him next. "Cadal, do you accept Mollie as your bride, your soulmate, one with you always?"

Cadal's mind spun. Such a question wasn't asked. Cadal had made his promise in wind dance. What he wanted was of no importance today. It was Mollie's day. He met his bride's eyes. It was important to Mollie, or Morda would not have asked the question.

"Yes, I do. You are my life until the end of Time." Cadal prepared himself for the seal, the kiss that would make them one.

Morda deviated again. "Traden, does Cadal offer a gift to his bride?"

Cadal started. The gift shouldn't have been offered until after dinner at least. He glanced at Mollie, but she was as confused as he was. Morda couldn't add to what Mollie wanted. The Fairy Mistress couldn't balk tradition that way.

Traden bowed and offered the carved box up to Cadal. He accepted it with a stern look at Morda. The lid carefully removed, he swung it around to present it to Mollie.

A fantastic change came over the bridal party. Valia turned a vivid scarlet and stared at Traden in some emotion that fell between shock and dismay. Gady gasped and paled slightly before averting her eyes. Harea snapped a startled look from Mollie to Cadal, then away.

Mollie grasped a handful of the front of her cloak reflexively with her left hand while she reached to brush the fingers of her right hand over the medallion in the box. Mollie's hands shook, and tears misted her eyes when she looked at him, an expression Cadal couldn't read etched on her pale face.

"You made this?" she whispered. Her mind was shut tight, hiding her thoughts from him.

"I designed it many years ago," he answered uncertainly. "The others did most of the work. They helped me craft it." What difference could it possibly make? Cadal was afraid Mollie didn't like it. The possibility of that outcome had never occurred to Cadal before, and it froze him for an instant.

Mollie looked at her grandmother, helplessly lost for some reason Cadal couldn't fathom, pleading with Morda silently to help her.

"Mollie," she spoke gently, "think of the Human ceremony. You know what comes next. You pretended it meant nothing to you, but it does. If you search your heart, you know it does. As you accept Cadal's gift, give him yours in return."

Mollie nodded and mouthed an unsteady 'thank you' to Morda before meeting Cadal's eyes. She let go of the front of the cloak and scooped her hands under the folds of the hood. As Mollie lifted a heavy chain over her head, the matching medallion slid out of the neckline and hovered before Cadal's eyes. Mollie had it. All along, she'd had it.

Cadal evaluated the medallion, ignoring the shock from his servants studiously. A century had made all the difference in Traden's craftsmanship. While the medallion in Cadal's hand was finely etched and feminine, the one in her hand, the one made for Xanthe all those years ago, was rough and heavy. It was more a man's piece of jewelry than something a woman should wear.

Mollie's voice cracked as she held up the medallion for him to see. "Accept this gift as a sign of my everlasting vow to you." She reached her hands toward him, and Cadal bowed his head to allow Mollie to place the chain over his shoulders.

Cadal removed the medallion in his hand from the box and passed the empty shell back to Traden distractedly. He reached his hands out to Mollie. "Accept this gift as a sign of my everlasting vow to you," he mirrored her words.

Mollie ducked her head to allow Cadal to drop the new medallion onto her shoulders. As she straightened, Harea pulled Mollie's hair from beneath the chain and smoothed her clothing in an air of devotion that Mollie would have found uncomfortable had she not been lost in Cadal's eyes. A fierce question burned in her eyes, a question Mollie was afraid to ask. They would have to discuss that question when the ceremony was over. But for now, Cadal was more concerned with the ceremony.

Morda smiled. "Let these gifts be an outward sign of the promises made between these two Fairies this day. And now, there being no reason why these two should not be ever one, I present to you Cadal and Mollie, dan e dannea Aiden, husband and bride." Morda placed a hand on each of their temples. "With this seal, I join you now and forever."

Cadal met Mollie's lips hungrily and groaned as they parted beneath his. The transfer began.

It was beautiful. At last, Cadal's understanding of his bride was complete. The missing scenes of her life took their place. This was why they were missing. The scenes allowed Cadal a sense of wonder that would have been denied him had he seen everything in his training. Many of the scenes had to do with the medallion, and Cadal wondered at the fact that it had been chosen as something not to be revealed to him until now.

Mollie gasped under his mouth as Cadal's life filled her mind. Cadal cringed inwardly at some of the things she would see. He sank into the sensations of Mollie's touch. Any upset the memories might cause her would be made right the first chance he had to correct it.

The transfer ended, and Morda's hands dropped away. Still, Cadal clung to Mollie and drank in the sensation of claiming her mouth with his own. When Cadal released her, Mollie buried her face in his chest for a long moment. She met Cadal's eyes, a shadowed cast hidden in the depths of her deep brown gaze. Then she smiled and touched his face, and Cadal relaxed again.

He barely heard the cheers that flew up from the crowd. Cadal understood now. Being one wasn't simply a matter of words, not merely rhetoric. In the seal of transfer, Morda bound their souls into a complete, stronger whole. Even if one of them lost the other, a part of the missing soul would remain with the soulmate left behind. They would never be alone again.

Morda sucked in her breath and raised her hands again to still the excited crowd. "On Cadal's announcement day, I promised this ceremony would be my final act as Fairy Mistress. I ask you now, Cadal, is your personal business complete at last?"

The crowd's excitement level rose at this unexpected bonus, another great ceremony on the same day.

Cadal nodded. "Yes, Mistress. It is complete."

"Do you accept the mantle of this office?" she continued.

"Yes, I do, freely and without exception." It was the traditional reply to the query.

"Mollie, do you accept Cadal's succession and the duties expected of you both?"

Cadal startled at that. It was a question that had never been asked before. A Fairy Master's soulmate's acceptance was immaterial to his place. Even as Cadal thought it, he knew it wasn't true for himself and Mollie. Perhaps, it wasn't true for anyone. Mollie smiled widely, and Cadal could tell she hadn't realized she would be consulted on this matter.

"Yes, Mistress, I do, freely and without exception."

Morda unclasped her cloak and fanned it out before her. Berner and Harea grasped the edges and settled it gently over the frozen ground. "We will conduct the transfer as we have Cadal's other training," she announced to the crowd.

Cadal looked at Morda in shock, but he nodded at the thought he grasped from her mind. There would be no more secrets from their people about unimportant things like this.

Morda led them both onto the cloak. Cadal sank to his knees then wrapped his hands around Mollie's waist. He steadied her, as Mollie sank cross-legged beneath her skirt, her hands on his shoulders. She wound her hands in his and met Cadal's eyes silently.

He kissed her cheek and laid his forehead to hers. "It won't be like the others," he whispered. "I promise it won't."

Mollie smiled. "I'll hold you to that."

Cadal sank back onto his heels and knelt taller. He met Morda's eyes and nodded. "We're ready."

Mollie nodded her agreement and squeezed Cadal's hands. Morda placed her hands from her spot behind him. Cadal met Mollie's eyes, then closed his in preparation.

Morda's voice rang out over the silent crowd. "Ten thousand years ago, The Harmony blessed the first civilized Fairies with the first transfer. She, Herself, appointed the First Fairy Master of Aiden who, in turn, transferred Her wisdom and power to the Fairy Master or Mistress of every other colony by special design of The Harmony.

"From that day to this, the Master of Aiden has been the Masters' Master. With each transfer of power, the history of our colony becomes richer and our Master becomes stronger.

"I can tell you now that Cadal is the strongest Master that The Harmony has chosen so far. She set him on a journey to accomplish the impossible, a journey which held in the balance the survival or extinction of Aiden itself."

The crowd murmured in alarm at that then settled to hear the rest.

"Cadal has done as The Harmony wished, and the colony of Aiden has been gifted a new beginning. The impossible has become commonplace for him."

A titter of laugher passed over the crowd.

"His journey took him far away and pitted him against terrors most of us cannot even imagine. He returned victorious with the greatest prize anyone could ever wish. Thus begins the second era of Aiden.

"Cadal kneels before me for the final time, the twenty-fifth Master of Aiden. Already one with no equal, after today, he will be stronger still. He will experience the transfer of power as all his predecessors have, but for Cadal, this transfer will be the easiest he has endured."

Mollie sighed in relief at the reassurance Morda added for her benefit.

"Cadal, your soulmate has seen you through those five horrible transfers which marked the sum total of your training."

The crowd erupted in exclamations of disbelief and concern, then fell silent, no doubt due to a scathing look from Morda.

"Never before has there been such a training, but The Harmony demanded this of you as She demanded so many other things of you and your soulmate. You willingly gave all She asked and more. No Fairy Master before you could have survived such a thing, even with the support of his soulmate. May Mollie guide you and comfort you this one last time."

The transfer began, and Cadal sucked in his breath at the strange sensation. A portion of Cadal's mind that had been locked away opened wide before him. His mind cleared, as the former transfers organized themselves into the new area open to him almost of their own accord.

That completed, new information began pouring in. There were so many gifts the Fairy Master possessed that Cadal had never dreamed of. The flowers Mollie carried were a result of one of those gifts. Cadal could contact the other Fairy Masters and his soulmate by force of will alone. No transfer was necessary. No physical contact or proximity at all. Messages of welcome, good will, and servitude flooded to him from the other Fairy Masters and Mistresses. There were three hundred and twelve of them in all.

His link to all the Fairies of Aiden solidified, and their thoughts and feelings coursed through that place in his mind like river rapids. Cadal's mind, now equipped to deal with the flood of information, sifted through it effortlessly.

Cadal felt the end approaching. The final thing Morda transferred was her consciousness of where every Fairy was in relation to himself. With it passed guardianship of every soul within the colony. She was

Fairy Mistress no more. Morda's hands fell away, and she stepped back from him. *He saw Morda's soul retreat in his new consciousness. She sank deep to her knees in a show of servitude to the new Master.*

Cadal opened his eyes, and the entire colony knelt to him. The motion sent a wave of dizziness through him, as the two portions of Cadal's mind attempted to establish a balance that would allow him each image without the hindrance of the other.

Mollie's hands left his as Cadal collapsed into her arms. She stifled a ragged cry in fear for him.

Cadal saw their servants jerk reflexively in an attempt to help them. They all cut the movement painfully short. They couldn't interfere in this. Cadal's recovery was in the Harmony's hands.

His mind cleared as the path to clarity, to duality, emerged from the massive transfer. *It is a tentative duality until your mind becomes fully integrated. A year at most,* his mind attested.

Cadal pushed back to his heels. Mollie's arms rested against him, ready to support him again if he required it. He kissed her, then stood confidently. Before he faced the crowd, Cadal took Mollie's hands and pulled her easily to his side. He wrapped an arm around her shoulder and scanned the crowd around them.

He smiled at the flow of comments from the Fairies old enough to remember Morda taking her place.

"Morda took ten times as long to recover." Dalen...

"Harmony, he's strong." Berner...

"The Harmony chose well." Zera...

Many others followed.

Cadal hugged Mollie to him and waved a hand to the crowd theatrically. "My friends," he called out, "please rise. This is a joyous occasion, and I have no wish for any to suffer from the cold. Join us inside where we will all be warm. My bride and I— Mollie and I invite you to celebrate our ceremony."

With that, Cadal took Mollie's arm in his own, turned to the entrance and led the procession of their servants into the tree-city. She squeezed his arm *to reassure herself that he was whole and well.*

Cadal patted her hand. "I'm sorry. I was dizzy from the sensations. They're very new. I didn't mean to frighten you again."

Mollie nodded. "For just a moment, when you collapsed..." She shook her head and swallowed a painful lump in her throat.

He wrapped his hand around hers. "I know. I am fine. And now that the work is done, we can celebrate. This day has been a long time coming."

She smiled and nodded in relief.

Chapter Twenty-nine

Cadal led Mollie to the Great Chamber and steered her to the smaller of the two thrones before taking his place to her right. They had a few moments of peace before the doors would open, while their servants prepared them for their first audience. *Mollie's nervous tension hung about her like a heavy curtain.*

Traden removed Cadal's cloak, while Harea unclasped Mollie's and Valia swept it from her shoulders smoothly. Cadal moved his eyes over his bride in appreciation. Only she could make such a statement so effortlessly. The bodice was cut to within inches of modesty, and the knotwork around the edges issued an invitation to his eyes. Waiting the proper length of time to consummate this ceremony was going to be a stretch.

Mollie met his eyes and smiled that impish smile that told him *she knew exactly what he was thinking and enjoyed the attention.* "Do you like it?" she asked innocently.

Cadal laughed heartily. "Only as much as I like you."

Mollie's smile widened at the memory before she bit it down again. "I suppose you're not very impressed then." She offered a fake pout.

Cadal laughed, then harder still at the shocked looks their servants were giving Mollie for saying such a thing. He wrapped his arms around Mollie and kissed her passionately. "I love you," he breathed close to her ear.

"I hope so. I don't go around having babies for men who don't love me."

Cadal smiled. He fingered the medallion that lay across the tops of Mollie's breasts. "You really like my gift?" He asked her only as a means of getting Mollie to ask her question.

"I always have. When I saw it, I realized that you must have given the other one to Xanthe."

That much was right, though Xanthe wore it out of friendship and never cared as much for it as Cadal knew Mollie did.

She dropped her gaze. "I was afraid you'd be upset to see it again."

Cadal shook his head. *This was her way of asking the question, if he would rather not wear the medallion.* "No. I told Traden the first medallion was made for my soulmate. I was simply wrong about who that soulmate was. It made me feel good to know giving it to Xanthe meant it found its way to you, and you loved it enough, without even knowing it came from me, to wear it today."

"I used to wear it every day," she began. Mollie faltered *at the thought of why she stopped wearing it* and looked away abruptly. That was the other topic she was afraid of.

Cadal cupped Mollie's chin and drew her eyes back to his. "You don't have to worry about that. You know from the seal of transfer that I know everything. I have for a long time."

Mollie nodded. "I understand those emotions now. The ones from the last training transfer. Why didn't you tell me?"

Cadal shrugged. "What would be the point? You only gave it a thought when someone reminded you of it somehow. At that point, you hadn't given it serious thought in almost a month. There was no reason to discuss the matter, was there?"

"I guess not. It's just something I would have spared you, given the choice."

Cadal smiled. "Oh, no. Then I would have kept making mistakes that hurt you because I didn't know what I was doing wrong. I hate doing that."

Mollie nodded. "It couldn't be easy, could it?"

"Nothing worthwhile ever is." Cadal sighed *at the musings of the restless crowd.* Their time was up. "Are you ready?"

Mollie nodded and took a deep breath, while Nolin and Gady moved to open the north doors and Harea and Berner opened the east.

Cadal felt Mollie's nervousness despite their joking. A last thought passed through his mind that he would like to ask before the bolts slid back. "Was the knowledge of what I saw in transfer what caused the look in your eyes after we were sealed?"

"Mostly."

Cadal peered at her.

Mollie's blush spread down into her bodice. "I was jealous...just for a moment. I had no right to be. I know that." She flitted her hand in dismissal of the subject.

"Not Xanthe," he breathed in disbelief.

"No." She smiled *at the absurdity of the thought. If she were going to be jealous of her ancestor, Mollie would have succumbed to that long ago.* "Benia and Flori—" Her eyes glittered under her lashes. "You used a few tricks on them I wouldn't mind experiencing." *Mollie was making less of it than there was, but she was being honest.*

Cadal's smile widened at the invitation. "Any time. Tonight, if you wish."

Mollie laughed *a genuinely happy laugh this time.*

This interaction between the two pieces of him was certainly an interesting way to think.

"We'll see," she teased.

The Fairies streamed into the Great Chamber. Cadal and Mollie stood arm in arm before the thrones. He held out his free hand to Zera as Mollie held hers out to Morda, who was dressed in a cool green ceremony dress now that she had retired her Mistress's blue and white.

Cadal calmed the crowd with a single raised hand, then looked to Mollie to give them welcome as the bride always did.

"My dear friends," she began in a strong voice, a voice worthy of her position. "My thanks to you all for sharing our ceremony with us. I hope you recover quickly from the weather."

She favored Cadal with a sidelong glance, and he smiled *at the move he read in her thoughts.*

"I know my husband harbors the illusion that this is my day and that nothing should interfere with it, but as his bride, I reserve the right to tell Cadal when he's wrong."

A laugh rippled through the crowd. *Enough stories had circulated about his headstrong bride that such a statement was not a surprise to most of the Fairies of the colony.*

"This is our day together. If any wish to make my day more happy, then don't ignore Cadal to favor me. For now, be warm, be happy, and soon — be well fed."

A cheer went up, and Cadal guided her onto the soft cushion on her throne before taking his place. Fairies approached to congratulate the couple on their ceremonies and on their baby. Many, who hadn't had the chance to meet Mollie at her last visit, welcomed her to the colony and asked questions about the Human realm, though none they all knew would upset her. Some offered small gifts to the Fairy Master and his new bride. Mollie was most delighted with gifts for Caden. Trays of food and cups of sweet milk and nectar wine were supplied to them throughout the day.

Cadal was amazed at the Human touches Mollie added to the celebration. The tower of cake stunned even her, and feeding each other the first slices they cut was a sensual experience which had Cadal reminding himself that it was far too early for them to disappear to their quarters.

When Valia explained the game of throwing the bouquet, Cadal was dubious, but the young Fairy girls were enchanted. To everyone's surprise *except Mollie's*, Gady caught the flowers. Cadal wondered at that. He would have to ask Mollie how she knew of Gady's wish.

Gady blushed deeply and cast Nolin a sidelong glance. Cadal nodded to him knowingly, and Nolin turned a deep scarlet before returning his nod.

Mollie laughed in delight at the interaction, and Cadal was reminded of how she pushed Liam to propose to Elizabeth. *That wasn't her intention in this case. She would let the couple take their time, but it pleased her that the game made Gady so happy.*

At a lull in the action, Cadal leaned close to Mollie. "Do they have other traditions at Human weddings?"

"Many. Some I like and some I don't," she admitted.

"For instance? What don't you like?"

"The bride wears a *garter* that the husband removes and throws to the eligible young men. The one who catches it will be promised next."

"Why don't you like that? It sounds like a good way to get the young men involved."

Mollie blushed. "The Human husband removes the *garter* in full view of the guests. That often embarrasses the bride. To make it worse, the man who catches it puts it, not on the leg of the lady of his choosing but on the lady who caught the *bouquet*. It is embarrassing for the woman, and often the man is permitted to push the *garter* much higher than she is comfortable with for the enjoyment of the other men. I don't like it, and I feel it is highly inappropriate here in the colony."

Cadal stared at her, shocked nearly beyond words. "I agree." Humans allowed such treatment of their women? No wonder men like Thornton and Tucker existed. "What ones do you like?"

Mollie's mood lightened again, and she smiled. "I'll show you one. Raise your cup close to your face."

Cadal did as she asked.

She picked up her cup and met his gaze. "Hold still for a moment." Mollie linked her arm through Cadal's. "Drink from your cup," she instructed.

The position of their arms placed them almost in the same position as for a kiss. Cadal felt her breath against his cheek. His elbow rested against the side of Mollie's breast as he drank deeply from his cup. Mollie smiled at him over her cup, and Cadal reached around it to kiss her.

"I see why you like that tradition," Cadal whispered. *Comments buzzed in his head from the crowd.* "The others see as well. They'll be doing it soon." He unhooked his arm *to relieve the tension in her back.* "What else?" Cadal was enjoying these lessons immensely.

"Dancing is essential to a Human wedding, like wind dancing here."

Cadal considered that for a few moments before he excused himself and, *trailed by Traden and Berner,* crossed to the musicians playing softly in the corner. *Valia, sensing Cadal was up to something, kept Mollie's attention on something else.* Cadal would have to thank her later. The artists closed the song they were performing and bowed to the new Fairy Master reverently.

"I have an odd request," Cadal informed them.

The head musician, Wealt, smiled widely. "Whatever would please the Master."

"If I transferred a song to you, the sound of it being played, could you recreate it?"

Wealt furrowed his brow. "From transfer? I suppose so. We would know the music as if we had practiced, and our hands would find the correct notes."

Cadal smiled crookedly. "Wealt, my friend, will you accept my transfer?" He asked it formally and with the same wide smile.

The musician laughed heartily. "As the Master wishes."

The transfer was quick. Barely a minute passed before Wealt nodded in reply. "It won't be perfect. The instruments are strange to me, but we can do a fine imitation of it with the instruments we have."

Cadal nodded and repeated his transfer to each of the musicians in turn. *Mollie wondered where he had gone. She would be looking for him soon, but for now, Valia had Morda distracting her for him.*

The musicians started preparing their instruments, and Wealt nodded to Cadal. "Should we play now, Master?"

"In a moment. I'll signal you. This is a gift for my bride," he explained.

"Then we are most honored to be of service."

Mollie looked at him strangely when he returned. "Is something wrong? You were gone for quite a while."

Cadal took her hand and kissed it lightly. "Nothing could be wrong with you by my side."

"Flattery will get you everywhere."

"I hope so. Come with me."

Mollie stood and took his arm, while Harea hurried to smooth her dress. The crowd parted around them as Cadal led her close to the musicians, *trailed by his two older servants and hers.*

Cadal laced his fingers through Mollie's and met her eyes. "Dance with me," he asked breathlessly.

Mollie looked at the ceiling in confusion. *It was high but not nearly high enough.* "How?"

Cadal laughed. "How quickly you've fallen into thinking like a Fairy. I want to dance with you, Mollie. The way we danced before we knew you were Fairy."

Her face darkened. "You want to *dance*?" She used the Human English word to be sure of his intentions.

He nodded. "As I recall, dancing with you is rather stimulating."

Mollie's smile widened. "But it means so much more, you know," she supplied the line.

"Yes, it does. Will you dance with me?" Cadal placed his hands on her hips.

Mollie wound her arms around his neck. "Guess you're stuck with me for the next five or six centuries," she sighed.

Cadal laughed and motioned to Wealt. The recreation wasn't perfect, but it was close enough that Mollie's eyes widened in surprise as they had barely begun moving. The gentle sway soon gave way to the gliding and whirling that marked their first dance. As they had that first time, their hearts kept them in harmony as they moved together.

Cadal smiled. Wealt and his musicians employed a trick of bridging the music to restart the melody smoothly. After three times through, they ended the song and sat back to watch the results of their efforts.

Mollie clung to Cadal and laughed. She curtsied to the musicians smoothly and thanked them before planting a playful kiss on Cadal's cheek for his surprise. Her chest heaved beneath the bodice of her gown and the color was high in her cheeks. Mollie reveled in the crowd's adulation.

He wrapped Mollie in his arms and kissed her in unrestrained passion. Dancing always seemed to have this effect on him. "Go to our quarters with me," he pleaded with Mollie in the barest whisper against her cheek.

She nodded, her breathing quickening in response. "I'd love to."

Cadal swung Mollie into his arms in the Fairy signal that the new couple intended to depart their celebration. He made the traditional announcement to the crowd. "Stay. Enjoy the food and drink, the fine music, and the fine company. My bride and I will see you all sometime after the dawn breaks."

The crowd roared their approval as Cadal carried his bride out into the corridor and toward their quarters. Cadal turned back to dismiss their servants. Some Fairies enjoyed having the servants available to pamper them as they wished through the night, but Cadal was sure Mollie wouldn't want that. It was time for privacy between them.

The bedroom was prepared for them. A lamp was lit and the quilt drawn back. A tray of food, drinks, and cakes sat by the bedside. Cadal sat on the bed with Mollie across his lap and kissed her with a deep longing. His hands found the small buttons down her back. He unfastened them gently, lest Valia never let him forget that she was forced to repair the dress due to his haste.

Cadal slid the sleeves down Mollie's arms and dipped his mouth to tease her breasts through the material of her *bra*. She cried *out in a combination of pleasure and discomfort at the tight fit of the garment,* so he removed it. Cadal supported her back with one hand while the other cupped a breast. He teased the nipples alternately with his tongue. Mollie arched her back and sank to the bed beneath his probing mouth.

Mollie reached to undress him, but he brushed her hands away and kissed her to still her protest. He backed away slowly and removed her dress and boots. His gaze wandered over the near-naked expanse of her. Cadal removed his vest and shirt, then dropped them over the edge atop her dress. His boots and socks followed.

He knew that Mollie ached to see him, but Cadal decided to draw out her excitement. He ran his cheek along the silky length of her hose and his tongue over the layer of fabric that hid her from his attentions. Mollie arched her back to offer herself better, and a moan escaped from deep in her throat. He lapped at the material and gauged her response closely.

Cadal hooked his fingers in the waistband of the panties and pulled them down to the tops of Mollie's thighs. He followed their progress with his lips until her hands grasped his head and she lifted her hips in something that resembled an invitation, *but was much closer to a demand.* Cadal favored her with a single, slow lick beneath the fabric before replacing his tongue with his expert fingers and massaging the tender flesh while she moaned and moved beneath him.

"Please, don't," Mollie begged him at last.

He moved his hand, then discarded the last of her clothing. Cadal bent to run his mouth over the sensitive area so recently vacated by his fingertips. Mollie cried out in frustration and pleasure, and Cadal sat back to remove the last of his own clothing.

She fondled him as soon as he was free of the trousers and moved over him, pulling gently while Cadal groaned at the way his arousal spiked at her touch. He laid back and allowed Mollie to pleasure him as she wanted. She started moving her hands over his body, used her mouth, then lowered the warm depths of herself over him.

Cadal placed his hands on Mollie's hips as she sat astride him and started moving against her, filling her completely every time Mollie dropped her body to his hips. He wanted it to last longer, perhaps forever, but Cadal lacked the self-control to execute such restraint. His arousal had been shelved for most of the day, and it screamed toward a release.

As his seed filled her, Mollie reacted as never before. *The feeling of his explosive climax within her sent a spasm of pleasure through Mollie with the power of a lightning strike.* Mollie cried out as she arched further against him. She dropped to his chest, and Cadal wrapped his arms around her, pulling her shaking form to him.

The reaction she had was erotic in its intensity, and Cadal was curious about its meaning. *He sifted back through the memories and feelings she experienced when he climaxed.*

Cadal filled her. The heat of him inside Mollie sparked a thought of Caden. Their son was within her because of that same hot fullness at the height of both their pleasure. It completed Mollie in so many ways. Cadal coupled with Mollie and completed her physically. He married her and completed her soul. His seed filled her and completed their son. All of it shot through Mollie's mind and heart in an instant, and she was abruptly, truly complete for the first time in her life. Mollie wanted the warmth and pleasure to last forever.

Cadal smiled and kissed her forehead. "That was the most Fairy experience you've ever had. It doesn't have to end, Mollie. We're not Human. We're Fairies. For us, this feeling will never disappear, even as we change. We are complete."

Mollie nodded and sank to his chest. *As she dropped off to sleep, visions of them dancing filled her mind.*

Cadal smiled at her memories. At last, there would be peace.

Chapter Thirty

Peace was not what awaited them the next morning. Cadal woke suddenly *to a feeling of deep discord.* Already? How could so dangerous a situation arise already? *Cadal groaned, as his mind replayed the situation for him. It was his doing...and Mollie's.*

Mollie moved beneath the quilt and reached for him. She snapped her eyes open and watched Cadal pulling on his day clothes in surprise. "What's wrong?" *Not Humans*, she begged silently. *He can't go chasing Humans now.*

"It's a disagreement. A rather bad one, as Fairies go. I have to mediate."

She nodded and started pulling on her own clothing. "Give me a minute, and I'll be ready."

Cadal looked at her in confusion. "I'll take care of this. Eat something. I'll be back soon."

Mollie laughed lightly. "A Fairy Master can always find The Harmony's will in his bride's eyes, right? What kind of bride would I be if I wasn't there when you needed to see my eyes?"

Cadal startled. "Who told you that?" he demanded quietly. This would be much easier without Mollie in the middle of it, and talk like that was not helping his argument.

"Valia. Is she wrong?"

Cadal found that his inability to lie did *extend to his bride.* Not that he'd seriously considered it. He wasn't sure how to answer for a moment, so Cadal concentrated on buttoning his shirt while he considered his options. "Yes and no. Our souls are one. When a Fairy Master gets lost in the facts of the case, sometimes what his bride *feels* makes the solution clear for him."

"Then what can it hurt to take me?" Mollie rationalized.

Cadal grumbled. He had to find a way to keep Mollie out of this. He could distract her. "You are a new bride. You should be allowed to relax in our bed, eat, and sleep with no hindrance today." It sounded weak, even to himself.

"Alone? I think not." Mollie fashioned a quick sandwich and poured a large cup of sweet milk. She pulled on her tennis shoes and gathered her tangled hair into a bun where it wouldn't show that she hadn't taken the time to brush it. "I'm ready."

Cadal regarded her with what he hoped was an expression of amusement to hide his dismay.

Misreading his look for one patronizing her, Mollie looked at him in annoyance. "We'll come back here when you're done. I'm not done with you yet," Mollie added in a teasing tone as she grabbed up her sandwich and cup.

Cadal sighed. Distraction had failed. "You're determined?"

She nodded in reply.

The truth was the only thing he had left. "I should warn you that this disagreement was caused in part by us. It will be difficult to mediate because of that fact."

"Because of us?" Mollie paled. "Which one of my Human traditions did it?"

"Several conspired together." *Cadal felt the urge from her to set it right.* He sighed. Mollie wouldn't be turned away. "You'll see. If you're coming with me, it must be now."

Mollie nodded and headed for the door, taking a bite from her sandwich. Cadal sighed again. At least she was eating. What Harea had to say would surely ruin Mollie's appetite before long.

The path cleared before them as they made their way to Berner's quarters.

Traden met them halfway there and fell in behind Cadal. "If you're here, you know the problem."

Cadal nodded. "I do."

"Can I do anything to help?"

"Have a proper breakfast ready for us when this is over. I'm afraid we were dragged from slumber rather abruptly, and Mollie is snacking to appease our son until we can take care of that. I'd like to continue our day together as soon as we can." Cadal glanced at her. "Would jelly pastries be all right?"

Mollie nodded through the last mouthful of her sandwich.

"As you wish," Traden answered. He dropped back and headed toward his quarters *to get Valia started on the dough while he stoked the fire for the baking dish.*

Fairies scattered as they reached Berner's quarters. Harea's voice let everyone within the closest three quarters know that she wouldn't be denied what she felt was appropriate. Cadal sighed and opened the door without knocking. Everyone froze instantly. Cessia and Harea faced each other across the table, while Nolin and Gady sat miserably aside under Berner's watchful eye.

Harea looked past Cadal's shoulder to Mollie and her features hardened. *The effect wasn't lost on Mollie.* His bride shivered at the silent accusation in those eyes.

Cadal looked from face to face. "There is a disagreement," he intoned the formal greeting. "I call you now to the Great Chamber. Will you accompany me?"

He met Nolin and Gady's gazes first, and they answered almost in unison *and in relief.*

Berner was next. "As you wish, Master," he answered with a deep bow to his nephew.

Cessia added her agreement.

Harea straightened her back slightly before answering. "As you wish." She stared at Mollie for a long moment and *gauged her response for...*

As it became clear to Cadal, Mollie sighed *in understanding.*

"As you wish," she said more to Harea than her husband.

Cadal looked at her in confusion. "You're not called. You are in no disagreement."

"I'm not, but Harea is, and she bears it against me. In my own *defense* and to offer testimony to clear up whatever havoc the Human traditions I introduced have caused, I ask to be included. If I'm not, Harea may never forgive whatever trespass she believes me guilty of."

Cadal opened his mouth to protest, but *he suddenly locked on her stream of thought.* Mollie was brilliant. Her understanding of Human nature served her well when dealing with the less complicated Fairies, and the general plan was inspired. Mollie couldn't offer testimony if she wasn't either one of the called or the mediator herself. It was perfect.

He looked to Harea. "Is Mollie correct? Will you bear this against her?"

Harea blushed under his scrutiny. *She feared Cadal would protect his bride,* but with Mollie's plan, that was the last thing he would have to do. "I will," she admitted, *knowing that she couldn't possibly lie to the Fairy Master.*

Cadal forced back his frustration. "Do any of you oppose this?"

Each Fairy in the room shook his or her head in acceptance of this strange request.

"Very well, you are called as well," Cadal informed Mollie. "There being no dissent, we will retire now."

Cadal took Mollie's arm and led the way to the Great Chamber with the rest of the procession at their heels. Once inside, Cadal bolted the east door and nodded to Berner to take care of the north. He took his place on his throne. To his surprise, Mollie didn't move to join him.

She met his eyes. "It wouldn't be appropriate for me to assume that place of honor while I'm one of the called."

Berner swore vehemently under his breath and placed a hand on her shoulder. "Yes, it would," he assured her.

Harea shook her head. "Another Human tradition, I'm sure."

Cadal's head snapped up *at the emotion of veiled disdain for Humans that Harea expressed.* Mollie turned to face her, before Cadal could investigate further.

"Would it make you feel better for me to face you from a throne than as your equal?" Mollie asked honestly.

Or was it? Mollie was leading Harea to expose something she knew was there beneath the surface.

Harea was confused by the question. "You're the bride of the Fairy Master. That's your place. Why should it bother me to see you there?"

Cadal felt her response. It did matter to Harea. It mattered a lot.

Mollie nodded curtly and took her place beside Cadal. He was stunned by her expertise at this.

Perhaps The Harmony chose Mollie for more than her spirit. She knew exactly what was on Harea's mind and led Cadal to it.

Cadal faced them. "Now I will mediate. Harea, your daughter is of age. What cause have you to react as you do?"

"My daughter has been wronged. I'm her mother. When she hurts, I hurt. You cannot deny that it should be so."

Cadal raised an eyebrow at Gady. This part was the easiest. The solution would be the difficult step. "Have you been wronged, Gady?"

The young Fairy blushed. "No, Master. I was upset, but it was of my own doing. Nolin—"

"Made a false promise," Harea interrupted angrily. "Gady cried pitifully because of it."

Nolin cringed, *and a sad sinking feeling assaulted Mollie.* Nolin spoke, while *Mollie held her tongue, so she could get a better idea of the problem.*

"I didn't mean to hurt her. I misunderstood," he whispered miserably.

Cessia cut him off cleanly. "He made no promise, Harea. Gady was the one who misunderstood."

Gady tried to make herself heard again, but Harea overpowered her.

Cadal held up a hand for silence. "Gady, tell us your version, with no interruptions this time." He offered the warning with a stern look at Harea.

Gady took a deep breath. "I was excited by the strange traditions. When I caught the *bouquet*, I was overjoyed." She looked at Mollie pitifully. "I know it was a silly game, but..."

Cadal glanced at Mollie. "You have something to add?" *He knew she did.*

"You said no interruptions, so I didn't dare, but since you asked..." Mollie smiled before she continued. "Even in the Human world, the women who *wish* to be the next wed try the hardest to catch the *bouquet*. Those who aren't hopeful try to fade into the background or refuse to play. That's what makes the game fun. Those who have the highest hopes try their best to win. Gady simply had high hopes, and she won because of it."

Gady nodded. "That sounds correct. I was enchanted by the Human dancing," she went on. "I remembered Mollie saying you two Human danced first and wished for it to mean the same as a wind dance."

Cadal cut in again. "But you knew it didn't mean the same thing?" he asked to clarify it for Harea and Mollie.

Gady nodded. "When Nolin asked me, he meant only to please me. I wished for more, but I knew no promise was made."

Nolin turned a deep crimson.

Cadal smiled *at his thoughts*. "Is she correct, Nolin? Was pleasing Gady all there was to your offer of a dance?" Cadal asked.

Nolin shook his head.

Harea seized on it. "You see? He admits it freely."

"Was a promise made, Nolin?" Cadal asked patiently.

"No, Master. No promise was made. Gady and I are far too young for promises. In a few decades, when my training is complete..." He blushed deeper.

"Gady, you knew his feelings? You knew Nolin felt you were too young to consider promising?"

She nodded. "I did."

Cadal turned back to Nolin. "You said there was more to the dancing than pleasing Gady. What more was there?"

Nolin smiled at Gady bashfully. "I was wishing it could be our promise as well."

Cadal looked at the secretive smile on Mollie's face. *Damn it! She can still do that.* He had only the faintest idea of what she was thinking. "You have insight on this?" he asked her.

Mollie nodded. "Unfortunately, it involves another Human tradition. I take it Nolin is courting Gady?"

Gady raised her chin indignantly. "How could I make such assumptions if he wasn't?"

Mollie laughed lightly, a laugh that reminded Cadal faintly of Morda. "You'd be surprised. Humans of the culture I was raised in have a tradition. When a couple is courting and believe they may be destined to wed, they *go steady.* They agree to court each other exclusively, with the understanding that something more may wait over the horizon. The woman wears a trinket of devotion given by the man on her person. Sometimes, he wears one from her as well. It is a sign that, though they are not prepared to wed, they believe they would like to make the promise someday."

Gady and Nolin leaned forward to take this tradition in.

Gady spoke first, voicing *what they both wondered.* "What happens if they're wrong?"

"Humans often are, but it rarely happens here in the colony." She glanced at Cadal's medallion and away quickly, *masking her embarrassment.* "At any rate, it's not something you would enter into until you were fairly sure of your heart, and it's not unbreakable. If you and Nolin discovered you weren't true soulmates, you'd be miserable together. To be truly happy, you would have to wed your true soulmates, and there would be no hurt feelings that you courted another in your search for that soulmate. Correct?" Mollie looked to Cadal for an answer.

He cringed inwardly but nodded. *Mollie wasn't thinking about Xanthe. She was referring to Benia and Flori, and while her feelings weren't hurt, there was significant unease at the sight of Cadal with them that Mollie experienced in transfer.*

Nolin nodded. "I think I understand. The couple agree that they believe they are to be promised without promising?"

Mollie nodded. "Exactly."

"What would be the point?" Harea interrupted.

Mollie sighed. "Gady and Nolin both crave something they cannot reasonably have for many years to come. If it puts them at ease, what can it hurt? You were upset that Gady was distraught about not being able to promise yet. I will pose two questions to you. Think carefully about your answers.

"If it will make Gady happy to know that Nolin feels the same for her as she does for him, why would you begrudge either of them that happiness? And, would you really want Nolin to promise to Gady, to seal it in wind dance and then to be miserably stuck in a situation neither of them can change because of it if they were mismatched? They would both be denied their true soulmates and those soulmates denied them in your haste to see them promised."

Harea stared at her in shock. "I would never begrudge my daughter her happiness. I would never force her into an unhappy relationship, but these Human traditions do nothing but cause upset to our order."

Mollie smiled, *which only infuriated Harea, and she knew it.* "Order is a fine thing. Rules and traditions are fine things, but sometimes people, Human or Fairy, need more. Gady and Nolin are unhappy with the current system. If it were perfect, they wouldn't be. A perfect system cannot exist any more than a perfect person can.

"If the Fairies of the colony were perfect, there would be no disagreements. There would be no need for a Fairy Master. The Fairy way of handling disagreements is infinitely better than any formal system Humans have, but you are so mired in tradition that you hold to it, even when it hurts you.

"I love the Fairy promise and the ceremony. But, why should it be forbidden for a man and a woman to admit that it would please them to wed someday — if they discover it really is their path, without being bound forever by that single word?"

"Because it has always *been* that way," Harea explained a little less than patiently. "These traditions have served us for ten thousand years, given to us by The Harmony, Herself. It would be an affront to The Harmony to balk them, but I wouldn't expect you to understand or appreciate that."

Mollie was crushed, though her face remained impassive.

Cadal accessed information at an astounding pace then shook his head. "You're wrong, Harea. Our traditions are our own. Some of them predate even the First Fairy Master of Aiden, from the dark times before civilization came to us. Some, we've added in the long years since then.

"Every decision made by every Fairy Master was made based on tens, hundreds, or even thousands of instances where something similar or even the same thing happened before. Occasionally, a Master was so disturbed by the suffering he saw that he decreed some decision openly and created a new tradition that we live by.

"Some traditions, like the one that keeps us from doing what Mollie suggests, are really neither. Over the years, it was deemed unnecessary to say anything aside from the formal promise. It grew into a ban over time. It was never decreed or even passed down. It simply happened along the way.

"What The Harmony gave us was our way of life. How we choose to use that life is our own decision. That is where the Fairy Master comes in."

Berner nodded in understanding. "What of this case? How many times has this happened before?"

"This exact thing? Never, but Human dancing was only introduced last night." Cadal added another stern look at Harea to ensure her silence while he finished what he had to say.

Harea smiled in percieved victory and pressed on, despite his warning. "You see? These Human traditions are disruptive. It can only get worse unless they are banished from the colony."

Cadal felt the mixture of anger and sadness from Mollie, but to her credit, she waited to see what would happen next.

Cadal hardened his features. "If I may continue uninterrupted," he prodded crisply.

Harea dropped her gaze.

"This exact situation has never occurred before, but situations where young Fairies and their families are unhappy for the same reasons as Nolin and Gady are almost too numerous to count. In Morda's reign alone, she dealt with a dozen such cases involving over fifty interventions on her part. It seems that this particular tradition is causing undue suffering to our people."

Harea bristled. "You would do away with the promise?" she demanded.

Cadal laughed, *and Harea's fury spiked again.* "Never. I don't advocate doing away with the current system. I think everyone here would agree that it is a beautiful and functional system."

Everyone, including Mollie, nodded his or her agreement.

"It was never decreed that two people couldn't express that they would like to promise someday. It is a strange twisting which came up over time. Such a proclamation need never be a ceremony. In fact, it should never be. It should be an expression of love between those involved which will put their minds at ease, and I think it might end these problems."

Nolin's eyes glittered in anticipation of such a decree, but Harea was still intent. "Why add undue Human complications to our lives?"

Gady eyed her critically. "If it were *your* pain, you would understand why," she countered acidly then blushed and looked away *in shock at what she had said.*

Cadal regarded the young Fairy kindly. "No, Gady. Go on. Would such an arrangement — such a system make you happy? At ease?"

Gady reached for Nolin's hand and smiled warmly. "It made my heart sing to hear Nolin say aloud that he wished it could be our promise. I would have liked to know that when he offered the dance." She met Cadal's eyes again. "Yes, it would make me very happy to have such a tradition."

Cadal nodded. "And you, Nolin?"

Nolin smiled at Gady, then at Cadal. "I've dreamed of the chance to say such a thing to Gady. Forever, it seems."

Cadal chuckled, bringing Mollie's hand to his lips. "I remember those days. Well, it appears that Nolin and Gady are no longer at odds or in pain. Cessia?"

The older woman nodded her head emphatically. "A wise decision, Master. I am content."

"Berner?"

"I am content, and I am overjoyed that my son is so happy."

Cadal sighed. "Harea, will you concede? Can you not simply be happy that Gady will be happy?"

"What of the tears she has already shed?" Harea demanded.

Gady looked at the pained expression on Nolin's face. *Nolin would give anything to take back every tear she had shed,* and Cadal knew that feeling. He'd had it a few times himself.

She squeezed Nolin's hand in comfort. "Forgotten," Gady assured him.

Were they not in company, Nolin would have kissed her for that. He still planned to do it at his first opportunity.

Harea crossed her arms over her chest. "Not by me."

Cadal smiled at her. "Harea, they were never your tears to protest or to forgive. We all feel. We would not be truly alive if we didn't. Sometimes, we must cry."

Harea glared at Mollie. "Some of us must. Some of us skate through blithely, causing upset in the lives of others."

Mollie turned a deep crimson. *Cadal felt her urge to either cry or strike back verbally,* but she didn't take the bait.

He fought back his initial response. Cadal was Fairy Master, and he couldn't enter into a conflict of interest, even for his bride. Still, the feelings Harea harbored for Mollie couldn't be allowed to fester.

"Harea, will you accept my transfer?" he asked quietly.

Mollie put a hand on his arm. "No, Cadal. Don't, please. Let her think what she wants. I was wrong to ask to be called. This goes deeper than Gady's tears. I can't heal this one."

"No, but I can. You have spent far too many years taking that road, my love. This time, I can correct what someone thinks of you, and that is what I must do."

"I don't care what she thinks of me," Mollie insisted.

Cadal hooked a finger under her chin and turned Mollie's face back to him. "Yes, you do."

Mollie cracked a sad smile and nodded. "I hate it when you do that, but I suppose you're right." She sighed in resignation and sank back into the cushion on her throne.

Cadal connected to her for his next comment. "I know what to transfer. I won't send anything you wouldn't want me to."

Mollie met his eyes in surprise, then nodded again.

He turned back to Harea. "Will you accept my transfer?"

The older woman looked uncertain. *Harea had heard the musings of Mollie's past and was afraid of what she might see, but she was not ready to back down, sure that whatever she saw couldn't be as horrible as the stories.*

Cadal felt a sort of pity for her. Even the fairly tame things he intended to show Harea were much worse than the stories she'd heard. Such was the life of a Fairy.

Harea nodded. "I must." She came to kneel before him and allowed Cadal to place his hands.

He transferred a montage of images. First, there was Mollie with broken bones and insect stings, followed by an image of the bruises the other Fairies hadn't seen when she came to them. He launched into images of Mollie crying in her bed with Xanthe's book held to her chest, in Cadal's arms after he'd confronted Tucker at the pond, and as Cadal walked away from her after the first time they danced. He added images of Mollie bleeding and exhausted after her days in the field, backing away from Zera's wrath when they first met, and sinking into her anger and sadness when she learned of Katie's death.

His next images were intended to truly humble Harea, if nothing so far had done the trick. Mollie screamed in pain and fear while Tucker kept a grip on her arm. Mollie sank to the ground in a daze after Tucker hit her. Mollie hit the ground harder when the vandal struck her, while Patrick launched over her fallen form to tackle the man. Mollie smiled at Cadal with the bruise from that encounter still fresh on her cheek.

Harea's own words flew back at her. "What's wrong? Cadal had his day. The ceremony is yours.

"He can't. Tradition says—

"What do you mean, no?

"Another strange Human custom, I suppose.

"Some of us must. Some of us skate through life blithely."

Valia's voice came next. "Harea isn't going to like this."

Mollie answered, "You shouldn't let Harea bully you."

Cadal ended the transfer with the conversation Mollie and Morda had while planning the ceremony about needs, traditions, and conformity.

As he released Harea, *he felt her deep embarrassment.* Cadal refrained from asking the standard question. Asking her if she understood sounded too much like "I told you so" for his comfort.

Harea nodded grimly. She kept her gaze cast down. *Harea couldn't look at Mollie. She wasn't sure she could ever face the younger woman again.* "I think I understand. I haven't been very gracious. I am at fault. I let my judgment be clouded. I must make amends."

Mollie nodded uncertainly. "I'm sure Berner and his family would appreciate that."

Harea looked at Cadal in confusion, still unable to meet Mollie's gaze.

Cadal took Mollie's hand gently. "Harea will, but she meant that she needs to make amends to you," he explained.

Mollie shook her head. "That's not necessary. I don't want it."

"For her, it's necessary. I know how you feel, but Harea's healing won't be complete until she does this."

"What exactly are we talking about? What's involved?"

"She'll be your servant for a week."

"You know how I feel about servants," Mollie warned.

Cadal laughed heartily. "If you do a single thing for yourself while she serves you, that much more time will be added on. There will be no blood, sweat, and tears this time. It won't be allowed here. Unless you want this woman serving you for the rest of her life, you had better let her do it the right way."

Gady was having a hard time hiding the smile on her face.

Mollie scowled at him. "You certainly have me cornered this time, don't you?"

"I hope so. You seem to have a way of slipping away just when I think I have you."

Mollie smiled. "Not this time, I assure you. You're not giving me any choice." She sighed. "All right. I agree, but we're not starting today. I want one relaxing day before I start this. It's going to be difficult enough reminding myself not to do anything for a week."

Chapter Thirty-one

Difficult turned out to be nearly impossible. Mollie tried giving Harea busy work to keep the other woman out of her hair. Mollie sorted out clothing, which she argued only she could do, and sent Harea to take the bags of things she couldn't use until after Caden was born to storage in their new quarters. That was when she ran out of ideas. That didn't stop the older Fairy. Harea seemed to be in perpetual motion. Just watching her made Mollie nervous.

Finally, Mollie couldn't take it any more. "Harea, sit down please. You're making me tired and keeping me awake at the same time."

"I'm here to serve you."

"You've done a week's worth of work in half a day. There is nothing left to do. Ever."

Harea smiled. "I'm sure there's something. For now, I'll make your lunch."

Mollie groaned and sank back to the bed with the book of Fairy poetry she was reading.

After lunch, Mollie couldn't sit still any longer. She pulled on the soft brown boots Morda had ordered for her and started toward the Great Chamber. Cadal would be working there, and she desperately needed to talk to him about this situation before it drove her out of her mind.

From the footsteps behind her, Mollie guessed that Harea was following her and making sure she did nothing for herself. Mollie uttered several harsh Human curses.

She faced Harea warily. "If I promise not to do anything for myself, will you go home for the afternoon?"

Harea chuckled. "Cadal told me not to believe that promise."

Mollie grumbled. The talk with Cadal was getting longer by the minute. "You're my servant. That means I can order you to go away until dinner," she reasoned.

Harea shook her head in amusement. "It doesn't work that way. Cadal told me you would try that. I'm not a *hired* servant like the Humans have. This is a duty. You cannot dismiss me."

Mollie spun back toward the Great Chamber and started stalking this time. "When I get my hands on that man, I'm going to commit the first murder in Aiden," she growled under her breath, punctuating it with several colorful Human curses.

Harea agreed to wait outside the Great Chamber, much to Mollie's relief. Mollie considered the possibility of napping in the small throne while her husband worked, but first...

Cadal smiled at her crookedly and dismissed the men surrounding him while he talked to Mollie. Thankfully, that meant the room cleared and the doors shut behind them. Mollie would hate to have to kill Cadal in front of his servants. She was fairly sure of that anyway.

Mollie placed her fists on her hips and regarded her husband in annoyance. Cadal relaxed back into his throne, and his smile widened. What else had she expected of him?

"I take it there's a problem?" he asked innocently.

"You're the Fairy Master," she shot back at him. "You know there is. You ordered Harea to stick to me like glue. You knew that would drive me *nuts*. Why did you do it?"

"This is a learning experience for each of you. The two of you have to learn to get along somehow, and you have to learn to let go and let someone else do the work."

"By annoying me? That's a lousy start, Cadal."

"Find something for her to do," he suggested.

"I have. She's too damned efficient."

Cadal laughed and reached out to wrap his hands around her waist. Mollie tried ducking out of his reach until they had settled this matter, but he was faster and more agile than she was now that she was pregnant. He drew her astride his lap, and Mollie felt a wholly inappropriate response for where they were. She sucked in a deep breath to steady her nerves, and Cadal's eyes glittered mischievously in response to her arousal.

"Why don't you try talking to her? You'll figure something out along the way."

"You try it. Harea never stands still long enough to talk. Maybe I should order her to talk to me..." Mollie wondered if that would work.

"In the meantime, why don't you take a relaxing bath and soothe your nerves?" He massaged at a stiff spot in her hip. "I'm sure Harea would be happy to help with that."

Mollie smiled wickedly. "I'd rather take one with you, if you're up to it."

Cadal looked at her in confusion, and Mollie pushed an image of what she had planned for them into the front of her mind. Cadal's eyes widened in surprise, and his smile bloomed with them.

Mollie knew she had his complete attention. She started to back off of his lap. "Well, back to work."

Cadal tightened his grip on her waist, raw desire in his eyes. "It's a *date*. Before bed tonight, I'd like to do exactly that."

Mollie smiled and kissed him, gasping at the response she felt when he deepened it. When she pushed away, Mollie sighed. "Wrong time and place for this," she decided. It sounded like an adventure, but it seemed irreverent at the same time.

He raised an eyebrow and pulled her hips to him in a way Mollie was sure Cadal knew would weaken her resolve.

"I can bolt the doors," he offered. "It wouldn't be the first time."

Mollie shook her head. "It would be for me. Another time." She crawled backward off of his lap.

Cadal feigned a pained look. "You're really going to leave me here to suffer without you, aren't you?"

She laughed lightly and walked away. "I ended that suffering two days ago. Besides, if I have to suffer, you have to suffer." Mollie added an extra sway to her hips for good measure, looking back to gauge its effect on him.

Cadal smiled despite the severe look he was attempting to give her. "If you keep this up, I promise I'll call you before me to answer for it," he warned her.

Mollie laughed louder. "You can't."

"Why not? I am the Fairy Master."

"You're not my Master. Besides, you have a definite conflict of interest. Your resolution would undoubtedly be to try to convince me to use that throne for something other than sitting in."

With that, she left the Great Chamber with a wide smile and her ever-present tail. Mollie sighed as she considered the possibility that Cadal would have been so stunned by her that he would have let her leave through the wrong door and ditch Harea.

Okay, honestly? None.

"Harea, is there any rule that says you can't walk beside me so I'm not talking over my shoulder?" Mollie asked in exasperation.

"If you wish it."

"I do. It will make me feel less self-conscious."

Harea fell into step beside her.

"That's better — sort of. Now, you have a life. Be reasonable. There must be something you have to do for yourself."

"Not at all. Gady is spending quite a bit of time with Nolin." She smiled. "He gave her the most beautiful token of love, a bracelet he has been working on for some time. Gady is working on a braided belt for him. I'm sure it's almost done by now."

"Don't you have any chores of your own to do?"

"Not many. Gady helps, so there is little to do."

"What about your work?" Mollie was grasping at straws, but she was running out of ideas to redirect Harea's attention.

"It will keep."

Mollie sighed. "What do you do for work?" Somehow, she never got around to asking that. Mollie had asked what Harea's husband had done before he passed away from a fever several years before and didn't go any further.

The topic of the meaters made Mollie a little queasy, so she probably didn't go any further for that reason. She supposed the arrangement of taking the lives of animals who were old or injured as a service, in exchange for the use of their meat and hides should seem more humane than what Humans did. Mollie decided, after several rocky meals picking at her meat, that it was easier not to think about eating something that you could have talked to a month ago.

"I'm a weaver."

Mollie looked at her in surprise. "You have a loom?"

"How else would I weave?" Harea asked solemnly.

"Would you teach me?" Mollie asked excitedly. She'd found weaving fascinating on her first visit, but there had been no time to learn the skill then.

"You're not supposed to be working. It defeats the purpose of my serving you," Harea argued.

"This would be a great service," Mollie pleaded. "I want to learn so badly. Maybe, it's different in the colony, but in the Human world, teachers are some of the finest servants. They put up with unspeakable hardships to serve in a way they love."

Harea looked at her in surprise.

"Please, Harea. It would mean a lot to me, and I'm truly unaccustomed to having nothing to do. If I get tired or frustrated, feel free to stop the lesson. Will you?"

Harea eyed her critically. "I have the feeling that you're tricking me somehow, but I'm not sure how. Can you promise me that Cadal won't be angry with me?"

"I promise," Mollie assured her. Cadal wouldn't be angry with Harea, but he was sure to be annoyed with Mollie. Harea didn't need to know that. That was between Mollie and her husband.

"All right, then. I'll teach you, if that is the service you wish from me."

* * * *

Mollie enjoyed her weaving lesson immensely. She got used to the foreign movements quickly and found only a slight stiffness and aching in her lately-underused muscles. It was close to dinner before Harea ended the lesson and directed Mollie back to Zera's quarters.

Cadal was at the table with a book open in front of him. He raised an eyebrow at his bride with a minimum of anything resembling amusement. "You did it to me again," he informed her.

Harea shot Mollie a look of dismay. "You promised me that Cadal wouldn't be angry."

"He's not," Mollie assured her.

"I'm not?" Cadal adopted the same stern look he'd used on Harea in the Great Chamber.

"No, you're not," Mollie replied calmly. "Tell Harea that you're not angry with her. You know you're not."

Cadal softened his look for Harea. "Mollie's right. I'm not angry with you, Harea. The Humans have a story about a man called The Pied Piper. The piper enchants people or animals to his will. I'm beginning to think my young bride is that piper. What you did is no fault of your own."

Harea looked to Mollie in disbelief. "What you told me about Human teachers was a lie?"

"No, Harea, it was absolutely true," Mollie assured her.

Cadal gave Mollie another severe look.

Mollie sighed. "I knew Cadal wouldn't approve, but I wanted to learn and I hate having nothing to do." She blushed and gave Cadal an impish grin. "Unless it's nothing to do with Cadal there," she added for his benefit.

He nodded his approval. "That's better. Now, you really are enjoying these lessons?"

Mollie nodded and her smile widened. "I really am. You aren't going to do something silly like forbidding it or something, are you?"

Cadal laughed and released a smile that Mollie was sure he had been hiding studiously since she walked in the door. "That would be ridiculous. It wouldn't do me any good if I did. With your *legalistic* Human upbringing, you'd find another rabbit hole to disappear through in less than a day."

"We called them *loopholes*. Am I really that bad?"

"You're determined, and you're accustomed to getting your own way. In this case, I don't think your idea is a bad one." His features hardened slightly. "I wish you would stop doing things with the thought of how I will disapprove at the outset. If this makes you happy and doesn't put you in danger or in pain, I wouldn't begrudge you finding something you like to do."

"In other words, Harea can continue as my teacher?" Mollie asked hopefully.

Cadal nodded.

Harea looked at him warily. "With your permission?"

"With my permission. With my gratitude, actually."

Mollie smiled and sank into his lap. She was going to have to show Cadal a very good time when they took that bath tonight. "Now you're trying to keep me busy? I thought you wanted me to sit back and let everyone wait on me?"

"Well, I'm not going to get that. You won't allow it. The best I can do is see you happily engrossed in an activity you care for, so you don't get yourself into more trouble."

Mollie laughed.

Harea stared at them in shock. "You talk as if Mollie's still a child. Really, Cadal. How old is your bride?" she scolded him.

Mollie laughed harder, then met Harea's eyes. "I'll be twenty-seven in the spring," she confided.

Harea started, then glared at Cadal. "How could you? I would have taken her for a hundred and fifty.

You married a *child*?" Harea had obviously forgotten that Mollie was Xanthe's descendent, or that Xanthe had only been gone from the colony for a little more than one hundred and ten years, in her shock.

"She's not a child," Cadal replied calmly. "Mollie lived as a Human and aged as a Human. By our standards, she's somewhere between one hundred and fifty and one hundred seventy-five. Now that Mollie's rediscovered her Fairy heritage, she ages as we do. As a Human, Mollie was sexually mature at twelve and mature at eighteen. However young that seems to you, Harea, I assure you that her Human experiences place her as my equal in most areas, and she surpasses me in more than one."

Mollie felt her impish streak building up steam. She wrapped her arms around Cadal's shoulders seductively. "You thought of me as a child once," she reminded him. "It's an honest mistake for a Fairy to make, don't you agree? You have to admit that Harea isn't the first to make it."

Cadal blushed. "I only thought of you as a child until I fell under your spell, piper. And, I was forewarned that you were both an adult and a formidable woman before I had the pleasure of meeting you."

"Warned by whom?" Harea asked.

"Katie, another of Xanthe's descendents. She was Mollie's great aunt, and she was a very dear friend of mine."

"Can you tell me about Xanthe's descendents? I'm sure the family would be interested to hear about them. How many generations passed for them?"

"Five, not counting Xanthe herself," Mollie supplied for her.

"So quickly? Did you know Xanthe? Did you meet her?"

Mollie shook her head sadly.

Cadal took over. "Xanthe lived for about forty or forty-five years after she left here. Not even Mollie's mother met her, and her grandmother and Katie barely remembered her. Xanthe died when Colleen and Katie were very young. All that remained were her medallion and her stories after that.

"Xanthe and her husband Bran had two daughters, Aine and Cecily Blake. Cecily married a man named Carrick MacHugh and," he paused and grinned at Mollie, "had two daughters, Aislinn and Blanche MacHugh. Aislinn married a man named Cairbre Barrett and..."

Mollie laughed when he paused.

"Had two daughters named Colleen and Katie Barrett. Katie married John Stuart, and though The Harmony granted her happiness, She blessed them with no children. Colleen married a man named Sean O'Bane and had a single daughter, Darcy O'Bane who married a man named William Hardy, Mollie's father."

Mollie nodded her agreement. "I brought *pictures*...likenesses of some of them with me. Katie and John, Nana and Pappap, my mother and father. I didn't want to leave without something of them."

Harea shook her head. "So your name is Mollie Hardy?" she asked, as if the concept that Mollie had a Human name surprised her.

Mollie shook her head. "I was named Mollie Marie Hardy. When I left the Human world, that was my name." She smiled and snuggled closer to Cadal. "Now, I am Mollie dannea Aiden."

Cadal laughed a husky laugh that told Mollie her proximity was getting to him slowly. "And how very long I've waited for that."

Harea sank into a chair. "What stories were left? I heard—" She looked away angrily. "I heard that Xanthe told the Humans all about us."

Mollie sighed. "That is not entirely true. She wrote a book of Fairy tales about Fairy life that was passed down from Aislinn MacHugh Barrett to me."

"Where is this book?" Harea asked pointedly.

Mollie blushed. "I left it behind when we came here."

"It's in the hands of Humans?" Harea demanded, paling as she asked the question.

Cadal took over, and Mollie sighed gratefully.

"It's in the hands of two of our Human friends. I've read it myself. Even if it leaves their hands, it's no threat to us. None of our secrets are revealed, and several friends knew who we were. They had no wish to see us trapped and helped us to escape. Traden can confirm that they knew and that they could have destroyed us if it had been their wish.

"The tales are as harmless as hundreds of others the Humans tell. Some of those stories found their way to Humans on the lips of Fairies. Others are pure Human creative fantasy. Either way, no one but our friends would ever believe them, and they will never admit that the stories are true to another Human soul."

"Are you sure? What if someone does believe them?"

Mollie chuckled. "It's not likely. The Humans who knew were a very unusual sort. Cadal spent a year there, and no one connected him to the Cadal of the stories, not even those who knew, until we were forced to trust them." She blushed. "I was infatuated with both the Cadal in the stories and the man I knew, but until

Thunder, I didn't realize there was any possibility they could be the same person."

Cadal grimaced. "Ah, yes. I remember that laugh and look very well. I wanted you to know and to believe what we both were. I hadn't counted on you having such a *crash course*. Forgive the pun."

"If you knew what I was thinking, why didn't you simply tell me right there on the road? I was having a *breakdown*, you know."

"You were injured and shaking so badly I was afraid your legs would give way any moment. I needed to see if your shoulder was broken before I tended to your mental and emotional stress."

Harea looked at them in shock. "Broken? Whatever did she do?"

Cadal turned a brilliant shade of red. "I promised not to tell that story again."

Harea eyed Mollie, and she sighed.

"I connected with a panicked horse and decided to help him. I lost my concentration at a critical moment, and he knocked me senseless." She glanced at Cadal. "While I was, but before I knew I was, carrying Cadal's son."

Harea's amazement faded. She tried to stifle an infectious laugh.

Mollie sighed again and sank into Cadal's comforting arms. "Don't say it, Harea," Mollie pleaded. "We're well mated. We know it."

Chapter Thirty-two

Mollie sat before her loom. She was still amazed at how quickly she came to enjoy the time she spent weaving. Mollie's current project was a length of dark green cloth Harea would help her fashion into a cloak to replace the tattered one Morda owned, the one she'd used to shield her granddaughter from the wind after Tucker attacked her.

In addition to her weaving, Mollie found she was in high demand as a teacher of all things Human. She taught higher *mathematics* that jewelers and designers used, art and literature, *psychology*, science, the Human condition, and traditions of Human cultures. A few of the older Fairies balked this course of action, but it soon became apparent that learning about Human culture from Mollie enriched the Fairies without laying them open to the terrors of the Human world that could easily snatch them from the fold of the colony.

To her surprise, Mollie found transcripts of her lectures were being stored in the repository, along with the Fairy teachings and literature. There were even requests for a *biography* of her life in both the Human and Fairy realms. Mollie was still considering the idea, though Cadal had given his blessing.

Mollie finally admitted to him that she wasn't sure she should share the more sordid stories with Aiden. Mollie wasn't worried about the Fairies repeating the Human brutalities, but she felt sure her Fairy friends would be ill prepared for the whole truth. After all, the brutality she feared most could never apply to them.

Cadal pointed out that a healthy knowledge of the Human dangers could be beneficial in keeping Fairies, who decided to visit the Human world, safe from its many pitfalls. In the end, he kissed her gently. "You have hundreds of years to make a decision," Cadal reminded her. "Don't let it worry you."

She faced her first true dilemma about what to tell the Fairies of Aiden when one of her younger students, Pela, a Fairy girl of about a century, approached Mollie after one of her speeches on Human poetry.

"Mollie, may I ask you a personal question?" Pela began reverently.

Mollie smiled warmly. "Why does every question after a lecture start that way? No, I don't mind, Pela. Ask away."

"Did you ever experiment sexually with a Human man?"

Mollie's stomach swirled. She considered her answer carefully. "Once. When I was still trapped as a Human. As a Fairy, it was impossible, and I didn't want to. I wanted my soulmate then."

"Did you love him?"

"I thought I did." Mollie shook her head. "I think I was more in love with the idea *of* him. With what I thought he was, but then I got to know him and I found out that what I loved was a mask he wore to hide what he was really like inside."

"Why would he do that? Why would he hide what he really was?"

"Because what he really was wasn't very endearing. A woman wouldn't be attracted to it, so he hid it and pretended to be something more appealing."

"No one could have no redeeming qualities. There had to be *someone* out there for him. If he hid who he was, how could he ever find her?"

"Perhaps. If he had redeeming qualities, they were few and far between. Unless he has changed considerably, I would pity any woman who accepted a promise from him." Mollie tried to make her voice impassive, but the thought of anyone falling for James was enough to anger her.

"Was it an enjoyable experience?"

Mollie took a deep breath and reminded herself that Pela was still very young. Pela hadn't developed the ability to evaluate her questions before she asked them and filter out the ones that were too personal or stop when the other person had had enough. This would be touchy.

"No, it wasn't," Mollie admitted. "As I taught you in poetry, Humans can have beautiful experiences, but that wasn't one of them."

"Why wasn't it?"

Mollie considered it carefully. She didn't want to lie to Pela, but Mollie didn't want to scare her either. She sighed. "Because I didn't want his attentions."

"But...you thought you *loved* him?"

"Yes, but in the Human world, that doesn't necessarily mean you should trust the feeling. Many Humans mask who they are. I was very young. I would have been about your age, Pela. Many Fairies aren't ready to experiment sexually at your age, correct?"

Pela nodded furiously.

Mollie smiled, mainly because she knew Pela was doing her share of experimentation with another student named Limor. "Neither was I."

"He seduced you?"

Mollie shook her head and tried to decide how to proceed. How did she end up here? Why didn't she simply tell Pela that she would talk to her later and give it some thought first? Mollie pressed on. "No, it wasn't a seduction, Pela."

She was still considering how to broach the subject when Pela launched into another question. "Then how did he get your permission?"

Mollie met her gaze. "He didn't, Pela. He had no permission." The answer came *off the cuff* and without forethought of how she would handle the *fallout.* Mollie's stomach churned more decidedly this time.

For several long moments, Pela didn't speak. "You mean he proceeded without your acceptance?" she asked in disbelief.

"Yes, Pela. That is exactly what I mean."

Pela seemed more confused than upset, and Mollie waited to see what she would do or say next. The young Fairy shuffled from foot to foot in the empty meeting room and met Mollie's gaze uncertainly.

"Did it..." Pela furrowed her brow.

"Hurt? Yes, Pela. It did hurt, but that was many years ago." She smiled and placed a hand on Pela's shoulder. "It's all right. Ask whatever you feel you need to." She'd allowed it to go on this long. Mollie couldn't *drop that bomb* on Pela and not answer her questions about it.

"What did you do?"

"I fought. I screamed. I cried. In the end, I couldn't stop it."

"None of that mattered to him? To the Human man?"

"Not really. I told you he didn't seem to have any redeeming qualities."

"Why would he do that?"

"I can't say for sure." *Because I was an easy mark?* Mollie shook her head and started again. "I think people like him are missing something in their souls. Not a soulmate they have to find to be complete, but something much more that means they either don't know right from wrong or they don't care. Either way, he did it and it's over now, so the *psychology* of why doesn't really matter. Unless you need to know more."

Pela looked uncertain, biting her lip as if holding in another question.

Mollie sighed. "Ask, Pela. Please, just ask whatever it is." It was unlikely that Pela would have been able to restrain herself for long. It was simpler to give her permission to ask.

Mollie's sick stomach intensified, as Caden started moving violently inside her. She was struck, yet again, by how strong her son was. He was so like Cadal. Mollie willed herself to keep going until she answered Pela's many questions, right up to the moment when Pela asked the question Mollie wanted to answer least of all.

"Did the man enjoy what he did?" she asked quietly.

"I believe he did," she answered quickly. Mollie knew James did. It wasn't something she had to consider.

"How could he? How could he force and hurt and—" Pela seemed frustrated by the concept.

"I don't know. I wish I had an answer for you." *An answer for myself, as well.* "I don't. Harmony help me, I really don't. He wasn't *sane*." Mollie rubbed her temples and laughed harshly. "*You don't understand insane. You don't understand criminal. You don't understand sadistic. Maybe it's better that you never do,*" she muttered bitterly in English.

"Maybe we can find a way to explain it together," Cadal said quietly.

Pela startled, then bowed deeply to him. Mollie saw the fear that she was about to be chastised for her avid questioning in Pela's eyes before the young woman started speaking. "I am sorry, Master. I will trouble Mollie no more."

Mollie patted her arm. "No, Pela. You deserve an answer, if I can form one for you."

Cadal shut the door to the meeting room and crossed to the two women. He ran his hand over the pronounced swelling of her seven-month pregnant belly through her maternity top and smiled. Instantly, Caden settled beneath his father's hand. Mollie heard his voice in her head, calming her as he calmed their son.

"Relax. I'm here, and we'll settle this together. If you're calm, Caden will be as well."

Mollie smiled and touched Cadal's cheek. "Thank you," she whispered to him. Mollie turned to Pela. "Now how can I explain this to you?"

Cadal looked at Pela. "You understand that people, Human or Fairy, sometimes get ill."

The girl nodded.

"Sometimes, that illness makes a person unable to function but it doesn't kill."

"Yes. That is a horrible thing, Master."

"In Humans, there are illnesses of the mind. Sometimes, those illnesses make a person think in a way the mind does not typically function. Unfortunately for those Humans he has to deal with, these illnesses do not always kill the sufferer. As a result," he met Mollie's eyes before continuing, "everyone he interacts with is forced to suffer the effects of his altered behavior."

Mollie nodded. "Excellent description. Thank you, Cadal."

Pela nodded. "I understand that. What I don't understand— He took pleasure despite Mollie's pain?"

Cadal shook his head sadly. "Not exactly, Pela. He took pleasure *because* of her pain."

Pela looked decidedly ill, and Mollie felt more than a little ill herself. She had never wanted to face the full force of that statement, though she knew it was true. Mollie felt the sudden urge to say something to make Pela feel better, to make herself feel better. Maybe if Mollie got clinical, she could gain control of her emotions.

"Pela, that is a particular mental condition called *sadism*. People who are *sadistic* are excited by or enjoy inflicting pain on others." Mollie left out that many sadists find an outlet that is not damaging to an unwilling partner. That was too hard to explain to a non-violent culture.

Mollie rushed into her description to block out the images and thoughts rushing at her. "In his case, he was also excited by the power he had over me. Because I couldn't stop him, it—" Mollie closed her eyes and took a deep breath as Caden moved abruptly, painfully within her.

Cadal moved his hands over her womb again, gently running the circles that were usually delicious in the relaxation they brought, but Mollie's emotions and thoughts were in a riot.

"Calm," he reminded her.

Mollie nodded and took another deep breath as Caden continued his assault.

Pela's voice rose to a panicked high. "Should I get Morda?"

Cadal's voice was as gentle as his hands. "No, Pela. There's no danger, but Mollie shouldn't continue this conversation. I will seek you out and explain everything to you another time."

"I'm sorry," the girl continued, sounding pitiful. "I didn't know."

"It's all right," Cadal assured her. "You've done nothing wrong, Pela. My son simply wants his mother to rest now. He's stubborn about such things."

"Like his father," Mollie added quietly. Caden hadn't settled, and she was suddenly very tired.

Cadal swept her to his chest and headed for the door that Pela swept open before him. "Enough of that," he chided her. "You simply need to rest."

Mollie nodded weakly and relaxed into the comfort of his arms. In what seemed like far too little time, Cadal laid Mollie on their bed and wrapped a quilt around her. Had she slept while he carried her? She must have. Cadal brought her sweet milk but didn't balk that Mollie managed only a few sips before nodding off to sleep.

In the usual manner of the colony, information, even misinformation, spread like wildfire. No sooner had Mollie found a comfortable slumber than she heard Cadal trying desperately to silence a riot of voices.

"Cadal, you're talking about my grandson." *Zera.*

Mollie felt badly for scaring her.

"Mollie is fine. Caden is fine. She simply needs rest," Cadal assured her.

"Cadal, I know you are Fairy Master, but I would feel better if I could examine Mollie to make sure Caden has no further plans." *Corea?*

Corea was a midwife and healer, but Mollie hadn't spoken to her about the pregnancy because of the older woman's feelings. Cadal simply checked Caden his way.

"Please, Cadal. Allow her." *Traden?*

Mollie considered burying her head beneath the quilt.

"If Mollie did collapse, at this point in a pregnancy, it is cause for concern, Cadal." *Morda?*

Have I upset everyone?

"Harmony help me," Cadal growled at them. "Mollie did not collapse. She felt ill because she got upset. It was nothing more than that. If anyone should know, I should."

"What upset her?" *Harea?*

Mollie groaned, pulling the quilt over her head. She was having trouble following the conversation, but it seemed half the colony was in their main room.

Cadal sighed raggedly. "The only thing that can," he mused wearily.

Mollie knew Cadal was being evasive. Only Morda would understand that comment, at least until Pela started talking to others.

"Harmony alive," Morda swore. "How could that ever come up in the colony?"

Mollie dragged herself from the bed and moved toward the door, but Cadal swept it open before she got halfway there. He'd no doubt felt her move.

Mollie met his gaze and spoke to the women over his shoulder. "It was my fault, Grandmother. I was asked a question I shouldn't have tried to answer, but I tried to anyway."

Cadal nodded grimly and hugged her. "Would you like Corea to check you?"

"If it will bring everyone peace of mind so I can sleep, she can, but I trust your assessment," she whispered.

Mollie could tell by his manner that it would put Cadal at ease as well. Elizabeth had told Mollie about Cadal's meeting with Doc Edwards back at the estate. Even his certainty that Caden was doing well hadn't calmed Cadal in the face of the fact that something could go wrong at any time.

Cadal steered Mollie back to the bed. "Corea, Mollie will allow your examination," he called over his shoulder, to sighs of relief from those assembled.

Not surprisingly, Corea's determination about Caden's safety matched Cadal's. Corea ordered Mollie's teaching schedule cut back to four times a month or less, daily rest breaks, and no more upsetting questions until her son was born. Mollie accepted it all without exception, grateful that it wasn't more restrictive.

Since then, Mollie had talked with Corea at least weekly. Four weeks later, the pains started. After that, Corea checked Mollie every few days to gauge her progress. Or lack of it, in Mollie's case.

"Cadal, will you rub my back?" Mollie asked Cadal that question more and more often as her pregnancy wore on. That night, a week past, was no different. Mollie's muscles ached constantly. "It isn't fair to be in pain that does nothing for me," she complained miserably.

Cadal chuckled. "It is doing something. You're a first-time mother. The women assure me that it takes a lot of work to prepare for a first baby. The next will be easier." His hands kneaded her muscles.

Mollie groaned. "Cadal, I love you, but you have a lot to learn about pregnant women."

"For instance?"

"Never point out a second or third child while a mother is in pain with the first. Wait until she's holding her healthy son first."

"Fair enough. I won't have to wait long. Caden is getting impatient."

"So am I," she growled.

Cadal kissed Mollie's shoulder and spooned behind her in the bed, then ran his hand over her tight abdomen in soothing circles. "As soon as you're ready, he will be," Cadal whispered close to her ear.

"You'll be there, won't you?"

"Be where?" Cadal crooned.

"Be with me when he's born," she qualified for him.

"It's not the usual way."

"What is usual about us?"

"Not a thing," Cadal agreed. "I'll be there. What would you have me do?"

"This. Be with me. Calm me. Hold my hand. Be there for me and for Caden."

"Gladly." Cadal hesitated before he continued. "You know, there *is* another thing that brings on a woman's *labor.*"

"Which is what?"

Cadal reached his hand lower and began to pleasure her. Mollie sank into the waves of ecstasy that mixed with a dull ache within her. When Cadal entered her, Mollie laid her head back into the hollow of his shoulder. Her climax was intense, and in the aftermath, the pains worsened considerably. For a few minutes, Mollie was sure it had worked, but there would be no such miracle cure.

Mollie rolled over to kiss Cadal's chest. His skin was covered in a sheen of sweat from their loving.

His hands roamed over their son in soothing circles again. "He's ready," Cadal assured her. "He's waiting for your body to prepare for his arrival. It won't be long."

"I like your treatment program. We should arrange this more often."

Cadal's eyes glittered. "As you wish, my little piper." He had been calling Mollie that as a pet name since he told Harea the story, and Mollie rather enjoyed it.

The treatment became at least a daily tradition that both of them enjoyed, but there was still no change, according to Corea.

"Mollie?" Zera's voice came from behind her.

Mollie snapped back to the present. "Yes, Zera?"

"Your class is soon," she reminded her son's bride.

Mollie caught herself before she could bring her wrist up. After almost six months in the colony, Mollie was still looking for a watch when she didn't actively remind herself she didn't own one anymore. She had left hers with Elizabeth. It served no purpose here.

"Thank you. I would have daydreamed through it for sure."

Mollie rubbed her lower back in annoyance. Ever since Caden had dropped, he had been lying uncomfortably over her hips and her spine, but this backache was new and draining. After her class, she would ask Cadal to rub out the tight spots again.

Zera eyed her in concern. "Are you sure you don't want me to cancel your class for you? You don't look well."

Mollie smiled at her concern. Ever since the day Corea first examined her, Zera had been on pins and needles, watching for labor or distress like a hawk.

"No, I'll be fine. Corea says Caden is still beating at a bolted door. I'll take a nap after my class and have Cadal rub my back for me."

Zera nodded and turned back to the embroidery she was working on at the table.

Mollie got to her feet awkwardly. *Is there any other way at close to nine months?* Her back spasmed painfully, and she considered taking Zera up on the offer of canceling the class. It was a lesson in geometry, and rescheduling for another day would not be difficult, but walking might help bring on labor. No. She wouldn't cancel. Mollie would simply put her feet up while she was there and cut it short if she was in pain. Cadal wouldn't fault her for that plan. Mollie waved to Zera as she passed the cook fire.

She walked slowly, in the uncomfortable gait Caden's position forced on her. Her back spasmed lightly several more times, and Mollie made a mental note to add a little extra fruit and sweet milk to her meal tonight. She kept walking and studiously ignored the backache.

Mollie was a hallway away from the meeting room when she encountered Nolin.

"How are you?" he asked, running a hand over the formidable mound of her son.

"Sore. This child is going to be huge." Even Corea agreed with that assessment. "I hope Caden decides it's time soon. Are you taking my class today?"

"Yes, I am. May I walk you?" Nolin put out his arm for her.

Mollie smiled at the gesture. "It would be—" She stopped as another spasm gripped her. Mollie dug her fingertips into the wall painfully and groaned as the spasm radiated down her back and stomach into her thighs. Canceling. Yes, canceling sounded like a fine idea.

Nolin leaned close to her face, as she sucked in her breath. "Mollie, are you all right?" he asked.

The tight knot began to unwind. The next pain came almost immediately, before Mollie could ask him to help her home. The gush of fluid that accompanied it confirmed her state to her. Mollie sank to the floor as the contraction ended and met Nolin's very frightened eyes. "Get Cadal," she told him. The next contraction hit, and Mollie groaned lightly as she struggled to control the deep breath she knew she needed to take.

Nolin's eyes were huge. "Harmony alive. Here? Now?" he managed in something close to a panic.

"Nolin," she cried out harshly, in her own panic to get through to him.

He nodded and sprang into action. As Nolin disappeared from sight, still another contraction gripped her.

Mollie leaned her head back against the cool wood and ran her hands over her womb as Cadal often did. "*Okay*, Caden, I get the point," she panted out. "Take a lesson from your father. Subtlety— Mom likes subtlety." Mollie groaned the last part as the contraction subsided again.

The next contraction had barely hit when Cadal barreled around the corner with Nolin on his heels. Cadal ran a hand over the tight muscles of her abdomen and watched her face. "Breathe slowly. Breathe deep," he crooned. "This is moving fast. Nolin, get Corea and Morda to meet us at our quarters. Then find Valia."

"Yes, Cadal." Nolin sprinted away.

Mollie chuckled, in relief that he was here and that she was blessedly pain free for a moment as much as in amusement. "Nolin forgot to call you Master. How did he find you so fast?"

A contraction hit, and Cadal smoothed her hair as Mollie sucked in a breath. "He didn't. I was on my way. I felt it when your *labor* turned serious." Cadal nodded to her unasked question. "I knew it was real all day, but you were relaxed. That was the best thing for you."

Chapter Thirty-three

Mollie nodded as the pain abated. Cadal didn't wait for another. He swung her up and took off at a run for their quarters. Cadal may not have been born in his father's bed, but that was not happening with his son. Not if he could help it. The way cleared before them. When a pain gripped Mollie, Cadal slowed to a fast walk while he soothed her through it, but there was not enough time to stop. As a result, news spread quickly.

Zera was pulling down the birthing cloths and making the bed for her delivery when Cadal settled Mollie there and started helping her out of her soiled clothes and under the soft birthing sheet Zera handed him.

Corea breezed in. She washed up in the hot water and soap that Zera had laid out for her as she watched the couple weather several pains together. "Fast," Corea commented. "Why didn't you send for me long ago?"

Cadal shook his head. "The pains weren't troubling until now. We thought we had much more time."

Corea nodded grimly, and Cadal felt a stab of guilt *at her assessment that Mollie may have to endure a birth like Zera's.* For his mother's sake, he prayed she wouldn't mention that in front of Zera.

"Were they regular?"

Mollie looked at him in confusion. *Cadal was the one keeping track. She had no idea if they had been.*

"Fairly," he answered, "but they were very light and in her back like a backache."

Corea nodded. "Are your pains still in your back?"

"Both front and back," Mollie replied in a voice that came out as a groan.

"Your baby's back is to your back. That is causing your back pain."

"Back *labor*. Great." She started sucking in another controlled breath.

Cadal looked at Corea. "Is it dangerous for Caden to face that direction?" he asked, wishing that his training had included full knowledge of every trade. Cadal hated not knowing something, considering how much he did know.

"No. It's painful, but not dangerous. He may turn and give her relief yet."

"Maybe I should ask him to turn," Cadal joked.

Mollie managed a weak laugh as a pain subsided.

"Cadal," Zera cried in shock.

"Will that work?" Corea asked, suddenly interested. She dried her hands.

Cadal shrugged. "No one has ever tried it before, but it wouldn't be difficult."

"Then don't," she decided. "We don't know why he's in that position. It may be important."

Cadal nodded and returned his attention to Mollie.

Morda burst through the door and rushed to wash. "Nolin says the pains are one on top of the other," she stated, waiting for confirmation.

Corea nodded and walked to the bed. "All right, Mollie. I need to check you. Be still if you can."

Cadal watched the expression on Corea's face carefully. He hoped she wouldn't find the same problems she found when Zera delivered. Cadal started as Mollie screamed, then met the midwife's gaze as he tried to soothe her.

"Breathe deeply, Mollie. I'm almost through. I know you're sore," Corea said softly. Her hand reappeared tinged with Mollie's blood.

Cadal searched Corea's memories frantically to reassure himself that it wasn't unusual.

"Mollie is doing fine. She'll be pushing in no time, and Caden is impatiently waiting."

"How far is she?" Morda asked, as Corea returned to wash again.

Cadal felt Morda's upset. After years as Fairy Mistress, not knowing was very hard for her.

"Far. The urge to push will be on her very soon."

"Good," Mollie managed. "I don't suppose there's such a thing as an *epidural* here?" she joked. Mollie grimaced as the next pain assaulted her.

Corea looked at her in confusion.

Cadal shook his head. "Don't ask, Corea. Trust me, we don't."

Mollie groaned in response.

"It sounds good to Mollie right now, while she is in pain, but you wouldn't like it." He turned his attention back to Mollie. Cadal placed his hands on her womb. "Don't push yet," he told her. "It will hurt worse if you're not ready."

"Try telling your son that," she faltered. "He's the one pushing. That's it. Next time—" Mollie didn't finish, the rest of the comment lost in the breath she started pulling in.

Cadal smiled as he checked on Caden.

"Is he all right?" Zera asked nervously. *She saw the parallels between this birth and Cadal's, and it frightened her.*

Cadal promised himself he wouldn't allow Mollie to be damaged that way. It was moving smoother than Zera's *labor* so far. It would continue to do so.

He nodded. "Mollie's right. My son is trying to speed things along."

Zera shook her head in amusement. "Just like Cadal. He was impatient to be born as well."

Mollie met her gaze. "This was information I could have used, Zera," she said *more harshly than Cadal knew she intended.*

Luckily, Zera knew it was the pain talking. Women in the pain of birth are not known for their patience.

The door opened again, and Valia sprinted into the room. "How much time do we have?" she asked. Valia dunked her hands in the hot water and started washing.

Cadal startled *at the emotion he was getting from Caden. It was complicated, something between relief and victory.* "None, I think. Caden is doing something new," he informed them.

Corea came back to the bedside. It took only a moment to confirm what Cadal already knew. She nodded at the couple. "Hurry, Valia. Cadal's son is more impatient than even he was. Mother, take one leg. Valia, the other. Zera, have the cloths ready and fresh hot water. We'll need them very soon."

"What can I do?" Cadal asked. The thought that his son could do to Mollie what Cadal had to Zera froze him in fear for her. Caden couldn't be allowed to hurt her like that.

Mollie took advantage of a brief moment without pain to look at him. "You're doing it, Cadal."

He felt the desperation from her at the thought that he might leave her. That steeled his resolve, and he nodded. Cadal wasn't going anywhere, but neither was he prepared when Mollie's eyes opened wide in a look akin to panic.

"I can't do this," she breathed.

Morda smiled warmly. "You can. Pushing is easier than not pushing. You can push now."

Corea nodded her agreement.

Cadal smoothed Mollie's hair away from her face as her eyes closed and she curled forward with a deep groan.

"That's right," Corea assured her. "Like I told you. Curl in and move with the pains. Don't fight them."

Cadal lost track of time. It seemed Mollie was always either pushing or recovering from a push. He touched her cheek and murmured to her almost constantly.

Corea's voice reached him. "Mollie, you need to stop. For just a few moments, I promise you."

He furrowed his brow. "Why?"

"Because, Cadal, I must check your son before his shoulders deliver," Corea explained patiently.

Cadal swung around to look. He smiled at the sight of the dark curls drying under Zera's tender touch with one of the many cleaning cloths she had set aside for this day. Cadal reached out to touch the silky hair above the slightly angry countenance of his son.

Mollie screamed *in frustration at stifling her urge to push.*

Cadal cupped her face. "Mollie, look. You must see," he crooned.

She looked at him wearily, but with a full measure of confusion, and he helped her shift to a slightly higher position.

"I can't see, Cadal."

He took Mollie's hand and brushed her fingertips over their son's hair. *A sense of wonder washed over her.* Cadal cupped her temples *and transferred his view of her ruffling Caden's hair.* Tears filled Mollie's eyes and she nodded. The next pain assaulted Mollie, and Cadal released her quickly to avoid hurting her.

Corea's examination ended at last. "All right. Caden is ready. Push with the next pain and I will try to ease him out gently."

Cadal alternated his attention between reassuring Mollie as she pushed and watching Caden's struggle to be born. One shoulder came free, and Caden slid instantly into Corea's waiting hands. Mollie sighed at the momentary reprieve, and a relieved laugh passed through the women in the room.

Corea passed Caden into the soft cloth in Zera's hands. "Mother, you will have to handle freeing Caden from Mollie while I finish here," she said.

Zera wiped the blood and fluids from her grandson with a wide smile on her face. Cadal couldn't recall ever seeing her so happy.

As the ceremonial knife used for the freeing found its way to Morda's hands, Cadal turned his attention to Mollie again. He kissed her gently. "You did a wonderful job. Our son is beautiful," Cadal assured her.

She nodded weakly. "Can I hold him?" Mollie asked, though she was still shaking from exertion.

Corea smiled. "In a few moments. Can you give me one more push for your birth parts?"

Mollie nodded and curled with the continuing pains. Corea nodded her approval. Cadal watched as Corea handed off the waste in a large, soiled cloth. She accepted a paste of numbing herbs from Valia in return and spread it over the small tear while the younger woman kneaded Mollie's stomach to help in her healing.

Mollie jerked as the paste touched her raw flesh.

Corea met her frantic eyes. "It's all right. This will take away the pain while I repair the damage. It should be working very shortly."

Mollie relaxed visibly and nodded. "When can I see Caden?"

Corea laughed lightly. "This is a good time for it. You should feed him while I work. It will help in the healing."

Zera smiled as she wrapped a clean blanket around her grandson. "Just a moment," she soothed Caden as he squirmed against her hand.

Caden answered in a fashion consistent with his impatience. He roared his displeasure.

Cadal laughed at the joy of hearing it *and at the relief flooding over Traden and the other men gathered outside in the corridor.* "I think Caden may be hungry after his journey," he told Mollie.

Zera joined in his laughter, turning with the squalling infant in her arms. "More likely, he's inherited your temperament. You were never happy until you could run."

Mollie glared at Cadal, *and he was hard pressed to determine that she was teasing and wasn't really annoyed with him.*

"What did I do?" he asked.

"You have a way of not giving me important information, Cadal. If Caden is up all night, half of it is yours," Mollie warned him.

Cadal laughed heartily. "Gladly." His gaze fell to Caden as Zera leaned across Cadal to Mollie. "I wouldn't hear of anything less," he promised over an earsplitting protest from his son.

She accepted their son with a wide smile. To his father's surprise, Caden calmed immediately into her arms, and Mollie smiled wider.

"No, Caden, you're no troublemaker," Mollie crooned. "You just wanted Mom, didn't you?"

Caden fixed his gaze on his mother with eyes that seemed impossibly huge.

"The pied piper," Cadal marveled, as Caden yawned and turned his face to brush against Mollie's naked breast.

Mollie chuckled, offering their son the nipple he sought. Caden grasped it in his tiny mouth and sighed in contentment as he ate. Mollie sang a Human lullaby quietly as she fed him. Cadal watched the scene with a mixture of pride, love, and amazement.

He barely registered that the women were cleaning up and preparing to get Mollie into a nursing shift and onto a clean catch-cloth until Mollie handed their son to Cadal while they accomplished the task.

Free to examine his son more closely, Cadal marveled at the tiny fingers wrapped around his own, the lower lip with a drop of Mollie's first milk still beaded on it, and the dark hair already showing lights of a vibrant red. He unwrapped the blanket to run his hands over his son's tiny feet. Caden moved his foot abruptly and nestled closer to his father's chest with a sigh, like his mother often did.

Zera watched the scene with a wide smile. "He's all there, Cadal. Ten fingers, ten toes, and a strong set of lungs," she teased him.

"I'm sure you would have mentioned it if he wasn't. I just can't believe how tiny he is."

Mollie laughed sleepily. "That's easy for you to say," she reminded him from behind closed eyes.

Corea looked up from packing her equipment. "Actually, Cadal, your son is very big for being newly born. Most babies are only three-quarters that size at birth. I'm surprised Mollie suffered so little tearing."

Mollie murmured something unintelligible in response. She dropped into a well-deserved sleep.

Valia nodded. "All those jokes you and Traden made about big, happy babies must have fallen on receptive ears when they reached The Harmony."

Corea shouldered her pack and ran a hand over Mollie's forehead. *Though she feigned a clinical interest, Cadal knew her worry and pride in the young woman she cared for. Corea's healing was close to complete. It wouldn't be long now.*

"I'll be back tonight to check on them," Corea told Cadal quietly. "Let Mollie sleep as much as Caden will allow, and make sure she eats and drinks well to build her milk and help in her healing."

Cadal nodded his agreement. "I will. Thank you, Corea."

She smiled. "I thought your birth would be the most memorable I ever attended, but I must admit that this exceeds it. She's a strong woman, Cadal. No one else could have made that birth seem so effortless."

Cadal nodded in understanding. *He had seen his own birth from several viewpoints in his final training transfer. It had been difficult for Zera. Even if Botor hadn't been killed, it would've been unlikely she could have carried another child after his birth. Zera didn't make Cadal's birth seem effortless. She couldn't have even if she tried.*

Cadal came fast, as fast as Caden had and with no warning. They took Zera to the closest place, Morda's bed, and called for Corea and her mentor, Lylie. In the end, there was barely enough time to catch Cadal as he rushed into the world, without benefit of the carefully prepared cloths or even proper washing.

The damage to Zera, both in the trauma of the birth and the fever that followed, was grievous. Botor feared he would lose his family then, and that made him all the more determined not to lose them later. As was said of

Cadal many times over, only The Harmony knew how he escaped unscathed. Zera only survived by the loving care of Morda, Corea, and Botor. Perhaps Cadal's destiny should have been apparent even then.

Corea glanced at Morda. "Mother, will you join me for a late lunch?"

Morda nodded happily and followed her to the door.

Good. Their healing was well under way. Corea held a grudge because Morda allowed Xanthe to leave, but the chasm was finally closing.

Cadal wrapped the blanket around his son again and kissed the baby's head gingerly.

Valia watched in amusement. "May I show Traden in?"

He considered how peacefully Mollie was sleeping. "I hate to make him wait, but..." It wasn't simply that Traden might disturb her when Mollie needed the sleep so desperately. Cadal knew she would be upset if she wasn't allowed to gift Traden with the first sight of his namesake.

Valia nodded. "I understand. What if I tell everyone that you will accept a few visitors after dinner? Will that be enough time for Mollie to receive a select few?"

"A few, Valia. Please, only a few."

"Absolutely. Would the servants from your ceremony be few enough?"

"Yes. For tonight, I think that will do nicely. Thank you, Valia."

"It's an honor, Cadal. You know it is." She pulled the quilt that Zera set aside for this day over Mollie and left quietly.

Zera watched Cadal with his son, her longing like a living being set between them.

He sighed. "I know you're aching to have Caden back in your arms, but I've waited so many months to hold him I find the idea of not holding him hard to contemplate." Cadal met her gaze and saw the sadness there. *She never had a chance to hold me when I was this newly born.* "I'm sorry. Please, hold Caden while he is still so young."

Zera nodded gratefully and took Caden from his father's arms. "He's beautiful, Cadal. I think he'll have Mollie's hair, but I hope for your eyes."

Cadal nodded. "It would be a striking combination. I can't say for sure, but I know Mollie's father had blue eyes, so there's a chance of it."

"Mollie did well today. I wish I had weathered as well," Zera commented quietly.

"Every birth is different. The conditions were not the same. I thank The Harmony that Mollie didn't have to suffer as you did, and I regret whatever plan She had that required it of you."

Zera smiled at him. "Still, Corea is correct. Your son is very big. Mollie carried him as well as she birthed him."

Cadal nodded and yawned deeply. He hadn't slept any better than Mollie had the night before. "If you don't mind, I believe I'll lay down with my bride for a while. Neither of us got much sleep last night. Wake me to help care for Caden if you need me."

Zera laughed lightly so as not to disturb her grandson's nap. "There is only one thing I cannot do for him. I will wake you if he requires it," she promised.

Cadal nodded and curled into the bed beside Mollie. He grimaced lightly as his arm crossed over her hips. As nice as it was to have Caden in his arms, Cadal would miss the tight swell of Mollie's pregnant belly beneath his hand. Perhaps, Harmony willing, he'd get to enjoy the sensations of running his hands or cheek over it and feeling one of his children moving against him several more times over the many years they would have together. Next time, Cadal would know to intervene in Mollie's *labor* much earlier.

Chapter Thirty-four

Mollie weathered well despite the aches and pains assaulting her. Cadal startled awake to find her attempting to make it to the comfort stand for the first time, the blood-soaked catch-cloth wrapped around her like a diaper. He rushed to aid Mollie, chiding her gently for not asking his assistance in the first place, considering her unsteady state.

After Mollie relieved herself, Cadal arranged a soaking warm wash to clean and soothe her battered tissues. He bundled her back to bed with a fresh catch-cloth and a clean nursing shift.

To her surprise, Mollie was ravenous, but Caden screamed in a way that made her breasts ache. She sighed in resignation that their son had to come first. Cadal didn't give up so easily. After their son latched on for his meal, Cadal brought a tray to the bed and sated Mollie's appetite with spoonfuls of stew, fruits, rolls with heavy jelly, and sweet milk. By the time Caden was sated, Mollie was as well.

Cadal smiled indulgently and wolfed down a meal for himself before requesting a turn holding their son. Mollie laughed lightly at Cadal's playful pouting complaint that Mollie had had Caden for nine months, and he simply wanted some time to catch up.

The visitors Cadal allowed for the evening started showing up shortly after they ate their dinner. As Mollie predicted, Traden and Valia arrived first. Traden breezed in with a beautiful rocking chair. He set it up close to the cook fire so that Mollie and Caden could enjoy the warmth when they were up to sitting in it.

Then Traden kissed her cheek and asked Cadal if he could hold his namesake. Cadal handed over the beefy newborn. Traden beamed, Valia said, as if it was one of his own. He congratulated Mollie on a wonderful job as he surveyed the baby, making sure Caden was really as perfect as he seemed.

Traden hated to leave, but Zera insisted that too many visitors at once would simply upset the baby, and lack of rest for Mollie would spoil the baby's milk. Mollie eased his upset by promising Traden the first visit of the morning. In the end, he handed Caden back to his father with a sigh and thanked Mollie for so precious a gift.

Harea and Gady came next. Gady carried a folded piece of cloth that turned out to be a carry sling. Harea presented Mollie with a nursing dress based on the design of her ceremony dress but with a front-opening bodice and done in a rich green that brought out the red in her hair and accented in a light beige.

After the women cooed over Caden for quite some time, they left and let Berner, Cessia, and Nolin in as they went out. Nolin was still wearing the braided belt Gady had given him as her token of love, and he looked extremely happy.

The young man hugged Mollie fiercely for a moment. "Are you all right?" he asked.

"Thanks to you and Cadal. If you hadn't found Corea and the others so quickly, it would have been a very different birth."

"I imagine. You frightened me." Nolin glanced at Cadal. "All births don't progress so quickly, do they?" he asked abruptly.

Cadal laughed. "Nolin, I wonder that you are over one hundred twenty-five. Such an impetuous question," he teased. "No, they don't all move so quickly."

"Only men of Cadal's line, apparently," Mollie teased her husband in return.

Berner smiled widely. "He's a fine son, Cadal. I'm overjoyed at this outcome. When Nolin told me about Mollie's condition and I saw his great upset, I feared her outcome would follow Zera's."

"No," Cadal assured him. "The Harmony has plans we don't always understand, but I think I understand this one. She simply wanted Mollie's experience to be as easy as She could arrange. For a birth, it went well, better than anyone imagined, considering its start."

Cessia handed a large bundle wrapped in a blanket of Master's blue to Mollie. The new mother was stunned to find a collection of outfits and light blankets in a variety of colors and sizes for Caden. "They're beautiful," she told Cessia. "Thank you."

"There's not an outfit for naming, yet. Valia and I will sew one now that we can fit it to your son."

Mollie blushed. "Would it be an insult if I requested to use an outfit I already have?"

Cessia furrowed her brow. "Not at all, but his outfit should mirror his father's. It should be white and Master's blue."

"It needn't be the same style?" she asked to be sure.

"No. It typically isn't the same style."

Mollie smiled widely. "Good, then what I have will do perfectly. It just so happens that Humans favor a shade of light blue very close to Master's blue for little boys. I bartered for several outfits in the Human blue and white before I came here. I'd like to use one of those if it would be allowed."

Cadal looked at her in surprise. "You never showed me any Human outfits for Caden. Can I see them?"

"All but the one for his naming ceremony. That one is a surprise."

Cadal smiled a smile that told her how much he enjoyed her surprises. "Can I see them?"

Mollie looked at the shift and the quilt and blushed deeper at the lack of anything else beneath it, then glanced at Cadal cradling Caden in his arm. She nodded. "If Berner will hand the bag to me. I'm hardly dressed for company."

Berner laughed uproariously. "Of course. You shouldn't be up yet."

Cadal joined in the laughter. "She already has been up," he informed them. "I made the mistake of falling asleep and woke to find Mollie halfway across the room."

Berner's laughter choked off, and they all regarded Cadal with nervous smiles. "You're making a joke."

Cadal shook his head.

Berner faced Mollie, hands on his hips and his jaw tense. "I think you need a keeper and leading strings. Tell me where this bag is."

"The purple pack below the shelves," Mollie requested. "Really, Berner. I slept for hours. I would've been on my feet much sooner if I had been in a Human *hospital*," she complained at his statement that she needed babysitting.

Berner handed over the bag and shook his head. "Now *you're* making a joke," he decided.

"Not at all. Human women are encouraged back to their feet as soon as they're able, with or without assistance. They care for themselves and their babies almost immediately. They do rest in bed for several days and have their meals carried to them for the first day or two, but they're not bedridden. They're walking to the comfort stand and even to get themselves drinks or snacks within hours."

Cessia stared at her in shock. "But childbirth is painful, debilitating for a time. Why would they choose to forego rest?"

Mollie shrugged. "They believe getting in motion aids in healing. Besides, once they leave the *hospital* and go home, they have to be accustomed to doing it alone. If a woman is lucky enough to have help at all, it rarely lasts for very long."

Berner huffed in disapproval. "Well, you're not Human and this is not a *hospital*. From now on, ask Cadal and Zera for anything you require."

Mollie nodded her agreement only because she was too tired to argue the point. She had no intention of agreeing to the pampering they wanted her to accept. After all, Mollie had science on her side. She started laying out the half dozen outfits that she'd purchased, less the one for naming.

Cessia sucked in her breath at the fine materials and styles of the various outfits Mollie had brought from the Human realm. "Such beautiful craftsmanship," she mused.

Mollie smiled. "These knit ones are, but the others aren't hand-made."

Cessia looked at her in confusion.

Mollie sighed. "Humans have *machines,* tools that work by themselves, to make cloth and aid in stitching. That's how these three were created. They are not as highly sought, though they still have charm."

Cessia looked at her in amazement. "Tools that run themselves and produce such fine results?"

Corea shooed them out when she arrived. She checked on Mollie's stitches and layered them with a mixture that would relieve pain and halt infection. She checked the shrinking of Mollie's womb before moving on to Caden. Her examination irritated the baby, who wailed his displeasure until Mollie appeased him with cuddling and another feeding.

"You both look well," Corea pronounced. "I'll leave the paste with you. Cadal can help you apply it as often as you need, but definitely after the soothing soaks. At least three times a day on those."

They nodded their agreement.

Corea regarded Mollie sternly. "Don't be in any hurry to get up and about. I've seen the way you push yourself," she warned.

Mollie blushed a deep crimson, while Cadal stifled a laugh. Corea sent her a scathing look, and Mollie passed it along to her husband.

"You're some help," Mollie complained.

Cadal stifled another gale of laughter. "Oh, but I am. I assure you I am. Wait until Berner tells Traden you've been up."

Mollie groaned.

Corea rolled her eyes and affected a harried sigh. "Well, don't do it again. Agreed?"

Mollie nodded.

"Good. Now that that is settled, I will see you tomorrow morning for another check." Corea hesitated for a moment and looked at them sadly before she turned away again.

"Are you all right, Corea?" Mollie asked.

She nodded quietly but didn't look back.

"Would you like to talk about something?" Mollie hoped she would. The sad looks Corea had given her the entire time she was acting as midwife almost broke Mollie's heart. She wished there were some way to make Corea feel better.

The older woman met her gaze, then sat in the chair by the bed slowly. "I must ask you to forgive me, Mollie. I haven't been very fair to you. To anyone, really. I blamed Xanthe for leaving. I blamed Morda for using her power to allow it. I blamed Cadal for not managing to convince her to stay." She blushed deeply. "That didn't last long when I saw his pain was as deep as my own.

"I was angry when you came here. Cadal and Morda seemed to have forgotten all about Xanthe. I avoided you, because you brought peace to everyone else. You were taking my daughter's place, and I couldn't accept that."

Mollie shook her head. "I could never take her place. I wouldn't want to. I'm not Xanthe. I don't want to be Xanthe. I thought that Morda wanted me to be once, but she doesn't want that, and I know Cadal doesn't see me as a replacement.

"I can see how it might seem that way. I'm *married* to the man Xanthe was courted by and call Xanthe's grandmother by that name. That's more because Morda would rather not hear all the greats involved, but..." Mollie shrugged hopelessly. It was a difficult situation.

"I know all of that now. By the time I discovered it, I wanted to get to know you for yourself, but I was at a loss for how to approach you after shunning you the way that I did. I hoped you would seek me out to midwife for you. When you didn't, I was afraid you and your baby would suffer for what I had done."

"To tell you the truth, I wanted to come to you, but I was concerned it would be too uncomfortable for you to midwife for me, considering the way you felt."

Corea nodded in response. "I was afraid that was the case. Once you needed me, I took advantage of it to get to know you. If I could have found a reason to see you daily without raising concern for you, I would have."

"How about friendship, Corea? You're still part of my family, though you're not my mother."

Corea looked at her in surprise. "You would have me after I treated you so badly?"

"Caden could use a grandmother to go along with Morda as his great grandmother, if you're interested." A sobering thought occurred to Mollie, and she met Corea's eyes sheepishly. "If you'd like another title— If that one is too painful for you, I'd understand," she added.

"No. I would love to be allowed to present myself as Caden's grandmother."

Mollie sighed in relief. "Well, you are," she reasoned. "You're a few generations removed, but you are still his grandmother."

"May I hold my grandson?"

Cadal laughed and handed the sleeping baby back to her. "I'm glad you two finally worked that out," he confided to them.

Corea regarded him strangely over Caden's head, her grandson cradled to her shoulder. "You knew and you didn't intervene?"

"I asked your mother that same question when she was Fairy Mistress. Morda told me she couldn't intervene until I was willing to listen to what she was saying."

"What was she saying?"

"That Xanthe wasn't my true soulmate, and I had tasks to complete before I could claim my true soulmate. Basically, she was saying I hadn't lost everything, and it took me more than sixty years to discover she was right."

Corea smiled. "My mother is a smart woman. That sounds like a reasonable way to look at the situation." She looked at Caden, and sadness filled her eyes.

"Ask, Corea," Cadal instructed her.

She nodded grimly and met Mollie's gaze. "I must know. Does my enjoyment come at another's expense? Your mother still lives. I've heard as much. Will she long for you as I have longed for Xanthe?"

Mollie swallowed a lump in her throat and shook her head. "No. She *disowned* me." She struggled for a way to put the concept into Fairy language. "She made me not part of her family. She withdrew from me and recanted her place as my mother." Mollie sighed at the inadequacy of her description, but Corea seemed to understand.

Cadal spoke up quietly. "Darcy has no wish to know her grandson. She said as much."

Mollie looked at him in surprise. She had never discussed that final letter with anyone. Mollie never told Cadal the assumptions her mother made, based on the lies Thornton and Joseph told her. From the twitching of the muscle in his jaw, Mollie could tell Cadal knew exactly what was said, probably from transfers, and it hurt him as much as it hurt her.

Cadal locked gazes with her and nodded to let Mollie know he'd heard the thought and that she was right. He wrapped an arm around her and pulled Mollie close as the sadness welled up within her.

"How could a mother do that? Withhold her love? Cast off a child?" Corea asked in confusion.

Mollie tried to explain it, though the concept was about as un-Fairy as you could get. "She's Human, Corea. It was the path she chose for herself. She didn't like what I did, so she shut the door. I wonder if she feels anything but anger, but—" Mollie shrugged again. There was no way to explain this to a Fairy.

Cadal nodded. "Sometimes she does, but it's fleeting. Usually, Darcy tries not to think about you or she thinks angry thoughts. You know it's the situation she fears and dislikes, not you."

Corea shook her head and straightened Caden's blanket. "What could make a mother so angry?"

Mollie laughed nervously. "Maybe I'm more like Xanthe than I like to admit. I left my home to work my land. She wanted me to come home, but I loved my land, and I loved Cadal. I refused to go home when she ordered it."

Cadal shook his head. "No, you weren't like Xanthe. You were both running, and you were running for the only places and people that would give you peace, but there was little for you to go back to. Xanthe missed everyone and everything, but she couldn't live without what she was leaving for. You were denied knowing the cost of your fondest wish before you made it. Xanthe was blessed with that knowledge to make her choice.

"The world you left behind was destroying you. You couldn't stay there. You know that, don't you?"

Mollie nodded. "You're right about that. I couldn't have survived there much longer. Already, I couldn't cope, and soon I would have been physically destroyed by Thornton and his vipers."

Corea smiled. "Is there a Human word for making someone a part of your family? For giving them a place?"

Mollie smiled. "Several. If you mean a permanent place in your family, it is called *adoption*. Humans who can't have children or who would like to help an unwanted child *adopt* a child no one wants." She furrowed her brow and sighed at Cadal. "That's a whole new issue to explain, I'm sure."

Corea shook her head. "I won't ask how someone could not want a child. It sounds far too complicated. I would like to suggest an arrangement of sorts, if you're interested."

"What arrangement did you have in mind?"

"You seem to be an unwanted child. I can no longer have children. Would you like me to *adopt* you?" She hurried on, and Mollie was sure Corea was afraid she would refuse the offer. "You wouldn't be taking Xanthe's place. I don't want to ever forget my daughter, but my heart has room for a new daughter, if that title isn't too painful for you?" The hope in her eyes was heartbreaking.

"I think I'd like that. I'm honored that you would make the offer."

"How do Humans accomplish *adoption?*"

Mollie laughed. "It's all very boring. And terrifying at the same time, or so I've heard. They make *legal* agreements, and then the child is theirs. I am sure this could be more of an informal thing, since I am an adult."

"You like to keep things informal, don't you?"

Mollie nodded. "I suppose so. It comes from years of being stuck in an *office*, dealing with numbers that don't mean very much. You get tired of seeing your life run by papers and numbers. I expect, after that, getting away from formalities of any kind does sound pretty good."

Cadal chuckled. "Living with numbers, working with numbers, identified by numbers. Yes, the Human system is tiring."

Corea regarded Cadal strangely. "Identified by numbers?"

Mollie smiled wider. "Silly, isn't it? In my lifetime, I have been identified by seven or eight different numbers for different uses. Humans are also identified by papers they carry. I brought a few of those with me. I don't really know why I did, but I did."

Cadal pulled her closer. "Probably because you knew no one here would believe you if you didn't bring them. I know I found it hard to believe they would lock me in a cage, because I didn't have them."

"It was probably simply force of habit to carry them with me. That's Humans, all right. Conform or suffer."

Corea looked from one to the other. "They would have imprisoned Cadal for not having these papers? I thought they sought to imprison him for—" She blushed deeply and looked away without completing the thought.

Mollie laughed. "Unless they invented evidence against him, they couldn't have held him on that suspicion. I called the horse in self-defense. There was no *malice*. They could have held him indefinitely on suspicion of why he was hiding his identity."

"But Cadal is still a fugitive in the Human world?"

"So am I. I helped him escape, remember?"

Corea shook her head. "Morda told me about your condition. You couldn't possibly have helped Cadal escape. You weren't capable of it."

Cadal laughed heartily. "She helped. Mollie planned our escape. She handled the Human *constable*, so we could leave in peace. She thought of bringing the quilt that kept her warm for most of the trip. For every objection I had, Mollie argued a solution. I might have ended up in that cage, if Mollie hadn't ordered and then practically dragged me out. Once her strength gave out, it was up to me to finish it. It was too late to turn back."

Mollie smiled crookedly. "I'm guilty of what I'm accused of. At least Cadal is innocent of everything but running, and since he was guilty of nothing else, that means he is essentially guilty of nothing. I'm guilty of aiding the escape of a suspected *felon* and interfering in a *police* investigation. If you *adopt* me, you're accepting a *criminal* as a daughter," she joked.

Corea laughed. "I imagine a Fairy *criminal* is still better than most honest Humans."

"I don't know about that. I've picked up some horrible habits in the Human world. I have a temper, and I've been known to defend myself violently."

"Your temper hasn't been a problem so far, and there will be no need to defend yourself physically here. Are you trying to convince me not to *adopt* you?" Corea asked suddenly.

"Not at all. I am simply making sure you know what you're asking for. I'm not an easy person to get along with."

"You're also an adult and married. How much trouble can I have?"

Cadal laughed uproariously at that one. "You don't know Mollie very well."

Corea stared at him in shock before it became evident that this was a joke that Cadal and Mollie shared. She smiled. "You and Xanthe weren't easy children to raise, Cadal."

Cadal leaned back on his elbows and smiled proudly. "That was recreation compared to my bride. Thankfully, Mollie hasn't had need of you medically yet, except for Caden's birth. I tended to her medically several times in the months before we came here."

"Almost all of them were minor," Mollie protested. "You'll have her believing I'm still a handful."

Cadal leaned across to nuzzle her neck playfully. "My little piper, with two hands and juggling, I still couldn't keep you out of trouble."

Corea laughed as Mollie blushed a deep crimson. "Then I suppose I must *adopt* you, after all. Cadal will need the extra hands to keep you out of trouble."

Mollie set her jaw in irritation. "If I hadn't promised," she grumbled. "Cadal, it's simply not fair that you can talk about what a handful I have been, and I'm not allowed to return the favor."

Corea smiled. "Don't worry, Mollie. Cadal's past is no secret here. Even if you don't say a word, we all know."

* * * *

After Corea left, Caden ate again, and they retired for the night. Cadal smiled at the sight of Caden asleep in the hollow of Mollie's arm. Through the night, Mollie handled feedings while Cadal took on the chore of changing and rocking the baby. They all got enough sleep somehow.

In the morning, Mollie stunned Zera by demanding to wear underclothes and blood rags under the nursing shift. Then she decided to sit, draped in a quilt, in her rocking chair. Mollie met all of the morning visitors that way.

Cadal felt Traden swaying from pride that Mollie was so pleased with his gift to concern that she insisted on being out of her bed so often. Cadal appeased him by promising Traden that Mollie would be safely in her bed when he visited again in the evening.

Corea returned with Toril. Xanthe's father hugged Mollie and called her daughter *to Mollie's delight as well as Corea's. Cadal knew that Toril honestly meant his words. The healing was complete for Xanthe's parents at last.* Toril brought carved wooden toys, some with little bells inside that were no doubt fashioned by Traden or

Berner. Cadal knew Toril had assisted Traden in making Mollie's rocking chair, and the pride he felt at seeing Mollie in it was obvious without any Fairy Master knowledge.

Linza and Marcan stopped by. Their visit was short, though they were delighted by Caden. Linza brought a gift of three outfits for the baby. All were beautifully embroidered in the same knotwork Mollie had chosen for her ceremonial garb, the knotwork that Linza had done herself.

Benia and Witten came next. Benia was animated, as always. She held Caden and made faces that only succeeded in making the baby angry.

Mollie suppressed a smile of relief. She was still jealous of Benia, despite her claims that she wasn't. Cadal smiled in the realization that he had succumbed to exactly that type of possessiveness over her.

Mollie accepted Caden back, and the baby settled before he was offered the goal he sought. Cadal was seeing it more and more often. Mollie and Caden shared a bond, but Mollie's true power went far beyond that. There was nothing as mystical as his own power about it, but her observation and her training in the Human world equipped her to read people and empathize with them in a way that was similar to Cadal's abilities.

From that point, Mollie could apply the knowledge to direct their behavior or lead their thinking in a way that stunned Cadal. There had never been a bride of the Fairy Master like her. There had never been a Fairy of Aiden like her. She could almost be a budding Fairy Mistress. No, Fairy Mistress and Fairy Master could not exist together, due to the nature of the transfer of power, but she was very close.

Benia and Witten stayed for a while longer, and Witten brought in a piece of furniture that made Mollie smile, though Cadal wondered at the cage-shaped device.

"What is it?" he asked.

Benia raised an eyebrow at him. "Your bride hasn't explained a *crib* to you?" she teased.

Cadal glanced at Mollie's sly smile as she fed their son. "Apparently not. Mollie, would you care to tell me?"

She didn't meet his gaze, but her smile grew more impish as she spoke. "Well, we won't need it for a month or more, but it has its uses."

"What kind of uses?" Cadal prodded.

Mollie looked up and arched an eyebrow in a way that sent a warm surge through him. "A sleepy baby or a playful baby with some toys and things get accomplished, even if grandmothers are busy with something and can't hold the baby. Caden can't flip out and hurt himself, and we can see him clearly, so we can pick him up if he needs us suddenly..."

Cadal wasn't listening anymore. He was lost in her eyes *and in the vision for them in her mind.*

* * * *

The three days until the naming ceremony passed quickly. Corea, Morda, and Valia arrived to take Mollie to shower before the ceremony. This time, Mollie didn't argue their help much. Caden slept well for a newborn, but Mollie was still exhausted and sore.

As she showered, Mollie surveyed her figure. She was sure that Cadal wouldn't mind the fuller breasts that her milk afforded, but the stretch marks and the loose skin of her abdomen were highly unattractive. *Okay, be honest. Am I stuck in post-partum depression?*

Mollie shook her head to escape the troubling thoughts. Cadal had helped her dress, soak, and apply the medicated cream many times in the last three days and Mollie had seen nothing but the same love in his eyes that had always been there.

Mollie wasn't surprised to find Caden squalling when she returned to their quarters to dress. She laughed lightly and took him from Zera. He snuggled into Mollie's shoulder without even the hint of a breast.

Zera shook her head in wonder. "How do you do that?" she asked with the slightest hint of desperation.

Mollie smiled. "I'm sorry, Zera. He's his mother's son. When anyone else will do, you will be acceptable. When only Mom will do, I'm afraid that only Mom will do."

"It's time to dress now," Zera reminded her.

Mollie nodded and deposited the calm baby back on his grandmother's shoulder. Corea and Morda rushed past Zera to collect Mollie's ceremony dress and started to help her into it.

"Wait," Mollie called out. "This won't work." She uttered a few Human curses. "I can't believe I didn't think of this before. I'll have to wear the green dress."

"Why?" Corea questioned her.

"My chest. My milk has come in. I'll work something out for later, but I need something that fits now."

"You won't match Cadal," Morda protested quietly. "I have a better plan. Valia, I need you to go to my quarters. Mollie, dress the baby while you wait."

Mollie nodded and changed Caden, while the other Fairies hurried about. Corea and Morda worked on Mollie's hair; she prepared her son for his presentation. By the time she had wrapped Caden in the Master's blue blanket Cessia had given him and handed him back to Zera, a second white dress had appeared. Morda and Corea settled it over Mollie's head and laced up the bodice over her ample chest.

Mollie smiled at the results. The dress was the same high-waisted design, but the blue vest and underskirt gave it a touch of color and classic appeal. "It's beautiful. Thank you, Grandmother," Mollie breathed.

Corea eyed it with approval. "I've never seen this dress, Mother."

Morda laughed. "It was my nursing dress. It hasn't been worn since you weaned, Corea. You are welcome to it, Mollie. It should be worn."

"Thank you again. I love it. Well, I suppose it's time to go now."

Valia laughed and led Mollie to her rocking chair. "As soon as Traden arrives. Relax until he does."

"Why is Traden coming?"

Corea wrapped a quilt around her carefully before she answered. "There's no set ceremony when it's the naming of a child of a Fairy Master or Mistress. The usual rules of ceremony do not apply, since it involves the Master performing a ceremony on himself, more or less. If Traden has been ordered to take you, I would guess that Cadal has a surprise in store for you."

Traden arrived a few minutes later. He smiled widely at the ladies. "Is everyone ready?"

Valia chuckled. "Waiting for the men to arrive, as usual."

Mollie stood stiffly, as Traden took his namesake from Zera's hands. Mollie smiled at the feeling of being under arrest. She fell in behind Traden with Morda and Corea to her sides and Valia and Zera behind her. The group moved at a speed that was comfortable for Mollie until they reached the doors of the Great Chamber.

Valia and Zera stationed themselves at the doors while Traden took Mollie's arm. As the doors opened, the four women fell in behind Traden and Mollie as they moved toward the throne where Cadal sat waiting for them. When they were an arm's-length away, Traden stopped and bowed his head over Caden's chest.

Cadal smiled at the move. "Traden, it seems that I spend a lot of time committing my bride and my son to your care. Thankfully, you seem quite adept at carrying out this chore."

Traden beamed. "It's a happy task to take. Ask it as often as you wish, Master."

Cadal stood and took Mollie by both hands. He guided her to her place and lifted her by her waist to settle her on the cushion on the smaller throne. Traden moved immediately to settle the baby in Mollie's arms, then took up a place to her left, looking like a guard at parade rest.

Cadal smiled warmly. "Mollie dannea Aiden, you bring a new life to be counted among the colony this day. What name do you choose for us to call him?"

"My son's name is Caden dan Aiden, if it pleases his father as well as myself."

"It most certainly does."

He laid his hand on Caden's tiny brow for a moment. Mollie knew from Cadal's description of the ceremony that this linked the baby to the Fairy Master as Cadal was linked to every Fairy in the colony.

"Caden dan Aiden is now a Fairy of the colony, counted as one of our own. Will the families come forward?"

The families of both Mollie and Cadal joined the semi-circle before the thrones. One by one, Cadal named them, told them their places in Caden's world, and asked for their aid in caring for and protecting him. One by one, they agreed.

Finally, Cadal turned to Traden. "Traden, leave your place and step forward," he ordered.

When he reached the center, Traden knelt before his cousin.

Cadal smiled. "Traden, I have trusted you to care for my bride and son in my absence and to see them home when they were in danger. My bride trusts you enough to give you our son as a namesake. You know what is involved in this. Do you accept your place as Caden's protector and advisor as his mother wishes?"

Traden knelt taller. "It will be an honor and a joy. I accept."

Cadal pulled a baldric of white and Master's blue from beneath his vest and settled it on Traden's shoulder. "You are my brother, Traden. Rise and take your place as such. My son is yours."

Traden moved back to Mollie's side.

Cadal knelt to one knee before Mollie. "The final question falls to you," he told her.

Mollie smiled. She was somehow sure this was something that had never been done before. "Cadal, I bring you your son, Caden. You are his father, and he is also your namesake. I named him for you for the same reason I gave him life, my love for you. Do you accept your place as his father as you did as my husband?"

Cadal smiled. "I do." He put his hands up to her, and Mollie placed Caden in his arms. Cadal kissed their son's head and rose to sit beside Mollie with their son cradled in his arm.

"One more thing, Cadal. Look at his outfit."

Cadal peeled back the blanket and gazed at the lightweight outfit of blue with white bears. A bib of white trimmed in the same blue lay over his chest. Embroidered across the front of the bib, in the Human English, was 'Daddy's Little Boy.' Cadal smiled widely. "My son," he beamed.

Epilogue

Elizabeth gazed at the tree line across the open expanse of the meadow. No matter how often she tried to coax Squirrel back to the stable, the mare seemed intent on hovering near the pond. Sean was having no better luck with Storm. Elizabeth was about to give up and send Sean back for Liam on foot when she caught sight of something moving in the tree line.

She leaned forward in the saddle to get a better look, and Squirrel surged toward the movement. It was simply going to be that type of day with the horses. Elizabeth waved to Sean to stop fighting Storm and follow her out.

"We might as well get a good look, since the horses seem intent on heading that way," she rationalized.

When they were about twenty meters away, a young boy of about five or six slipped out of the trees and glanced around. Elizabeth stared at the fiery red hair. He wasn't one of the children from Ballynaclogh. She would have noticed a child with hair like that.

He wore soft brown leather boots, green trousers, and a fine white shirt that was open at the neck. When Elizabeth came alongside him, he flashed her an almost angelic smile, and his blue eyes glittered. His eyes were hauntingly familiar. "Hello, Elizabeth," he greeted her.

Elizabeth started at his use of her name. "Hello. Are you lost?"

"No. Just waiting."

"Waiting for what?"

The boy laughed a tinkling, infectious laugh.

Sean looked at her in confusion. "Mother, who is he? I've never seen him before."

Elizabeth shrugged. "I have no idea," she admitted. "He does look familiar somehow, but—" She looked at the child closer. "What's your name?"

A booming laugh echoed from the woods. "His name is Caden, Elizabeth." Another form moved from the trees. It was a tall man dressed like the boy, a man with snow-white hair and those same blue eyes. He placed his hand on his son's shoulder proudly.

"Cadal?" she breathed in disbelief.

He nodded.

"You look so young. Where's Mollie?"

The Fairy put his hand back into the trees and helped his wife out to stand next to him. Elizabeth's breath caught. Mollie hadn't changed a bit except for the hugely pregnant belly beneath the green high-waisted dress.

"Hello, Elizabeth. Sorry I'm late. Being pregnant tends to slow me down."

Elizabeth slid off of Squirrel's back and walked to them. She hugged Mollie and ran a hand over her stomach. "Another one, huh?" she teased.

"Yes. You remember Caden, of course."

Elizabeth looked at the child in shock. "It's been..." She nodded in understanding. Cadal and Mollie looked no older. Caden would look young despite his age.

"Well, I never got to see him," Elizabeth managed with tears in her eyes. "You left before he was born. This is my youngest. His name is Sean."

"How many children do you have?" Mollie asked.

"Three. Patrick is thirteen, William is eleven, and Sean is eight."

Cadal smiled. "How are Liam and Patrick?"

"Wonderful. Patrick is in Kinvarra today, but Liam is at the house. Would you like to come up?"

Mollie shook her head. "We'd like to, but another time. We have to get back. We don't have much time this trip."

"Sean, fetch your father quickly. Tell him Mollie and Cadal are here."

Sean nodded and set off at a run on Storm.

Cadal watched him go. "He's a fine boy, Elizabeth. You should be very proud."

"Yes, he is." She hesitated. "Fifteen years, Mollie— It's been so very long."

Mollie nodded and sank to the grass awkwardly. "This is Caden's first long flight." She settled her hand on her belly and eased it in large circles. "He's faster than I am right now. We'd stay a few days, but Mother threatened violence if I dared take such a chance at this point. Mother has picked up several bad habits from me, I'm afraid. Human curses are one of them."

Cadal laughed and stretched out beside her to stroke his hands over the baby inside her lovingly. "She almost threatened violence that I would allow you to take this flight at all."

Elizabeth ran a hand through her graying hair. "Is it very dangerous for you to travel now?"

Mollie chuckled. "I have fast labors. She worries. All mothers worry."

Elizabeth sat next to them. "Your mother? You mean Cadal's mother?"

"No. She was Xanthe's mother. She sort of adopted me after Caden was born."

"Caden is a pretty name. Is it a common one at the great tree?"

"There are no common names for Fairies. Many names, like Caden's, are patchwork names. He was named for Cadal and Traden." Mollie smiled and looked at her distended belly. "This is Bethlia. She's named for you and Traden's wife, Valia."

"A girl this time?"

Cadal grinned. "We needed a little girl. I promised Mollie another boy next time." He put out his hand to Caden, who happily pounced on his father.

Mollie laughed. "Cadal, I think we discussed this."

"You've held one of my babies now. Is it so unbelievable to you that you would want to give me another?"

"And another and another. I could happily give you dozens."

"Is the trying distressing?" Cadal raised an eyebrow, and his glance heated in invitation.

"So distressing that I enjoy it every chance we get."

Elizabeth grinned at their banter. "It's nice to know some things never change." She looked up as Liam returned with all haste on Storm. "Ah, here he is."

Liam pulled Storm up short and dropped to the ground in a smooth motion he'd learned from Cadal all those years ago. "I couldn't believe it when Sean told me. It really is you." He clasped Cadal's hand and laughed. Then he surveyed Mollie. "I see you're still enjoying each other's company."

Caden popped up from behind his father's shoulder and waved. "Hello, Liam," he called, then scampered over to take the man's hand.

Liam lifted the boy to his shoulder. "And who would you be, my young man?"

"I'm Caden," he answered seriously.

"And how old are you, Caden?"

"I'll be fifteen this summer."

"Then you would be the baby your mother was carrying when she left us."

He nodded. "And you would be the people who helped us go. You protected Mom, and you kept our secret. You're good Humans."

Mollie laughed heartily.

"You know about all of that?" Liam asked.

Caden nodded gravely. "Mom is writing a book about it all. Is the bad Human still here?"

Liam glanced at Cadal for his nod of approval before continuing.

Some things never change, Elizabeth mused.

"Mr. Thornton died a few years ago. His son is better. Not much, but better. He had a limp, you know." Liam smiled at Cadal. "It was a riding accident that he had not long after your Mom left us. He was never very happy about the way things turned out."

"I imagine," Cadal commented acidly.

"What happened with John McConnell?" Mollie asked.

Elizabeth smiled. "Not much. John decided that no one was riding Thunder, based on some forensics tests about the weight on Tucker or some such thing. There was still evidence that you weren't alone out there. Everyone agreed we were not responsible for your escape. Everyone except Thornton. We had a few run-ins with him over the years, but nothing serious. He tried to convince the authorities to return the land to your family. Luckily, the paperwork was done. You knew it had to be."

"Yes, I did. I knew Thornton would get the land somehow if I didn't do it quickly." Mollie looked away. "Did my— Did Darcy ever contact you?"

Elizabeth shook her head. "Never directly and never in a civil way."

Mollie nodded silently at that.

"So," Cadal mused, "we're technically still criminals here?"

Liam laughed. "Technically, I suppose, but John would release you himself if you were ever caught. He still tells me about the night you left when he comes out for a drink or for dinner."

Mollie winced lightly and rubbed her back.

Cadal startled and met her gaze before standing abruptly and lifting her by the waist to her feet. "We must go now," he said quietly.

Caden started to complain; he looked at Mollie curiously and wiggled out of Liam's arms to hold her hand.

"So soon?" Elizabeth asked.

"I'm afraid so," Mollie offered by way of an apology.

Liam sighed. "I would say to let us know when the baby is born, but..."

Cadal smiled crookedly and touched Mollie's belly lightly. "Based on the last time, I'd guess very early tomorrow morning, if the stress of flight doesn't speed her labor."

Liam regarded him in shock. "Then you can't leave," he protested.

Mollie shook her head sadly again. "We must." She offered Cadal a weak smile. "I shouldn't have come. Mother is going to really hurt me this time. Enough threats from her."

Cadal laughed. "Only if she takes you outside my tree-city. Besides, she wouldn't dare. I'll carry you in, and we'll plead for her help. She'll roll her eyes, utter a few choice Human curses, and get to work."

Mollie laughed uproariously and hugged Elizabeth and Liam. "I guess we should go," she managed tearfully.

Liam clapped a hand on Cadal's shoulder. "Next time, don't forget the nectar wine."

Caden darted into the woods and returned with a sack, handing it to Liam. "He didn't forget this time."

With that, they disappeared back into the trees. Elizabeth and Liam watched them go.

Liam wrapped an arm around his wife's shoulders. "Think we'll ever see them again?" he asked.

Elizabeth laughed heartily. "I intend on living that long. Next time, I'll get to meet Bethlia."

"Who is Bethlia?"

"The baby Mollie is having tomorrow. She's being named after me."

Liam smiled and opened the sack to take out the nectar wine. "Guess I better call John out for dinner. It's been a long time since we've enjoyed nectar wine together." His gaze settled on a stack of papers. He put the bottle back in, then took the papers.

"What's that?" Elizabeth asked.

Liam smiled. "They are new stories to be transcribed into the book of Fairy tales."

She took them from her husband and thumbed through them. "Mollie's gift to us. Could life really be so perfect?"

Liam laughed. "Maybe that's why they live so long."

Elizabeth kissed him passionately. "Here's to a long life."

The End

About the Author

Brenna Lyons wears many hats, sometimes all on the same day: former president of EPIC, author of more than 100 published works, owner of Fireborn Publishing, columnist, special needs teacher, wife, mother...and member in good standing of more than 60 writing advocacy groups.

In her first ten years published in novel-length, she's won 3 EPIC e-Book Awards (out of 15 finalists) and finaled for 3 PEARLS (including one Honorable Mention, second to NY Times Bestseller Angela Knight), 2 CAPAS, and a Dream Realm Award. She's also taken Spinetingler's Book of the Year for 2007.

Brenna writes in 26 established worlds plus stand-alones, poetry, articles and essays. She's a bestseller in indie/e fantasy and horror, straight genre and cross-genres thereof. Brenna has been termed "one of the most deviant erotic minds in the publishing world...not for the weak." (Rachelle for Fallen Angels Reviews) Milieu-heavy dark work is practically Brenna's calling card, with or without the erotic content.

She teaches classes in everything from POV studies to advanced editing, networking to marketing. Brenna enjoys hearing from people who read her work and can be reached by email.

Website: http://www.brennalyons.com/

Facebook: http://www.facebook.com/brenna.lyons

Email: brennalyons4168@live.com